MW00776629

ASSASSIN: RISE OF THE GEIST

THE BOOK OF BAWB
BOOK 3

SCOTT BARON

Copyright © 2024 by Scott Baron

All rights reserved.

Print Editions:

ISBN 978-1-945996-73-3 Paperback

ISBN 978-1-945996-74-0 Hardcover

No part of this book may be reproduced in any form or by any electronic or mechanical means, including information storage and retrieval systems, without written permission from the author, except for the use of brief quotations in a book review.

Cover by Jeff Brown

"Vengeance is in my heart, death in my hand. Blood and revenge are hammering in my head."
~William Shakespeare~

CHAPTER ONE

The tapestries were ornate, hanging to the ground. Almost tasteful yet crossing the line to overly opulent and clearly quite costly, as were all of the things belonging to the lady of the house. In fact, the overall feel of the expansive compound was one of wealth, power, and order, and everything within her walls was always in its place.

That is, except for the two guards who now lay quite dead, their bodies hidden out of view beneath a large ornamental table in the main entertaining hall. Master Kopal, the assassin responsible for their unexpected demise, had been fortunate the oversized tablecloth hung all the way to the ground rather than partway. The stronghold's owner having a penchant for opulence and overkill rather than understated good taste helped him in that regard.

He had spent days infiltrating the series of connected buildings, carefully maintaining his disguise as he slowly worked his way through the layers of internal security his target had set in place over the years.

Emmik Forbin was her name, and she was a low-level player in the Council of Twenty. But what she lacked in power of her own, she made up for in connections. Connections and information. And now it seemed someone wanted her removed from the equation, the likely result of blackmail gone wrong.

Whatever the case, the contract was good, the money held safely in escrow by a trusted intermediary. All that remained was the completion of the task. And with Kopal on the job, it was as good as done.

His shimmer ship was so close he could throw a stone from the compound's rooftop and hit it, but no one was any the wiser, the cloaking spell holding strong and true. The ship safely hovered inches above the roof of a nearby structure, ready for his departure. All that remained was one thing.

Kill Emmik Forbin.

It was a straightforward mission, simple and to the point. But even so, his infiltration was slow and steady. The Ghalian took no chances. That was what kept them alive.

On the fifth day inside the emmik's walls, he finally took the identity of Markis, one of her closest assistants, hiding the slumbering body of the man beneath the clean linen in a nearby supply closet. If he had timed it right, no one would be changing the sheets for at least another day. That gave him ample time to complete his task and make his silent escape.

There were a series of interconnected chambers in the emmik's personal quarters, but few guards, if any. She felt safe here, deep within the layers she had protecting her every waking and slumbering hour. It was that overconfidence he would use to his advantage.

The two guards had been a surprise. No one was supposed to be patrolling the receiving area. But he was a Ghalian Master, and he had learned long ago that plans changed on the fly quite often. He would simply adapt and carry on. Once he dealt with them, of course.

"You there! You are not supposed to be in here!"

"It's me, Markis. You know me."

"Then what's the pass phrase?"

Master Kopal hadn't heard anything about any pass phrase.

"Don't be ridiculous," he said, a broad grin on his face as he drew closer to the two guards. "I don't use a pass phrase," he continued, hoping his bluff would work. "Come on, now. You know that."

The guard nearest seemed to relax, his shoulders lowering slightly. "Just had to check. You know the new rules."

"Yes, of course. And a good thing you did."

Kopal felt the other guard drawing his sword before he saw it, his senses honed to a razor's edge. He spun at once, driving his concealed dagger into the man's throat, silencing him in an instant. The blade flew into the eye of the other guard a moment later, ending their game as soon as it had begun.

This was unexpected. Something had changed. But there was no time for leisurely investigation. He had planned on no extraneous casualties on this contract, but with these two dead, he was now on a ticking clock. It would only be so long before their absence was noted. Kopal dragged the bodies beneath the table and wiped up their blood with their clothing before stuffing the soiled rags into their wounds. It wasn't much, but it would at least keep them from leaking out everywhere and revealing their location.

He rose to his feet and continued on, faster now, well aware of his new time constraints. He reached the hallway connecting several anterooms to the emmik's main suite. Kopal straightened his clothing and walked calmly ahead, his disguise in place, acting as normally and calm as the real Markis would have.

He reached the end of the hall and stopped. The emmik's door was ajar. It seemed fortune was favoring him after all. This would only serve to speed his completion of the contract. He pushed the door open and stepped inside.

"Emmik Forbin?" he called out. "It is Markis. I have a message I've been tasked with delivering to you."

The emmik walked through the far door leading from her bed chamber.

"Markis? Yes, what is it?"

"A message. Shall I share it with you?" he asked, walking closer.

The emmik's lips curled in a wicked grin. "Oh, you will not be coming any closer, Assassin."

She cast a fierce series of spells, both offensive and defensive, sending Kopal diving aside before he could launch an attack of his own. It seemed they had some additional pass phrase he was unaware of. There was little to do now but fight and kill the woman before she could raise an alarm.

As the other doors burst open, he realized it was much too late for that.

Scores of guards rushed through, along with additional casters, all of them targeting the lone intruder. Kopal was hit hard, the magic cracking his defensive spells, spears and thrown blades penetrating his projectile-obstructing spells. Enchanted blades, he realized, as he felt hot blood seeping into his tunic.

This wasn't an assassination gone wrong. This was a trap.

He shifted his plan at once, the plan for his assassination a thing of the past. All that mattered now was getting out in one piece. That meant *everyone* was a target now. Drawing both his concealed blades, he flew into battle, laying waste to the onslaught of guards as best he could. But he was tremendously outnumbered. Whoever had planned this knew the skills of a Ghalian, as well as their limitations. And with multiple casters safely behind layers of defenses, they could bombard him with magic with impunity, wearing him down until, eventually, one of the blows he took would prove to be fatal.

Kopal, a great warrior if ever there was one, turned and ran.

There was no shame in it. In fact, he was a staunch supporter of flight when warranted. And it had never been more so than right now.

Spells and spears impacted with his defenses, the magic at his back barely stopping the onslaught. This was overkill. The number of forces committed to stopping this one man would have been ridiculous for anyone, even a Ghalian Master. More wounds opened, and precious blood seeped out as attacks landed. There was simply no way he could block all of them, and likewise, the odds were so stacked against him, he could not hope to take on so many opponents.

The routes to all three exits he had planned to use were now choked with guards, bristling with weapons and ill intent. He was trapped. There was no way out.

Kopal felt himself growing weaker. He drew deep from his konus and healed the most severe wounds as best he could, slowing the bleeding if he couldn't stop it entirely. On the run, there was only so much he could do. His head pivoted, searching for something, anything that might aid him in his time of need. Only one thing presented itself.

And it was going to suck.

He barely dodged a slicing sword, disemboweling its owner as he dove aside. But he didn't stop to retrieve the fallen weapon. He ran full speed ahead, casting the most powerful force spell he knew. He just hoped it was enough to break the spell holding the window shut.

Kopal burst out into the nothingness of open air, tumbling rapidly toward the street below. He cast a protective spell as best he was able, doing all he could to cushion the impact, but even with the magic softening the blow, he felt bones break and organs tear from the hard landing. Ignoring the pain, he forced himself to his feet at once, managing an awkward run until he ducked into a low building. Guards were already on his trail, hurrying in after him moments later.

A burst of wind greeted them when they reached the roof, the shimmer-cloaked ship blasting invisibly into the sky with great speed and force. The guards called for aerial support but knew it was too late. The assassin had managed to escape. But the emmik was safe, and her attacker would likely not survive their flight to wherever it was they were fleeing.

Master Kopal managed to activate the Drookonus in his ship long enough to jump the vessel clear of the planet. He then sent a distress skree on the secret Ghalian wavelength, calling for help and giving his position before finally slipping into unconsciousness.

CHAPTER TWO

Demelza stepped quietly out of the healing chambers, closing the door gently behind her. She had a class to teach, but Master Kopal was a colleague. A friend, even, and she needed to know he would survive the day before she could properly focus on her planned lessons. That, and she knew the students would have heard of his misfortune by now and would surely ask of him.

They were an impressive group, the young adults who made up the ranks of Adepts, and she had known them all since their earliest days at the training house. Since they had first been thrust into this demanding life, either failing horribly under the unrelenting pressure or flourishing, evolving into more than they ever thought they could be.

Those who remained were most certainly the latter.

They had all graduated to the ranks of full-fledged Ghalian, each of them devising and demonstrating their own unique fighting style to the assembled masters before being raised from Vessel to Adept. It was at this level that some would remain, carrying on with their training the rest of their days, ever improving their skills. But they would also be sent on contracts, as Adepts, just as the Mavens above them.

The differences between the two ranks were seemingly minor, but a few were significant, akin to an undergrad degree compared to a graduate's. Adepts were now true Ghalian and could conduct missions, but Mavens could also plan them. Adepts could study, but Mavens could teach, and some of them might very well become teachers one day.

Then there were the spells, Mavens having access to even more dangerous and arcane magic than their lesser brethren. Only Masters knew more, but that was a path that was reserved for the top among them. And at the head of the class was an Adept named Bawb. The very same who stepped away from his classmates and hurried to greet Demelza as she entered the training chamber.

"How is he?" Bawb asked, his face remaining far more neutral than he had been able to maintain in his youth, but a clear hint of his concern shining through nevertheless.

"He will live," his teacher replied. "But it will take time. The injuries were severe and extensive. Had there not been one of our own near enough to receive his distress skree, he would have perished."

Bawb nodded solemnly. Master Kopal had become almost like a friend to him over the years, flying him and the other students to training outings in his shimmer ship. A highly skilled and personable man, he was also one of the few rumored to be on the short list to perhaps one day become one of the Five.

But now he was lying in a bed clinging to life.

Demelza could read Bawb's emotions without even needing to be a reader. She had known him so long it had become second nature, even as he learned how to better conceal them.

"Do not fret, Bawb. Even the most talented among us sometimes face these trials and hardships. It is the way of things in our world."

"I know. It is just hard to imagine anyone getting the better of him."

"Oh, they paid a heavy price."

"They?"

"I am not at liberty to go into details, but let us just say Master Kopal made quite a showing for himself. One that will be long remembered by the survivors who faced him."

Motion at the door caught her eye. Master Hozark poked his head inside, giving her a little nod.

"If you will excuse me a moment," she said, stepping outside into the hallway and closing the door behind her.

The other students had heard Demelza and Bawb's conversation and quickly fell into hushed discussion about what had happened. They all knew Master Kopal, and all were just as stunned as Bawb had been.

"I can't believe Master Kopal fell," Usalla marveled. "He is such a fierce combatant, and so skilled."

"He should have been more careful," Elzina suggested. "Even a Master cannot be careless."

"I doubt he was careless."

Elzina chortled. "How else would you explain one of the Masters being overcome by the enemy? And a lowly emmik, from what I hear."

Bawb stormed across the room right up to his classmate's face. "You should not say these things about Master Kopal. He has always been cognizant of the dangers he faces. He would never be sloppy. It was not his way. You know this."

"Perhaps. But do you have a better explanation?" she shot back. "No? I thought not." Elzina turned and walked away, leaving Bawb annoyed, as she was fond of doing. Now, however, she knew his skills, and unlike in his youth, she had to acknowledge he was no pushover to be bullied and harassed, no matter how much she still enjoyed it.

The faint sound of voices redirected Bawb's attention, pulling him back to the doorway. Hozark and Demelza were still just outside, barely within earshot. Casually, not drawing attention to himself, Bawb cast a minor enhancing spell, amplifying the sounds.

"I know it is hard to believe, but it is all but certain," he heard Master Hozark say.

"I hate to admit it is even possible," Demelza replied, actual emotion in her voice.

"As do I. But it would appear we have a traitor in our midst. Someone is helping someone within the Council of Twenty target Ghalian operatives."

Bawb felt his stomach flip at the words. A traitor among them? It was so incredibly unlikely it made his head spin.

The door abruptly snapped open, two Ghalian Masters staring hard at the young man caught in the act. Hozark studied him a moment, his unsettling gaze employed to full effect for a few seconds before he reached in and pulled Bawb out to join them, closing the door firmly.

"You must always mute your steps, Bawb. Even when you feel you are safe. You never know who may be listening," he said.

"Like you?"

"Or worse."

"I am sorry for eavesdropping, Master Hozark."

Hozark and Demelza shared a slightly amused look.

"Do not be sorry," Demelza said. "But next time, do not get caught."

"I will not. But tell me, did I hear right? A traitor in our order? Is that even possible?"

The glance the two masters shared this time was of a different kind. One of painful memories and regret. Hozark rested his hand on Bawb's shoulder, locking eyes with him.

"This has happened before, but many years ago. Treachery

from an ally we believed to be loyal. I personally took care of that situation, but not without great cost."

Demelza nodded, the adventures and tragedies of the encounter dredged up from the place they'd been dormant a long, long time. "Visla Tozorro Maktan was a very powerful, and very clever man."

"Wait. I know the name Maktan. He is one of the Council of Twenty."

"That is his son, merely exercising his birthright, enjoying the fruits of his father's labor, as so many in the Council have done over the years. He was no more than an innocent boy when this all occurred. But his father? Well, Tozorro Maktan was *powerful*. So powerful, in fact, that he managed to hide his power completely, as well as sensing it on others. A dangerous combination."

"He could prevent you from sensing it?" Bawb asked, amazed. More than most, Hozark was particularly skilled at sniffing out even the weakest of natural power users. The ability to block one's magic signature entirely was incredibly rare.

A sad look flashed across the Ghalian Master's face, but only for an instant. Some memory dredged up then quickly locked away once more. "He did far more than hide his power, Bawb. He infiltrated my most trusted of allies."

"Bud and Henni? And she let him? She's a powerful reader."

"Yes, she is. But even she could not detect him. Not when she finally met him. But this was all put into play before her time. In fact, Bud and Henni first met during the incident, and we nearly lost both of them because of it. Others were not so fortunate."

Hozark was speaking calmly, but Bawb could feel something just beneath the surface. A tension in Hozark's throat subtly changing his tone. Was it anger? Sadness? Regret? Master Hozark never showed emotion, but for just a split second he had felt something from him. Some spark that to this day burned him to the core.

"What happened?" the student asked.

"Hozark happened," Demelza replied with a cold grin.

The master assassin shrugged, as if shedding the heavy thoughts that had intruded on his day. "Let us just say it took quite some doing, and a *lot* of patience. But eventually, I ended the threat quite permanently."

"You killed him?"

"Very much so."

"But you said he could sense power."

"Oh, that he could. Even the slightest whiff of it on me and I would have failed. No, I had to do it entirely without magic, all accomplished without his guards, staff, or even family being any the wiser to my presence."

"But you are sure he is dead."

"On this you may rest assured. Tozorro Maktan is dead and buried, never to threaten us again."

"But now it has begun happening again," Demelza interjected. "Slowly at first, just small incidents. But over the last few years, missions have been going wrong, the frequency increasing at an alarming rate."

Bawb was confused. "I have not noticed such a thing."

Hozark shook his head. "Because you are an Adept, Bawb. You are quite skilled, but the contracts you are offered are fitting your ranking. No, these incidents are occurring at the highest of levels, targeting the most skilled among us. Our brothers and sisters are finding themselves in jeopardy, injured or worse, and it is happening far too frequently for mere coincidence. Someone is leaking information, and we must do all we can to stop them."

Bawb stood up a little taller, a feeling of righteous anger

igniting within. "Can I help? Just ask, and I will do whatever is required."

"Admirable initiative, my boy, but no, dealing with this sort is exceedingly dangerous. Dangerous beyond your years. I need you to keep this to yourself for now."

"I will, Master Hozark."

"I know you will. You are trusted, but we have no idea who may be the leak, or if they are even from this compound or perhaps another. While it seems many who have passed through these doors of late have encountered problems, a Ghalian does not assume."

"Of course. I will keep my ears open for any sign of treachery, all the same."

"As I assumed you would. But now you should go join your classmates and train, Adept Bawb. Soon you could very well be facing your toughest mission yet."

Demelza flashed a knowing look at the Master then turned and opened the door. "Yes, come along, Bawb. Class awaits. Time to train. You never know when you will be called away on your next task."

As it turned out, that would be much sooner than later.

CHAPTER THREE

Bawb was in space, off on yet another task, pulled from the training house and his classmates only a short while after his discussion with the two Masters. It seemed he was needed for something quite soon indeed.

He had completed the two jumps to his destination some time ago, but rather than descending to the planet below, he lingered in space, hiding in the shadow of a passing asteroid. This wasn't a training exercise. Not anymore. He was an Adept, and the contracts had been coming with increasing regularity, and he was to complete them on his own, as was the Ghalian way.

Yes, they all trained together back in the safety of their compound, as well as on various excursions, each of them always striving to improve and perhaps one day reach not only the rank of Maven, but that of Master. And they did still compete with one another with an intensity that put even the toughest of gladiator academies to shame. But when it came to actual wet work in the real world, the Adepts had reached the dangerous transition point in their training.

The point where they truly worked alone.

Most of the time they were sent on intelligence gathering and item recovery tasks, something the Ghalian secretly handled frequently, though they were best known for their assassination skills. But not all missions were exciting and dangerous. Some were actually quite benign, at least compared to the rigors of their training.

This, however, was not one of those. This was one of the most challenging ones yet, and as a result, he would make sure to take as much time as necessary to ensure its completion would not cost him his life. As Teacher Griggitz often said, "We do not spend years of time and resources training you only to have you go and get yourselves killed on a fool's errand."

Bawb was going to take those words to heart.

The ship he was piloting was fast and stealthy, the Drookonus running it moderately powerful, but nowhere near what the Masters used for their craft. It was also decidedly *not* a shimmer-capable ship. He still had much practice to go before he could properly master that particular set of very useful, but very difficult spells. He was somewhat proficient with a shimmer cloak around his person, but a whole ship, even a small one, was an entirely different matter.

He had found himself tasked with this mission while his classmates trained, the contract handed to him by Master Hozark himself. It was unusual, but Bawb had been told in no uncertain terms that with a traitor somewhere in their organization, he did not wish to take any chances, even with lower-tier quests. Not when the younger and more vulnerable of their ranks—at least by Ghalian standards—were not yet fully battle-hardened.

But Bawb had proven himself in combat, and to an advanced degree his fellow students were not aware of. Hozark, however, was quite certain of the young man's skills, having fought beside him on more than one occasion now. It was training, yes, but the fights had been quite real nonetheless, and as a result, the two had become quite close, for a Master and a pupil. No amount of training in controlled circumstances could replace the bond forged in battle.

And so it was Bawb had been selected for a task normally reserved for those above his level. This was to be a straightforward but somewhat difficult assassination. One that would require time, finesse, and skill to accomplish.

On its face the mission sounded simple enough. Stalk a certain Emmik Mollin, a modestly powered magic user who was not particularly threatening on her own, and assassinate her, ideally leaving no trace. But as an Adept, that was not a rigid restriction for Bawb's mission. If things got messy, he was to complete the task regardless, even if that meant things were not exactly subtle.

Mollin was a relatively underpowered bit player and did not seem like the sort who would warrant such a contract, especially not one the Ghalian would accept. And normally, the she wouldn't be. But as a key element in the underworkings of the Council of Twenty in his system, this emmik had managed to leverage that standing to become far more influential than there would ever have been without the affiliation. Power corrupted many a good person, but it just so happened that Emmik Mollin was a terrible one.

It was for this reason the Ghalian had accepted the contract. An interested party had paid a handsome sum to see her removed from the system's workings. The Ghalian had, of course, done their due diligence before taking the job. The one footing the bill, though she had attempted to remain anonymous, using multiple intermediaries to make the arrangements, was hoping to fill the void Mollin's assassination would leave behind.

That was up to her. Whether she could manage to do so was

up to her own skills, contacts, and machinations. The Ghalian would play no part in the political side of things. They would merely address the task at hand, and they would do so with the utmost discretion.

Bawb had inquired about the task and how it would be forcing the Council of Twenty to rearrange their operations in this system. The Council was ever-growing in power, he was told, and the Ghalian made it their mission to do what they could to slow that increase when they could. As the Council's policies and tactics were generally quite contrary to the order's beliefs, it made sense. And on occasion, that meant becoming directly involved with their inner power struggles.

"The enemy of my enemy, I suppose," Bawb commented when Hozark informed him of the target and purpose of the contract.

"More or less," the Master Ghalian replied. "If this woman does succeed in assuming Mollin's position, it will be a marked step down in the level of danger the Council poses in the entire sector. Mollin's ambition is dangerous, not only to his own system but those nearby. This would be trading the removal of a greater evil for a far lesser one."

"She is not a danger, then?"

"Oh, she may very well become one, someday. It seems to be the way with those aspiring to power in the Twenty. But by the time she does, we will have our spies well embedded in her staff to keep us apprised of any real problems she may pose."

"But we do not have any within Emmik Mollin's people?"

"We did, but Mollin has been a low-level player for some time, and when more pressing matters arose, we re-tasked our operative accordingly. Though we have influence far across the systems, the Ghalian cannot be *everywhere* at once."

"Though the public does not know that," Bawb said with an amused grin.

"All part of the reason we have retained our reputation," Hozark agreed. "And that reputation can open more doors and achieve greater ends than mere violence of action ever could. But with our spies not active within Mollin's ranks, I wish for you to not only complete your task, but also keep alert for anything that may be of use to the order within her compound. Intelligence of any sort you would deem important. The overly confident often leave sensitive documentation unsecured, and we would do well to know of whatever the emmik and the Council might have in the works."

"Of course. I will take note of anything related to Council business."

"Good. We may be required to return to this system one day, and every bit of intelligence makes the next Ghalian's task all the easier."

"Understood."

"Good luck, Bawb. I wish you safe travels, and great success."

"Thank you, Master Hozark. I will not let you down."

And he had really meant it. Bawb had no intention of failing, no matter how hard the effort would be. Now, days later, quietly orbiting the surprisingly small world he was about to infiltrate, Bawb felt confident he would uphold that promise. He would make his mentor proud.

CHAPTER FOUR

Bawb started his mission with calm confidence, his faith in his blossoming abilities well-founded, bolstering his steady resolve. He had excelled in recent years, and he'd completed tasks more difficult than this. It would be a long infiltration, yes, but nothing beyond his capabilities.

Of course, unlike prior years, now, as an Adept he was entirely on his own.

Bawb took his ship down from his vantage point in orbit, settling into a casual approach from across the continent, appearing to any who might happen to observe his craft to be just another local traveler, and not one arriving directly from space. Anything to throw potential pursuers off his trail, just as he had been taught.

His konus was running at moderate capacity, feeding his disguise spell a steady stream of magic the moment he set down in the landing area near Emmik Mollin's modest but fortified estate. He had been afforded a good view of it from above on his approach, and the unusual layout, with multiple exterior courtyards and sprawling gardens within the compound's walls, would both afford him ample opportunities to complete his task, but also undoubtedly hinder him in the intelligence gathering portion of it.

There was simply a lot of ground to cover, and it was all spread out, not interconnected as a single building might be. And with the emmik possessing a well-trained guard staff, that meant he would need to move slow and steady, blending in for long periods of time.

Bawb set his resolve. So be it.

To begin, he had selected the appearance of a golden-tan-skinned courier, his eyes shifted to silver, his hair now a brassy orange, all thanks to his disguise spells. It was not one of his favorites, but this persona was striking, and as such, would be afforded a bit of leeway. Typically, people doing shady things tended to avoid drawing attention to themselves, not the opposite.

Bawb had crafted a document, forging the seal of a relatively wealthy patron of the arts from a neighboring system. It was an invitation for the emmik to attend a well-known gathering—one that actually *was* taking place. He had learned of it in his reconnaissance, the idea to use it to his advantage springing to mind as soon as he'd found out the details.

Emmik Mollin might very well be invited to this event, but no invitations had yet been sent out. As such, he had a unique opportunity to use this bogus invite delivery to gain entrance to her compound. And if by some twist of bad luck and timing the real invitation should arrive while he was still there, it would merely seem as if she had accidentally received two of them.

"Hello, friend!" he called out loudly as he approached the guards standing casually at the front gate to the entry gardens. "I have a delivery for the emmik!"

"Leave it with me," the woman in charge replied.

"I'm sorry, but I've been instructed to hand it directly to someone named Horka. Her personal aide, I believe."

"Horka's out for the afternoon on an errand for the emmik."

Bawb was quite aware of that fact, having watched the woman depart not long before his approach. He had memorized the names, faces, and jobs of most of the staff, and that happy coincidence had been precisely the sort of opportunity he had been looking for.

"Yes, well, that's a bit of a problem. My employer will absolutely kill me if I don't do as she instructed. But I have a few hours before I have to return. Will Horka be back by then? Perhaps you could tell her I am here?"

"We've got a shift change coming up."

"Oh, I see. I hate to be such a bother. I wonder, is there any chance I could just wait in the garden?" Bawb asked, peering through the gate at the lush grounds. "It would be much more pleasant than standing out here on the street. And that way I will see Horka the moment she returns."

The guards looked at one another questioningly. The garden was completely secure, part of the compound's design. This was just the first entryway, but one that led to an easily defended and encircled area if someone did manage to breach the front gate.

"Yeah, I don't see any problem with that," the guard replied. "Just stay close to the front, and you should see her when she's back."

"Thanks," Bawb said with a chipper grin. "I really appreciate it."

The guards stepped aside and opened the gate, allowing the assassin into the compound without the need to shed a drop of blood. The gate closed behind him, but that was fine. There was a shift change happening soon, and once that had happened, he would make his entrance to the inner sanctum.

Bawb had taken careful note of the guard and her attire. Her manner of speech and the way she moved. Her partner was a rather large fellow, and Bawb decided it would be far less of a magical draw to disguise himself as the smaller of the pair. He walked into the garden and settled into a comfortable spot in the shade beneath a small tree. He was out of sight of most of the area, but was afforded a straight view of the guards up front. This was going even smoother than he had anticipated.

He waited casually, leaning against the tree, staying still long enough that any who had initially noted his arrival would have just unconsciously accepted him as part of the landscape by now. Motion attracted attention, and he kept his to a minimum. Of course, he did move a little, but just enough to not seem like he was trying to hide but was waiting comfortably in the shade.

A little over an hour had passed when movement at the front gate caught his eye. The guards were changing shift, the pair he had met heading for their barracks to get out of their heavy gear while the relief took their places.

Bawb stood absolutely still and cast a minor obscuring spell, not making himself invisible, so much as making all but active magic users' eyes sort of glance past him. The trick wouldn't work against any real scrutiny, but if he had done his job right, no one should be paying him much heed at all.

He pulled from his konus and cast the new disguise spell, his intent crystal clear, having spent the past hour focusing on the details to get it all just right. His new appearance in place, he then stepped out into the sunlight and strode confidently across the garden, away from the door to the barracks, heading right into the heart of the facility.

He simply gave a nod to the guards just settling into their positions, having only relieved their counterparts a few minutes before. The face of the woman he wore was a familiar one, and they knew her shift had just ended, as this was a daily routine.

"Just dropping this off," Bawb said, waving the sealed invitation at them, his voice and cadence matching that of the woman whose identity he was wearing perfectly. "Courier dropped it off for Horka, but she's out on errands."

"Of course she is," one of the guards said with a knowing chuckle as the disguised assassin walked right past him.

That was it. Bawb was inside, and no one was any the wiser. He knew the basic layout thanks to the older data the previous spies had left, but the interior configuration was a bit different than he had expected. Detailed plans had not been requested when the spies were pulled to other duties and he would just have to make do on his own.

As it turned out, the estate was far more complex a residence than he had anticipated.

For one, there were magical wards between buildings. Guards and staff each had specialized access spells bonded to their konuses. Without them, moving from one building to the next was incredibly difficult. It could be done. Bawb had the requisite skills to eventually bypass the mechanism long enough to proceed, but then he would just have to do the same in the next structure.

With little in the way of options, however, that was precisely what he did. Over and over. And it was miserable.

What he had foolishly begun to believe would be a relatively quick mission had morphed into a tedious task. One that saw him spend days within the compound walls, shifting disguises, hiding, slowly sneaking past warded thresholds, and, of course, gathering intelligence in each area he gained access to.

Then he would do it all over again.

After seven days he had managed to slowly work his way to the emmik's personal chambers without tripping any of the alarm spells or protective wards. He got inside the main rooms just fine, but her private study remained locked, a chamber within a chamber, sealed with several very challenging spells. Had she been present, he would have just slain her, used her power to open it, and been done with it, taking what he could before making a slow and deliberate escape from the estate, his victim's power drained and added to his own, helping him bypass the wards fast and easy.

But there was just one problem. During his delayed approach, the emmik had left the compound. It had taken too long.

Bawb felt a flash of frustration in his gut when he discussed it with a kitchen staffer, having switched to disguising himself as a guard for the moment, allowing him to simply grab a little snack without drawing attention. It had also provided him the opportunity to talk casually with the workers, gleaning what information he could.

Emmik Mollin had left for a few days, but she would be back shortly. Bawb pretended to be as glad as the others, musing aloud that it must be nice to have a little break in their lavish cooking duties. While they enjoyed their jobs, many voiced their agreement, having a nice bonding moment with one of the typically stoic guards, feeling a bit privileged he had even come into their kitchen. Normally, the guards were aloof. Treated them like lessers. But this? It was a pleasant change of pace.

It also afforded Bawb a chance to not only eat a proper meal, but also gather a lot of information in a relatively short time.

He took his food, thanking them for their generosity, then headed out, allegedly preparing for a long day of work, fortified by the delicious treats they had provided him. Instead, however, he headed back to the emmik's chambers and settled in for a long wait.

Bawb took up a position near the entrance, planning to take her down the moment she stepped inside, before she even had the opportunity to react.

He waited for days.

"This is ridiculous," he finally said after his fourth day. "I may as well try."

He crossed to her study door, feeling the layers of wards and tripwire spells like a dangerous tingle across his senses. But Bawb was nothing if not persistent. Slowly, with great care and ample caution, he began unwinding the magic, putting his training to work one ward and spell at a time.

It took even longer than he had anticipated, forcing him to use more magic and more focus than he had thought. Hours and hours went by. This was no ordinary room, clearly. Whatever was inside must have held significant value. After a very long time, he finally felt the last of the defenses fall.

"Finally," he said with a sigh.

Level up: Wards, traps, and defensive spell nullification, his konus told him. But it sounded unimpressed. Annoyed, even.

"What?" he asked, opening the door and stepping into the study.

You used a lot of power.

"Yes. It was required."

Not if you had stuck to the plan.

"Plans change."

You made them change.

Bawb ignored the device, quickly riffling through the belongings in the small but opulent room. There were enchanted items stored here as well as correspondence locked away in cabinets, sealed with even more spells. He got one open, took the contents, and was moving to the next when a sound caught his attention.

The hallway door was opening.

Bawb felt a flush of adrenaline hit his system. He hadn't heard anyone approach, but he could feel the magic now that it was nearby. The emmik had come home. And as the door opened, revealing her surprised face as she saw him standing in her violated personal space, he realized she was not alone.

"Get him!" Mollin shouted, casting attack spells immediately.

The aides and guards carrying her possessions dropped them at once, shifting role from porters to warriors in a flash, charging at the intruder, their employer's spells narrowly missing them in her haste.

Bawb jumped aside, the magic slamming into the desk behind him, smashing it against the wall.

He shifted into a crouching run, placing Mollin's staff between them. She held back, unable to cast, at least for the moment.

Bawb did the math. Guards, staff, and a pissed-off emmik, all in a fortified compound. His choice was clear. He immediately turned and ran. His sprint took him to a window. It was closed, but he dove through it anyway, flipping in mid-air, landing on the ground two floors below with a diving roll, the momentum scrubbing the force of the impact.

He did not slow down, running as fast as he could, tripping alarm spells as he went. That didn't matter. Not now. All that did was getting out alive.

Digging deep, he cast the most powerful defensive spells he knew, layering them over himself as he charged through warded gates into adjacent gardens and courtyards, a magical bull in a proverbial China shop. But his magic was waning as the defenses pummeled him. He had been counting on having the emmik's power as his own, and he had expended a lot of it in his breach attempt.

I told you, the konus chided.

"Help or shut up," he growled, pushing hard for the final obstacle. The main gate. Unfortunately, the alarms had given the guards plenty of time to amass there. He was facing nearly a dozen of them, and they knew he was coming. He couldn't take them. Not all of them. Not fast enough to avoid the rest hot on his heels. This was not the time for combat. It was the time for escape.

Force spell, the konus said flatly.

"What?"

I said, force spell.

Bawb didn't know what the device had planned, but he let the other more deadly spells slip from his mind, focusing all of his intent on the strongest force spell he knew. "*Malovicta!*" he said, casting as hard as he could.

A twinge pulled through his body, the konus feeding his spell far more magic than it ever had before. The spell ripped out, slamming into the guards, throwing them aside like rag dolls. They would live, but the impact had stunned them, leaving an opening.

Well? Don't slow down to gawk. Run!

Bawb didn't need to be told twice. He increased his run to a full sprint, leaping past the fallen guards and out into the streets at full speed. He ducked down an alley and shed his disguise, changing into the shape of a house servant. He pulled coin from his pocket and purchased a large quantity of vegetables from the nearest vendor he could find then redirected to a nearby roadway and altered course again, taking the fast path back toward his ship. Now he was in the form of a lowly servant carrying an armload of produce, and his hurried pace didn't draw anyone's attention. He was just another peon doing his master's bidding.

Guards raced through the streets, not paying him any mind as they passed. Bawb forced himself to maintain a steady gait and not run. That would only get him captured. Instead, he turned to look with curiosity on his face, just as everyone else was doing. Once they passed, he worked his way to his ship and boarded as soon as he felt sure there was no undue scrutiny. Safely inside, he shed his disguise, dropped the produce in a heap, and leapt into his pilot's seat.

He lifted off casually, flying across the region rather than up, watching the emmik's security detail pursue the ships attempting to reach orbit, as they were the ones likely trying to escape. Bawb simply stayed low, flew slow and casual, and crossed the landscape, heading to the next major city before shifting course upward. Once in space, he jumped immediately, heading back home. Returning a failure.

Teacher Demelza was waiting when he entered the training house. Notable, as there were so many possible entrances, yet she knew precisely where he was.

"Master Imalla wants to see you," she said calmly.

"Not Master Hozark? He was the one who—"

"Master Hozark has something of a soft spot for you, Adept Bawb. Master Imalla, however, does not, and she is *not* pleased."

The student nodded once, a ball of tension in his belly, almost worse than when he had been discovered in the emmik's chambers.

"I will go to her at once."

"Do. And Bawb? Do not hold back. Tell her everything. It will be better for you if you do."

CHAPTER FIVE

Master Imalla.

Bawb rarely saw her in all his years at the Ghalian compound. She ran things here, and while other high-ranking Ghalian would come and go, she was the one who had her finger on the pulse of all the goings-on for the multiple systems under her watch. As a result, training was left to the teachers. They were more than capable of the task, and there was no need for her micromanagement. As the saying went, micromanagement leads to macro screw-ups.

So she remained hands-off, going about her business until the time came where she had to step in. With Bawb's spectacular failure on a contract under her purview, this was one such occasion.

He felt his stomach tighten involuntarily. Imalla was not just the ranking Ghalian in the house. She had been there when he was young, assessing him as she did with all the new recruits. And when he showed a reluctance to taking another's blood, it was she who deemed him too soft for the Wampeh Ghalian. It was she who had suggested they just kill him and be done with it.

Fortunately, he had proven himself countless times since then, and slaying their own was not the Ghalian way. But nevertheless, Bawb couldn't help but feel on-edge as he entered her receiving chamber.

"Yes?" she said, not looking up from her desk.

"You requested to see me."

"Ah, Adept Bawb," she said, her eyes still on the scroll in front of her. Casually, she rolled it and put it aside, her gaze slowly rising to meet his. She stared silently for a long time. Even though he had learned the very same trick, which was quite useful in making the reticent speak up, he found himself having the same visceral reaction anyone else would.

Namely, he was on edge, wanting very much to break the silence. But he was an Adept. He knew better. Bawb bit his tongue and remained silent.

Master Imalla watched with curiosity, finally giving him the slightest nod of satisfaction. It had been a test, apparently. One he had passed.

"So, Adept Bawb. It seems your mission was quite the spectacular failure. Not only did you fail to complete your objective, you also alerted pretty much the entire city to your presence. Not exactly the stealth one would expect of a Ghalian. So, tell me. What happened? What went wrong?"

He noted that while her words spoke of failure, her attitude was calm. Not angry, not disappointed, just matter-of-fact, asking him the necessary questions to force him to analyze his mistakes and learn from them.

"I was unable to overcome the guards, and as a result the emmik remained out of my reach."

"Yes, there is that. But what of the *why* of the situation. What was your error, Bawb?"

He thought about it a moment, though he didn't really need to. Truth be told, he'd done nothing but replay the whole thing in his mind over and over ever since he had managed to escape the pursuing forces. At the end of it all, one thing led to his failure.

"I was impatient," he said. "I rushed."

"And what happened?"

"I was nearly caught. The emmik surprised me as I was searching her study."

"And yet the gathering of information was secondary to your primary task. Namely, the elimination of Emmik Mollin."

"I am aware. It is just, well, I had encountered many unforeseen difficulties on my infiltration, and as a result, the emmik had departed. That meant I was forced to blend in and wait. After a long period of time, I decided to break into her study rather than wait and force her to open it. As a result, I was out of position to remain concealed to take her."

"So it would seem," the Master said, her face unreadable and calm. "And you were nearly caught."

"Nearly. Please, Master, let me try again. I have learned from my mistakes."

"No. Not now."

"But why? I know the estate and am certain I can do better."

"Oh, of that, I am sure. Your lesson was hard-earned, and I doubt you will make that mistake again."

"Such is my intention."

"The problem, you see, is the estate is on high-alert now. The entire region is, in fact. You made quite the impression."

"Yes, well—"

"But there is a positive outcome of all this."

"There is?"

"Thanks to the specifics of your misfortune, namely the damage caused to the emmik's personal possessions, they actually believe this was a robbery gone wrong, not an attempt on the emmik's life. A fortunate side effect of your blunder, and one that keeps the Ghalian free of suspicion."

Bawb mulled over this little tidbit. Of course Master Imalla had dispatched spies to report back the status of their target. She knew everything of significance within her sphere of influence. What impressed him was just how quickly she had managed it.

"Will I be able to right this mistake?" he asked, hopeful for the chance to redeem himself.

"Will you? Perhaps, in time. But, for now, we must step back and allow them to relax back into complacency. Only then can we hope another opportunity presents itself." Her expression hardened, her gaze now more intense than it already had been. "But know this, Adept. While failure is a part of our profession, continued errors of this magnitude will have serious repercussions on your standing within the order. Is that clear?"

He felt his stomach clench, fighting the wave of acid wanting to burn his throat. "It is, Master. Thank you."

"Then get out. Go clean up and get a meal in you before you rejoin the others. You have much to think about."

CHAPTER SIX

Bawb sat alone in the dining hall for a long, long time, hardly touching the food in front of him. He knew he had to eat. He had spent a long time exerting both physical as well as mental energy, and his body needed the nourishment just as much as his mind craved it. But hunger was lacking. Something had shrunk his stomach into a tiny knot, and he knew what it was.

Anger. Frustration. The emotions he normally kept under control were exerting uncharacteristic sway on him. He had been a fool. Hasty. Impatient. Yes, he had managed to escape with his life, but this had been an important contract, and he'd blown it.

He forced himself to swallow the mouthful he'd been chewing for minutes, lost in thought, replaying the whole fiasco over and over in his head.

"You are being a fool, Bawb," he chided himself. "Mistakes happen, even stupid ones. Learn and move on."

His words were true, but he also knew all too well some things were easier said than done.

Bawb shook it off and focused, then forced himself to power down the rest of his meal by sheer force of will. There would be training today, no matter his failures outside the compound, and he would need the energy.

As it turned out, he was in luck, to an extent. When he located the other trainees, he found they were occupied with the dungeon training course for the day. Yes, it shifted constantly now that they were Adepts, but this had always been one of his strongsuits and as a result, he could typically clear the obstacles with his eyes closed, both figuratively, and occasionally literally, if the teachers were feeling particularly sadistic.

Bawb joined the others without a word, quickly setting to work on the course. As he ran, shifting his attention as he began vaulting over deadly traps, avoiding pitfalls and magical snares, the lingering anger finally began to truly subside. He was typically in complete control of himself, but this mistake and his reaction had changed his perception of the reality of things. It had struck him just how easily his emotions could well up and threaten his calm, even to this day. It was something he would need to continue to work on with even greater effort, it seemed.

At least the others didn't see his inner fire burning so hot. One thing he had definitely achieved in his time with the Ghalian. He had gotten *very* good at hiding his emotions, no matter the state of his inner turmoil.

"You were late joining us, Bawb," Teacher Rovos said when the student had finished his second straight time through the dungeon course.

"Yes, you were tardy," Teacher Pallik agreed. "We were concerned, but you made exceptional time through the course today."

Bawb nodded, bowing slightly. "Apologies for my tardiness. Master Imalla requested to see me."

The two teachers' demeanor shifted almost imperceptibly, but for Ghalian Masters that was significant. If Imalla had called him, it must have been something serious.

"I see," Pallik said, her demeanor softening slightly. "Carry on, Bawb. You have several rather difficult tasks today. The other students will fill you in on the way."

Bawb followed the others from the training dungeon as they ran to their next stop in the day's challenges.

"Glad to have you back," Finnia said as he fell in with the group.

"And unharmed," Usalla added.

The others gave nods of agreement, carrying on with the run through the subterranean tunnels to their next stop. None asked of his mission. They were all Adepts now and knew full well their personal contracts were their own business. They could speak of them if they so desired. Their secrets were safe among the group, but they typically didn't discuss their tasks. Not even with their classmates.

Finnia, however, did have something of another nature to discuss.

"Bawb?" she said quietly, barely winded as they ran.

"Yes?"

"I have a message for you. From Dullin."

Something in her tone put him on edge. That, and the fact that the message was from their local spy teacher, one of Finnia's instructors. One from whom Bawb had requested a favor some time ago. To keep tabs on a certain someone he held dear.

"What is it, Finnia?"

"Dullin asked me to relay to you that a friend of yours has had an *encounter*."

Bawb felt his anger bubbling to the surface before the next words were spoken.

"Alara?" he asked.

"Yes."

"Is she dead?"

"No. Not dead. But injured, and significantly."

35

Bawb's face remained neutral, but it took every bit of restraint to not show the emotions now roaring back to the surface. Alara was a friend. A *dear* friend. She was a very selective Ootaki living in hiding on this world, and she had gladly taken his virginity, a test and rite of passage. She was the first to teach him those skills. Bawb had followed Hozark's words and not continued their physical relations, not forming a bond —as Ghalian could not—instead training further in those skills with Usalla. He had nevertheless remained good friends with Alara, visiting when he could, enjoying her company and many fascinating discussions.

She had seen a lot in her *very* colorful life. And she was happy to talk about all things without shame. An open book glad for the meeting of minds. As such, Bawb learned much of not only the interactions between lovers she had gathered from years of experience, but also an objective, unrestrained outside opinion on all manner of other things.

And now someone had harmed her.

"Healers?" he asked.

"Seeing to her. She will recover physically, but it was traumatic."

Bawb's jaw flexed, his heart pounding a little harder as they ran. "Do you know who did this?"

His tone concerned her, but this was her friend. "I do. But we have challenges to focus on, Bawb. Resistance training. Heat, cold—we must be at our best."

He knew she was right. Nevertheless, his anger burned bright. "Tell me when we have finished, then."

"Very well."

They arrived at the next chamber shortly thereafter, Bawb running in silence the remainder of the way. The blast of cold air hit them as soon as they entered. It was a smaller cavern, one with an icy stream running through it. More than that, there was an underwater tunnel that led to an adjoining cave. One that had but one air pocket roughly halfway through its long swim.

"There you are," Teacher Warfin said. "No delays. Into the water. No protective spells."

The Adepts did as he said, jumping in at once, the cold water hitting their skin like a rude slap with an icy hand. Without even the most basic of temperature-regulating spells they were entirely exposed to every uncomfortable sensation of the freezing water. But that was the point. To overcome their bodies' natural reactions and enter a Zen-like state of complete control over themselves.

Or, as Teacher Warfin had said on several occasions, "Cold is not cold, hot is not hot, and pain does not hurt. These are all perceptions, and a Ghalian learns to control them."

The Adepts were forced to tread water for a while, fighting against the gentle current as they did. That actually helped them, keeping their muscles active and preventing a total locking up of their limbs. And this was the easy part.

"All right. To the next chamber," Warfin finally commanded.

The Adepts swam to where the slightest shift in current told them the underwater tunnel lay. It was completely dark, and they were to traverse the obstacle without the aid of illumination or air bubble spells. Sometimes, they would be out of magic, forced to rely on only their own physical abilities. It was why they trained so hard in their compound, because the more they sweat and bled in training, the less they died in combat.

Elzina dove at once, eager to take the lead. As she had grown older, her competitive streak had only strengthened. And with Bawb rising above his classmates, it made her push herself even harder. It was a character flaw, but one the masters overlooked simply because she was incredibly talented in all other respects.

The others simply carried on. Skilled and constantly

improving, but competing with themselves, not others. Among them all, only Elzina seemed to have that conflicting personality flaw.

Usalla flashed Bawb a little wink. "See you on the other side," she said, submerging calmly beneath the frigid water.

The others followed one at a time, spaced out, ensuring they would not kick one another in the face as they swam through the long tunnel. Finally, Bawb took a deep breath and slid beneath the surface.

The icy water on his face made his heart slow even more, the natural diving response to the cold water built into his physiology, making the task at least a tiny bit easier. He kicked hard, propelling himself headlong into the darkness, the rock walls sliding by under his fingertips.

That was one of the difficult aspects of the tunnel. It was not a straight line, and with no illumination, one had to be very careful not to swim headfirst into a wall. The Adepts had to rely on mostly their legs and torsos, the undulating motion propelling them forward while one of their arms and hands spent most of the time extended, feeling for the right path.

Fortunately, they had swum this challenge a great many times and the basic course was memorized by now. But variations in both current speed and their own energy levels could change their rate of progress rather significantly.

Bawb felt his lungs begin to burn. This was sooner than usual. Normally, he experienced the discomfort's onset at about the halfway point, where the small air bubble could be found if one surfaced carefully. But in the dark it was near impossible to locate it, their freezing fingers too cold to discern the feeling of air versus water as they groped ahead.

He would have to fight through it and persevere.

Bawb swam on, doing his best to keep his thoughts from the pain in his chest. The good thing about the growing agony was it was helping take his mind off what happened to Alara. The bad was that it made it quite clear he was exerting himself far more than usual, his emotions making his heart beat faster, burning through his precious oxygen more rapidly than he should.

Worse, he had no air bubble cast around his head. Even if he did want to cheat and use magic, he simply couldn't. No spell could be uttered underwater. He had to make it to the end or die trying.

On he swam, his hand gliding along the stone wall. A turn was coming soon, and after that, the straight shot to the open water of the next chamber. He swam and swam, but the turn didn't come.

Bawb's lungs were convulsing with burning agony, his body desperately wanting to take a breath. Had he made a wrong turn? Was there some new variation to the course he hadn't known about? Bawb's mind raced as he kicked steadily, barely keeping himself calm, fighting the urge to flail wildly in a desperate effort to go faster.

His hand bumped into an angle, and he turned immediately. A faint light caught his blurry vision. That was it. Precious air was just up ahead, so close and yet so far. He kicked faster, ignoring his training, both arms pulling as hard as they could. He bumped his head on the rock above but did not stop. He couldn't.

Bawb's vision was starting to dim, and it had nothing to do with the tunnel's illumination. He was out of oxygen. If he didn't make it out immediately, he never would.

With a desperate surge of energy, he swam even harder, arms and legs working together as fast as they could, propelling him ahead. Things were going dark when he cleared the tunnel into the pool, giving one last mighty pull with his arms as he forced his head above the surface.

Bawb sucked in air loudly, flopping onto his back in a

survival float until his senses cleared. When he finally opened his eyes, he saw his classmates and teacher staring at him. This was not like him. Not at all.

"I am fine," he said, brushing it off. "I merely hit my head, causing me to lose some of my breath."

It was a lie, but given the scrape on his forehead, the others seemed to accept it at face value. What had really happened was far more embarrassing. His emotions were jeopardizing his training, and in so doing, his very life. He would have to get himself under control. More training requiring his full attention was ahead, and it would be just as hard.

If not harder. And hotter, as the case may be.

CHAPTER SEVEN

The Adepts jogged at a leisurely pace through the adjoining caverns, tunnels, and passageways, their clothes still soaked from their swim when they reached the sealed entry to their next challenge.

"You know what to do. Standing only. And no magic," was all Warfin instructed. And yes, they most certainly did know what to do. And it was not going to be pleasant.

Bawb and the others began stripping at once, shedding their soaked clothing as fast as they could before gathering it up and unsealing the chamber door. Once inside, it would seal tight behind them.

They walked in, the brutal heat of the geothermal cavern blasting them like a blistering wind on the hottest summer's day. While they had all wished for warmth in one manner or another as they tread water, shivering and cold, this was not exactly what they had in mind.

All were well hydrated, fortunately, and that would be crucial to making it through this challenge as they began to sweat almost immediately. The heat was far more than a mere sauna. This was dangerously hot, and that was the entire point.

The shedding of their clothes had been automatic, but in their first visits to this chamber many learned the hard way that while wearing their damp clothing might feel good at first, the water would quickly evaporate, and the resulting steam would burn their skin in a most painful manner.

It had been a lesson they'd only had to learn once.

The brutal temperature contained in the thick stone cavern was natural, not magical, generated by both hot springs as well as thermal vents, both funneling the heat from the planet's core. While the springs created a miserably humid pocket of air, the vents blasting their breeze to the ceiling kept any condensation from forming.

Combined, it was a perfect duet of pain and suffering. One the entire class of Adepts would now have to face for as long as their teacher saw fit. And they had to do it all without any magic. Fortunately, their konuses naturally maintained a neutral temperature without their having to cast any spells. Otherwise, the metal bands would have become painful *brands* instead.

They had actually used magic in this place on many occasions. Most notably, when dealing with the air around the hot springs. They had received a few burns at first, their magic shaky, but in short order they learned how to best cast to protect their skin from the scalding steam without wasting too much power in the process. It was a minor comfort in the back of each of their minds that here, above water and able to breathe, they could, if they absolutely had to, cast a spell to save themselves.

But that was not the point of the exercise. This was all about endurance, and nothing could create it but extended periods of discomfort and effort.

Bawb felt himself beginning to wilt after only a short while, the heat taking its toll far quicker than the cold had. Of course, the cold had also weakened his, and everyone else's, bodies from the strain, making them more susceptible to this latest torment.

He looked at his classmates, each and every one of them standing, wishing they could lie down on the hot floor, which would at least be a few degrees cooler than the hotter air at head level.

No one spoke. Even if they could, to do so would be exhaling precious moisture with every breath. As it was, breathing through their noses, while painful, at least helped moderate the air's effect a tiny bit. Had they been animals with long snouts, their physiology would have cooled the air before channeling it into their lungs. But they lacked any such natural adaptation, and so the misery continued.

They stood absolutely still, not locking their muscles and joints but rather settling into as relaxed a position as they could. Every bit of effort they could avoid would keep their body a fractional amount cooler. It wasn't much, but it added up, especially as the clock ticked by.

Bawb slipped into an almost meditative state, forcing himself to think about anything but the heat. His anger was making things difficult, but as the heat overwhelmed his senses, even that internal blaze began to seem cool by comparison. He was still upset—even this exercise would not put that out of his mind —but he began to envision a clear lake, a refreshing breeze, and a frosty drink even as his muscles burned with accumulating lactic acid. But his aching limbs held still despite the mounting pain and weakness.

He reminded himself of his prior experiences on real worlds where heat was a very real enemy. He had survived, but if not for his training, he very well may not have. And that was easy compared to what he would face moving forward in his pursuit of mastery. If he was on a contract in a hot location he would not be able to just take a break whenever he felt like it. And if a sensitive caster was about, using even a little magic could blow his cover and cost him his life.

And so, he and the others suffered through it in a test of pure willpower and mind over matter, pushing themselves to the limits but in a location where failure would at least not cost them their lives.

But no one failed. Not today. A few came close, but all remained conscious and upright. Barely.

"Out," Warfin commanded as soon as he unsealed the door. "Recover on the move."

There were water bladders waiting for them, not cold, but refreshing nevertheless. They downed them slowly, not allowing their thirst to cause an overindulgence that might bring about nausea and vomiting. Another lesson they had once learned the hard way.

They walked silently, doing their best to slow their heartrates and relax their cramping, weak muscles. No one made a sound when Teacher Warfin stopped at their next destination, at least not out loud, but the collective groan in their minds was almost palpable.

"Yes, you know what is next," their teacher said as he opened the door. "Three circuits, beginning with knife throwing. Swordplay is second, followed by two laps around the chamber carrying a classmate. Switch after each lap then begin again." He took in the exhausted looks on their faces with satisfaction. Good. This was what it took to grow stronger. "Well? What are you waiting for? Begin!"

The Adepts hurried to the weapons racks and gathered up their knives for the exercise. While their arms were like jelly, they had to hit a small target several long paces away. Then sword work, and finally, the heavy lifting. It was a test of fine muscle skill as well as brute strength, all done at the end of multiple challenges that each would have laid out any normal person.

But these were not normal people. Not by a longshot.

"After you," Usalla said to her friend with an exhausted but amused grin.

"So thoughtful," Bawb replied with a pained chuckle. "Very well. Let us get this underway. The sooner we start, the sooner we finish. Hopefully, it will be our last task."

It was his deepest hope at the moment. It was all of theirs. But it was not meant to be.

One more challenge. One more task before they could finally rest. And it was not even a physical one. At least, not exactly. But exhausted as he was, Bawb was not looking forward to it. Not one bit.

He had felt his body begin to recover during the brief respite the students were given before they were to begin. It wasn't a lot, but it was enough for him to start to regain his sense of equilibrium. With it, however, also came his anger at what had happened to Alara, a steadily growing ball of heat spreading through his psyche.

"No," he chided himself. "Control yourself."

"What was that, Adept Bawb? A problem?" Warfin asked, standing much closer than he realized.

"It is nothing. I am fine."

"Ah, nothing. Well, as you are fine, I suppose that makes you ready to begin. You shall be first up."

Bawb nodded once and headed to the circle, where four teachers now stood at the perimeter. He walked to the center and settled into place, waiting for the command.

Warfin let him wait a while before speaking, studying the young man with a curious gaze, sizing him up, as he always did.

"Hover," he said, tossing a stone orb to the student.

Bawb cast the spell at once, catching the ball and holding it aloft with a minimal use of power. This was a tricky spell but one that could come in handy in all manner of situations. And now Bawb was to hold it. Hold the spell no matter what.

Warfin nodded to the other teachers.

They started light, taking turns hitting him with spells of their own. Annoying ones to begin. Itching spells. Foul smells. The sensation of stinging insects. All the sort of thing he might encounter in the real world. Also the sort of unusual spells that might one day serve him in his pursuit of a goal, distracting someone enough to complete his task.

But Bawb was very much on the receiving end today, and it was not pleasant. Nevertheless, he persisted, his intent solid, his spell holding.

Warfin gave the others a look. They shifted to more distracting spells. Punches and pulls making Bawb shift on his feet. But he still kept his focus, not allowing them to make him fail. He didn't have the extra bandwidth to even think about the abuses they were heaping upon him. Not today. What little free capacity he had was slowly creeping back to thoughts of Alara. How he had not been there to protect her. How he would make whoever did this to her pay.

He felt his grip on the magic slipping and quickly redirected his attention, forcing the spell to regain its hold on the orb. A blast of cold and hot hit him from two sides, the teachers teaming up on him, layering their attacks at the same time from different directions. The feeling of sharp sand whipping against his face came next, followed closely by solid thumps to his back.

Bawb felt his annoyance grow. He had better things to be doing than this. He needed to—

The orb fell to the ground.

The teachers ceased casting at once, falling back to a neutral stance while Teacher Warfin stepped into the circle, approaching the student.

"This is failure, Bawb."

"I am aware, Teacher Warfin."

Warfin stared at him silently yet again, almost as if he could smell some sort of disturbance on him. "This is typically a strongsuit of yours."

"It is."

"And yet you stumbled. Lost your focus on what should have been a simple exercise for you. We had not even reached the difficult distractions, and yet you faltered. This is not acceptable."

"I realize that, Teacher. I am sorry. I will do better."

"You most certainly will. You are clearly distracted," Warfin said, aware of Bawb's recent failed mission, but unaware of the incident that had truly unsettled him so close to home. "Do whatever you must to put your head right. You are fortunate this weakness was exposed during training. It was a mistake that could have seen you killed in combat."

Bawb gave a little bow. "I will gladly take care of it, Teacher," he replied, a look of calm resolve in his eyes.

If only Warfin had known what he actually meant by that, he might have dissuaded the young man.

CHAPTER EIGHT

Bawb stalked through the city, disguised, determined, and armed to the teeth.

He had eaten ravenously after training, fueling his body for his off-hours quest. Then he geared up and slipped out into the streets, leaving his classmates to their own devices, training or resting the remainder of the day, depending on their whims. A bit of freedom afforded them after so grueling a training session.

Bawb, however, had other ideas. Teacher Warfin had suggested he do whatever he needed to get his head straight. And he was doing precisely that.

Thoughts of Alara were at the forefront of Bawb's mind as he navigated the crowds, the Adept flowing through them like water, blending in and passing without anyone the wiser of his deadly intentions. It was second nature now, and that was a good thing, because his thoughts were most certainly elsewhere.

While Alara had been the first to teach him the ways of the bedroom, that had only been one time. An impressive time, but a lone occurrence nonetheless. But he and the disguised Ootaki woman had remained in contact, a friendship forming that both of them grew to cherish. It had been an entirely platonic one with no ulterior motives, which, for Alara, was a novelty coming from a male. But for Bawb it was just natural. She was a good person, a knowledgeable lover, perfectly capable of sharing her insights in conversation rather than skin-on-skin practice, and on top of that, she was an all-around pleasant person to simply spend time with outside the training house.

Of course, he kept their meetings secret. He would never dream of bringing attention to her doorstep. She was hidden, but she was still an Ootaki, and her hair was valuable enough to put her at risk if any ever found out about her.

They sometimes discussed her romantic liaisons over the years, Bawb learning more about the habits and weaknesses of all manner of otherwise powerful men and women who sought her out for her services. It was valuable insight into the psyche of all sorts of people that this unusual woman taught him in a way no classroom instruction could ever rival. And she gladly shared that knowledge with her young Ghalian friend at no charge.

Despite their first meeting, what they had developed was a chaste, healthy, deep friendship, and neither would have it any other way.

After she had faced one rather upsetting encounter, Bawb had requested that the local spy network keep tabs on a woman living far across the city. No one had asked why; they simply did as he asked. The subject was someone who had powerful visitors from time to time, so it made perfect sense they would be tasked with such a thing.

And when he called upon them now, a name was what Bawb had received from them. A name and likely location. He was a Tslavar slave trader named Argotz, and he was already off world, visiting a nearby system to sell his most recent acquisitions.

It made the Adept's blood boil. Slavery was abhorrent to the Ghalian, and that his friend had been assaulted and beaten by one of the slave traders only served to increase Bawb's rising ire. But he was a professional. Angry as he was, he had to be smart about this.

Argotz was not just a slaver. He worked for the Council of Twenty. A low-level player in their slave trade, acquiring and selling at their behest, but still under their umbrella. It was mostly Ootaki and Drooks he dealt in, but he also ran a healthy side business of his own, snatching up men and women alike, selling them off as gladiator fodder, sex workers, or even Zomoki food if the price was right.

His affiliation with the Council afforded him a degree of protection most Tslavars did not enjoy. Security came with the arrangement, and only a fool would dream of pushing back against him. That was both a challenge and a benefit from Bawb's perspective. Argotz would be difficult to reach, yes, but he would also be overly cocky and sloppy as a result. And that could be taken advantage of.

First, however, he would have to get close to him.

Bawb crossed the city to Alara's place, entering through a window on the side. One that only he had access to. The wards were still in place against all others. Only her Ghalian friend could come and go without tripping them. Once inside, he saw telltale signs of her abuse. Broken furniture and smashed personal items spread about. There was also dried blood.

He knew she was alive and being healed, but that was beside the point. Her home, her inner sanctum, had been violated, and he felt his anger burn even brighter. He took a deep breath and put it aside, forcing himself to reach out with his konus's magic to sense the use of power in this place. It took a moment to clear his mind, but once he did, he could feel it easily.

There was an almost imperceptible trace of Alara's familiar konus, its magic keeping her disguised and safe at all times. There was also something else. An enchantment of sorts. He crouched and touched the dried blood. Tiny hints of magic could be felt in it. Alara had been cut with an enchanted blade.

It was enough for him. Too much. He did not need any more. This man, this savage, would pay.

Bawb exited the window and headed straight for the nearest tavern. He scanned the patrons, but there were no Tslavars for him to disable and steal their identity, nor were there any at the next three he stopped at.

"Fine," he grumbled. "I will just deal with it when I get there."

It was time to shift tactics. He would just fly to the planet Argotz had last been seen and handle acquiring his false identity on-site. He would need to take the face of a Tslavar, specifically. Any of them would work, so long as they had high enough ranking to be of use.

Bawb would have to infiltrate to get to him, and it would be tricky. Tslavar crews were notoriously suspicious of outsiders. Any non-Tslavar wouldn't stand a chance of making it into their base of operations. But a fellow Tslavar? Well, if he got all the little details right, from the way they walked and spoke, down to the obscure things like how they ordered food and drink counting up with alternating fingers on both hands rather than just one, then, and only then, would their guard be truly dropped.

Fortunately for Bawb, he had spent a long time perfecting exactly those habits. Tslavars were found all across the galaxy, and people tended to steer clear of them whenever possible. It was what made them such a useful disguise. And Bawb could slip into that mindset in an instant, adopting the movements and slang of the brutal race with ease. All he had to do now was find the right person to be his patsy.

He paid extra for the fastest flight and reached his destination in no time, the Drooks powering the transport ship using a fair amount of magic to jump them there in short order. It was an expenditure he was more than happy to make. His time was limited.

The world was a rather unimpressive one. Not particularly lush, not particularly big. But what it lacked in those regards, it made up for with a reputation as a trading hub. One where anything could be found, for the right price. Perfect for Bawb's needs.

Bawb moved with relaxed ease as he walked the landing site, appearing to be out for no more than a casual stroll. He located Argotz's ship easily. It was big for a slaver. More than that, it was also parked in the main landing field in an area reserved for Council vessels. Definitely Argotz's ship.

Bawb watched the craft for a short while, noting the comings and goings of a few of its crew, and more importantly, the markings of their badges and ranks. Each ship was a little different, and knowing who served aboard which one of them was a vital part of his plan.

That done, Bawb headed off toward a rougher part of the city, walking the area around the dive bars and taverns until he came upon a group of *very* inebriated Tslavars stumbling down the footpath. They always traveled in packs, the safety in numbers bolstering their aggressive behavior. Of course they did.

But that would be of no help to them now. Not with the Ghalian in their midst.

Bawb brushed past them, noting their insignias in a glance. These men were not from Argotz's ship. Perfect for what he had planned. He turned around and followed them quietly.

No one even noticed when one of their friends went missing. They would just assume he had passed out somewhere along their tavern crawl and go find him later, unaware a Ghalian had taken him, knocked him out with a powerful stun spell, and then assumed his identity, leaving the slumbering Tslavar in a pile of trash behind a cheap rooming house.

Bawb moved faster now that he was in disguise. People moved out of the way of the Tslavar they perceived stomping down the road. He smiled to himself. It was exactly the reaction he needed.

Argotz's men would almost certainly be frequenting one of the taverns nearest their ship, their reputation scoring them favorable rates on food, drink, and whatever illicit services the proprietor might offer. It only took Bawb three tries to find a group of them with the right insignias on their uniforms.

He noted their location in the establishment when he entered, then veered toward the bar. He purchased a large ale and turned back to the milling patrons, moving through them closer to his targets.

"Hey! Watch your damn feet!" he bellowed in the deepest, most intimidating Tslavar growl he could.

The man he had bumped into spun with panic in his eyes. "I-I didn't mean to. I didn't see you there!"

Of course he hadn't. Bawb had walked right into him from behind. But that was the entire point.

"Idiot!" he shouted, backhanding the man, sending him flying. He hit the wall hard, slumping to the ground. No one sensed the stun spell Bawb had cast, making the injury seem far worse than it had been. He needed it to look real, but he had no desire to harm an innocent.

It clearly looked real enough. The table of Tslavars laughed uproariously, pleased with this newcomer's attitude.

"Hey, you! Yeah, you. Come join us!" the leader of the group called out.

Bawb spat on the unconscious man, poured some of his drink over the poor fellow's head with a laugh, then took a seat with them.

"I'm Yakko," Bawb said, flashing a particular chest bump sign with his fist and giving a little nod. It was a small thing, but one that told the Tslavars he was not just a trader but came from a mercenary sect.

"I'm Toggz," the group leader replied.

The others then responded in kind, introducing themselves, showing their own secret signs, bonding with the newcomer immediately over their shared love of mayhem and carnage.

"It's good to find friends on this shithole of a world," Bawb said with a jovial laugh. "Lemme buy the next round."

"No argument here," the nearest, very drunk Tslavar said with a slur.

Bawb flagged down a cowering barmaid and dumped coin on her tray. "Whatever they're having," he said, giving her a lascivious grin as he eyed her up and down.

The others laughed uproariously. "She's not having any of it," the group leader noted. "We tried."

"Tried? We take what we want!"

"Yeah, but the captain wants us on our best behavior here. Can't go messing up our cushy situation with the Council."

"You have a Council gig? Lucky bastards!" Bawb replied, slamming his drink down hard enough to make it splash across the table. "I'd kill for that kind of work."

"We've done plenty of that!"

"I bet you have," the disguised assassin said with a laugh.

He carried on like that for some time, plying them with drinks, drawing out all of their stories, endearing himself to them by being a great listener, though it was done so subtly they had no idea they were all talking extensively about themselves. They were also very, very drunk.

Bawb expertly weaved in his own story in bits and pieces. Tales of adventures, killing, and eventually winding up stuck on this shitty world, with his ship nearly destroyed thanks to a pirate attack.

"It's gonna be forever before I get off this damn rock," he grumbled. "I need action, dammit!"

"Hey, why don't you join up with us?" one of the Tslavars still sober enough to speak suggested.

"Really? A spot on a ship with a Council gig? You'd do that?"

The leader of the group seemed to sober up just a little bit as the idea churned through his intoxicated head. He liked this new guy. He was rough, violent, could hold his alcohol, and seemed like he'd fit right in.

"I don't usually make the offer to strangers—"

"Who are you calling a stranger?" Bawb shot back with a laugh.

"You're a good one, Yakko," the man replied. "We all like you already. Hell, I know the captain'd like ya too. Why don't you come with us? I'm sure he'd offer you a temporary spot with us."

Bawb slammed both hands on the table and rose to his feet, wobbling just the right amount as he did. "You are the best damned people I've spoken to in ages! I accept!" He spun toward the bar, knocking a passerby down in the process. "Another round!" he shouted with a carefully applied slur. "Another round for my new shipmates!"

CHAPTER NINE

Under the guise of the man called Yakko, Bawb traveled back to the secure landing site and was ushered aboard the Tslavar ship without having to spill a single drop of blood. His disguise was holding up well, and these overly confident slave traders could simply never dream of someone being crazy enough to try to sneak aboard their ship. As a result, no one had taken the precaution of casting detection spells.

It was to prove a costly mistake.

Bawb spent several hours with his new shipmates, talking up his past exploits as they showed him the workings of the ship. He then volunteered to help them deliver some slaves their captain had sold, returning with the supplies and coin from the exchange. Though Bawb was appalled by the interaction, this was not the time to act. He had to let things play out as expected, no matter how distasteful it might be.

"There's the captain," Toggz said, nodding to the sturdily built Tslavar with a fair collection of scars on his visible flesh, including a few fresh gouges on his neck. Apparently, Captain Argotz had been through quite a lot in his climb up the ranks.

But that made sense. In Tslavar society, brute force was often respected above most else.

"Captain, this is Yakko," Toggz announced as he handed over the bag of coin he had collected from the transaction. "A solid man in need of a job. Me and the boys thought he'd be a good fit."

Argotz pocketed it without counting its contents. He trusted his crew. More than that, they all knew that stealing from him would result in the harshest of punishments, if not worse. And for a Tslavar, this Council gig was about as cushy as it could get. No one wanted to jeopardize a good thing.

The captain sized up the newcomer with a typical Tslavar leer. "Too weak."

"I'm not weak, Captain." Bawb replied with just the right amount of threat to his tone.

A tiny glimmer of approval shone in Argotz's eyes. "Maybe not. But we don't need another mouth to feed."

"I'm not a beggar. I've got coin of my own. It's just my last ship was run by an idiot and now I'm left stuck on this godsforsaken rock. I'd hoped to join a better ship with a better captain."

"Well, that you've certainly found. But why would I take you on?"

"Because I realize what I'm asking, and I know the expense. That's why I'm willing to cover the cost of my food and lodging while you make a decision," Bawb replied, pulling a small pouch of coin from his pocket and tossing it to the captain.

This time, Argotz did inspect the contents, and he found them acceptable. While not the most common occurrence, bribes to get a better assignment were not exactly unheard of in Tslavar life. It was just most crew didn't have enough saved up to make one. But if this newcomer had coin of his own to spend, he must have been good at his former job.

"Yakko, you say?"

"Yes, Captain."

Argotz stared at him a long moment, sizing the man up. He was strongly built, had somehow endeared himself to his most trusted crewmember, and had even come up with coin for him. In other words, he was about as good an addition to the ship as he could ask for. And if he didn't work out? Well, Argotz could always simply have his men strip him of his remaining coin and toss him out on the next planet.

"All right," he finally said. "You've got yourself a spot on my ship. But I expect you to pull your weight."

"I always do."

"And what I say goes. Go against my wishes and you're off my ship. Possibly before we make planetfall."

"Understood. Just one thing."

"What?"

"Well, I have certain, uh, needs. How flexible are you with a man seeking satisfaction?"

At that, Argotz let out a deep laugh. "I'm all about finding pleasure where we can. Just be sensible about it. And don't get carried away."

"Carried away?"

"See these?" he asked, pointing to his freshest injuries. "Stupid bitch dared turn me away. I was just going to take what I wanted and leave, but now it's personal."

Bawb felt his anger glowing hot in his belly but forced it down, maintaining an amused expression that was quite the opposite of what he truly felt.

"Some whore attacked you? Who would be that stupid? What's her name? I'll take care of it for you."

"Nah, this I'll handle on my own. Alara's her name, and she's all mine."

That was all the confirmation Bawb needed, but Argotz wasn't done talking. "Beat her good," he said with a laugh. "Maybe a little too good. I was so pissed off, I decided to snatch her up then and there. Sell her off at a slave market somewhere far away."

"But you didn't?"

"Nah. Bitch sounded some kind of alarm when things got rough. I had to get out of there in a bit of a hurry. But not before I made her regret it."

"Maybe it's for the best you left. No sense getting tied up with locals over some woman, especially if they've got some sort of loyalty to her. I know I've had a few experiences like that over the years."

"Oh?"

"Let's just say I may have made quite an impression on them when I did."

The captain grinned wickedly. "Well, I don't think she's worth much to them after what I did to her. She shouldn't have upset me like that. But you know what? I'm gonna head back and snatch her up once she's healed. I'll still get a decent price for her, I wager."

Bawb laughed loudly, an evil sound rumbling from his lungs. And it was genuine, but not for the reason Argotz might have believed. He was thinking not about the Tslavar's braggadocio, but rather about what he was going to do to him as soon as the opportunity presented itself, and the violent image in his head was truly amusing, in a horrific sort of way.

He found his thoughts briefly shift to the powerful konus she had been gifted by Hozark. How it had protected her, keeping whichever disguise she had been using in place even while Argotz did his worst. Had he known she was actually an Ootaki, he'd have taken her as a slave at once, consequences be damned. Her hair was full of powerful magic, and that alone would have made his Council masters very pleased. Enough to quash any problems with the locals, even.

But Bawb was no local. He was a Ghalian.

"It sounds like you've been having quite a good time out there," he said. "I bet you have a *lot* of good stories."

"Ha! That I do," the captain said with a laugh.

Bawb looked around, then acted as though he'd made a tough decision. He pulled an old, opaque black glass bottle from his bag, presenting the label to the captain. "I've been saving this for a special occasion," he said, noting the man's very appreciative reaction to the very high-proof and extremely expensive booze. "I think maybe this is the time to finally crack it open."

"That's a thirty-year-old bottle of Deemal," Argotz mused. "Private reserve, no less. Alcohol blended with arcane magic, fermented to perfection. Where'd you get something like that?"

Bawb shrugged with an amused grin. "Let's just say its owner won't be drinking anymore. Ever again, in fact. But perhaps—if you have time, that is—you might be persuaded to tell us all some more of your stories over a few cups."

Argotz knew what the man was doing. He was buttering up his new captain, and he was really pulling out the stops. This was a very rare, and very expensive bottle. But while Tslavars had no problem taking coin from one another, drink was something they all took very seriously. A sort of bonding rite, the likes of which Bawb had already achieved with the crew, albeit with a far less pricy libation.

But this? Each cup would be worth a month or more's wages. And while the newcomer was willing to share with all, the expenditure clearly calculated to foster further goodwill among his new crewmates, *this* was the sort of thing the captain wanted to keep all for himself. Not to mention, it would serve to cement the pecking order aboard *his* ship.

"Put that away," he said, wrapping his arm over the newcomer's shoulders. "You want stories? I've got the best. Visit my ready room later, and we'll talk and drink, just you and me. No sense wasting the good stuff on the rabble. Just be sure to leave your blades at the door. It is a weapon-free chamber."

"Thank you, Captain. I look forward to it."

"As do I," Argotz said, already thinking ahead to the delicious treat awaiting him. One he would not dream of sharing with his crew. "You're a good man, Yakko. I think you will fit in here just fine."

CHAPTER TEN

The new crewmember came to the captain's ready room with a broad smile on his face and the pricy bottle in hand. Argotz invited him in and sealed the door, his chamber's privacy notice set in place to ensure none of his men would disturb them. If for some reason one of his people came in and saw an open bottle, the captain would be somewhat obligated to share some of the precious drink. It was a Tslavar thing.

But the newcomer had no problem keeping this bottle between the two of them. Yes, the man mused, this Yakko fellow was going to be a fantastic addition to this crew. Of that he felt quite confident.

That opinion changed quite rapidly as soon as the door shut behind him. A sharp pain cracked across his head, followed by unexpected darkness.

Argotz woke a short while later, his head aching. Judging by the sensation, he had been struck by something solid. And hard. No magic here. This was a good old-fashioned bludgeoning. Of course, with his defensive spells layered about the ship, any magical attacks on him would have been met with alarms at the least, and responsive counterspells at the best. Apparently, his attacker had taken that into consideration. At least he had come unarmed.

The captain shifted in his seat, his arms bound firmly behind him, he noticed. He opened his eyes, not bothering to feign slumber. If his captor was clever enough to take him hostage, he would be well aware of any such tricks.

"So, this is your plan?" Argotz growled, eyeing his personal items lying on the nearby table, stripped from his person just in case the captain might have some unexpected tricks up his sleeves. Sleeves that were now fastened behind his back along with the arms inside them. There was more. His hidden stash of valuables was also there. Apparently, this man was just a common thief, though a fairly good one at that.

Yakko simply sat in front of him, staring. Argotz didn't flinch. He had not risen to his position by being easy to fluster. If this fool wanted a staring contest, he was a more than capable participant. Or so he thought. But after several minutes even the great Captain Argotz began to feel uncomfortable, though he did a good job hiding it.

The man in front of him seemed to sense it, though, a decidedly unsettling smile creeping onto his lips.

"Fine, you got me," Argotz finally said. "What is it you want? Coin? You know I have plenty. But you need to remember, I am not some victim off the street. I work for the Council of Twenty. Do you realize what that means for you, thief?"

The man called Yakko let out a small chuckle. It was not a cheerful sound.

"It means the Council will find another lackey to fill your boots," he said in a threateningly calm voice.

"This makes no sense. Why are you doing this? You could earn more than you can steal under my wing. I took you in. Gave you a new home. You're one of us now."

"No. I will never be one of you," was the reply. Yakko picked up the bottle and began picking at the label, slowly peeling it off.

"Then why are you here? Why go through all this, for what? A ransom?"

"Not a ransom, no," Yakko replied, tucking the crumpled label in his pocket. "Do you remember that story you told me? How you got those gouges on your neck?"

"What? The whore? What of her? You want me to give her to you when I take her? Is that it? You want a woman?" Argotz said, almost laughing at the absurdity of it all.

"Alara," his captor replied. "Her name is Alara. And she is a friend of mine. A *very* dear friend."

It was then that Argotz began to get the slightest inkling of the trouble he was in. This man must have taken a special liking to her, for whatever reason.

"Look, I can pay you."

"I do not want your coin."

"I'll get her fixed up all nice for you, is that what you want?"

"She is already being treated by the most talented healers in the city," Yakko said, his fingers manipulating the seemingly smooth glass of the bottle as he turned it upside down. A hidden seam opened up, the bottom of the container sliding open easily, the liquid staying inside the upended vessel as the bottom came free. He pulled something out. Something the wards on the door would have alerted to had he been carrying it on his person.

A slender glass dagger, dripping with precious alcohol. The drink's magic content had masked its presence. Clever. *Too* clever for a Tslavar merc. This man was clearly something more.

"I'm well connected," Argotz blurted. "I have information. Valuable information."

In his anger, Bawb almost let his disguise slip as he pressed the tip of the blade through the Tslavar's tunic and muscle, sliding it into the man's chest, stopping just short of his heart. Almost.

"There is nothing you can tell me I do not already know," he growled.

"Then what do you want?"

"What I want? I want my friend to know she is safe. That you will never be coming back to trouble her again."

"I'll leave her alone, I swear!"

"But there is more."

Argotz forced himself to hold still despite the pain of the cool glass embedded in his flesh. "Anything! Just name your price."

Bawb grinned, his fangs sliding into place for just a moment. Just long enough for Argotz to realize what he was actually dealing with.

"What I want is to rid the galaxy of filth like you," he said, driving the blade the rest of the way into his captive's chest.

Argotz shuddered as it pierced his heart, his eyes wide with terror. Then he fell still, staring sightlessly, slumped in his chair. Captain Argotz would never trouble anyone ever again. What Bawb had said was true. Another would just take his place. But hopefully the next captain would show more self-control than this one had.

Bawb cut his bonds and carried the body to his couch. He wiped up the spilled blood carefully, then put the rag on the captain's chest before splashing the man liberally with the high-proof alcohol. He pulled the glass blade free and smashed it, dumping the pieces on his victim's lap, setting the half-empty bottle atop them. With a word, he ignited the body, fire engulfing the man in an instant. The heat would shatter the bottle, leaving his weapon's remains hidden in the aftermath, undetected.

He moved fast, prepping the next spell in a hurry. It was a

SCOTT BARON

tricky piece of magic, but in his anger Bawb's intent was laser-focused, and the spell was cast without a problem, an invisible containment bubble quickly forming around the captain. One that would keep the flames and smoke hidden for about an hour before dissipating and sounding the alarm. By the time the rest of the crew realized there was a problem, he would be long gone, and to whomever found the captain, it would seem that he had fallen asleep drunk and burned himself alive. That it was the newcomer's alcohol that caused it would just make his disappearance seem like the panicked flight of a man worried he'd be blamed for the mishap.

Bawb gathered up most of the coin and the most valuable items, then left several in plain sight in a few locations around the compartment. No one would consider foul play if there was currency left lying around and a nice profit to be made from the captain's demise. But he wasn't worried about being followed. He had scouted out departing shuttles before he had even begun his infiltration, and one was leaving well before his spell would fade.

His disguise intact, Bawb casually strolled off the ship—no one would be questioning anyone coming from *inside*—and made his way to a public restroom facility. The man who left a few minutes later looked nothing like the Tslavar mercenary who had gone in.

He paid his fare and boarded the shuttle, departing for a nearby moon from which he would acquire his much faster ride home. He could certainly afford it. Even leaving behind a considerable amount of coin at the scene of the crime, Argotz's death had provided him a small fortune.

It was very late when Bawb returned to his home city, but he headed straight for the healer regardless. Given the healthy payment he slipped to the attendant, not a word would be said

66

about his late-night visit. Alara had a private room, he was pleased to note. No one would be disturbing them.

"Ah, Bawb," she said, lying awake, her injuries healing nicely, but slowly. "I'm glad to see a friendly face."

"And I yours, Alara."

"Though mine is a bit worse for wear," she said, grimacing as her smile made her split lip open again.

Normally, the repairs would have been finished by now. But whoever had brought her in had somehow made sure the healer would do their job with much smaller infusions of power than normal. It had likely sounded like an unusual request, but the concern that her Ootaki nature might inadvertently take over and simply absorb the magic rather than allow it to be applied to her injuries was a very real one. One that might lead to her discovery. Given the nature of her hidden-in-plain-sight status, it was almost certainly a Ghalian who had seen to it. He wondered who.

That didn't matter now. All that did was that his friend was alive. Alive and getting better.

He placed his pack on the small table beside her bed. "This is for you."

"Gifts? Why, Bawb, if I'd known there were presents involved, I would have gotten beat up sooner."

"Do not jest, Alara. You could have been killed."

"But I wasn't," she said, opening the pack.

Her eyes widened at the sight of the contents. A wealth far beyond any get-well present. She reached in and pulled out a small sack of coin. One of many. This one, however, had faint traces of blood on it.

"Bawb? What did you do?"

"It cannot make up for what was done to you, but they will trouble you no more."

She nodded, slipping the pouch back into the pack and sealing it up tight. "And you are unharmed?"

"I am fine, Alara," he replied, both his concern and relief clear on his face. Maybe not to others, but she had known him a long time now and was one of the few outside his order he considered a confidant. Perhaps the only one, for all she knew.

"You are a most unusual Ghalian, Bawb. Has anyone ever told you that?"

"You, on many occasions," he said with a grin.

Alara laughed, ignoring the pain in her lip and body. It was good to see her friend, and despite her conflicting thoughts about a killing being carried out on her behalf, she felt a deep sense of relief knowing she was safe. Truly safe.

"Well, it is *very* late, but I bet you have some stories to tell. Share some tea with me before you return home. I would hear all about your travels and adventures. What you can share, of course."

"I would like nothing more," he replied, resting his hand gently on hers. "Where shall I begin?"

CHAPTER ELEVEN

Bawb spent an hour with his convalescing friend before he finally took his leave. Alara had a new sense of peace around her, knowing she was well and truly safe. With that came her first truly restful slumber in days.

Bawb left once she had nodded off and walked the empty streets, accompanied by nothing but his footfall in the darkness of night. It was a long way home, but he found himself sliding into a sort of moving meditation as he walked, his thoughts flowing with a comfortable ease now that the disconcerting anger that had flooded him had finally dissipated.

Now, after the fact, the reality of what he had done was sinking in, and he could not help but find himself a little concerned. His reaction had been drastic, as were the lengths he had gone to seeking justice. His emotions had gotten the better of him, he was forced to admit. Even after all this time, rising steadily in the ranks of the Wampeh Ghalian, he still had that emotional streak that had concerned the Masters since his earliest days in the order.

He had learned to shut it down externally. To keep everything in check and locked up tight. But, apparently, there were still some things that could get a rise out of him. And along with it, a severe reaction. Deadly, as this particular case may be.

Bawb pulled himself from his thoughts as he drew close to the compound. He silently entered via one of the lesser-used doors and made his way to the bathing chamber. The hot water felt marvelous, washing away the last remnants of the stresses of his impromptu adventure.

Clean in body and spirit, he quietly crawled into his bed and settled in, the soft pillow a welcome embrace upon his weary head. He fell into a restful sleep almost immediately.

"Adepts, up!" a voice called out, interrupting his sleep only an hour later. It was Teacher Griggitz. "Prepare for travel."

Bawb moved quickly, dressing at once and falling in with the other students. Despite his truncated rest period, he actually felt good. Refreshed, even. Taking care of this problem for Alara had not only helped protect his friend, but it had also given him an unexpected sense of confidence, for only after the fact did he really think about all he had done, and on a moment's notice, without support, and with no intel to speak of, no less.

Teacher Griggitz directed the students to different chambers across the compound. Even at this painfully early hour, it seemed the teachers and Masters were hard at work setting whatever they had in mind in motion.

Bawb reached the room he had been sent to and found Master Hozark waiting for him. He'd thought the legendary Ghalian was in another system. That he was here gave Bawb a slight flush of concern. Had Hozark found out about his unsanctioned assassination?

"Good to see you, Bawb," his mentor said with a casual air. "Come, take a seat."

The young man did as he was told, wondering if and when the other shoe would drop. But Hozark said nothing of his little adventure. Even so, Bawb would not have been the slightest bit surprised if he had. The man always seemed to know things.

"You possess many skills of a Ghalian. You have trained hard, and the results are clear. It is only natural that you would be sent on more frequent and more difficult contracts."

"Thank you, Master Hozark. I—"

"I am not finished. Things have taken an unexpected turn of late."

"I can explain."

"I am not speaking of your recent failure. Master Imalla has relayed all of the details, and while you most certainly acted in foolish haste, your performance up until that one critical error was exemplary. But you need to learn more. To be better prepared to defend yourself against more dangerous adversaries."

"We are training hard."

"You are, as are your cohort. But you need another perspective. A different kind of instruction. As I am sure you have heard rumor, Ghalian are being targeted more frequently of late. The other Masters and I fear this is the doing of the leak in our organization. There is no way to know yet, though we are working on it. In any case, we are concerned the traitor's actions may lead to even Adept-level Ghalian being at risk. As such, you are all to receive specialized training."

"I noted we were separated," Bawb observed.

"Astute of you. Yes, you have gathered correctly. You will each be taken to train away from your classmates."

"I have not seen Master Turong in some time. It will be good to—"

"You will not be seeing Turong," Hozark cut him off. "I have decided you are to train with none other than Ser Baruud."

Bawb didn't show any reaction externally, but on the inside, he felt a rush of excitement. Ser Baruud was something of a legend. A former pirate, captured and forced to fight as a gladiator. One who excelled in the combat arms and eventually earned his freedom through his marvelous exploits. To train with him was an honor.

"He will train you in pirate combat skills. It is an asymmetrical style, shifting and flowing with the tides of battle, often using the most unexpected of methods to overcome and overwhelm far larger adversaries."

"Bud and Henni have shown me a bit," Bawb noted. "But nothing like you are suggesting."

"Those two are quite skilled in piracy, and you would be wise to heed their instructions. But there is far more to Baruud's training. You will also become proficient in the gladiatorial arts. It will be an entirely new style of combat for you, Bawb. Gladiators are similar to Ghalian in one very important respect. They train with a single-minded ferocity, because theirs is a life of combat, and failure means more than mere disgrace and injury. If the cost of healing is too great, they may very well be sold off for Zomoki food."

"It sounds like it will be quite the learning experience."

"It will be. And know this, Bawb. You may be in the best condition of your life, but nevertheless, his training will push you to your limits."

"I look forward to it."

Hozark grinned. That was the response he had hoped for. "You will travel there with me under the guise of being my slave. A recent acquisition who shows promise and whom I wish to have trained in the gladiatorial arts. That story will allow you to keep your konus. I have informed him that you are bound to me with it as my servant and property and that it cannot be removed."

"Like a control collar, sort of?"

"In a manner of speaking. But this way you have access to

magic, though you are only to use it when instructed by Ser Baruud."

"So, a slave? He does not know what I am?"

"No. You will need to maintain a basic disguise spell for the duration of your time with him. This is another reason you will need your konus. Choose your disguise wisely. You will be powering it for the entire time and must maintain it no matter what. Do not select anything you might lose control of, but also nothing he would sense."

"He is a natural power user?"

"No. But Baruud has not survived as long as he has by any lack of perception. If you falter, he will sense it. This is a skill you will use often in your life, Bawb. Learning to hold a disguise spell for a long period of time in a real situation and under great pressure will serve you well one day."

Bawb wanted to make mention of the Tslavar disguise he had just successfully used to trick the devious slave trader but thought better of it. Even if Hozark did actually know of his actions, he had chosen not to bring them up, and only a fool would draw attention to their violation of Ghalian rules like that.

"When do we depart? Immediately, I assume?"

"Go eat a good breakfast first," was the amused reply. "Normally, yes, we would leave at once. But this is Ser Baruud we are talking about. You will need all the energy you can muster."

CHAPTER TWELVE

Bawb heeded the Master Ghalian's words and ate the most energy-rich meal he could manage, filling himself almost to the point of discomfort. Some would say he was overreacting to the suggestion he eat well, but this was Hozark. He would not make the recommendation lightly.

The pair walked across the city to one of the smaller landing sites, where they boarded a relatively regular ship. It was still a very nice vessel, as one would expect of someone with the resources to hire Ser Baruud to train his slave, but it had no resemblance whatsoever to a Ghalian craft.

Hozark had slipped into a disguise before they left the training house, as had Bawb. The Master had selected the name Oralius, a man of his normal build but his skin possessing a light blue coloring. To use a lot of magic in this instance would not only be wasteful, but could also draw attention. If Ser Baruud was as good as he said, there was no telling if he would sense more than the most basic of spells.

For that reason Bawb followed suit, his skin now a ruddy orange color, his hair a deep brick-red. For the duration of this task, he would be called Drenn, he decided.

The craft was powered by a small team of Drooks, the group focusing their power with an ease that made it quite clear they had been together in this configuration for some time.

"Free Drooks," Hozark said, noting Bawb's curious gaze back toward their compartment as they lifted off with grace and precision. "A team we saved in the process of destroying a Council vessel some years ago. A skilled group we have used quite often. This ship is theirs, in fact. Rented out to generate income for them while allowing them to utilize their gift."

"And the Ghalian?"

"We pay for the use of their services like anyone else. They are never made aware when we are passengers aboard the craft. So far as they are concerned, we are just another charter. Better for their safety, as well as ours."

Bawb rose from his seat and moved about the cabin, studying the craft with curious eyes. Drooks owned this ship outright. Yes, it would appear as though they were under the control of the blue-skinned man now posing as the owner and captain, but the truth was anything but. It never ceased to fascinate him how this order of killers were also likely the single greatest power for good in the fight against slavery and the Council of Twenty in all the galaxy. Quite the dichotomy by any standard.

The flight went relatively quickly, allowing Hozark time to further brief his pupil on the legendary man who would be taking him under his wing for a while. By the time they landed just outside Ser Baruud's compound, Bawb was almost a little starstruck at the thought of getting to train under someone of his reputation.

"Remember, you must maintain your disguise at all times," Hozark reminded him. "Learn all you can, but under no circumstances make your true nature known."

"Understood," the young man replied.

"Good. Then let us go and meet the man, shall we? We would not want to keep him waiting."

Hozark led the way, exiting onto the soft soil with an even stride, walking right toward the imposing gate leading into the training compound. But this was just one of many. From what he had told Bawb, Ser Baruud had all manner of training facilities at his disposal. This just happened to be the one most people knew about.

"You must be Oralius," a ridiculously fit young man with red skin and equally red eyes said as they approached the gate. "I am Togo. Ser Baruud asked me to see you in. Please, follow me. He will be with you shortly."

Togo led the pair into the compound's entry courtyard. Both Ghalian appreciated the layout. To the common eye it seemed like nothing more than a pleasant outdoor space leading to the main living areas. But they could see it for what it really was.

A killing field, if so needed.

The magic wards and defenses layered here were strong, likely the work of decades of patient casting. Ser Baruud was not in the habit of making enemies. But those he trained sometimes did, and he would be damned if anyone would get the drop on him on his own premises.

Fortunately, by the feel of the resting magical potential, no one had been that foolish in a very long time.

"Ah, Oralius," a voice called out from the shadowy doorway directly ahead of them. "I am pleased you reached my humble home without difficulty."

The owner of the voice stepped out into the light, and Bawb almost allowed surprise to show on his face. Ser Baruud was a middle-aged man with an incredibly fit physique, his every movement calm and smooth, but radiating a bundled energy waiting to be unleashed. That wasn't the unusual part. What had so startled Bawb was that Ser Baruud was a Wampeh.

He could sense the man was not a Ghalian—he lacked the almost imperceptible feeling of one capable of stealing power as Bawb and his fellow assassins could. But he could well have been mistaken for one by any not in the know. His pale skin bore a few small scars, souvenirs of his life of combat. His hair was pulled back in a tight ponytail, the tension making his face seem a little younger than he actually was.

Hozark strode right up to the man and shook his hand warmly, handing him a hefty pouch of coin as he did. "So nice to see you again," he said, and to Bawb's ears, it sounded like he actually meant it. "This is Drenn, the one I told you about. I'm hopeful you can make something formidable out of him."

"We shall see," Ser Baruud replied as he looked over at the orange-skinned youth. He stared a while, assessing him like a piece of livestock. He nodded once, satisfied.

"Strong enough, though he could do with a bit more muscle," he said.

Hozark nodded his agreement with a chuckle. "He eats well, let me tell you. But he's got that youthful metabolism. Just burns right through it."

"Well, rest assured, by the time you collect him, he will have gained a bit more mass," the gladiator said with a grin. A curious look crossed Baruud's face. He lifted Bawb's arm with a questioning look. "A konus?"

"Ah, yeah, that. It's bound to him and can't be removed. On pain of death."

"But why not use a control collar? It is the norm."

"Sure, but I find a konus works better. A bit of the carrot as well as plenty of stick. He has some power to make himself useful but nothing more. But if you want to release more for him to work with in your training, just use this spell," he said, slipping a folded piece of parchment to Ser Baruud.

"We will see about utilizing magic. That sort of training comes later, and it is on a case-by-case basis."

"You hear that, Drenn? Do well and you might even get to use some magic. But for now, off you go. I'm sure Ser Baruud has a lot in store for you. Train hard."

"I will, Master. Thank you for the opportunity."

Baruud nodded. "He understands respect. A good start. Very well, come with me. Oralius, I will skree you when he is ready for your retrieval."

"Thank you. I look forward to that day," Hozark said, then turned and walked away.

Just like that, Bawb was on his own. And it was not going to be easy.

"Come. This way," Baruud instructed, leading his newest student through the doorway and into the compound proper.

What Bawb saw impressed him, which said a lot coming from someone who had spent years of toil in the Ghalian training house. There were dozens of men and women training, some full-grown adults with scores of battle scars crisscrossing their bodies like badges or ranks, earned from the gladiatorial matches from which they had emerged victorious.

Others were younger. Aspiring gladiators. Or, at the very least, those whose owners wished them to be so. It was among them Bawb would likely first train. And watching them spar, he felt he could hold his own.

All were fighting, practicing forms, wielding all manner of weapons, and running through the familiar-looking misery of quite difficult obstacle courses.

"A bit skinny, but you seem wiry and strong. Let us see what you can do," Ser Baruud said.

Bawb jogged to a rack and picked up a sword, twirling it about his body with ease, showing off a little, hoping to make a good impression.

He did not.

"No, not that," Baruud said, shaking his head. "This."

He pointed to something Bawb had not seen before but nevertheless knew quite well. It was a variation of one of the most torturous series of challenges the Ghalian teachers had subjected him to in his younger days. Not a test of fighting skill but one of strength, endurance, and most of all, the will to press on no matter how much it hurt.

"Well? What are you waiting for, Drenn?"

Bawb nodded once and walked into the gauntlet. Running would not make a difference. This was not that sort of challenge.

He lifted up two buckets of water and gazed up at the steps leading to the top of the platform the other students were climbing, each dumping their load and returning to refill once again. It brought back memories. Painful ones at that. His shoulders almost started to burn just thinking about it.

But he did not hesitate, holding the buckets in his hands and climbing the steps, just as the others were doing. Baruud had him do this for an hour before moving on to the next element. This was precision work.

"You are to take this staff and put the tip through that ring," Baruud said, handing him a very long but slender length of wood and pointing at a metal ring suspended nearly its entire length away.

Bawb lifted it up and began aiming for his thrust.

"Not like that," Baruud said with a knowing look. "With *one* hand."

Bawb did as he was told, his hand gripping as tightly as possible. The staff wasn't all that heavy, but its length made it wobble violently with every amplified move he made. Bawb thrust and missed. Ser Baruud seemed to expect this.

"Come see me when you have succeeded," he said, then walked away to check on other pupils.

Bawb tried over and over until his wrists were on fire, his forearms swollen and tight from the effort. But he persevered, calling deep within himself and forcing his aching limbs to work in spite of the agony. At long last, when he wondered if he would ever succeed, the tip slipped into the ring, but only barely. Bawb held his breath, willing his arm to hold still. The slightest tremor and it would fall out, and he didn't know if he had the strength to push it through.

You really wanna fail? his konus asked.

It was not a question.

"Not now," he grumbled.

Then do it already. I'm getting bored watching you flounder around here.

Bawb felt a little flare of anger in his belly and channeled that into his arm, thrusting forward and sending the staff flying through the ring. It landed on the dirt with a rather anti-climactic thud.

You're welcome, the konus said, then fell silent.

Bawb ignored it and hurried along to find Ser Baruud.

"Done already?" the man asked.

"Yes."

"Good. Only twelve more challenges to go."

Bawb kept his face neutral but felt his stomach drop. He ignored his emotions and shook out his hands, holding them over his head until the blood began to flow out of them, reducing the swelling.

"I am ready," he said.

Baruud seemed pleased with that reply. "Good."

Bawb spent hour upon hour being pushed through all manner of trial, from endurance to strength, to even having to fight off several quite dangerous beasts with little more than a wooden sword and his wits. Finally, Ser Baruud called him over.

Bawb walked to him, head held high despite his exhaustion.

"Not bad," the gladiator said. "How do you feel?"

"I feel—"

Ser Baruud launched into an attack, fists and elbows flying fast and hard. A few hit, but Bawb's reflexes kicked in, defending and blocking as fast as his drained body would let him. He even attempted a counterattack, though his energy was clearly flagging.

Abruptly, Ser Baruud stopped, giving him a satisfied nod. "Not bad at all," he said, walking around the sweat-soaked young man. "Yes, this I can work with. Togo will show you to your quarters and the dining area. Bathe, eat, rest. We will begin your training in earnest in the morning."

CHAPTER THIRTEEN

Bawb, or rather Drenn, as he was known to everyone in Ser Baruud's compound, had cleaned up quickly and hurried to join the others training under the legendary gladiator's tutelage for the group's much-anticipated hearty dinner. This was when he would learn more about this place and its residents, the end-of-day meal often being the one where exhausted and bruised students would bond over their shared hardships.

As the newcomer, Bawb found himself bombarded with greetings and unrequested suggestions, everyone having some little tip or tidbit that might make his stay better. They fought one another hard during the day, sometimes to the point of requiring a healer, but when the weapons were down and the training finished for the day, these people all had the deepest of respect for one another.

Those who bore the scars of gladiatorial combat also realized that for the professional gladiators among them, one day they may be forced to face one another in a true contest, and unlike the lower-tier events, it could very well be to the death.

"You made it," Togo said, the first face Bawb had

encountered at the training grounds taking a seat beside him. "Not everyone makes it through the intake process."

"It was a bit of a surprise."

"Just Ser Baruud's way of making sure anyone who comes to train with us doesn't need to be hand-held through basic fitness kinds of things, you know? We're all here to improve, not start from scratch. There are plenty of places someone could go to for that sort of training."

"Tell me about it. I've been run through it for ages. But I guess that's just our life," Bawb replied.

Togo's fingers toyed with the band around his neck. "Indentured fighting. Not what I envisioned when I set out looking for adventure."

"None of us did, I'd wager."

"Not true. There have been a few who got into the whole gladiatorial life because they found they were good at fighting and killing but not much more. Hey, Rahalla, come sit with us," he called out to a tall, violet-skinned woman with jet-black hair close cropped on the sides, the remainder woven into a tight braid hanging between her chiseled shoulders. Bawb noted the faint gleam of a darkened blade tied into the end of it.

"It's not happening, Togo," she said with a roll of the eyes, walking right past him to sit with a group of hardened fighters.

"A friend of yours?"

"She likes me," Togo said with a shrug. "She's just playing hard to get."

Bawb read her body language and could tell at once that, no, it was not a game, but he wasn't going to be the one to break the news to the poor guy. Besides, he was here to train and fit in, and while he might not make friends, per se, he was determined to become a welcome part of the group. And that meant not upsetting people unnecessarily for starters, especially on day one.

It was funny, that. How tough warriors would sometimes go to pieces over a romantic interest, putting all of their brute strength and drive aside and becoming as vulnerable as a child. It was a trait the Ghalian exploited when they could, and noting the interactions of others for future manipulation was almost second nature now.

Togo introduced Bawb to a lot of other people as they dined and laughed, most of them giving him a warm welcome and jokingly lamenting the day's labors, well aware the next day could be worse. By the time he turned in for the night Bawb had nearly a dozen new names and faces locked into his mind, and another dozen or so he planned to meet in the following days.

The bunkhouse he found himself in was quite similar to what he had grown up with, a large group of trainees sharing a communal space. The only difference was the bunks were more comfortable here. Larger as well, likely to accommodate some of the bigger residents' mass. At least half of them were unoccupied as well. Other than that, it was a pretty familiar setup, and Bawb drifted off to sleep with ease.

It was dark o'clock when Bawb felt the hairs on his neck tingle. He lurched from sleep, defending himself from an unseen attacker in the dark. But this was Bawb's element. Ghalian thrived in darkness, and he was no exception.

His attacker, however, was clearly using a night-vision spell, putting Bawb at a disadvantage. But he could not cast one of his own. He was entirely prohibited from using magic while in this disguise. That is, unless Ser Baruud made him. That meant fighting relying entirely on his senses and nothing more.

Bawb could hear the others waking from the sound of fighting, but no one came to his aid. Bawb was on his own. He parried and blocked, launched counterattacks and even landed a few light shots of his own.

"Lights!" Ser Baruud said, the bunkhouse illuminated in an

instant. He looked at the newcomer with a satisfied nod. "You did well. Most do not rise so quickly from their slumber."

"I've always been a light sleeper," Bawb replied, almost amazed he had managed to maintain his disguise in the unexpected chaos.

"A good trait," Baruud noted. "Come, we join the others."

"At this hour? Where?"

"You will see."

Bawb dressed in a flash and followed, the rest of the group going back to sleep. Apparently, whatever this exercise was, it was for him and him alone.

They headed out of the compound walls and into the wilderness surrounding it. The duo trekked hard and fast, Ser Baruud moving with the ease and speed of a man half his age, barely breaking a sweat as they traversed streams and gorges, climbed hills, and circled cliffs. Finally, they came upon their destination atop a low mountain just as the sun crested the horizon.

It was a mountaintop training site, and quite an extensive one at that, hidden far out in the wilds, away from prying eyes. A group had camped there, Bawb noted. They were already up, and a few were preparing their morning meal while others took the opportunity to practice their skills as it cooked, balancing atop staggered wooden poles, leaping to and fro as they fought one another at a relaxed speed.

Others were engaged in some light wrestling at ground level, tossing, rolling, and pinning one another in a friendly bit of practice at an easy pace, warming up their muscles for the day to come while priming their bellies for the cooking breakfast.

It was a motley group of older fighters and younger ones, made up of all manner of races, shapes, and sizes. One thing was certain at a glance. Whatever their morphology, every one of them had a certain sort of confidence in their movements. A feeling of skill and power hidden just below the surface. Bawb knew it well. They all had the air of a warrior.

"This is Drenn," Ser Baruud announced to the group. "He will be joining us for a while."

With that, Baruud turned and headed to the group atop the tall poles, watching but not critiquing, allowing them to practice unfettered. This was just their morning warmup, after all, and a little sloppiness could be forgiven. But with the way he watched them, Bawb could see he was taking notes, and once the day's real training began, he would be adjusting their work accordingly.

"Hey, welcome," said a particularly large man with a deep rumbling voice and shoulders that looked as though someone had hewn a couple of large rocks in half and stuck them on his body. He was an imposing figure, to say the least. "I'm Borx. Lemme show you around."

"Thank you. I appreciate it."

"Heh, no worries," the massive man said with a good-natured chuckle. "Okay, those are the poles. We fight on top of them. That's the ground work area over there. That's where we sleep. And over there's the shitter. Questions?"

"Uh…"

"You'll be fine. Usually we spend a few days out here before Baruud swaps us out. Likes to keep training fresh, ya know? Doesn't want us falling into routines. As he says, 'You never know what you'll face in the arena, so be prepared for anything.'"

"I've heard a similar saying: 'Expect the worst, hope for the best, and prepare for both.'"

Borx clapped him on the back with an amused grin on his face. "I like that one! I'm gonna use it, if you don't mind."

"Knock yourself out."

"I actually did that once."

"Really?"

"Just a stun spell gone awry. I'm not the best with magic. But if you need heads cracked," he said with a gleam in his eye as he slammed his meaty fist into his palm. "Well, that's something I've been good at since I was a little boy."

"I doubt you were ever little," Bawb joked.

"Yeah, my ma would agree with you. You'll fit in just fine, Drenn. Glad to have you with us. Now, come on. Food's almost ready, and I don't know about you, but I could eat a Malooki!"

CHAPTER FOURTEEN

Breakfast was hearty and clean, filling the gladiatorial students with plenty of healthy energy to get them through the morning's training. Lunch was sure to be just as robust, as dinner would no doubt also be. For what these fighters' owners were paying for this schooling, no expense would be spared.

They started their day's work shortly after breakfast, beginning with balance skills to allow their food to properly digest as they warmed up their muscles. Ser Baruud would train them to their limits, but that did not mean he was an unreasonable man. And unlike the Ghalian, these fighters were preparing for arena combat, not unexpected confrontations in the streets. Going into their fights at their best was the way their lives functioned. A novel change from the impromptu and often uncomfortable sessions Bawb and his cohort so often faced. Training with proper rest and meals would be a delightful novelty, and almost relaxing in a way.

The hard work, however, would be anything but.

"Who's that?" Bawb asked, nodding toward a slender, pale-green-skinned woman in a long frock.

She crossed in front of the group, all of them giving waves or nods of greeting. It seemed everyone knew this woman. Bawb couldn't help but wonder why.

"Get ready," Borx said with a grim chuckle as they were instructed to head to the sparring circles. "Plamanna's here early today. Looks like you're gonna have a trial by fire."

"Fire?"

"Not literally."

"Is she an instructor?"

Borx laughed at that. "Oh, hell no. She's the healer. Ser Baruud keeps her *very* busy."

"So, it's going to be *that* kind of training?"

"If you mean hard and violent, then yes, you're right. Maybe they'll start you out lighter since it's your first day."

"You think so?"

"Nah, you're screwed. But hey, at least they'll fix whatever you break."

"What a relief," Bawb said with a sarcastic shake of his head.

"Just have fun. And good luck out there."

"You too."

"Luck? Ha! I've been at this a long time, Drenn. I don't need luck."

Judging by the way Borx moved, Bawb felt pretty confident this wasn't just empty bragging. Despite his size, he moved with the grace and body awareness of either a dancer or a warrior. Both were in complete control of their bodies, it was just one tended to leave death and pain in their wake rather than cheering audiences. Though, technically, fans of the gladiatorial bouts would cheer too, only theirs were in reaction to bloody carnage.

Bawb found himself separated into a group of less-seasoned fighters at first, the ones with the most experience in the arena separating off to run through a vigorous weapons warmup before diving right in and sparring at full speed. The only difference between their fights and true combat was they would stop short of killing blows, but only just.

Bawb noted that size, age, and gender mattered not here. In fact, smaller opponents often seized the advantage that afforded them, using their speed and smaller target profile to land multiple blows on their opponents. For their part, the larger of them fought back with surprisingly nimble countering techniques, landing plenty of hits of their own. One and all, they barely held back, but at this level, one was bound to get hurt, and quite seriously at times.

Hence the on-site healer.

Bloody, broken, whatever the cause, she would patch them up and send them back into the fray for more abuse. Bawb marveled at the amount of power the woman was wielding to handle this many patients in such short order. It was more than he'd seen even the Ghalian healers use.

"You are to train at full speed," Ser Baruud said to Bawb's group. "You have free access to whichever weapons you wish. But you will be fighting a targeting dummy rather than one another. Do not hold back. Show me what you are capable of."

The students nodded their understanding and spread out across their own section of the sparring area, gathering up all manner of weapons then launching into their moves, wailing on the sturdy targeting dummies at full speed.

Bawb started with a short staff, spinning it with ease, battering the dummy in a flurry of moves. He carried on like that for a little while, his limbs moving with practiced ease.

"Switch weapons," Ser Baruud instructed them.

The group returned their weapons to the racks and grabbed something else to work with. Bawb switched to daggers, a favorite of his, throwing them, slashing with them, not holding back. Hozark had told him to give it his all. Ser Baruud could only help improve his skills if he knew what he was really dealing with.

They went on like this for a while, switching out to all manner of weapons. Spears, swords, chain whips, knives, Bawb showed a great proficiency with all of them. Not master level yet by any means, but he was good. Surprisingly good, in fact.

Ser Baruud gave the slightest nod of approval. This one he could do something with.

"Sparring," he called out to the group. "All weapons. All styles. Let us see what you can do."

This was the sort of thing Bawb was familiar with. He partnered up with a woman twice his size, her green skin shiny with sweat, making her impressive musculature stand out even more. She carried a sword and a dagger and had the bearing of someone who could most definitely take care of herself. Interestingly, he noted she had an extra joint in each of her arms. Her attack angles would almost certainly take advantage of that rather unusual physiological trait.

"Ixxna," she introduced herself with a little bow.

"Drenn," he replied in kind.

"A pleasure meeting you," she said, launching into a flurry of attacks without further ado.

"The pleasure is mine," he said, deflecting her attacks with the twin daggers in his hands.

As the two of them locked blades, a little grin crept onto his lips. This was actually fun. He was getting to show his stuff—like, *really* demonstrate what he could do—and to someone other than his Ghalian classmates and teachers. And it felt *good*. Ixxna, however, seemed a bit at a loss. This new opponent was apparently far more skilled than his years would imply. And yet, she did not seem concerned. Bawb was processing that tidbit when she quietly uttered a few words, a moderate force spell slamming into his chest as another pummeled him from above, sending him hard to the ground.

He reacted immediately, pushing up and diving aside, rolling to his feet and charging her with a zig-zag pattern, avoiding most, but not all, of her magical attacks. Bawb moved fast, landing a kick and maneuvering himself behind her. He could smell her magic and felt the Ghalian urge well up within him. He had to fight hard to keep his fangs from sliding out and taking her power.

His indecisiveness allowed her to shimmy free, throwing him hard, creating distance. Bawb rolled to his feet, daggers at the ready but dusty from head to toe.

"Stop," Ser Baruud said calmly. No yelling instructions from this one. He commanded everyone's attention with the quietest of words. The sign of a true leader, in that regard. "Drenn, what happened? Analyze your mistakes."

"I wasn't expecting magic. She has no konus, so it came as a surprise."

"Indeed, it did. And this is why you must always expect the unexpected. Ixxna may be unusual in her possession of natural magic, especially as a gladiator, since the rest of you must rely on external aid." He looked at the dull band on Bawb's wrist. "Your master said that cannot be removed."

"It can't."

"But he also said it has a little power in it. Is that correct?"

"It is."

"And can you cast with it?"

"My master unlocked additional power within it for me to use while under your tutelage."

Baruud nodded his head. "Very well. Let us see if it is sufficient for our lessons. If not, you will be training at a disadvantage."

"Why is that?"

"Because we will be practicing incorporating magic into the remainder of today's drills." He turned to the others. "Everyone, put on a konus and prepare yourselves. We are going to ramp up today's lessons."

The remainder of the morning's exercises were a test of everyone's endurance, but also a learning opportunity hidden just beneath the surface of the violence at hand. Ser Baruud was quietly guiding each student, correcting form and giving them instructions on how to better utilize their strengths and overcome their weaknesses. This was not about any one person winning outright. Each of them would fail repeatedly over the course of the day. This was about making sure they learned each time it happened. Learned and improved.

Of course, the healer was kept plenty busy fixing the combatants' injuries, Bawb included, though his visit came later in the day after the group's lunch break.

Ser Baruud had both groups of fighters working hard in their mountaintop training ground, and toward the end of the day, he decided to switch things up a bit yet again.

"You are to fight Orlax."

Bawb looked at the mountain of an opponent, the man's arms thicker than his legs and his chest so broad it would take two of Bawb linking his hands just to reach all the way around him. It seemed Ser Baruud was giving the lesser students a bit of a trial by fire. Sink or swim, thrown in the deep end to see what they would do when pushed beyond their perceived limitations.

Bawb, however, was more than some trainee. He was a Ghalian, and he would push himself until he either triumphed or dropped from the effort.

Orlax proved to be nimble for his size, and his strength was ridiculous compared to Bawb's. What's more, he was a skilled caster, his spells peppering his opponent and creating gaps for him to strike or kick, using his physical abilities as well as his magical ones in a devastating combination.

Bawb took the brunt of the attacks well, casting shield spells, defending himself until the right moment arose, just as his teachers had instructed him. He even managed to land several powerful knees and elbows on his sparring foe, but Orlax just shook them off as if they were nothing. Given the size difference between the two, that might as well have been the case.

Bawb was pummeled, heavy fists slamming him harder than the brutal spells raining down on him. He felt his body breaking from the stress and saw the healer watching with interest, likely making note of what she would need to fix before his inevitable defeat.

But Bawb was not having that. A flare of emotion surged in his gut, forcing his mind and body to act as one, delivering a vicious series of spells and fists to Orlax's chest, actually driving the man back a few steps. He didn't stop there.

A swarm of buzzing, stinging flies swarmed Orlax's head as Bawb's unusual spell flew true. The man swatted at them, a momentary lapse in his defenses forming as a few flew into his mouth, causing him to gag, cutting short his spells. Bawb leapt at the opportunity, quite literally, driving his shin down on his opponent's leg with a rapid series of brutal kicks. No matter how big and strong he might have been, Orlax's body reacted on instinct, the leg twitching and jerking back from the barrage.

It was just enough to lower his head a few inches. All that Bawb needed for his coup de grace. He jumped up, his head cracking the man across the chin, opening up a gash in Bawb's hairline even as he brought blood to Orlax's mouth. Bawb spun hard, driving an elbow followed by a hammer fist into the corner of his jaw. The impact nearly fractured the bones in his hand, but he poured everything he had into another two punches in rapid succession despite the pain.

Orlax staggered, stumbling to his knees. Bawb slid onto his back and locked in a tight chokehold rather than attempt to simply beat the man into submission. More likely than not, he would break all the bones in his hand on that solid block of a jaw if he kept that sort of attack up. Instead, he squeezed his arm around his neck hard and fast, cutting off both blood flow as well as air.

It was a risky move. With his reach, Orlax could pick him off with his massive hands, and that would be the end of it. But Bawb had practiced this technique hard and often, and it came to him as naturally as breathing. Just as his teachers said it one day would, he realized.

Orlax struggled a moment then toppled over. Bawb released his hold at once, rolling the man onto his side to ensure he had a clear airway until he awakened. He then stumbled backward, landing on his ass, his own head spinning. It seemed he was more than a little concussed, and now that the adrenaline was fading, he realized that, yes, he had likely broken a few bones as well.

Ser Baruud nodded to Plamanna the healer. She had a few students help carry the two off the sparring area and set to work on them, mending their injuries with speed and efficiency. When they were both restored, she got Ser Baruud's attention, and the two found themselves paired off with other fighters at once.

No sense sitting around. There was training to do.

It went on like that for a few more hours before Ser Baruud announced that was all for the day. He instructed the assembled group to run back to the compound together. Once there, they were to bathe, eat, and relax. They had done well and, as a result, would have the rest of the night off.

Sitting in the large sauna hours later, Bawb felt the remaining aches and pains of the day slowly leaving his body.

Orlax's massive shape filled the doorway as he entered, a mountain among them. A mountain Bawb had somehow defeated.

He sat next to the newcomer and clapped him hard on the back. "You're quite a fighter," he said with a grin. "I underestimated you."

"People do that," Bawb replied.

Orlax laughed, as did the others sweating away in the sauna. "I bet they do. I won't make that mistake again, that's for sure."

Bawb wasn't quite sure where this was going. He'd defeated one of the more formidable of them, and quite publicly. Not all would take that well. Not well at all. But as Orlax leaned back, his body language that of a man totally at ease, Bawb realized he wasn't taking the defeat personally at all. He turned to face him.

"You know, that was one hell of a fight. You nearly had me a few times."

"Oh, I know. But you're a tricky one. And that insect spell? Bloody clever. Unheard of!"

"Thank you?"

"I mean it. That was some damn original thinking. Well done, little brother. I'm adding that to my arsenal, no doubt about it, though if it works, I'm totally claiming it was my own idea."

The others in the group laughed, enjoying the relaxed, sweaty bonding among warriors, and Bawb felt relief flood his body. He was one of them now. Accepted. A welcome addition to their merry band of gladiators. A true brother-in-arms, just like the rest of them.

If only they knew what he truly was. But if Bawb did what he was supposed to do here, they never would.

CHAPTER FIFTEEN

The days of training grew longer and harder, but despite the brutal workload, Bawb pushed himself even more, impressing Ser Baruud with his determination and skills. Enough so that he found himself sparring with the professional gladiators more often than not. Something that would normally take a student months, if not years, to achieve.

But Bawb had been pulling out the stops little by little, not showing *all* of his Ghalian skills, but enough to make every day a challenge, and that was the entire purpose of this visit. He could have sandbagged and held back, enjoying some easier training with the lesser fighters, but Master Hozark had brought him here for a reason. To make him into the best possible fighter he could become, and that was an honor and responsibility he did not take lightly.

Days turned into weeks, and, just as Ser Baruud had predicted, Bawb's lean musculature began to fill out from the hard work along with the substantial meals he and his new cohort downed several times a day. One thing was for sure; in this place, no one went hungry.

"The well-fed warrior is often the successful one, facing an equally skilled foe," Ser Baruud mentioned when Bawb complimented him on the quality and quantity of food he provided his students.

It was not always feasible to dine in such a manner when facing the realities of outside settings, of course, but there was a reason the top gladiators in the game were continuously at peak levels. Namely, the way they were cared for by their owners. They may have been enslaved fighters, but like prize animals, when they were not fighting, they were extremely well taken care of, anything to keep them in peak condition.

And as most of the top fighters' patrons had paid very good coin to have their prize specimens undergo the rigors of Ser Baruud's training, it only made sense that the cuisine would be both satisfying and hearty. And did they ever need it.

As the weeks stretched on, the group trained all over the region, Bawb almost always accompanying the top fighters once he had proven his worth. They were the ones pushed the hardest, for unlike the lesser trainees, when these men and women returned to the arena it would not be a mere contest of skill. It would most likely be a fight to the death.

Up the mountains they ran, sometimes carrying rocks, logs, or even each other, depending on their instructor's whims. Other days they would race down into the deep ravines, learning to maintain their balance on the mossy rocks and in the swift waters pulling at their feet as they sparred. Far more than once, Bawb found himself requiring the healer's touch.

Forest sessions were his favorites. The balancing atop poles and practicing of magical techniques while keeping oneself centered falling in line with the Ghalian ways he had been training in for so long. The larger of his newfound friends had a harder time of this particular labor, their mass making it difficult to keep balance with feet so much larger than their perch.

Bawb, however, thrived in the constantly changing environments. It was just like home in that regard, though he never said a word about that. Lips shut about his real life and his disguise firmly in place, Bawb carried on just like any other trainee, though he did seem to draw the special notice of Ser Baruud on more than one occasion when he let a little of his own technique slip into his sparring.

It wasn't sloppy, exactly. Just instinct kicking in when body and mind were exhausted. Just as it was intended, at least in any other situation. But here he had to maintain his cover story, and that meant his own special technique, crafted and refined, though not quite complete, needed to be kept under wraps. Fortunately, he only made that error once, and no one said a word about it, chalking up his unexpected victory to a lucky shot taken in the heat of the moment.

The training days often went into the night, but not always, and it was after a particularly rigorous afternoon of muscular endurance, full-force sparring, and the most dangerously powerful magical practice, that Ser Baruud approached his prize students.

"Shore leave," he said to the assembled group as they prepared to run back to their compound.

The gladiators let out a gleeful roar, but Bawb was confused. Borx noticed the look on his face and clapped him across the back with a rumbling laugh. "No, we're not on a ship," he said. "But he was a pirate once, so Ser Baruud calls it that all the same."

"So, shore leave is what? Downtime to ourselves?"

"Oh, more than just that, little brother. We are free for the night to leave the compound walls. To go visit the local taverns and dining halls."

"We're free to go as we please?"

"Well, within limits, obviously," the massive man said,

fingering the golden control collar fastened around his neck. "We stay in the nearby village but don't venture all the way to the city. And it goes without saying we don't engage with anyone. No fighting, no matter what. If we do, we face not only banishment from the compound but also Ser Baruud's wrath. And let me tell ya, I've seen what he can do. You do *not* want to bring shame on his house."

"Noted. What now?"

"Now? Now we bathe—I know we all must smell like beasts of labor after today's trials. And then we head to the village for a night of fun and festivities. But don't overdo it, Drenn. Tomorrow it's back to hard work, just like every day."

"Thanks for the tip. I'll be sure not to go too overboard, then."

"Smart fella. Now, c'mon, the sooner we get back, the sooner the fun begins."

The group wandered into the nearby village with joy in their hearts and smiles on their faces, and it was a good thing. While most knew of Ser Baruud's facilities in the area, coming face-to-face with a gaggle of very tough-looking gladiators on the common footpaths would be disconcerting for even the most stoic of citizen.

But this group was out for fun. Libations and food, and perhaps a few other treats, should the local talent prove successful vending their wares. Bawb laughed and caroused with the best of them, but he remained quite sober, his jovial behavior masking his alert gaze taking in everything around them.

It was a few hours later that conversation among a nearby table of drunken flight crew from one of the small transport ships caught Bawb's attention, and quite firmly at that. He shifted in his seat, casually turning his head just right and calling upon his konus to power the smallest of hearing enhancement spells. Nothing so grand it would risk his cover, but enough to let him hear them clearly. And what he heard chilled his blood.

"Yeah, he said he did it without even getting hurt," one of the group slurred.

"No chance. Slaying a Ghalian? I don't believe it."

Bawb rose from his seat to move closer under the guise of making a trip to the bar, conveniently near their table.

"I'm telling ya what I heard. And Narbahl from the Toridian trading outpost said he heard it too."

"He's lying. There's no way some fool could have done that."

"Hey, friends," Bawb said, fresh drinks in hand. "I heard you say something about a Ghalian being slain? That's pretty impressive. Who did it?"

"I'm telling you the same thing I told him. That guy's a liar," the drunk replied.

"Who's a liar?"

"Some common mercenary fella."

"Did you get his name?"

"Kid, *everyone* got his name. Wouldn't shut up about how brave he was and how he got the drop on one of those assassins and killed her stone dead. People would be talking about Zallin's amazing feat for years to come, he said. Over and over and over."

"Zallin?"

"Yeah, that's what he said. Fekkin' loudmouth. But why do you care?" the man asked, a little suspicious.

"I'm training up at the compound with that lot," Bawb said with a shrug, nodding toward his gladiator crew. "I just thought it was almost impossible to slay one of them. If he was local, I'd love to hear his story."

"Well, lemme tell ya, kid. Them Ghalian? Scary fuckers, sure. But they bleed just like anyone else."

"I suppose they would. But hey, do you know where I might find this guy? I'd really love to hear his story."

"He'd be more than happy to tell it, yet again," the man said with a chuckle. "In the city, last I saw him. He was hanging out near the Barulian marketplace."

"Oh, so he's not here?"

"Nah. But the city's not far."

Bawb considered his options. They were not to go to the city. They were to stay in the village and not stray. But no one knew his konus was not really a form of control band, and he could go wherever he pleased, so long as he took the right precautions. But if Ser Baruud found out and ejected him from the camp, Hozark would not be amused.

He weighed the options a long moment then set his drinks on the table. "Thanks for the conversation. You can have these. I think I've had too much."

That cheered up the men to no end, and he was confident any suspicions they may have had were gone, washed away for the measly price of a few drinks. Bawb staggered back to his group, holding his stomach.

"Whassa matter, Drenn?" Rahalla asked. "You overdo it?"

"My stomach doesn't feel good."

The table laughed at his misery, but in good-natured jest. He was much smaller than they were, so it was only natural his drink might take its toll sooner than later.

"Just don't puke on the table," Orlax said with an amused gleam in his eye.

"Or shit your pants," Gibbitz said, all four of his hands holding either food or drink. "Do that outside where we won't smell it."

Bawb shook his head and did his best to look as sick to his

stomach as possible. "I'm gonna head out and get some air. Maybe take a walk."

Rahalla let out a snorting laugh. "Yeah, walk it off, Drenn. Walk it off. Poor kid may be able to fight, but he's still got a weak stomach."

"It must've been something I ate," the Ghalian said, his obvious lie seeming like any other attempt at saving face. "I'll see you all later."

"See ya, Drenn. Don't soil the bunkhouse!" Gibbitz called after him.

Bawb stepped out into the fresh air and stumbled a few blocks until he was well clear of the tavern. He stood up straight and changed course toward the city proper, a name on the tip of his tongue, and its owner destined for the tip of his blade.

CHAPTER SIXTEEN

Bawb had trained long and hard under Teacher Demelza's tutelage, and shifting into a new disguise as he was on the move was now second nature. When he left the little town, he appeared as one person—though certainly not as his cover story, since he was not allowed to venture out beyond its borders—and when he reached the nearby city after a decent trek, he sported an entirely new look.

Multiple disguises even when you thought no one was looking was simply standard Ghalian protocol. "Assume someone is watching even when they are not, and you will be prepared for the occasion when they actually are," Teacher Rovos had once said. Words all of his students took to heart.

Bawb walked quickly but with a deceptively leisurely appearance to his stride, making it seem as if he was moving much slower. It was a trick he had learned from Master Hozark, a way to cover a little more ground when in a rush without drawing attention to yourself. It was hard at first, relaxing and forcing his body to move in a languorous manner even as he took longer and faster strides, but once he got the hang of it, it came as naturally as breathing.

He adopted the name Vinngo for this impromptu outing. He'd never used it before and would likely never use it again. A throwaway persona for a mission none would ever know he had undertaken.

It was Vinngo who inquired casually if anyone happened to know the whereabouts of Zallin. He employed a variety of similar but slightly differing cover stories depending on whom he spoke to. If any compared notes, it would simply appear as if one of them had their story a little off.

After the first few people he casually talked with mentioned they knew he was in town but not where, he got the distinct impression that the man was living a bit large off his newfound reputation and was stiffing people he owed for food, drink, and more. Naturally, Bawb implied that he was owed coin as well, and if he did happen upon the man, he would make it abundantly clear he needed to pay his debts.

Those to whom coin was owed but who lacked either the time or skills to reclaim it seemed quite thankful for his offer, and after several misses, he finally tracked Zallin down in the most unlikely of places.

A temple.

Bawb didn't care. He was a Ghalian, and while he respected the sacred places of others in a broad sense, he had absolutely no qualms about doing his business within those allegedly consecrated walls. In the end, no matter which invisible sky person one believed in, a Ghalian's blade would always find its mark.

He had gathered more information about the man who had killed one of his kin as he spoke with people on his search, and now it was relatively easy to pick him out among the worshippers scattered throughout the building. Bawb adopted the wide-eyed appearance of many visiting the structure, taking in the architecture and overall feel of it. Casually, he meandered about for a while, taking note of everyone in the building, their locations, and which of them appeared to be able to handle themselves, as well as those who posed no threat.

It was always fascinating the way fighters would carry themselves without realizing. A tension in the shoulders, a pivot of the feet, the squaring of the hips unconsciously when someone approached. All things that had likely gotten them out of scrapes in the past, but also a plethora of bad habits they didn't even realize they were projecting when trying to keep one's abilities under wraps.

Luckily, there were no killers lurking here today. The survey of the temple had gone as easily as he could have asked. That task accomplished, Bawb strolled closer to his target, a dozen ways to either kill him here or lure him outside to do the deed there scrolling through his mind. Whatever the case, the killer of Ghalian would not be drawing one more breath than necessary on this day. The order would have its revenge.

"Amazing detail," he said casually, nodding toward a sculpture towering over them both. "I can't imagine the years of training needed to get good enough to do that, can you? How do you even begin to study to learn that?"

He asked both a simple yes and no question, followed with one that would elicit a more detailed response. A tactic that he had found to be fairly effective in getting people to engage. Even if they weren't the chatty sort, the yes or no reply would give him an opening. This one, however, seemed like quite the talkative type.

"One of my favorites," Zallin replied. "The sculptor is actually from my homeworld. Have you heard of Moranghis?"

"I haven't. Is he still sculpting?"

"*She*, actually. And no, she died a long time ago. But the quality of her work ensured she'll live on forever. Pretty amazing, when you think about it. Immortality, just not like we usually think. Not a bad legacy."

"I'll say. I don't have any skills like that, I'm afraid. When I'm gone, I don't think anyone will even notice."

"That's okay. Most people live unremarkable lives. Now, me? I wouldn't know how to do that. Excellence is simply in my nature. But if you don't feel that way, well, don't you worry about it, if that's not your calling."

"Thanks. I try not to concern myself too much with that sort of thing, ya know? A bit beyond my way of thinking, if you know what I mean."

"I do. Like I said, it's not for everyone."

"But it is for you, it seems. It must be a great feeling, being special."

"Being *famous* is just who I am," the man humble-bragged.

Bawb extended his hand. His right hand, not his left, which was poised to draw a dagger and strike as soon as the cluster of worshippers close by moved away. "Vinngo," he said.

"Zallin," the man replied, shaking his hand with a strong grip. "Nice to meet ya."

"Wait, *you're* Zallin?"

"That's what I said."

"*The* Zallin? I've heard of you. Tales of your exploits are on a lot of people's lips, you know."

The man smiled, pleased to hear of his notoriety. "You know how it is for people like me. I have so many stories to tell. Adventures only a handful of people would ever dream of attempting."

"Oh?"

"Yeah. Like the time I went up against a full Council death squad single-handed and got away without a scratch."

"You really did that?"

"Yep. Or there was the time I stole a small fortune right out from under Nixxa's nose. That's a good one. Pirating from a pirate, see?"

"See what?"

"The irony."

Bawb was tempted to explain what irony actually meant, but refrained. He also knew that if this man had actually done that, he would have likely been hunted down and killed by now. Nixxa was not the sort to let that kind of thing slide.

"You've led an exciting life. Far more than I could ever dream of."

"Just who I am," Zallin said with a cocky grin.

"I heard someone saying you even slayed a Ghalian. How did you manage that?" Bawb asked.

Zallin's expression faltered. It was only a microsecond, but Bawb clocked it at once as the man's eyes darted involuntarily as his mind crafted the tale. Bawb's left hand relaxed, sliding away from his concealed dagger. This man hadn't killed a Ghalian. He likely hadn't done any of the things he claimed. Zallin was no more than a braggart and a liar. And while he had confirmed from others that a Ghalian had been slain recently, this was clearly not the one who had done the deed.

"Uh, yeah, that's right," Zallin said, barreling ahead with his lies. "I was on Gorlax. You know the planet?"

"I don't. I haven't traveled much."

"You're not missing much. Pretty boring world, if you ask me. But that's where I ran across the fella. He was a tough one, let me tell you. And the battle we had? Oh, it was epic."

"You went head-to-head with a Ghalian and lived? You must be an incredible warrior," Bawb gushed, already looking for the cleanest way to make an exit and head back to Ser Baruud's compound. The lies were coming fast and furious. For one, he'd heard from a couple of people that evening that the Ghalian reportedly slain was a female. And beyond that, even if he had managed to win in open combat, the clearly unscathed man would have paid dearly for it.

Zallin just blustered onward. "Not to brag, but yeah, I'm kind of legendary. I mean, to beat a Ghalian? It was hard. But just when it looked like he would get the best of me, that's when I used my secret weapon."

Bawb smiled big and bright, an impressed look on his face even as he groaned on the inside. The man was ridiculous. Faking it all to create what? A persona that only a fool would believe? But then, he realized, most people lacked the requisite skills and powers of deduction to catch on to the deception. It had simply become so ingrained in him with his years of constant training, that to *not* see the man for who he was would have been virtually impossible.

"You see, the key to fighting a Ghalian is to know their weakness," Zallin rambled on.

Bawb, bored with this as he was, actually wanted to hear this ridiculous tidbit. At least he could get some amusement out of the otherwise wasted time.

"Oh? What's that?"

"They're sneaky. Sneaky and fast. But their overconfidence makes them vulnerable."

"How so?"

"I just had to play it up like I was tiring, which, to be honest, I was. Not a lot, mind you. I'm too fit to get worn out like a normal man. But I let the Ghalian think I was. And then he moved in for the kill."

"But you're still here."

"That I am. You see, he wasn't ready for my little friend." Zallin turned his palm up, flashing a small dagger he had palmed.

Bawb wasn't impressed; he had seen the telltale movement. But he did have to admire that the man actually had a bit of skill with sleight of hand. However, making a blade appear in one's hand and knowing how to use it were two very different things indeed.

The disguised assassin skillfully maneuvered their conversation in a manner that allowed him to probe for any real information the man might have possessed about the killing, but he came up empty. All Zallin knew was that a Ghalian had fallen. He didn't even know the gender or age, from what Bawb could tell. He let him ramble on a bit longer then extricated himself from the conversation and made his exit.

He then ran the whole way back to Ser Baruud's compound, working off the frustration of the failed outing. He was in disguise, of course, so he didn't care who saw him. And when he was safely back in the small town, he tucked into a public restroom facility and shifted back to his Drenn persona, then wandered back to join the others as if he had merely been out for a long walk, his stomach settling from the fresh air and long outing.

No one suspected a thing.

CHAPTER SEVENTEEN

Bawb managed to draw no suspicion when he arrived somewhat late back to the training compound. Ser Baruud had no intention of treating his charges like children. They were gladiators, fighting for their lives on a regular basis. He would not hand-hold them like some child's nanny.

That they were also bound by their owners' control collars played into his leniency on their rare night out. They would come back or they would have to deal with the consequences, and no matter their skills, that would be most unpleasant for any who crossed that line.

Bawb spent most of the next several days practicing with the more advanced students. Ser Baruud felt comfortable enough with his rapidly improving skills to allow him to face adversaries with quite a lot more experience than him. That he held his own even against the toughest of them was a testament to his growing abilities.

He still visited the healer daily, however. The sheer violence and brutality of the training at this level was beyond even what he and his Ghalian cohort endured on a regular basis. They fought hard back home, but injuries were generally avoided, with the exception of the no-holds-barred dueling sessions they would periodically have.

But for the gladiator students it was a way of life, being truly harmed every single day and not flinching at the thought of it. Now he saw why Hozark had said he would learn a lot in his time here. It was one thing to intellectually know how an opponent with this sort of instinctive fighting background would react. It was something altogether different to have experienced it firsthand.

Their lack of fear or hesitation, combined with some rather impressive fighting skills, made him almost wish a few of his new comrades were of his kind. They'd have made fantastic additions to the order. But Ghalian were rare. More so than even these talented gladiators. People he had actually come to consider friends, much to his surprise.

He had sweated, toiled, and bled for many weeks before word came that his "owner" had finally arrived to claim him. Bawb's new gladiatorial comrades took the opportunity to say their affectionate farewells in a manner only this group of lifestyle warriors would find appropriate. They jumped him as a group, forcing him to fight them all off at once. It was something they did, but only for the ones they were truly fond of. A bonding sort of brutality among the toughest of the tough.

Ser Baruud watched them with a calm but assessing eye. He'd seen it before, and while he would not tolerate any serious damage done to someone about to depart, he let them have their fun. This group was close-knit, and in any other situation they would be a formidable fighting force. But they were gladiators. Indentured or outright slaves, and one day, even these friends might be forced to face one another. A bit of levity, in the meantime, was well-deserved.

"We'll miss you, little brother," Orlax said as he and his departing friend exchanged blows. "Be safe out there."

"Yeah, have some fun, if you can," Borx added as the whole lot of them attacked at once. At least, as best they could, given their size and numbers only allowed a few at a time to get close enough to lay hands.

Bawb replied with a laugh accompanied by a fierce flurry of kicks and elbows, transitioning between styles in a way that took his comrades by surprise. He powered through them all, delivering brutal parting shots to their heads, bodies, and limbs as he deftly avoided their counterstrikes.

He was pushing himself hard. Harder than he had previously, truth be told, because unlike the lessons they normally endured, this was a free-for-all attack, and anything went. Bawb was sweaty and bruised when Ser Baruud finally called for an end to their fun, but he was not bloody. His opponents could not say the same, more than one of them leaking from their lip or nose.

"I'll miss you lot," Bawb said, embracing them one by one, all of them breathing hard from the violent farewell in which they had just partaken. "You all take care of yourselves, you hear?"

"You know we will," Orlax said with a wide grin as he wiped the blood from his nose. "It's been a good time, Drenn. I hope to see you again."

"But not in the arena."

"Ideally, no," the man agreed.

Bawb saw Ser Baruud waiting for him and hurried his goodbyes. Ser Baruud then led him through the compound to the outer courtyard, where his "owner" would be picking him up.

"You have trained hard, Drenn."

"Thank you, Master."

"Not all put in the effort. Not all fully commit to the process. But you? You have done well."

"Again, my thanks to you. You have been an inspiring teacher."

"I am glad you have benefitted from my tutelage. But I must say, your little parting scuffle just now? It was most unusual. Your fighting style, where did you learn that?"

"It's just what came to me in the moment," he lied. "I was reacting to the situation without thinking about it. That many coming at me at once, it was kinda all I could do just to stay on my feet."

"Hmm. An impressive showing, for *instinct* alone."

"Thank you, though I've got to say, you stopped it at just the right time. Any longer and I'm pretty sure they would have just all piled on and squashed me like a bug."

"Perhaps. But perhaps not," his teacher said with a curious look in his eye. "Regardless, I wish you the best of luck in your future endeavors, whatever they may be." He shifted his attention to the man waiting for them at the courtyard entryway, waving a casual greeting. "Oralius, welcome back," he called out.

"Thank you, Ser Baruud," the disguised Ghalian Master replied, handing the man another hefty sack of coin. "I take it Drenn was no problem?"

"A delight to instruct."

"I'm glad to hear it. Hopefully he'll fare well in upcoming bouts."

"I am sure he will. Come, I will walk you out."

The three men headed through the gateway and out into the streets. They drew a few looks, but that was all. The locals were not only used to the comings and goings of dangerous-looking sorts from those walls, but they also knew better than to stare for any length of time.

"Drenn, you go ahead to the ship. I wish to speak with Ser Baruud a moment."

"Of course, Master," Bawb replied, taking off at a jog.

Hozark watched him go, noting that Bawb actually seemed more confident, though he had already been quite sure of himself. Despite that, this was a good test for him and his blossoming skills. He turned to the seasoned gladiator.

"He seems no worse for wear. And as you promised, he has indeed put on a bit of muscle."

"He trained *very* hard, and without complaint."

"I am glad to hear it."

"I figured you would be. Not all are as willing to undergo the rigors of my training house. You will be pleased to hear, Drenn was an exemplary student. Quite the trainee, I must say. He will go far in this life, of that I am quite confident."

"Again, thank you for your tutelage," Hozark replied, pulling out an additional pouch of coin as a tip. "Your knowledge and skill is greatly appreciated."

Baruud accepted the currency and tucked it away in his pocket with a little nod. "You know, he is more skilled than he lets on."

"Oh?"

Baruud smiled. "Quite. But he blended in well. In fact, he nearly let his disguise spell slip only once, and believe me, I sent my best at him."

Hozark's expression remained calm and cheerful, but his eyes took in the man with a fresh assessment. Ser Baruud knew what Bawb was. That he was a Wampeh Ghalian. And that meant he likely knew what Hozark truly was as well.

Ser Baruud remained perfectly at ease, with no trace of tension in his composure. "A safe journey to you both," he said. "If you should ever have others in need of my services, you know where to find me."

With that, he did what no one ever did to a Ghalian. He turned his back to him and walked away, utterly unworried.

Hozark watched him go, a grin creeping onto his face,

followed by a little chuckle. Baruud was quite a piece of work, and even his impressive reputation didn't do it justice. Hozark turned and headed to his ship, his parting moments with the gladiator replaying in his amused mind. He'd been fond of him before, but now he *really* liked the man.

The Ghalian Master boarded his ship and took his seat, connecting with the Drooks powering the ship and lifting off into the sky, happy his boy had done so well, and ready to enjoy a little time with him, even if he still could not tell him who he really was. Mentor and father figure would have to suffice. At least for now. One day, perhaps, he would tell Bawb of his origins.

But that day was not today.

CHAPTER EIGHTEEN

The flight was to be a fairly short one, so Bawb was as direct as possible with Master Hozark. He had known the man many years by now and looked up to him as more than just a mentor, but almost a father figure he had never had at the orphanage. As such, he felt he could speak openly with him about just about anything. Even the most painful and sensitive of matters.

"I heard talk while I was there," he said, still a little uncomfortable bringing it up.

"Yes, there is always gossip among the gladiators. You know, they hear far more than people would think. Their owners often treat them as items they own rather than people, and as a result, they are quite loose with their tongues in their presence. It is as if just because they wear control collars and fight for a living, that people believe they do not have minds of their own."

"Oh, I realize that. A few of the people I befriended in the training facility are exceptionally well-read. Of course, there are those who are quite the opposite."

"The slow-of-wit-but-quick-of-sword types? Yes, I have encountered quite a number of those as well over the years."

"I am sure you have," Bawb said with a little grin, the

awkwardness melting away. "But that wasn't where I heard things."

"Oh?"

"We had a night of liberty, and there was talk in the tavern of a Ghalian being killed. A woman. I pursued a lead to the city and found the man who claimed responsibility."

"You did? And what did you find?"

"He was a braggart and a liar. Somewhat skilled, from what I could make of him, but he lacked the abilities to kill one of our own. He did, however, speak of it as though it had truly happened, and rumors were floating around town to that effect. Was one of ours struck down?"

Hozark's face remained the same, but Bawb could feel the mood shift in the command compartment.

"So, it was true," the young man said, shaking his head, not in disbelief, for theirs was a violent and dangerous profession, but in sadness at hearing the news confirmed.

Hozark took a deep breath. "This is not something to share with the others. The details I am about to tell you are for your ears alone. Is that clear?"

"Of course. I will keep this to myself."

"Master Kolinga was her name. A younger Master, only recently ascended to that rank. Skilled, smart, she was a talented woman, though I did not spend much time with her."

"How did she perish?"

"That, my boy, is the problematic part. What you heard rumor of was correct. At least partly. It was a targeted killing, not a contract gone awry."

"She was assassinated?"

"In a manner of speaking, yes. It *was* a contract, and as such, it did possess certain risks. But Kolinga had ample intelligence on the location provided well in advance—the target, the guards and spellcasters protecting them—all of the things one would rely on for a task of this degree of difficulty."

"If she had all of that at her disposal, what happened?"

"She was betrayed," the Master Ghalian replied grimly. "This confirms what we have been investigating. Someone within the order is a traitor. Kolinga was led into a trap. A trap she very nearly escaped, from what I'm told, but in the end, the odds were stacked too strongly against her."

A knot twisted in Bawb's stomach. Someone really was working against them. Someone on the inside. But who would have a bone to pick with the Ghalian? And who would have access to the sort of information required to effect this kind of trap? They all had the same resources, but somewhere in that chain was a toxic, weak link. And if they didn't weed it out, more would surely die.

Hozark read the expression on Bawb's face and reached over to pat his shoulder. "Do not be concerned. Strange things are most certainly afoot, but rest assured, the Masters are looking into them. And so far as we can tell, Adepts are not at high risk. Whoever this is, they appear to be targeting higher ranks. Those on the more difficult and dangerous contracts."

"That is bad."

"Yes, it is. But there is no need to worry yourself about it. You are training hard and improving by leaps and bounds, and Ser Baruud tells me he feels you can more than handle yourself in unexpected situations against older, more experienced fighters."

"I am glad I did not disappoint him."

"Quite the opposite. He does not show outward favoritism, but I can tell he likes you, Bawb. You made an impression, and if you ever wish to train further with him, I am certain he would be glad to have you back."

"Perhaps I will, one day."

"I think you would enjoy it, though as you now know, he would drive you harder than most. But for the time being, you are still an Adept. Once you have achieved Maven, then you can consider taking time to yourself to further your training with outside instruction. For now, however, you will have more than enough to do in the Ghalian compound. The skills to level up to Maven are difficult, and they will require absolute dedication of time, energy, and mental bandwidth. In your case, I am not concerned. A few of your classmates, on the other hand, may have a harder time of it."

"As it has always been."

"Indeed."

Bawb was curious what the Masters were planning to do to seek out the traitor within the organization, but he had read Hozark's tone and language clear enough. He had already been told more than he should have been allowed to hear. No matter how bad things seemed, at least he was confident the Masters were on the job. That would have to suffice.

Hozark landed at one of the closer fields, affording Bawb a short walk back to the training house. Entering, he found that the others had all returned from their outside studies some time earlier. He was the last to come back, and by a few weeks at that.

"Held behind?" Elzina asked with a sarcastic smirk.

"In a manner," Bawb replied calmly.

"I bet you were."

"As I said, in a manner. They were so pleased to have me, I was asked to remain beyond my original time allotment. When was it you returned?"

Elzina gave him a sour look and stormed off without a reply. The others who happened to be in the bunkhouse, however, were happy to trade stories of their adventures, along with sharing the new techniques they had acquired. Bawb refrained from revealing everything he'd picked up, but he did contribute as much as he felt appropriate.

All of them would soak in these new lessons like a sponge, adding what worked best for them into their own personalized martial forms. They had already developed their styles enough to level up to Adepts, but even the Mavens and Masters still grew their learning and refined their fighting techniques. No one ever stopped improving. Not among the Ghalian.

He learned that the group had apparently been training hard earlier in the day, and as such, the teachers allowed them the evening to themselves to rest, eat, and recover. To do so meant they had truly been driven hard indeed, but now as young adults, the Adepts had finally developed the stamina Ghalian were legendary for. And all of them seemed quite fresh, in fact, and eager to share stories of their time away and the assignments they had most recently embarked on.

They were all conducting real contracts on their own now. No longer overseen and babysat by teachers, Adepts were expected to behave as true Ghalian. That meant going on missions, killing targets, and whatever else the contract required.

But they were not yet Mavens, and therefore, they still had a curriculum to follow and skills to practice. More often than not, they worked alone these days, but the teachers still had them team up on occasion. But they also set them against one another as well, and as their skills improved and bodies strengthened, some of those interactions became not only heated in their competitiveness, but also the levels of violence and damage they inflicted on one another.

The healers, as a result, were kept busy, though not as busy as at Ser Baruud's facility.

Bawb felt a sensation of warm comfort fill him. He was enjoying hanging out with his friends once more. While the gladiators he had spent so much time with were an amusing, jovial, and surprisingly clever lot, these were his true peers, and it was here he could let his guard down and be himself to the fullest, and the stories shared over dinner were a source of great joy to them all.

As the evening's meal wrapped up, Bawb and Usalla were the last to finish, lingering over the remnants of their dinner.

"Are you up for a bit of that practice we discussed?" Usalla asked. Her face was calm, as usual, when she made the offhand comment, but there was a heated gleam in her eyes that was unmistakable.

Bawb took a swig from his mug and began stacking plates. "Yes, I think I am," he said with a hint of a grin.

"Excellent. The usual spot?"

"I will see you there."

Bawb bussed their dishes, the whole exchange casual and taking but seconds, none of their classmates the wiser. This had now been going on for years, but they had remained absolutely discreet about their liaisons. It was just training, after all, albeit of a different sort.

Bawb took his time making his way to the designated chamber. It was a rather large one on the third subterranean level. A place illuminated naturally by bioluminescent moss growing from the walls and ceiling, the whole thing lending the location a cozy air. It also had only one way in or out.

Bawb stepped through the door and secured it behind him, then cast the strongest muting spell he could at the threshold before striding to the far end under a short, lush, purple-leaved tree where he knew Usalla would be waiting.

Sometime later, the two stepped out into the corridor, their clothing and hair perfect, seeming as though nothing had happened at all.

"Thank you for the practice. I will see you back at the bunkhouse," Usalla said with a little nod, walking away casually as if eyes were upon them at all times. Her training kept even the slightest of affectionate gestures firmly restrained outside of the security of the chamber.

"I will see you there," he replied, watching her walk off down the corridor until she rounded the corner and was out of sight.

Now that *was a showing*, the konus said with a chuckle. *Level up—*

"I do not need to hear it," Bawb silently replied. "Just let me enjoy the moment."

Fine. Fat lot of fun you are, the device griped.

Bawb didn't care. He and Usalla had developed quite a shorthand over the years, and they knew each other *very* well. But for the konus to make that announcement, this must have been truly special. Bawb had thought so at the time, but this was objective confirmation. It seemed there were always new skills to be learned, even when you didn't expect to.

A contented glow in his belly, he casually strolled back to the bunkhouse to bathe then turn in for the night. Tomorrow would undoubtedly be another tough day.

CHAPTER NINETEEN

After so many weeks of grueling work under Ser Baruud's watchful eye, Bawb found his first group lesson back at the Ghalian training house to be more than a bit anticlimactic. He had just been fighting not quite to the death, but definitely to the pain, visiting the healer on a near daily basis, taking his licks from the skilled and resilient fighters refining their techniques at the master gladiator's compound.

Thinking about it, he had probably bled as much as he'd sweated, the training with sharp weapons leading to so many cuts and slices that he'd stopped counting after the first few dozen. *That* was quite possibly why Ser Baruud charged what he did. Not just for room, board, and training, but to pay the healers for their non-stop work putting his students back together again.

Of course, that was not how they all trained, and even when the toughest of the tough did come together to fight, more often than not, Ser Baruud had them battle with dummy weapons simply so they could go for killing blows without actually ending the life of their opponent. To die in battle was one thing, but to perish in training was simply foolish.

Bawb had taken quite a few serious hits during those sessions, but it was the live weapon work he truly enjoyed. The practice of landing blows but with control and restraint. It made up perhaps five or ten percent of the training, but Bawb had been lucky enough to arrive just as the training cycle shifted to that more dangerous sort of work. That he had proven himself skilled enough to be allowed to participate said more about his skills than he had realized at the time, but Master Hozark knew what it meant. It meant Bawb was beginning to truly excel. To ease into the effortless execution of the most difficult of techniques without really thinking about it. All of his private tutoring over the years was paying off, and one day, it seemed likely Bawb would perhaps even have a shot at becoming what he aimed to be.

One of the Five.

But that was still far off in the future. For now, he would work hard, focused on being the best at everything, expanding his mind to more than just the ways of assassins and spies, but all manner of things outside the order. He possessed a voracious intellect, and while he did not discuss it within the compound walls, Bawb had developed quite the fascination with a great many other cultures, especially those possessing tight social networks. He spent hours upon hours disguising himself and infiltrating them, learning to walk among them even though it might not ever serve him in his Ghalian duties.

The truth was he simply enjoyed fitting in with these groups, participating in their songs and dances, being accepted as one of them. It was the one thing the Ghalian lacked. A sense of family. Yes, they were all brothers and sisters of the order, and they cared about one another with a bond deeper than mere blood, but Ghalian were not prone to outward expressions of affection, and while Bawb had changed since his youth, deep inside, something about that feeling of connection resonated.

His life, however, was not about that. Not now. This was an existence of hard labor and dedication, though today's work was, despite his knack for it, rather boring.

It was a codebreaking, cypher, and puzzle lesson, taught by Teacher Dimmak, a slight woman with a piercing gaze, almost as if her formidable mental skills were somehow sharpening her perception in a way the outside world could see. They say the eyes were the window to the soul, and if so, hers were honed razor-sharp.

"Yes, I know what you are thinking," Teacher Dimmak said, surveying her students. "This is not exciting. It does not get the heart racing and the blood thundering through your veins. And while I am your instructor in these arts, I must also admit that much is quite true. Few derive a thrill from breaking ancient codes and deciphering obscure runes and texts. But in our line of work, the manner of thinking which is employed in the creation of these things is one we must know. Many of you have already used a variation of these skills since your earliest days here. Bawb, I believe it was you who found Master Olafitz's hidden passageway to the training dungeon."

"I did."

"I know. And what you did was achieved by recognizing markings. Deducing the pattern and meaning, even if you were too young to know exactly what they meant at the time. And since then, you and your classmates have faced many other challenges, many requiring similar reasoning skills. There are puzzles *everywhere*. It is a part of life on all worlds. More than that, the Council of Twenty has a particular fondness of using cyphers and riddles to obfuscate their messages and hide otherwise apparent truths. Now, look before you. Each of you has a small tablet. Turn it over and study the glyphs. Are they simple markings, or do they have more meaning? And if they have a message, what could it actually mean beyond the obvious?"

"I see a pattern," Usalla commented. "It appears to be using an old script hidden within a decorative glyph style."

"Jindaaran, obviously," Elzina scoffed. "Birds fly with the wind, soaring high and crossing the expanse."

Dimmak nodded. "Good. You are getting the hang of this. The hidden message within the message."

Bawb shook his head.

"What is it, Bawb?"

"There is more."

"Oh?" she said with a pleased grin. "Do tell us."

"It is a technique instruction," he replied. "Stillness is motion, and slow is fast."

"How did you come to this conclusion?"

"Because, a bird flapping its wings exhausts itself, while one soaring in position glides with ease, using the power of the wind to its advantage rather than fighting against it. Efficiency in effort."

"Well done. You saw beyond the obvious. But then, you do seem to have a knack for this sort of thing, I understand."

"I do not know. Perhaps."

You do know. And level up, by the way, his konus announced in his head. His invisible display flashed up in front of him, minimized, but still quite clear for him and him alone. He noted he had just unlocked multiple new skills in codebreaking and a few other related subsets, but this was not the time to take them in. He was being scrutinized by a Master Ghalian. He would survey the list later.

Bawb's face remained blank, as if he did not have a semi-sentient magical device talking silently to him.

"*Perhaps?* Your teachers would say it is more than perhaps. But that is beside the point," Dimmak said, circling the room, depositing another tablet, this one blank, on each of their tables, along with a folded piece of parchment and a small carving implement. "For today's lesson you are to take the phrase provided to you and devise your own means of concealing it in a message carved onto the tablet you have been provided. Take your time; think it through. When we are done, we will try to decipher each of them as a group. Let us see if any of you can stymie the others."

The Adepts set to work studying each of their texts, taking as long as necessary to come up with an appropriate means to conceal the message as they had been instructed. Some leapt into it quickly, but those were the students who tended to be a bit more obvious in their techniques. Those who would likely advance to Maven one day but never beyond.

For those on the Master track, a bit more thought went into their designs, and in Bawb's case, a secondary and tertiary decoy built in as well, concealing his true message in what he hoped would be both an artistic as well as subtly complex manner. He picked up the carving tool and began sketching out the rough outlines on the tablet. Soon enough, he found himself deeply engrossed in the task, the lines flowing as easily as if he were writing with ink on parchment.

The konus knew he was leveling up but kept that tidbit to itself for now. Bawb had hit the flow state where instinct and knowledge blended together and everything just seemed to come out naturally without effort.

As for the rest of his class, some were making better progress than others. Usalla was hard at work, always having something of a talent for the cerebral of their tasks. Elzina, on the other hand, was making good progress as well, but through sheer force of will rather than elegantly instinctive abilities. Say what you would about her, she always found a way to advance, and always remained at or near the head of the class no matter what it required of her.

Even as Bawb began overtaking her more and more—much to her annoyance—he persisted, convinced she would remain at the peak of their group no matter how talented any of the others might be. And most days she did manage to jump ahead of the rest.

That she was not above sabotaging her classmates on occasion might have had more than a little to do with that, but in her mind, all was fair in her pursuit of greatness. It was not a typical Ghalian mentality, and her teachers had expressed concern on more than a few occasions, but none could argue one thing. She was gifted, and one day would make one hell of a killer, perhaps even finishing at the top of her class.

That was her belief as well, and what drove her so hard. And heaven help anyone who got in her way.

CHAPTER TWENTY

Bawb had discovered that he actually rather enjoyed the codebreaking, cypher, and puzzle class with Teacher Dimmak. Despite his initial reluctance, still running high on his recent gladiatorial experience, as they dug into the material and began crafting their own hidden messages, he found this, like so many things of late, was coming to him naturally, and the feeling was great, albeit different than thriving in combat.

The group worked on their projects for some time before their teacher collected them, studying their work as she added each to the stack in her arms.

"Interesting," she said as Bawb added his to the mix.

"Wait, is that a Palavlovian mating rune?" Finnia asked, catching a glimpse of his work as the teacher moved on to the next student.

Their teacher nodded. "You will have an opportunity to try your hand at deciphering it in time, Finnia, just like the rest of the class. But to answer your question, yes, that is a Palavlovian mating rune. You have quite the eye for this."

"Because all she thinks about is mating rituals," Albinius joked.

"Shut up, Albinius," Usalla said with a groan. "Do you never tire of these jokes?"

"Nope. Pretty much never."

Usalla shook her head but let it go. He had kept up this persona for so many years, she didn't think he could step out of it even if he tried, though he had on occasion showed moments of more serious behavior. Usalla considered that to be the exception, not the rule.

"You will be a great spy," she said to her friend. "Ignore him."

"Oh, I do not let him get to me," Finnia said with a cheerful grin. "As you said, spying is my calling, and dealing with fools will be the least of my worries."

Albinius sat up a bit straighter. "Hey! Are you calling me a fool?"

"I did not call *anyone* a fool. But it is interesting you immediately thought I had been speaking about you. I wonder, what could that say about what you truly know of yourself?"

"Enough," Dimmak said, dumping the tablets on a table. "It is time to begin the next part of this lesson." She picked up a tablet at random. "Who made this?"

"I did," Zota replied.

"Fair work. A bit simplistic, perhaps, but let us see if your classmates can figure it out. Raise a finger to let me know when each of you is done."

She handed the tablet to the nearest of them and allowed them to pass it around, studying the message hidden on it. She then cast a minor display spell, projecting the image in the air for further investigation.

Bawb was the first to get it, raising a finger then sitting back to wait for his classmates. Elzina followed close after him, then Usalla, Finnia, and eventually the rest. Teacher Dimmak went through all of the tablets in this manner, and the students made quick work of them until she reached Elzina's. Hers was more complex, featuring some clever diversionary markings woven into the overall design. She smiled broad and bright, enjoying her moment of glory, besting her classmates.

"No one?" Teacher Dimmak asked, looking across the group. "Come now, not a single one?"

"Well…" Bawb said, drawing a sharp look from Elzina.

Dimmak's brow twitched slightly upward. "Yes, Bawb?"

"It is a mathematical variation utilizing musical reference for a linguistic key."

"And?"

"And it says the chalice in the palace holds the brew that is true."

"That's not what it says," Elzina hissed.

"No, it is not. Not the direct translation, that is. But while the message itself is a riddle, the meaning of it is clear enough."

Teacher Dimmak actually chuckled. "Impressive, Bawb. Beyond the scope of what was required, but impressive all the same."

Bawb's friends gave congratulatory nods, while Elzina stared daggers at him for upstaging her moment. It had been happening more and more often of late, and she was increasingly acerbic as a result.

"The last one," Dimmak said, passing Bawb's tablet around the room. "Let us see how you fare."

Usalla glanced at Bawb, recognizing his handiwork at once. She shook her head. This was impossibly good. The way multiple languages, both dead and alive, were woven together with shapes and decorative lines, all carved with a steady hand.

The others soon realized it was futile as well, sighs of frustration escaping a few tight-pressed lips. Teacher Dimmak let them work on it for some time before finally asking for the correct answer. None had it.

"Elzina? Would you care to take a guess?" she asked.

Elzina's simmering ire was almost palpable. "No, Teacher, I would not. I do not know the answer."

Dimmak looked at each of them, giving them one last chance to come up with the correct reply. None did.

"Bawb, will you please explain this rather ingeniously hidden message?"

"Of course." He gestured to the hovering image displayed in her spell. "May I?"

"Please."

He cast his own modification to the spell, stripping away letters, runes, and decorative lines until nothing but the stars in what had looked like a somewhat simplistic sky scene remained. It was then the others realized what he had done.

"A star chart, utilizing system names," Finnia said, clearly impressed.

"And if I am not mistaken, the third letter of each system's name is used to form the cipher," Usalla added.

Teacher Dimmak nodded, pleased they caught it so quickly once the decoys were removed. "A very clever design, Bawb. Your knack for concealing messages is impressive. And this was a most creative use of design to draw the eye away from the actual message." She waved her hand, extinguishing the spell. "We have gone a little over our time, I am afraid. You will need to run to your next lesson. Teacher Griggitz is waiting for you in the lower fifth level hot spring chamber."

The students left as a group, jogging quickly through the hallways and corridors, descending the stairs quietly, each of them practicing their muting spells on their feet as they ran. Bawb felt Elzina's angry eyes on him but didn't turn to look. There was no point. It had become clear ages ago that they would likely never be friends. Such was life. But they were Ghalian, and as such, they would face each other in training hard and often, and as they grew more powerful, each encounter would pack a little more punch.

They had both sent one another to the healer more times than they could count, but the teachers allowed it, almost urging them to keep pushing each other harder. Sometimes, having a nemesis could make one excel beyond their own expectations, and with these two it seemed that was precisely the case.

"You are late!" Teacher Griggitz bellowed as they entered the steamy, hot spring chamber, his words echoing off the walls despite the humidity in the air dampening their voices as well as their bodies.

"We were delayed," Martza said. "Class ran long, and—"

"I do not want excuses. I want punctuality. If you finish late, you run faster. Is that clear?"

"Yes, Teacher."

"Good. Now listen up, and listen closely. Your task today is dangerous. You possess the skills for this, but if you falter, you may be harmed or even killed if you truly botch things. Understand that going in. You are not children any longer, and this is going to require *all* of your attention and effort."

The Adepts didn't say a word, each of them giving him their full attention. Griggitz, of all their teachers, was not prone to hyperbole. *Ever.* If he said a lesson might kill them, then it very well could. Of course, at this level of training, danger was just a part of the deal, even death, but typically, that degree of threat was still relatively minimal. Not today, it seemed.

"You will infiltrate a dungeon, but not just any. This will be done both above as well as under water. There will be hazards of all types. Traps. Snares. Beasts. Your task is to reach the end in one piece. Do that, and you get the rest of the day off. Fail, and you are mine for as long as it takes." He turned and pointed to a steaming hot spring. "That is the entrance. You know how to cast bubble spells, and you have learned to moderate extremes of temperature quite some time ago. Let us hope you have not forgotten those skills. Begin."

Teacher Griggitz turned and walked out of the chamber, likely taking a simple, short, and direct route to the finishing area. The Adepts, on the other hand, were going to get to do it the hard way.

"He said beasts," Albinius noted. "Underwater beasts."

"They could be on land. We do not know for sure," Zota countered. "Only part of the dungeon is submerged."

Bawb strode to the steaming water's edge and gazed down, scanning for any clues or signs of traps. So far as he could tell, there were none. There was what looked like a natural lava tube big enough for a person to fit in. That had to be the way. He cast a cooling spell, a foggy mist forming around him as the heated air rose up to meet his far colder body.

"No time like the present to begin, I suppose," he said to his friends. He turned back to the water and cast his air bubble spell with all the intent one well aware he could quite possibly die a wet death could muster. "*Oblio fama manititzi*," he intoned, then without hesitation, stepped off into the water, plunging deep and beginning his long swim, hoping his bubble spell had enough air to get him to the next chamber.

Fortunately, it did. But that was only the beginning of his ordeal.

CHAPTER TWENTY-ONE

Bawb's head emerged from the water silently, having long ago used up his last breath within his bubble spell. The magic, however, still helped him remain quiet as he surfaced. As it turned out, that was a very good thing.

He was in a dark chamber, the only illumination cast by glowing violet crystals sprouting from the walls. The whole cavern was no larger than one of their mid-sized sparring facilities, meaning it was big enough for all of the class to fit comfortably with plenty of room between them, yet not so spacious as to be considered anywhere near expansive.

The ground was solid stone, he was glad to see. None of the crushed crystal or rock that some of the other chambers possessed. Given the nature of the creatures creeping along the periphery, it was a very good thing indeed.

He'd dealt with them before. Shanzin, they were called. Long, lizard-like creatures with gaping jaws, powerful limbs, and whip-like tails, the smallest of them easily larger than their biggest student. They moved slowly, relying on scent and sound to track their prey, their eyes barely functional given a life in the relative dark.

Bawb pushed himself up onto the stone ledge of the shore, timing his movements to coincide with the natural lapping of the water. Given the swim he and the others had just had, scent would not be an issue. Sound, on the other hand, most certainly would be.

He looked back over his shoulder as he squeezed the water out of his clothing as best he could while still wearing it. A few drops here and there would likely not catch the Shanzin's attention. Squishing footsteps, however, most certainly would, and he wanted nothing more than to pass all the way through without having to fight them. A single Shanzin might engage, and that could be dealt with, but once blood was spilled, the others would be drawn in a hurry.

Bawb pointed out the camouflaged lizard to the others as they surfaced. Competition or no, this was one occasion where *none* of them wanted the beasts roused. Even Elzina took heed. The others began emerging as he did, spread out and cautious, moving with the utmost stealth they could manage. Unfortunately, to voice a muting spell in this space would draw attention to themselves by even the quietest use of their voices. Were they Master Ghalian they would have had the skill to cast in but a whisper, but as Adepts, they simply lacked the requisite talent.

Entirely magic-free it would have to be.

Bawb was ahead of the others a fair bit, but he stopped in place, motionless in the dim light. He felt his skin cooling naturally after the hot waters of the swim. It was more than that, though. There was a breeze. Slight and subtle, but it was there, making one cheek colder than the other. He turned his head and scanned in that direction. The gap in the rock wall was well concealed by the shadows the glowing crystals cast, but his eyesight was particularly good, and he picked it out with little effort. He nodded his head toward the opening, signaling to

137

Usalla. She nodded and passed the silent message along the line until all of the group was dialed in on the exit route.

The climb was going to be a little problematic, he realized as he drew closer. There were a few Shanzin basking on the warm stones nearby. They appeared to be slumbering, but he had learned the hard way just how fast they were to wake and react if something caught their attention. The healer had made him whole again, and it was a juvenile that had done the damage, but the memory of the pain he'd endured was more than enough to make him extra cautious as he moved near.

Bawb pointed to the creatures. Zota slowly waved his arms, pointing to a loose stone by his foot. He gestured toward the other side of the chamber, his intention clear. Bawb nodded his agreement and stood ready. Zota gently picked up the projectile, careful not to make a sound as he did, then hurled it hard to the intended location.

The sound seemed almost deafening in contrast to the silence in which they had been laboring, though it was anything but. The Shanzin reacted at once, all of them scuttling in a run toward the sound in a frenzy of hungry teeth and snapping jaws. Sometimes they would even attack one another, which would further aid the Adepts' advance if they did. Bawb hoped this was one such occasion, but he didn't wait to find out.

He jumped up and hauled himself into the opening, turning to help pull up the others in rapid succession. Usalla first, then Finnia and Zota. Elzina *accidentally* kneed him in the face as she gained her feet, but Bawb said nothing, remaining silent as he helped the rest to safety. That accomplished, he turned to join them in the tunnel.

"Shanzin," Albinius grumbled. "I hate those things."

"We all do," Usalla agreed. "But we managed all right, thanks largely to Bawb's keen eyes. He should take the lead again as we resume. It is only fair given his sacrifice of time to ensure all our safety. Once we enter the next chamber it will once more be everyone for themself."

Finnia shook her head. "I guess Elzina did not get the message."

Bawb looked around. It was true, Elzina had taken advantage of the situation to sprint ahead of the group. While technically allowable, it was bad form and sat poorly with the others. But then, this was Elzina, so no one was really surprised. She had always been all about herself since their earliest days together. Why should that change now?

"So it goes," Bawb said with a resigned sigh as he began walking fast through the tunnel, scanning for traps and obstacles as he moved. "Good luck to you all."

The group moved as one for a time. It was the only way to progress in the tunnel anyway, so there was no sense jostling one another. There was a fork in the tunnel, one branch clearly marked as the emergency egress, the other their next challenge. All headed on toward further difficulty without a second thought.

When they emerged into the next chamber, they discovered it was almost entirely submerged with only a small pocket of air at the cavern roof. The rest was underwater, and the water was frigid.

Of course it was.

Bawb didn't hesitate, casting a robust bubble spell once more and submerging as he slid into the deep, clear waters. He didn't swim immediately, though. He sat still a moment, floating motionless, taking in the environment.

Yes, there was air at the surface in pockets that looked mirror-like when underwater, but to utilize them would mean remaining vulnerable to attack from below. At first, he thought this might be a simple water hazard and nothing more, but he knew better than to act too quickly. The teachers always had tricks up their sleeves.

Motion caught his eye. Elzina was at the far side to his right, deep underwater but holding still behind a rocky outcropping. This alone confirmed his suspicions. If *she* wasn't moving, there was definitely something else down here. Something that would make even Elzina pause in her quest for victory.

Nothing was in sight at the moment, so Bawb began his dive, hugging the stone wall as he did, ensuring his body remained not only close to protective rocks, but also sticking to the shadowy parts in a way Teacher Griggitz had instructed them so as to break up their silhouette should anyone or anything be looking their way.

The others followed suit, diving and spreading out. Soon enough, the lurking hazard made itself known in a rather dramatic fashion.

Zota was swimming deep, staying out of sight as best he could, when a silver flash shot out of a crevice in the rock, swirling around him in a flurry of sharp teeth as it whipped him to and fro. Zota had enough air to cast a few spells but was too busy fighting the beast to properly cast. He strained and struggled, swimming back toward their entry point, bleeding and winded. The creature could have continued to attack him, but it seemed more interested in the other interlopers foolishly trying to cross its domain while it was occupied.

It swam incredibly fast, pummeling each of them as it wove among the Adepts, biting them as it passed. Bawb watched, holding still and conserving his air. His heartbeat was still slow and steady. He had trained far too long for this to cause panic, and he had several breaths left should he need them. But more than that, he noticed this was creating an opportunity. The animal had not noticed him yet. Him, or Elzina. Lack of motion had made them of lesser interest. At least, for the moment.

They both had the realization at the same time and made a break for the far end. It seemed there was a reflective air bubble that was slightly different from the others, likely leading up into an actual cavern or passageway. Whatever it was, that had to be the next leg of this endeavor.

Elzina reached it first by virtue of having been down there longer. In her haste, however, a rumbling magical impact slammed into her as she triggered a hidden tripwire spell, breaking her bubble spell and leaving her without air. She struggled up to the nearest pocket of air, her face hitting the stone hard as she broke the surface, sucking in air hard and fast.

The creature immediately shifted its attention and swam right at her, wrapping her up hard and pulling her deep, back toward the other side of the cavern, where it flung her into the stone wall, protecting its domain with brutal efficiency.

Bawb gauged his air and made a decision. He had enough, but only just. He swam ahead, making his approach as fast as he could, but then pulled up short. There was a tripwire spell, yes, but also something else. This wasn't just a single hazard. Multiple traps had been layered upon one another, guaranteed to stymie the impatient.

He began working methodically, disarming the first as cautiously as possible while the toothy obstacle was occupied with forcing the others out of its home. The second hazard fell soon after, leaving two more to go.

A shift in the water flow around him drew his attention, his daggers drawn in haste as the creature flew straight for him.

He was close to getting through, but would he have time to complete the disarming process before the attacker reached him? He simply couldn't be sure, so a fight it would be.

He lashed out, his arms slow in the water while the beast

moved through it effortlessly. But Bawb nevertheless managed to land a blow, and the beast reacted with more caution than when it attacked the others. Apparently, *this* interloper was a more formidable foe.

It mattered not.

The beast renewed its attacks, swimming around him faster and faster, the current it caused forcing him back across the cavern without having to actually get close enough to be cut. Bawb reacted by casting attack spells, but he found them woefully inadequate underwater. Griggitz had taught them well, but this was not his normal sort of adversary, and in all their underwater sparring, none had ever faced a foe who could move like this, deftly avoiding spells while serving up a beating with its body and teeth.

Bawb cast and cast but felt his lungs abruptly unable to cast any further.

Fool. You used up all of your air, his konus chided, well aware he would be unable to cast another air bubble spell in the absence of breath.

Bawb didn't panic, but he did realize how dire the situation had just become. He knew he could function at full capacity for at least two minutes without air. Training had made that much clear over the years. But more than that, he had to *find* air when that time did finally arrive, and the pockets were few and far between.

It turned out he didn't need to worry about that as the creature seized upon the moment and bit him hard, pulling him from his goal and slamming him into the far wall with astounding speed. Bawb felt his last breath forced from his lungs from the impact.

He no longer had minutes to function. He had to get air, and soon.

He pulled hard with his arms as the beast battered him

relentlessly, his getting too close to the next chamber seemingly enraging it even more than it had already been. Sharp teeth broke his flesh, his blood coloring the water as he struggled to the surface. Bawb felt as though he was going to black out, his energy dropping with every second.

Rock met his hand.

Rock with an edge to it. His fingers felt the warm air above, his body somehow finding just enough strength to pull. His head broke through the water, his lungs sucking in air with ragged gasps. He felt hands grab his arms and pull. A moment later he was sprawled out on the wet stone, exhausted and bleeding just like the others. He lay there until his head stopped spinning then looked at his classmates. All were there, and all were injured to varying degrees. One thing was clear. None were in any shape to make another attempt at the challenge. Not without a visit to the healer first.

Reluctantly, he rose to his feet and trudged back down the tunnel toward the emergency egress with the others.

They had all failed.

Teacher Dimmak stood waiting for them at the exit, along with Teacher Griggitz. Interestingly, neither seemed terribly surprised they had not progressed farther than this chamber. That was telling. Telling in that it seemed quite likely *no one* did on their first attempt.

Even so, Bawb was frustrated with himself. He'd been so close, only to come up short.

"How did you fail?" Dimmak asked. "You each know the spells. Teacher Griggitz assures me you even have some degree of proficiency with them. So what happened?"

"We were ambushed," Zota replied.

Dimmak shook her head. "And? You are Ghalian. You *will* be ambushed on occasion. And you will have to overcome."

"It was too fast," Elzina grumbled.

"Fast if it is aware of your presence, you mean. And even then, some of you still had the opportunity to move forward," she said, her gaze falling squarely on Bawb. "So, what did *you* do wrong?"

He knew the answer. He'd been mulling it over since the moment he ceased wondering if he was going to die.

"I chose poorly," he said.

Griggitz almost seemed to grin, though Bawb thought it might have just been a trick of the light. "How so?"

"I had limited air, but enough to finish disarming the trap spells. Instead, I chose to try to fight the creature."

"It is called a Lempett," the man replied. "And how was fighting it the wrong choice?"

"For one, it is too fast for the usual underwater combative techniques you taught us."

"And?"

"And I should have saved my air for casting to complete the task rather than engaging a simple beast. I allowed myself to focus on the possibility of the attack rather than disarming the tripwires."

The two teachers shared a glance. "Good," Griggitz said. "But the spells you know, they are enough to handle the Lempett. You need only learn to properly apply them to this type of opponent. And given today's failure, you will all have plenty of opportunities to perfect them. Now, go see the healers and get yourselves put right. You have the rest of the day to yourselves to reflect on this failure. Some of you may be sent out on assignments, but for those who are not, I suggest you continue your studies of these skills, for obvious reasons."

The Adepts trudged to the healer, leaving a trail of water and blood behind them, along with the entirety of their egos. Just when they started to get cocky, it seemed the teachers would always have some new means to remind them they were still a long way from being Masters.

Bawb took it in stride. He had to. This was just one more step on the path to his ultimate goal. To one day become one of the Five.

CHAPTER TWENTY-TWO

Bawb's injuries were relatively minor, all things considered, and the healer had him sorted and out the door in no time. While the damage to his body was repaired, his psychological issues remained, a lingering sense of frustration with himself for being foolish with his use of power.

Yes, it was a test, and yes, the Adepts were expected to fail the first time through. But Bawb had been excelling so much more of late. Moreover, as Adepts, they were no longer confined to the training house, and with that independence, a sense of graduation into normal adult life had found its way into his mind.

This had been a harsh reminder to them all that while they were now free to come and go as they pleased, they were still students. Not until they became full-fledged Mavens would they be able to permanently leave if they so desired.

Of course, those on the Master track would train often and hard, but they would be able to do so at any of the Ghalian facilities in the galaxy, as well as the non-Ghalian locations their kind often frequented, albeit in disguise.

In any case, Bawb felt the sting of his failure acutely, and as a result, he needed to clear his head. What better for that than a walk among normal people? Those not preoccupied with all things Ghalian.

He slipped into a simple disguise spell, changing his skin color, eyes, and hair, adding in a shift in his perceived body size as well just for practice, then stepped out into the city to walk, think, and process the day's events.

Bawb had no set route he liked to follow. The hazards of having a routine had been drilled into his skull since his early days. It was something he would use to his advantage against others, but one he'd be sure not to allow to be used against him. As a result he just walked aimlessly, following the flow of pedestrians, letting the throngs of the city carry him from street to street.

He passed the fragrant cooking stalls of the marketplace, picking up a little treat on a skewer before continuing through the sparkling-clean rows of shops closer to the main landing site. On a whim, he decided to go look at the various ships that had come in since he was last there. The Ghalian typically used the peripheral sites, as they were both less conspicuous as well as easier to maneuver.

This one, on the other hand, was a veritable showroom of expensive craft, their owners jostling for prominent landing spaces to show off their ships while they carried out their business in the city. He walked among them for a bit, noting the guard patterns and structural weaknesses out of habit more than any conscious plan. One ship in particular caught his eye. It looked like any other high-end vessel of its size, but a few lingering spells had a familiar feel to them.

This was a Council of Twenty ship, its passive defensive spells blending in seamlessly and virtually undetectable. That is, until something triggered them, at which point they would become *very* apparent.

"A Council ship here?" he mused, wondering what it was doing on this planet. The Council did show up from time to time, naturally, but this wasn't some ordinary cargo ship. This had a different feel to it. This ship carried someone of importance. And by the look of it, the ship had only just arrived. It was entirely possible the Masters had not even heard of its presence yet.

"I will pass the information along," he decided, turning back the way he'd come from. Yes, the spies and information brokers would relay the message soon enough, but this was the sort of thing they would likely rather know sooner than later, even if its presence was benign.

He walked down the roadway from the landing site, making a straight shot back to the training house, when something caught his attention out of the corner of his eye. He turned the opposite direction and looked at the reflection in a store's window. There, in reverse image, was Elzina. And she was not alone.

She was talking to a burly man in a crisp uniform. The insignias were unclear at this distance, but it seemed very much like a Council uniform, though one typically worn by envoys and agents of the vislas. Bawb stepped into the nearest store and began browsing, his eyes taking in the scene outside with his well-honed peripheral vision.

Ghalian did not have to look directly at someone to know what they were doing. It was just one of the many tricks of their trade. And now, here, of all places, it was being put to good use in the outside world. He just had not ever thought he would be using it on one of his own.

Elzina and the man seemed to be engaged in quite the conversation. She was heated, from what he could see, but then, when wasn't she? The man took her attitude in stride and gestured down the roadway. The two began walking toward the landing area, their discussion now mobile.

Bawb had a decision to make. Leave her to her own devices or follow. With anyone else it might have been a tough choice, but with Elzina, it was as easy as breathing. He stepped out onto the street and followed at a distance.

With the ambient chatter of the crowd, even his sound-enhancing spells were of no use to him. He could see them talking but could not hear them, nor could he read lips, as they were now facing away from him. He would just have to follow and see what unfolded.

They stopped at the edge of the landing site, turning to face one another. Bawb tucked into another shop and watched from afar. Elzina shook the man's hand and walked away, their conversation now at an end. Bawb was faced with another choice. Follow her, or stick with the newcomer. In the end, he decided to see what Elzina might do next. He waited a moment, then stepped back out onto the street, falling in with her pace, keeping her in sight from a distance.

She walked with a relaxed air to her, looking in shops, window shopping. She was doing what he had planned on earlier, making a casual loop of the city, her path back home anything but direct. The smell of freshly baked bread wafted to Bawb's nose as she eventually drew closer to the training house. She'd taken the route that passed one of his favorite bakeries.

Elzina stepped inside. Bawb thought a moment, then entered a residential structure. The lobby area was empty. Perfect. He let his disguise melt away, and a moment later a handsome young Wampeh stepped out onto the street. He made his way to the bakery and walked in, jingling a little coin in his hand.

"Elzina, I see you had the same craving I did," he said, acting surprised to see her there.

Interestingly, her usual dour attitude was somewhat diminished. In fact, she was almost pleasant.

Almost.

"I thought a little treat was warranted after earlier," she said, taking her parcel from the cashier.

"Indeed. That was quite the morning," he agreed. "Has yours been an interesting day otherwise?"

"Nothing exciting. Just taking a walk and getting some air."

"I am doing the same. Some days it just feels nice being out wandering the city."

"On this we agree," she said, heading for the door. "Well, you have a pleasant rest of your day. I will see you later."

"That you will."

He watched her leave, then purchased a few small pastries while he was at it, not only maintaining his cover story, but because the smell of them really was quite enticing. Treats in hand, he exited the bakery and headed back to the training house, more than a bit perplexed, wondering whom Elzina had been meeting and what it could possibly mean.

CHAPTER TWENTY-THREE

As he walked home, taking the longer, scenic route, Bawb solidified the beginnings of a plan to do a little casual digging into Elzina's mystery meeting when he finally returned to the training house. She had been pleasant to him at the bakery, and her unexpected civility was unsettling in just how out of place it was.

Something was up, but he had no idea what. So he would dig. Ideally, after she had relaxed into a sense of complacency after dinner. She was a tough one, and always on guard, but there was one pattern he could somewhat reliably count on. After a long day and a large meal she tended to be less dour, at least for a short while. With luck, after dinner he might even be able to have an actual conversation with her.

Was it food affecting her blood sugar levels? Who knew? All that mattered was it was the most likely time he could perhaps pry a little information out without her realizing. He'd have to be careful and discreet, whatever he tried. She wasn't on the spy path within the order, but that did not mean she was lacking in those skills by any means.

Bawb entered the compound through one of the peripheral doorways on one of the many nondescript buildings linking into their hidden training house, a plan of action forming in his mind. An unexpected encounter stopped him in his tracks, derailing that thought quite effectively.

"Hello, Adept Bawb," a familiar voice greeted him.

"Master Imalla. I did not expect to see you here."

"Of course you did not."

She said no more, staring at him quietly in that unsettling way she was so good at, knowing full well Bawb would be the first to break the silence.

"Um, did you wish to speak with me?" he finally asked.

"Funny you should mention that. Walk with me."

She turned and strode off, leading the way through the disguised doorway leading into the compound proper, sealing it tight behind her. Once they were absolutely out of anyone's earshot, she continued.

"You failed at a task not so long ago."

"I know. It was foolish to waste my air battling the creature, but I will not make that mistake again."

"Not that failure. A far more important one. A contract."

Bawb felt his stomach sink a little. Now he knew exactly what she was talking about. His blown attempt on Emmik Mollin's life.

"Ah, that."

"Yes, *that*. It has come to my attention that there will be an opportunity to complete your task. You—"

"I am ready."

"You did not let me finish."

"My apologies, Master."

"Do not get ahead of yourself, *Adept*. While you are skilled, this is a particularly difficult piece of infiltration work. One I dare say is well above your level."

"I wish to make my mistake right."

"And I am not ordering you on this mission, Adept Bawb. I am offering it to you."

"Master?" he asked, confused. It was highly unusual to be given a choice in these sorts of things at his rank. The Masters told you what to do and you did it. But this? This was something different.

"As I said, this will be particularly difficult and of exceptional danger. You may very well perish if things go awry."

"I understand," he replied. "And I am ready if it is my time."

She studied him a moment, assessing his commitment to the challenge, finding him unwavering in his conviction. "Good. A Ghalian does not fear death. It is an inevitable part of life that eventually visits us all. We simply do not know when."

Bawb nodded solemnly, recalling the words Hozark had repeated to him on many occasions. "We are already dead, and that is why we live with no fear. To fight as such, we fear no man."

"Or woman," Imalla added.

"Or woman," he agreed.

"Gather your basic kit. You will be entering into this endeavor unarmed but for your konus. All other weapons will be provided to you upon your arrival."

"I do not understand. I am to be given weapons at the location I am to eliminate Emmik Mollin? What sort of mission is this?"

"One where you will be posing as a gladiator. One of many in a training facility. You will be briefed fully en route. There is a small window for your insertion into the ranks of the gladiators there, and you must leave at once."

Now it made more sense. She had obviously heard of his time with Ser Baruud. Posing as a gladiator would actually come somewhat easily thanks to that training.

"I am on my way. And, Master, thank you for the opportunity."

"Thank me *after* you return," she replied, leaving him to wonder if he would.

The flight was a relatively short one. Bawb could have just flown himself, but he needed time to go over all the details during the trip, absorbing the minutia of the gladiatorial compound's inner workings as best he could, given the limited time at hand.

The ingress would be straightforward enough. A new batch of fighters were arriving to bolster the ranks, as others had just departed to rejoin their owners to be deployed for real gladiatorial bouts. This meant he could simply filter in with the newcomers. This was the easy part.

The hard part would be positioning himself to take down the emmik while not standing out as he endured days of hard training, blending in with the other gladiatorial hopefuls. If he was discovered, he could be facing dozens of hardened fighters. And if the emmik found out about him, there would be no daring escape like last time. This would require finesse.

The pilot set down just outside of the gladiatorial training facility. This was not a stealth insertion. It was all about timing. He walked Bawb to the gates of the training compound and gave him a shove to make a show of it.

"Work hard, and do not embarrass me," the man growled. "I'll be back to retrieve you in a month."

"Hang on. Who are you?" the guard at the gate asked.

"What the hell do you mean, who am I? Do you have any idea how damn far I had to travel to drop this guy off?"

"We don't take in randoms."

"Well, good thing he's not a random. Check your records,

idiot. Look what day it is. I was told specifically to have him here by today, this afternoon, no later."

"I don't—"

"Have a brain? Clearly." The disguised Ghalian turned to Bawb, also sporting a different skin tone and modified appearance. "You, get inside and get settled."

"He can't—"

"You heard me. Go. I'll deal with this fool."

Bawb simply nodded, his false control collar firmly around his neck, allowing him the luxury of pretending he was simply following orders lest he receive a nasty shock from it. This was the tricky bit. Bluffing past the guard. But once he was past him, it would be smooth sailing.

The thing was, this was the day new arrivals were permitted, and it was entirely possible there had been a screwup somewhere in the record keeping. All the two Ghalian had to do was make it uncomfortable enough for the guard to give him an excuse to just kick the can down the road and let someone else deal with it.

Bawb shouldered his way past the man and into the compound. No one stopped him. He was in.

He glanced back over his shoulder, but the guard already seemed beaten by the encounter. It would only be a matter of time before he would say whatever he had to, to get the newcomer badgering him to just leave him alone. And by then Bawb would be safely ensconced in the gladiator ranks.

He walked into the bunkhouse and found an empty bed, dropping his stuff and immediately heading out to the training area. The other new arrivals were already there, being assessed and sent to train. All around them, fighters of varying skill levels were practicing with great ferocity. It seemed the healers here would be kept busy. From what Bawb saw of their skills, it also seemed that the instructors couldn't hold a candle to Ser Baruud's tutelage.

"You're late," the overseer noted.

"Sorry. My master's transport got here late."

"Tough shit for you, then," the man sneered, sizing up the fresh meat. "I'm Overseer Krall."

"My name is Topor."

"Whatever. Topor, you're in with Orkus. Let's see if you've got any worth," he said, gesturing to one of the sparring rings, the perimeter carved into the stone floor, a minor spell in place to warn combatants if they stumbled out.

The man standing in it was massive. A sweaty, tan-skinned brute with as much blubber as muscle. But for his size, he looked as though he actually moved well, and his sheer mass likely made him a difficult one to take down in anything but armed combat.

"Well? Don't just stand there collecting flies. Get moving," Krall snapped. "Empty hands only."

Seems you are a bit screwed, the konus noted, choosing this of all moments to voice its opinion.

"We do what we must," Bawb muttered under his breath.

Orkus lived up to Bawb's concern and then some, light on his feet and fast with his hands. The hard-fisted flurry hit like an iron club, knocking Bawb clear out of the sparring ring. He rose and dusted himself off. So, this was how it was going to be, eh? He'd faced worse.

Bawb launched into an attack of his own, forcing the larger man to pivot and retreat as he threw kicks and knees, relying on power against the man's sheer mass.

Don't get cocky. You know you need to blend in, the konus reminded him. Bawb, however, was well aware of the situation. He was going to have to take a beating. Many of them, in fact, over the next several days until his target finally arrived. Until then, he had to appear to be a fair fighter but not an elite one of high value. That was the sort of person who could get close to his target, while the top fighters were treated as the valuable, deadly tools for their owners' profit that they were and would be kept in other circles.

Emmik Mollin, for all her refined appearances, was actually a rather vicious woman. And one of her favorite pastimes was visiting gladiator facilities such as this to test her mettle against people who were both skilled but also of little consequence. These were enslaved fighters, and if one or two of them should be seriously harmed or even killed in her fun, so be it. She had plenty of coin to compensate their owners if it came to that.

So it came to be that Bawb suffered at the hands of lesser fighters over and over and over, avoiding serious injury with great skill, but making himself seem just a middle-of-the-road combatant in the process.

He spent three days as a living punching bag before rumors began to spread of the arrival of a powerful fighter coming soon. Bawb acted just as surprised as everyone else, though he knew full well precisely when she was scheduled to land. When Emmik Mollin finally did strut into the facility, it was almost anticlimactic. Here they had been anticipating some brute of a warrior, and all they got was an average-looking woman of normal build.

Then they learned *why* she had her reputation.

"Billix, you're with the emmik," Overseer Krall ordered.

Billix was a good fighter. Not amazing, but skilled. Bawb had nearly beaten him a few times, always pulling his punches and losing, of course. Billix stepped into the ring with the emmik and set to work. Or, rather, he tried to. Emmik Mollin made quick work of him without even using her magic.

"Really, Krall? Do make it a challenge," she said with a bored sigh.

Three more fighters were sent to challenge her, and while they now had an inkling of what they were up against, each fell in turn. The emmik had broken a sweat at least, and that was enough to satisfy her for the moment.

"Let us work with weapons tomorrow," she said. "It will be ever so much more fun."

"As you wish, Emmik," the overseer replied. "Ixniss, show the emmik to her suite."

The servant bowed low and scurried ahead, leading their esteemed guest to her chambers. If intelligence was correct, she would likely stay for two to three days before heading back home. Bawb had that long to complete his task. And having seen her fight, he realized just how lucky he was to have made his escape from her compound. Even without all her guards, she would have been quite the handful, and his training at that point was lacking. His death would have been a very real possibility facing her alone. Fortunately, that gap in his skillset had been filled by Ser Baruud quite nicely.

The next day Mollin worked with swords and spears, injuring a few of the fighters quite seriously. But it was when one of them landed a blow on her arm that something truly unsettling occurred. Emmik Mollin lashed out hard and fast with her magic, an instinctual reaction to the injury. The gladiator, though stout and strong, was flung hard against the nearest wall, his body breaking from the impact.

This one, the healer would not be able to fix. The emmik's eyes shone bright, the thrill of killing arousing her blood lust.

Strong magic, the konus noted. *Very strong. I don't think you can take her head-on.*

"I am aware of that," Bawb replied, already altering his plan. His original idea had been to simply make it look like an accident. A fatal blow landed by an inexperienced gladiator student. Now he realized he would have to come up with something much different.

"Topor, you're up," the overseer called to him. It seemed Bawb was going to have to think on the fly.

He had been allowed to use his konus in training, casting the usual magical shield spells and attacks, although with less skill than he actually had. But this? He couldn't sandbag against this opponent. At least, not like he'd planned.

The emmik rolled her neck and attacked hard and fast, swinging a spear in slicing arcs, barely missing her opponent. Bawb and Usalla had trained extensively with spears, and he had developed a great degree of skill at dodging her blows. A skill that was now being put to very good use, though as inconspicuously as possible.

He allowed her to land glancing strikes, mere scratches, but enough to make it appear she was winning easily. Bawb knew he couldn't land a shot on her without incurring her magical wrath, so he settled for somewhat wild swings of his sword, pressing his attack as best he could against his opponent.

The emmik responded with a little stun spell. Nothing major, but something fun to spice up the contest. She was actually surprised to find her opponent had already cast a blocking spell around himself before he attacked, her stun spell sliding off it harmlessly. She grinned. Maybe this one wasn't quite as pathetic as he seemed.

She had killed with magic, but as the fights wore on, Emmik Mollin found herself wanting to experience the visceral feel of hot blood on her hands. That meant getting up close and personal with her target. Dropping her spear and pulling twin daggers from her belt, she had just the plan in mind.

She charged him, overconfident in her power, peppering Bawb with a series of spells designed to cause him to drop his guard, allowing her blades to find a warm sheath in his body. Bawb pretended to struggle with them as she raced toward him. Abruptly and without warning he tripped, making a show of losing his footing. Her blade flew past, meeting empty air as his shoulder caught her in the sternum, knocking the wind out of her, preventing her from voicing a spell.

Bawb rolled with it, as if surprised and knocked over by the impact. This was it. This was his one chance. He would have to time it just right so no one could see, but rolling with her like this, the opportunity presented itself.

His fangs sprang out, latching onto her neck hard as he sucked with all his strength, pulling out as much power as he could while his face was obstructed from view. The surge of power was intense. Delicious. Invigorating. He didn't want the flow to stop, but much as he wished to drink her dry, he forced himself to unlatch from her neck, casting a healing spell, immediately sealing the wound on her neck as he slid his sword's point under her breastbone.

They rolled a moment before a gush of blood spread out across the stone. Overseer Krall shook his head.

"Gollip, you're next. Dinzus, clean up the—"

He fell silent as the combatants rolled apart. Only one of them was moving, and it was not the emmik.

"What happened?" Bawb cried out as if utterly horrified at what he'd done. He shook the emmik's lifeless body, as if hoping it was all some terrible mistake. But it wasn't. This had gone exactly as he'd planned, albeit with a few modifications on the fly.

Level up: Subterfuge, magical combat, concealment of a kill, healing, the konus announced.

Bawb ignored it, acting stunned at the blood all over him, looking at the dead emmik with a look of panic. A panic

Overseer Krall most certainly shared. This wasn't supposed to happen. This was bad.

"I didn't mean—"

"Shut up!" Krall bellowed, the consequences of this mess flashing through his mind. "Topor, you are out of this training house, never to return. Leave at once."

The gladiator was off-limits to a degree. He was owned and paid for, and no matter how violent life here was, there were rules. Rules that would see his livelihood shut down if he didn't follow them. But if he couldn't offer up another's property as recompense, at least he could banish him. Hopefully, that would somewhat lessen the wrath of whomever would collect the emmik's body. But she was a connected woman, and this was bad.

"But my master—"

"Fuck your master. Summon him on your own. You are out. Now!"

Again, as Bawb had intended.

He hurried to the bunkhouse and quickly washed the blood from himself, donning the only clean clothes he had before trudging out the front gate, head held low as though he had the weight of the world on his shoulders.

Bawb walked for a time, eventually shedding his disguise, opting for blue skin as he made his way to the waiting transport. He felt good. Better than good. He felt *amazing*. He'd never taken power from someone this strong, and it was an incredible sensation. And with that, there was also the feeling of contentment at a mistake righted and a job well done. And all without anyone knowing it wasn't an accident.

He boarded the ship and took a seat, relaxing as they lifted off into the skies.

You may actually have what it takes, you know, the konus said.

Maybe not to become one of the Five. But a Master? You've got a way to go, but keep performing like that, and it's a very real possibility.

"Thank you, Konus," he replied, a little surprised at the device's positive words. Usually, it was a sarcastic little shit, but today it seemed even the konus had been impressed. And who knew? Perhaps this would be the beginning of a new phase in his path.

CHAPTER TWENTY-FOUR

Bawb's return to the Ghalian compound was a quiet one, the flight uneventful and his walk through the streets he now knew so well a refreshing chance to take in a bit of fresh air before heading underground for whatever today's lesson might be. He made his way to the entrance at a leisurely pace, stopping to pick up a little snack as he walked.

Energy was flowing through him. Emmik energy, and a lot of it at that. It was a heady feeling, the raw power he had taken from his target now ready to serve his wishes. He had taken power many times by now, of course, but never from someone this strong. She may not have been a visla, but now that he had sampled her magic, he realized she was only just below that rank. He'd gotten lucky things worked out in his favor, of that he was certain.

But luck and the how and why didn't matter in the end. He had done his job and gotten out, just as required, nothing more. Yes, it had been a particularly challenging contract, and he had suffered greatly in the process. But that was what it took to achieve his goal, and pain was temporary, whereas glory was forever. He had done a good job. More than that, he had been able to stop his bleeding without much effort or expenditure of magic as he made his escape.

Now that he was home, however, he would need to visit the healer for a proper stitch-up. Or, given the power he now possessed, maybe he would even do it himself this time. The practice would surely prove useful one day.

He reached a small shop and stepped inside, nodding to the lone disguised employee as he made his way to the back. There he walked through another door into a storage room. He waved his hand, casting the opening spell with barely a breath. The wall parted, admitting him to the inner realms of the Ghalian training house. He entered without hesitation, the wall sealing behind him in an instant. Now he just had to see Master Imalla.

It was a funny shift from his early days, he mused as he walked to her receiving area. In his youth, he might have first sought out his cohort, eager to talk up his adventures. Now, however, he was acting like a true Ghalian without really thinking about it. He would report his success then carry on with his day, as simple as that.

"Adept Bawb," Imalla's voice rang out from just behind him.

He turned slowly, impressed with her degree of stealth, though not surprised. She didn't become the Master overseeing the entire facility for no reason, after all.

"Master Imalla."

She looked him up and down, though he was quite certain she'd already assessed him before saying a word. "You seem well. Injured, but not terribly."

"It was a challenging task, as you anticipated. But in the end, all fell into place."

"I sense you are carrying a significant amount of power. You were not observed, were you?"

"While it was a bit of a daunting task, no, I was not. I managed to drain her and cover my tracks in the process. To any who will come looking, it will appear as if she was killed in an unfortunate sparring accident. No foul play. No questionable circumstances. There were many witnesses to the event, and all will state the same thing."

Imalla's face remained blank, but Bawb could have sworn he almost felt a hint of a smile beneath that serious exterior. But Master Imalla was not one for outward shows of emotion. Or flattery, for that matter.

"Well? Your task is complete," she said plainly. "Go join your classmates."

"Of course."

"And do not visit the healer. I would have you use up some of that excess power practicing your healing spells."

"That was my intention."

"Then your instincts serve you well. Be quick about it though. Your classmates are already heading into the crafting room. Today is something a bit different from your usual fare."

"I look forward to it."

Imalla gave the tiniest of shrugs, then turned and walked away. Bawb's curiosity was piqued after her off-hand comment. Something different? Different could be fun. He hurried down the corridors, casting his healing spells as he walked. If he was going to use this as an opportunity to train, he may as well do it in a manner that replicated a real-world situation. Namely, healing on the fly.

His bruised muscles and strained tendons recovered quite quickly, he found. The cuts he had sustained required a bit more focus. The thing about mending sliced and torn flesh was it could itch terribly as the tissue knitted back together. It was uncomfortable, and more than a little distracting. In a way, it was worse than the injury itself. He had trained long and hard to ignore pain to complete his task. But itching? It was a different and quite annoying sensation entirely.

Of course, that was how he had come to the idea of employing annoying but otherwise harmless spells in combat. He'd done it since his youth, but now the tactic had been refined, and he could send buzzing, stinging insects, annoying dust clouds, or itching bug bites with little effort.

But this was crafting day, and he would be using his unusual thinking skills for something quite different.

"There you are," Teacher Warfin said as he entered the room. "A bit late, but I understand you were away on a task for Master Imalla, so I will let it slide."

"Thank you, Teacher. I do apologize for my tardiness regardless."

"Forgiven. Think no more on it. I am pleased to see you return to us unscathed."

Bawb noticed the way he had said that. It was clear Warfin had an inkling just how dangerous his mission had been. He also had the tact not to mention it during class.

"All went well," he replied, not mentioning the bit of healing he'd done on the way there.

"Good. I think you will enjoy today's lesson. This is something quite unusual, and we will not be spending much time on it beyond a few additional lessons to practice what you have learned."

Albinius perked up, his curiosity running at full-throttle. "Are we going to learn to make konuses?"

"No, Albinius. Don't be foolish. You know that is a very specialized bit of skill that takes years to master. But you are on track in a way."

"I am?"

"We are going to work with *this*!" he declared as he whipped the cloth covering the nearby table free, revealing hunks of stone of various sizes.

"We're learning to throw rocks at people? Are we making slings?"

Warfin sighed and shook his head. "Again, no. Can anyone tell me what I have here on this table?"

"Rocks," Zota said.

"Yes, clearly. But what else? Anyone? Think beyond the table. Think of your setting."

Bawb looked around the room as his classmates struggled to come up with what Warfin could possibly be getting at when his eyes fell upon something new set up at the far end, a small flicker of flame emitting from within. It was a forge, and next to it, a small crucible.

"Ore," he said confidently.

"Very good, Bawb. You are correct. This is raw ore. The most basic components in the creation of the weapons you all carry. Any metal object started out as this, or some variation. And today you are going to learn how to identify different metal ores in nature, as well as how to prepare them for smelting."

Elzina somehow managed to contain her annoyed sigh, but she seemed quite unimpressed with the day's lesson. "Why would we waste time melting rocks when we can just buy or steal weapons?"

Warfin turned his gaze fully upon her, staring silently a few moments.

"Imagine you are stranded far from a city. There is a traveling band of mercenaries, and you must eliminate one or more of them, but you possess nothing. No blades, no konus, just the clothes on your back."

"I would kill one of them and take their weapon," she replied confidently.

"No, no, that is not the point. The point is, you need to be able to craft weapons in an emergency. Will you ever find yourself needing this skill? I certainly hope not. But more than one Ghalian has used these techniques to great success over the years. And now, Elzina, you will *all* be learning them."

"Blending in," Bawb said.

"What was that?"

"Blending in. Knowledge of blacksmithing is also a useful skill if we ever have to blend in as a laborer. It is a rather particular type of knowledge."

"Well put. This training will also prepare you for that circumstance, as well as giving you the skills to forge weapons in a pinch."

"So we melt the ore and pour it into a form. Everyone knows that," Elzina interjected.

Warfin shook his head. "Oh, dear Elzina. *Knowing* how things are made is far different than actually doing it. And remember, knowledge is power, but only if properly wielded."

"And sometimes the difference between life and death," Bawb added quietly.

"Indeed, it can be that as well. But, enough chatter. Let us begin. We will start with identifying the different types of ore before you. Then we will move on to the smelting process, at which point we will discuss how alloys are formed. It can be quite a trick to get right, especially in the case of primitive forging, but you are a clever lot, and I am confident you will pick this up rapidly. Now, Elzina, would you please step forward? You shall be my assistant in this demonstration."

Bawb and Usalla shared an amused look, inspired by Elzina's less than thrilled one. She would do as she was told, but she would not like it. Bawb, on the other hand, was excited. Whether it was the unexpected magic flowing through him or just a natural progression in his psyche as he reached the higher levels, whatever the case, he was eager to fill his cup of knowledge with ever more skills.

It was a deep-seated love of learning that would stick with him all his days.

CHAPTER TWENTY-FIVE

A full week passed after Bawb's successful mission, and he spoke of its details to no one but Usalla, their casual pillow talk a constant source of unexpected comfort after their training sessions in the horizontal arts. They had practiced together for some time at this point and knew each other better than any other. Regardless, they were Ghalian, and therefore, there were rules to follow.

This was training. Pleasurable training, but training nonetheless. To be anything more would go against the ways of their people. Ghalian did not bond. And so it was they learned from each other, developing their skills, enjoying the frankness of conversation that often followed.

Usalla had been rather impressed when she learned of Bawb's self-control in the face of brutal beatings and so much misery endured just to get close enough to complete his task in the most unusual of ways.

"Was it amazing? All of the emmik's power flowing into you?"

"I was nearly overwhelmed, to be honest. In fact, I almost failed to relinquish my bite and heal the wound."

"That could have ended quite badly."

"It could have. But that is why we train. To prepare our minds as well as our bodies for whatever may come our way."

"And I thank you again for your vigorous efforts in helping me train," she said with a little gleam in her eye. "You know, it really is something, preparing to rise in rank. We are very nearly Mavens, Bawb. And when that happens, we will be full-fledged Ghalian, out in the world doing the order's business."

"You will be amazing, I am certain," he replied, absentmindedly caressing her shoulder.

Usalla slipped from his touch and gathered her things. "Aren't you forgetting something?"

"What might that be?" he asked, admiring her as she dressed.

"That we have a task this afternoon. A *real* mission, Bawb."

"I have not forgotten. I was merely enjoying the moment."

A little grin creased the corners of her lips. "Yes, well, there is a time and a place for our training, but right now, it is time to prepare for this exercise. You do realize it is going to be a group outing."

"I do."

"Which means it is almost certain we shall be competing against one another to complete whatever the objective may be."

"Indeed. And I look forward to the challenge," he said, donning his clothes in a leisurely manner. "Rumor has it we are to bring weapons with. We are to be ready to kill."

"How did you come by this knowledge?"

"I learned long ago to keep my mouth shut and my ears open. I could be mistaken, of course."

"But knowing you, you likely are not."

He cracked a wry grin. "Why, thank you for the vote of confidence."

"It was nothing of the sort. I was merely stating a fact."

"Nevertheless..."

They gathered with the others in the upper courtyard. The instructions were simple. Though the Adepts were skilled at flying, they would be ferried to their destination in a group of shimmer ships. They would need to arrive as stealthily as possible, and while they could pilot the craft, maintaining a shimmer spell was still out of their grasp.

The group spread out, all of them in disguise as second nature at this point, wandering through the streets, eventually boarding one of the waiting craft. Only once inside did they let their disguises down, saving their magic for the task at hand.

They were to compete against one another, all of them vying for the prize, in this instance, a collection of a dozen small, masterfully crafted enchanted daggers, perfectly weighted and just the right size for concealing on one's body. And Ghalian *loved* carrying hidden weapons.

The task was to be two-fold. They would infiltrate a covert konus fabrication facility, retrieving the power source used to charge the devices and interrogate the low-powered emmik overseeing the location if possible. He reportedly possessed information about the ultimate destination of the konuses. Something an interested party would pay handsomely for, and which the Ghalian were quite curious about. But as time was of the essence, retrieving the power source was the most important part of the task. And if they could not pry the information from the emmik, in a timely fashion, he was to be eliminated in whatever manner necessary.

Some days a cover story was essential. In the case of an illegal facility such as this, no one would think twice if the man was slain in his duties.

Zota had seemed a bit shocked that all of them would be

going. It was to be an infiltration, after all, and if they were each working individually, that meant there was bound to be incidental overlap.

"Figure it out," Teacher Griggitz told them. "Do what you must to win. Sometimes there may be others attempting to complete the same task as you. It is rare, but not unheard of, and you will need to deal with those situations as they arise."

"We take out the competition," Elzina said with a malicious smile.

"In those cases? Yes. But not now. In this instance there are to be no fatal actions taken against your cohort. You are competing, and you may interfere with one another, but that is all. Beyond that one rule, anything goes. But remember, do not get carried away with competitiveness amongst yourselves. The contract *always* comes first."

At this point, the Adepts were comfortable with being sent on missions, and the flight was not one of concerned plotting but rather a time to rest, collect their thoughts, and prepare for what would undoubtedly be an interesting challenge. When they saw their destination as the ships dropped into the atmosphere and activated their shimmer cloaks, their hypotheses were confirmed.

The landing site was atop a mountain, the peak jutting out from the mists surrounding it, spreading low and covering the entire area. How far down it went was anyone's guess, but judging by the people in the small town atop the mountain, it couldn't be too far. The air would have been much thinner if they were at an exceptional altitude.

The ships came in slowly. So slowly that their passengers actually began to get a little fidgety. The reasoning was clear, however. Shimmer cloaks did not work well in smoke, mist, or clouds, and with the weather being what it was, they were forced to make their approach painfully slowly so as not to stir the air and alert anyone to their presence.

After far too long a wait, they finally set down in an empty field off to the side of the township. The Adepts stepped out of the cloaked ships and quickly made their way to the cloudline, moving down into the mist and out of sight of the locals.

The clock was now ticking.

"Seems obvious why they chose to set up here," Zota commented as they walked into the thickening mist.

"Oh?" Finnia replied. "How so?"

"No one will ever find this place unless they know exactly where it is."

Bawb shook his head. "These are low clouds, nothing more. Look at the vegetation around us. It requires sunlight to grow this lush. What we are experiencing now is merely a fluke of weather."

"Huh," was all his friend replied.

Finnia pushed ahead a bit, the three of them following the same path down while the others had spread out to other trails. As they had no idea which was the more direct one to take, they simply decided to fan out and descend en masse. No one knew how to find their destination, so they opted for an unspoken truce for now as they traveled down together.

Once they reached their target, however, all bets would be off, and they would separate into their individual approaches.

They hiked for some time, the cloudcover thinning as they dropped lower, shifting into mist, then simply slightly damp, foggy air. The valley was lush with violet foliage, which they could finally see, and the township where the konus-forging compound was located was now clearly visible. This was the end of their cooperation. The Adepts peeled off and began vanishing into the woods, each plotting their own line of approach.

Bawb glanced over at Usalla not far away and flashed her a little hand signal they used when speaking was not an option. "Be safe and good luck," he said. She gave a little nod in return and vanished.

Okay, Adept. This is it. You ready?

"Yes, Konus. Compared to recent events, this should be relatively straightforward, if not easy."

The key word there is relatively. *You know things never go right, right?*

"Of course."

Well, as long as you think you've got it all under control. Let's see what you can do.

"That was my intention," Bawb replied, briefly calling up his greatly expanded list of skills and techniques he had leveled in over the years.

There were a lot he could potentially use in this situation, but he would have to select wisely and on the fly. With the others involved, he would have to adjust as the situation unfolded, but at least his options were far greater than in his youth.

He made his way down to the base of the mountain quickly but cautiously, muting spells cast at his feet to silence his footsteps just in case. As it turned out, it was a good thing, he realized as he came upon fresh tracks. Tracks with claws digging deep in the soft soil. He knew the beast that had made them. Not a terribly difficult one for a Ghalian to deal with, but a confrontation he would rather avoid if he could manage it. If he did happen to notice one, he would first use local mud to mask his scent and simply let it pass. If it did, however, decide he was of interest, it would be the last mistake the creature would ever make.

The locals, on the other hand, would have a hard time with the beasts. He noticed the vast Malooki pens were spread out all around the periphery of the town, creating a massive buffer of open fields of muddy ground. The Malooki were grouped in clusters, the herd always on alert, the larger males facing outward, protecting their mates and the young.

Bawb realized what was going on and, suddenly, it all made sense. The empathic animals' changing hair color would alert their keepers if danger was close. A living alarm system of sorts, allowing the populace to save their magic for other uses. It was quite clever, actually, and Bawb heartily approved.

He would also have to move carefully so as not to spook the gentle creatures with his unexpected arrival. He lessened the spell at his feet, allowing them to make a little noise as he walked. He also stood up taller, moving smoothly with no jarring motions as he stepped out into the open. The Malooki nearest him looked up from their grazing, their hair swirling slightly with a hint of concern as they assessed the interloper.

"I am of no concern to you. I mean you no harm. Be calm, my friends," Bawb said quietly as he drew closer.

The Malooki's coats shifted again, settling into a comfortable shade of lilac. It seemed they were feeling more at ease than before, now that he had arrived. Apparently, they recognized him not only as a friend, but a protector.

Level up: Empathic communication with animals the konus announced quietly. *I have to admit, I wasn't expecting that.*

"Nor I. But it seems these Malooki are particularly sensitive to my skills."

Apparently. But don't you have something more important to be doing than playing with the critters?

"I am moving, Konus. Do not rush me. You get bad results when you rush."

Yeah, yeah. Just don't let the others get the jump on you, is all I'm saying.

"Judging by the muddy nature of the approach, I feel confident my cohort will have a slow and arduous approach."

You will too.

"Perhaps," he said, an idea forming in his mind. "But perhaps not."

CHAPTER TWENTY-SIX

The Malooki calmly walking across the muddy field was a massive one, clearly one of the male protectors of the herd judging by his size. His coat was rippling a calm wave of silver, pale violet, and the lightest yellow. No one from the town gave him a second look. This was a creature utterly at ease.

No one noticed the young assassin riding its back, matching its colors as best he could with limited magic. He didn't have a disguise spell to fit this bill, so he had to improvise. But with some mist in the air and no one on alert, it was enough.

Bawb scanned the fields from his perch atop the impressive steed, lying flat on its back as it walked through the mud with the ease of a creature well adapted for this sort of terrain. In the distance he saw shapes low to the ground. His classmates, spread out far, each making the most stealthy approach they could. It seemed no one had opted to attempt the main road. Getting in that way would be difficult, but leaving? There would be no scrutiny on people heading the other direction.

But for now they were all ankle-deep and worse in the sucking mud, trudging along as quietly as they could. The Malooki in those fields saw them and reacted a bit, but their colors never shifted to those of actual panic, and as a result, he felt the others were likely to make it all the way to the township without notice.

Bawb did observe that a few of them appeared to be muddier than the others, likely having taken a tumble in the difficult terrain. It was certainly not an easy approach by any standards.

The towering Malooki slowed as it drew close to the edge of its enclosure. Just on the other side of the fence were the town streets proper. Bawb slid off its back, shifting his coloration and improvised clothing disguise back to normal.

"Thank you, my friend," he said quietly, gently rubbing the beast's massive neck.

The Malooki gave a little snort and casually turned back to its herd.

You do have a way with animals, the konus admitted.

"And a good thing," the Ghalian agreed, slipping through the fence and into the town's streets, his boots and clothing mud-free.

Bawb had arrived well before his cohort, but he did not rush. Instead, he walked the town casually, blending in with the locals, adopting the physical look as well as behaviors, tics, and vocal patterns of the people he encountered. If he had to make an escape, it would be far easier if he didn't look like an interloper.

Finding the illicit konus fabrication foundry was relatively easy. Normally, he would have used one of his specialized spells to pinpoint the source of particularly strong magic, but as he still had a sizable amount of emmik magic flowing through him from his recent kill, he found he could just sense it without effort. It was an eye-opening experience. Not all magic users had this ability, but knowing firsthand what the ones who did possess it could feel would help him better protect himself from others who possessed the gift in the future.

The building was a thick-walled structure of black, bricklike material, as many of the structures in the area were, but the windows were opaqued and the main entrance doors sealed up tight. It stood out a little from the other buildings in that regard, but otherwise drew no attention.

Surely there were guards inside, as well as the power source and the target emmik, but no one would know from looking.

Aren't you going in? the konus asked.

"Not yet."

But the others will have reached the town by now.

"I would think so. But there are too many unknowns. The prudent move is to wait and observe."

Someone else will win the prize. Get moving, Adept!

"No."

Are you telling me you're really going to just sit by and let someone else snatch victory from you?

"Also no. I am going to run my own race and do things in my own time. You have been with me a long time, Konus. You know as well as I do that sometimes slow is fast."

That's just nonsense motivational speaker mumbo-jumbo.

"Caution, more often than not, trumps speed for its own sake. And taking one's time can ultimately lead to a faster end result. Just trust me, okay?"

Do I have a choice?

"No. So please, do be quiet," Bawb said as he observed a familiar shape moving closer to the building. "I must concentrate."

It was Elzina, disguised as a Pillarian, with their characteristic reddish-gray skin and black eyes. But Bawb could sense the disguise thanks to the emmik magic flowing through him. It was so helpful he found himself wishing every kill could be like this. Not only giving him access to power, but enhanced senses as well.

He watched her lurk for a bit until she pulled up and chatted with a medium-sized person wearing an inclement weather cloak. He couldn't see who was in it, but Elzina seemed to be quite interested in their conversation. Then, as quickly as it began, she gave a nod, and they both went their separate ways.

"That was interesting," he mused, thinking back to her prior encounter before he'd been sent on his gladiatorial task. But he would think about that later. For now he watched as several other classmates approached the area, all in varying disguises, and all of them heading to the same general location.

A fluttering of color caught his eye. A trio of saddled Malooki were tied near the konus facility's entryway. While his classmates had successfully infiltrated the town so far, he could sense the animals' disquiet as they drew near. Empathic creatures, they could feel something was amiss, and they were beginning to stir. Any moment they would react, and loudly.

Bawb called up the most powerful muting spell he knew to his lips, concentrating hard and casting it from a distance, enveloping both his classmates and the Malooki they were passing. The power flowed from him in a rush, the stolen magic within him boosting his konus's power exponentially in a way he had never done before. The spell blasted out of him, silencing their steps and the Malooki's loud vocalizations.

Sweat began beading on his brow as he strained to maintain the spell. Unlike his konus, which was easily recharged, when the stolen power in his blood was used up, it would be gone until he stole more. He had to hold on. Just a little longer and they would be clear enough for him to pass, making his attempt at the small service door he had located on the side of the building. But first his classmates had to get clear. He poured all he could into the spell and started moving, hoping it would hold long enough for him to get into position.

He rushed along at a quick walk, clearing the front of the

structure and making his way to the side without incident as the others milled about near the front. No alarm had been raised. Not yet, anyway, but he knew the spell would wear off soon enough. Even so, he was thrilled it actually worked.

Okay, that was impressive, the konus commended him. *Big-time level up: Use of stolen power, distance casting, muting spell level nine.*

"I am not finished yet," he muttered, quietly unlocking the door, casting a detection spell for tripwires or hidden guards, and then slipping inside.

Just as the door closed, he heard a loud commotion out front. The Malooki were reacting, and they were doing so very vocally. It seemed the spell had finally broken. Voices shouted, and he heard feet rushing from within the building, all of them heading to the front door. Some would step outside, others would remain within, guarding their stronghold.

Bawb hurried down the hallway, following the visceral pull of whatever was being used to power the newly forged konuses. Even with his stolen emmik power dwindling faster than he'd anticipated, he could still feel it plain as day. He didn't know what the source was, but it was powerful. In no time he reached the foundry room. It was warded with strong protective magic, but nothing he couldn't work his way around given a little time. And with everyone rushing to the front door, that was exactly what he got.

The commotion outside had played to his advantage, and in short order Bawb had the warding spells disarmed without leaving a trace. He moved inside, hugging the walls of the steaming-hot chamber. Molten metal was in the crucible as new konuses were being forged. But he didn't care about those. What he was here for was their power source. When his eyes fell upon it, however, his stomach sank like a stone.

"Ootaki," he gasped to himself, horrified at the sight.

Normally, Ootaki were shorn, their cut hair taken to fuel someone's magic, the loss taken from cutting the hair just a part of the trade-off. But this was different. This was an atrocity.

Sitting on the focusing pedestal was a massive coil of braided Ootaki hair. By the look of it, someone had been growing it for many decades, the power within slowly increasing every day of that time. That part, while distasteful, was still relatively normal. What wasn't, however, was the other thing; the scalp the hair was still attached to.

Someone had scalped an Ootaki, likely in hopes of reducing the loss of magic from cutting the hair. If an Ootaki died, the magic in their hair died with them. But it was entirely possible to survive scalping, horrific as it might be. Bawb felt a flare of rage replace the hard ball that had formed in his gut, his anger burning as hot as the molten metal heating the air around him.

He grabbed the hair, scalp and all, and stuffed it into his bag of holding, compressing it into a size he could conceal and carry easily. He then turned for the exit, wanting very much to stumble upon the emmik who did this.

"Hey! You there! What are you doing here? Stop right there!" a *very* unfortunate guard shouted from across the room.

He was dead before he hit the floor, the dagger thrown and embedded in his eye before he even saw the intruder move a muscle.

Bawb hurried to the man and retrieved his blade, wiping it on the man's clothing before resheathing it. He hefted the body and dumped it into the molten metal, the fresh corpse catching fire immediately then turning to ash in an instant. The evidence gone, he moved to the door but stopped, a thought running through his mind.

Bawb had heard the man's voice. That meant he could copy it.

Bawb laid a powerful tripwire destruction spell on several

key elements of the facility then cast a new disguise spell in a flash, adopting the dead man's look as well as he could given the haste in which he was forced to work. It was far from perfect, but he hoped it would work for his rapidly improvised plan.

Bawb felt a flare of power as defensive spells were cast at the front door. Apparently, someone had been foolish enough to attempt a frontal attempt on the building. Now everyone was on high alert. But if he was lucky, they didn't know they'd already been infiltrated.

He rushed through the structure to the group at the front. It sounded like many were outside fighting his classmates, at least those who had gotten caught up in the whole mess. The bright side was that left only about a half dozen inside. Them, and the emmik casting his defensive spells, protecting their hard, illegal work.

Bawb mussed his appearance, making himself look sweaty with a bit of blood spattered on his magically altered clothing. It wouldn't withstand close scrutiny, but given the circumstances, it would have to do.

"There's an attack at the second-level rear windows! We need more hands to fight them off!" he yelled, his seemingly injured state immediately grabbing the attention of everyone present.

"You four, get over there!" the emmik shouted.

Four of them took off at a run while two remained. Bawb leaned on the wall, appearing weakened from the fight. The emmik approached him, a sharp look of concern in his eyes.

"What happened?"

"The front is a distraction. They were coming in the windows."

"What about the—"

A loud rumble shook the whole building. The other guards had tripped the spells, destroying the forge and everything in it.

The emmik's expression shifted in an instant. It was no longer about defending. The plan now was escape and survival.

"Kitchen! Now!"

He took off at a run, the guards sticking close by. Of course he had an emergency egress plan. And Bawb was being invited along for the ride.

They raced through the building, hot smoke filling the air as the fire from the destroyed chamber spread. They reached the kitchen, and the emmik held up his hand at the wall next to the food-cooling chamber. The wall cracked and bucked, then slid aside, revealing a hidden door to the outside.

It wasn't nearly as well-crafted as the ones in the Ghalian training house, but it would more than do the trick for their needs.

Out they ran, heading away from the building. The emmik was leading them deeper into the city. That was the last thing Bawb wanted. He'd been burning through his magic faster than he expected, and it was with the last of his stolen power that he cast a hard pulling spell, hoping the emmik wasn't a magic-sensitive sort. The wall of the building ahead yanked free and crashed before them.

"It's a trap!" Bawb shouted. "This way!"

He wasn't supposed to be in charge, but in their panic, the emmik and the guards heeded his words and followed. Bawb ran with a limp as he guided them toward the perimeter fields, allowing the guards to pass him and take protective positions in front as they hopped the fence.

The emmik stayed close to Bawb as they came up from the rear. He never saw the fangs coming.

Bawb drank fast and deep, stealing his power in a flash but not killing him, just rendering him useless and unconscious. He slung the fallen target over his shoulder and vaulted the fence, then called out to the guards. "The emmik is hurt!" he yelled, carrying the man away from the town.

He would have to take these guards down with one hand, but they still thought he was one of them, so the task would be easy enough. Easy for a difficult one, that is.

The guards unexpectedly dropped to the ground, stunned unconscious by an invisible hand. Teacher Griggitz uncloaked, as did Demelza and Warfin. Demelza nodded to her counterparts.

"Retrieve the others."

Griggitz and Warfin moved in a flash, their shimmer cloaks engaged, hiding them from sight once more.

"On the ship, hurry," Demelza ordered, the hatch to the hidden ship suddenly appearing at her command.

The shimmer ships had been brought close, it seemed. While they were infiltrating, the teachers had brought the evacuation plan to them. And it seemed it was a very good thing. Demelza secured the captive and took off at once. The others could cram in the other ships. The priority was getting their prize back to the compound for interrogation. Knowing what that entailed, Bawb had little doubt they would get the answers they wanted.

Once they were in flight with their cargo secured and thoroughly stunned, Demelza took a seat beside her student.

"You did well out there, though you spent a lot of time before entering the structure."

"You were watching us?"

"The whole time," she admitted. "We are not to interfere, just observe. You are Adepts now, Bawb. But that does not mean we do not keep an eye on you."

"Fair enough."

Demelza dug out a pair of cool refreshment containers and

popped the lids, handing one to the young man. "Drink. You expended a lot of energy out there."

Bawb did as he was told, draining it in a flash.

"You protected your opponents," his teacher noted, a curious look in her eye. "You silenced their approach as well as the reactions of the Malooki. And it cost you nearly all of your remaining magic."

Bawb reflected on his actions and found no fault in them. "Sometimes we need to help an adversary in order to attain our ultimate objective."

Demelza let out a little chuckle. "Well-put, Bawb. Very good, indeed. And you have replaced at least some of the magic you expended, so it was not a total loss."

"Though this emmik was far less powerful and lacking the natural sensitivity of Emmik Mollin."

She nodded her understanding. "Still, it is a fair trade. And the power source? I assume you retrieved that as well?"

Bawb's grin faded as he pulled the bag from his tunic and withdrew the horrifying contents. He could see by the look in Demelza's eyes that she was as tempted to kill the emmik as he had been. But he possessed knowledge. Punishment for this atrocity would have to wait.

They flew in silence the rest of the way home, and Bawb remained that way as he bathed and dressed in clean attire. Only when his classmates showed up at the dining hall some time later did he slip from his quiet introspection. He noted a few had bruises and cuts from their altercation, but nothing life-threatening. It had been quite the outing, but in the end, it had turned out all right.

And he had a glorious new set of daggers as a result. Something Elzina was clearly miffed about, even though he kept them in his equipment locker and didn't say a word about them to his classmates.

"I bet you just *love* your new blades," she said, sitting down at the table with him, a respectable plate of food piled high after the exertion of the day.

"They are nice, but the experience was the real reward," he replied.

The comment would surely annoy her, but that was fine. Really, he was somewhat surprised she had chosen to sit with him. But sometimes she enjoyed their verbal sparring as much as the physical kind. He, however, was tired and really didn't want any part of it. Not today. A redirect was very much in order, and he had just the topic for it.

"So, I hear there were Council ships nearby recently," he said. "That is concerning. They normally do not visit our world."

"Oh, there were?"

"Yes. Why do you think they might have landed here? And in our city no less?"

Elzina shrugged innocently. "I have no idea. The Council works in mysterious ways."

Bawb had to admit, she was a talented actress. But he was also skilled, and she had no idea he had seen her talking to a Council agent. This was no time for hard prying, but he could drop comments and see how she reacted. That might give him at least some lesser clues.

"Bawb, there you are," Usalla said, interrupting his train of thought as she sat down beside him. "Quite a show you put on back there."

"Just completing the task."

"In impressive fashion, I would add."

"Oh, give it a rest," Elzina grumbled, rising and walking away with her plate and plopping down at an empty table.

"What is her problem?" Bawb wondered aloud.

"Do we *ever* know what goes on in her mind?"

"I suppose we do not."

"Precisely. She is always bitter about something."

"That is true."

"So, did you hear the news? Mavin Tiggal was slain."

Bawb had not, and his shock was apparent. "Tiggal? But he was so skilled."

"I know. But it looks as though he was ambushed. Not a contract gone awry, but an intentional targeting of one of our order, just like the other one. And this happened only two systems from ours."

"It was close, then."

"Very. And given the proximity, there is talk that the leak may very well be coming from *our* compound."

Bawb's face remained neutral, but he looked around at the others in the chamber in a new light. A questioning one. Of course, the facility had far more people within its walls, but the mere suggestion of a traitor among the Ghalian ranks was enough to unsettle him. This was simply not supposed to be possible. And yet, here they were.

His mind flashed to Elzina's recent encounter. Encounters, plural, if he included the unusual conversation she had during today's mission.

"Excuse me, Usalla. I have something I need to discuss with Elzina. I will return in a moment."

He rose and walked to her table, sitting down across from his sulking nemesis.

"What?" she snarled at him.

"I was just wondering if you could help me out. There was something that I wanted to ask you. I noticed you delayed your approach to the smelting facility to speak with that cloaked individual. Honestly, I do not think I would have beaten you inside had you not been sidetracked. The prize likely would have been yours otherwise."

"You are damn well right it would have. You just got lucky."

"I know. It was a fluke, really. But I was curious. What could they have said that would cause you to delay like that? I was sure you had me beaten."

He was playing to her ego, but Elzina's expression remained relatively calm. She wasn't going to let anything slip. Whatever they'd talked about, and whomever it had been, he was not getting any answers from her lips.

"It was just some guard, is all," she replied, shoveling food into her mouth. "I had to talk my way out of being searched and detained," she continued as she chewed. "Just bad timing."

"It really sounds like it. Well, thank you for that. It was bothering me, knowing you had the advantage but I still won."

"You want to give me those daggers, then?"

Bawb laughed his most convincing chuckle. "I think I will be keeping those. But we shall see who prevails next time, eh?"

"*I* will," she replied.

Bawb just grinned and walked back to join Usalla. Elzina's story made sense, and if it was anyone else he'd have taken them at their word. But in her case, he couldn't shake the feeling he was being lied to. For now there was nothing he could do but keep his eyes and ears open, wondering if it was truly possible one of his own cohort could be a traitor.

CHAPTER TWENTY-SEVEN

The next several days were business as usual at the compound. The Adepts trained, but nothing particularly grueling after their recent adventure. At least, not for a little while. The days of brutally hard training, while not behind them, were less frequent now. They were rapidly approaching Maven status, at which point they would be able to decide how much they wished to participate in additional training. Some would possibly opt out entirely, choosing a life of service but not striving for more. Others would carry on, working toward becoming Masters.

But their path would be up to them.

Of course, in their youth, they were all pushed hard. Incredibly hard, in fact, but it had all been for a reason; weeding out the weak of body and spirit while forging the best of them into the strongest, most competent versions of themselves. The teachers were still challenging them, of course, and soon enough they would undoubtedly be given a new project that would tax their skills, but for now, the Adepts were allowed to spend their increasing amounts of free time training as they saw fit.

Finnia had seized the opportunity, vanishing into the city in disguise, eager to practice her spycraft in a non-deadly situation. She'd become impressively good at it, and once she blended into a crowd, it was near impossible to pick her out again.

Yes, the teachers could find her, but her classmates were not nearly as successful.

Albinius and Zota tended to stick with the comfort of familiar environs, opting to run their obstacle mazes and dungeons, but at their own pace, working on the puzzles and traps they still found most troublesome.

Elzina vanished more often than not, but she did seem in good spirits when she knew there would be a decent chunk of free time in which to do so. Bawb wondered where exactly it was she was heading off to, but as of yet he hadn't followed her. One day soon, however, he very well might.

As for Bawb, his time was spent refining the skills he felt were not up to snuff. Hozark would help him, when he was available, but Bawb knew by now he would ultimately have no one but himself to rely on. If he wanted to excel, he would need to push himself. Fortunately, he had no problem doing just that.

He was training in swordplay with Teacher Demelza when Finnia abruptly appeared beside them. Close, but not so close as to be cut down should the combatants be startled.

"Finnia," Demelza greeted.

"Hello, Finnia," Bawb added. "Would you care to join us? We were just doing a bit of bladework."

The spy shook her head, a concerned look in her eye. "I was actually looking for Master Imalla, but I thought you should know as well."

"Know what?"

"Usalla has been injured."

Bawb felt his gut tighten. "What happened? She was not on any mission that I know of."

"No, she was not. She was frequenting one of the taverns, practicing her infiltration and seduction skills on harmless merchants."

"But?"

"But when she accompanied one of them back to his room, apparently several of his friends joined them without her approval. They did not know who they were dealing with, and she made a fair accounting of herself, but not before they roughed her up rather significantly."

Bawb knew Usalla took lovers from time to time, practicing what they had learned together in the real world. He did the same on occasion, perfecting his skills with non-Ghalian. There was no jealousy or possessiveness. It was simply what they might be called upon to do in their line of work. But now? Now he felt something far different swirling inside him, and heaven help whoever had done this.

"Where is she now?"

"With the healer. She will be fine."

Bawb knew that already, but there was no way he was putting this distraction out of his thoughts. "Teacher, if you do not mind, I would pay a visit to Usalla. May we continue our training later?"

"Go, Bawb. See to your friend," Demelza replied, picking up on his agitated energy. "Just remember, she is in good hands."

He nodded once and hurried on his way. He found Usalla reclining in the lone occupied bed in the healer's chamber. By the look of it, much of her hurt had been taken care of already, but she still had a few bruises lingering. Likely, the healer thought them non-threatening and a waste of magic given there was no active task or mission for the Adept to return to. She would finish her healing naturally, and quickly, given her youth and resilience.

"What happened?" Bawb said, sitting beside her, taking her hand in his.

"It is embarrassing. There were five of them, and for obvious reasons, I was unarmed at the time. I should have sensed the others before they entered the room."

"You were not expecting that sort of a situation."

"No, but we must always be ready. It was a slip of focus on my part."

"So, it was good until that point?" he asked.

"Not as good as you and I, but quite satisfactory," was her reply.

It was something they were not shy about discussing between themselves, sharing notes and improving their skills with what they learned individually. But for all the lack of jealousy, Bawb did feel one thing very acutely. He felt protective of his friend, assassin or not.

"I am glad you managed to escape."

"As am I. That has always been such a comfortably safe place, I think I allowed myself to become a bit complacent."

"Not good in our line of work."

"No, it isn't."

Gears turned in her friend's mind, but his expression remained calm and neutral. "I am sorry this happened to you, Usalla. You should rest. Your body will heal quickly, I am sure."

"Thank you for your concern, Bawb. And, as always, for your friendship."

"Of course," he said, heading to the door. "One last thing. Where did you say this was?"

The tavern was a bustling place Bawb knew well. He had frequented it on many occasions for much the same reasons

Usalla had. And normally it was the perfect sort of place for that. Not too high-end, but not for ruffians and unsavory sorts. The numerous lodging houses nearby were also convenient locations for more private forms of training.

The gregarious man who walked boldly into the building was not the trader character Bawb enjoyed playing, though his persona was similar in many respects. Bawb's favorite disguise would be inappropriate here, and he could not risk burning the identity he had rather enjoyed crafting. So Urtok would be this fellow's name, and his coloring and build was a bit different as well, ensuring there would be no correlation between him and Bawb's preferred trader disguise whom many knew well by now.

Urtok walked up to the bar and ordered a tall drink, then made his way into the bustling crowd, walking around a bit before flopping into an open seat near a group of burly men. Men matching the description Finnia had provided him. Men with a few tell-tale signs of a recent physical altercation.

"Did you say women?" he blurted drunkenly at one of the men's comments. "Sorry, I didn't mean to eavesdrop, but when the finer sex are the topic of conversation, well, I can't help myself."

"I know how that is," one of the men replied with a laugh.

"They always say, Urtok sometimes thinks better with his little head than his big one."

"Little one? Speak for yourself," the man said, prompting a raucous uproar from his friends.

Bawb laughed along with them and soon enough had ingratiated himself to their band of merry drunks, plying them with a few rounds of drinks, happy to treat his new friends. It took hardly any work at all to get them talking about their aborted attempt at a good time earlier in the evening, though they wouldn't go into details.

Even so, it was the opening Bawb needed.

"You know, I've got a couple of working girls waiting for me back in my lodging," he told them. "I was going to head back on my own for round three—I paid for the whole night, after all— but now I feel selfish. Let me share with my new friends. That is, if you don't have anything better to do."

The eager replies of the men were exactly what he had been anticipating. The Adept currently called Urtok moseyed up to the bar and settled up his tab as the men finished their drinks, then led them out in one cheerful, rowdy group, weaving their way to the nearby lodging house. Their expectations were high, planning on a satisfying end to an evening that had otherwise been a bust.

They were in for quite the surprise. Unlike his friend, Bawb was well aware how many adversaries he faced. And *he* was armed.

"This way," he said, stumbling down the corridor to the room he had rented for the night.

The drunkards followed, none of them noticing as he cast a robust muting spell on the chamber's door and walls. What happened in the lodging house stayed in the lodging house.

Bawb opened the door and ushered them inside, the room only barely lit by the dimmest of illumination spells.

"Oh, ladies," their defacto leader slurred. "We've got a surprise for you!"

The door shut behind them silently. Moments later the men began to fall, brutal attacks coming at them from all sides in the dark. Their assailant had night-vision spells at his disposal. They, on the other hand, did not.

Bawb moved through them in a dance of violent action, refraining from landing killing blows, but only just, his fists, elbows, and knees doing most of the damage, though a blade would occasionally make its way into the assault, adding another flavor of pain to the blistering retribution.

In no time all of them were on the ground, their bodies broken and bloody, but still drawing breath.

"*Lumaris*," Bawb said quietly, illuminating the room fully with his spell.

The men lay at awkward angles where they had fallen, their limbs likewise bent in ways they were not really meant to. A few were still conscious, the pain keeping them alert. Their friends, on the other hand, were out cold. Looking at their injuries, deciding whether that was a blessing or a curse was up for debate.

"Why?" the man closest to Bawb asked, staring up at the person he had thought to be his new friend.

"You assaulted someone quite dear to me," he replied, his drunken cheer gone from his voice.

The man's eyes shifted, locking onto the gleaming blade casually grasped in his attacker's hand. Bawb looked down at it, as if he had forgotten it was even there, so accustomed to its presence had he become. The Adept considered the situation a long moment, tempted to bury the weapon to its hilt in each of their chests. Soon, however, reason and logic took hold. Bawb slid the dagger back into its hidden sheath.

"You can't just leave us like this," the man whined, mistakenly believing he was safe now.

Bawb felt his anger flare.

"Like you left my friend?"

"I didn't mean—"

The flurry of brutal kicks would have been enough to kill the man under normal circumstances, but Bawb was casting a healing spell even as he lay into him, causing massive damage but setting it right before doing it again. He wanted him to suffer. All of them. He spent a few minutes more working them over before finally heading for the exit. He glanced back over his shoulder once, spitting in disgust, then stepped out.

The lodging house staff would find them in the morning and get them to a healer. And after what they had just endured, Bawb felt quite confident this particular lot would not set foot in the city again.

CHAPTER TWENTY-EIGHT

Bawb stood quietly in the healer's doorway a long while, watching Usalla as she slept. She was recovering well, from what he could see, and her visible bruising was already fading. Apparently, the healer had decided to show a bit of kindness and apply a little healing magic to the lesser injuries as well. And now that Bawb had seen firsthand the size and nature of the group of men his friend had fought off, he was glad for it.

Usalla stirred, sensing someone near even in her light slumber. She opened her eyes, alert in an instant.

"Bawb, you have come to visit me again so soon."

"I was concerned for your well-being. I see you appear to be healing well."

"I will be fine by morning. Technically, I am fine now, but the little extra rest will not hurt any."

"Indeed," he agreed, a relieved grin curling his lips. She truly would be fine, and that was what mattered.

Usalla's expression shifted, her eyes drifting downward, focusing on the cuff of his tunic.

"There is blood on your sleeve."

"As is so often the case here."

"But it is a down period for our class. There are no group exercises for at least another day, and no one is training. Not at this hour."

"It is nothing."

She stared at him, his friend's questioning gaze unexpectedly making him slightly uncomfortable. Usalla noted the subtle shift in his demeanor. It was not like him. Not at all.

"What did you do, Bawb?"

"As I said, it is nothing."

Her brow twitched upward. "You know, you never could lie to me. Not with any success, anyway."

"Let us just say it has been handled and leave it at that."

"What has been handled, Bawb?"

He gestured to her remaining bruises. "This could not go unpunished."

Realization dawned, and Usalla looked at him more closely. There was more than just a splatter of blood on his cuff, she realized. Most would not see the signs, but there were droplets on other parts of his person. Signs of a fight as well, scuffs and smudges, though no injuries of his own. She inhaled deeply, taking in the smells still clinging to him. Alcohol, smoke, sweat. And it was familiar. She had smelled those same things earlier this very evening. She knew where he had been, and she wondered what he had done.

"Did you kill them?" she asked, her eyes locking with his.

"No. Much as I wished to, they still draw breath. But they will not attack innocents in that manner again."

"I am *not* an innocent, Bawb."

"You know what I mean."

Usalla's face flushed, her eyes sparkling with a mix of gratitude and anger. Frustration and even a little resentment.

"This is *my* fight, not yours."

"I realize. But you were injured, and—"

"*I* handle my own business, Bawb. What were you thinking?"

"To make things right."

"You risked yourself over such a foolish thing."

"It is not foolish to me. They hurt you."

"Yes, they did. But we have been hurt countless times over the years, and you know as well as I do that I will be fine. This was something else, Bawb. You overstepped."

"I can see how you might feel that way," he protested. "But this could not go unpunished."

Usalla began to speak but fell silent, holding her tongue as she instead sized up her friend. They had been through a lot together. Had grown up together. And she could see in his face that no matter what she said, he would always consider himself her protector of sorts, though she needed no such thing. She took a deep breath, then another.

"Bawb, this should not have happened."

"I understand your feelings on this, but—"

"Allow me to finish. I think it is time for us to cease our, um, *training*."

He felt her words like a punch to the gut, his insides twinging sharply, but remained silent. Interrupting would only make this worse.

"I appreciate you, Bawb, and we have both learned much from one another, and for that I am grateful. But that time in our lives is over. It is time to move forward."

Bawb felt an unfamiliar flush of emotion pump adrenaline through his body. This was not fight or flight, however. This was something else. He kept his expression neutral, his pulse steady and calm, but he was *not* all right. Not for the moment, at least. But he would be. He was a Ghalian, after all, and their time together had just been training. It always had been. At least, that was what he told himself.

He nodded once, then let it go. A little smile creased Usalla's lips. He would be okay.

"Friends?" she asked quietly.

"Always," was his reply. And to his core, he meant it.

Bawb did not go to bed for some time after that. His mind wasn't exactly racing, but it was unsettled. Processing. Running through scenarios and replaying parts of his life, assessing them, trying to understand his subconscious interpretation of things as well as what had been his surface understandings.

He found himself in the most unlikely of places in the dark hours—a violently churning volcanic cavern, the lava flowing and melting stone and ore as it rumbled from one side to the other. There were several precarious stone outcroppings the students used in their training, sharpening both their physical reflexes as well as their mental ones. Tension would lead to mistakes. Relaxing would lead to ease of action, both mentally and physically.

It was atop one of these he sat, eyes closed, his mind processing as his heart rate slowed with the deepening of his meditative state. His sweating diminished, his body cooling naturally but slowly as it slid into a state of easy relaxation. He sat like that for some time, a pinpoint of calm in the center of a tempest of deadly energy.

Finally, after a long while, he rose and headed to the showers then slid into his bed, falling into an uneasy sleep.

The next morning he woke poorly rested but a bit clearer of mind.

"Up for some sparring?" Albinius asked him as they headed to breakfast.

"Perhaps later. I have something I need to do," he replied,

diverting his course. There would be time to eat later. Right now he required something other than food.

"Teacher Demelza?" he said, entering the empty sparring hall.

Demelza was often there at this time, sharpening the weapons one by one, her own form of moving meditation. She looked up from her task, utterly at ease.

"Yes, Bawb? What can I do for you?" she asked, noting his unease in an instant.

"May I speak with you?"

"Of course. Come in and close the door."

He did so, joining her at the table.

"Here, you can help me with these. There are quite a few to sharpen today."

Bawb noted the particularly clumsy nicks and dings to the training blades. "Aspirants?"

"You guess correctly."

"Not much of a guess. I recall the poor form I had at that age. These bear the marks of poor attacks and poorer defense."

Demelza chuckled as she ran the sharpening stone across the blade in her hand. "And what a long way you have come since then."

"Thanks to your tutelage," he noted, picking up a stone and setting to work removing the ragged burrs on the edge of a long dagger.

She let him work in silence a moment, giving him space to gather his thoughts. "What troubles you, Bawb?"

He hesitated, searching for the right words. He had thought he had them when he came to her, but now he realized his plan was poorly formed. He knew what was going on inside him, but he needed a way to express it out loud.

"Teacher Demelza—"

"Just Demelza, Bawb. We are not in class. Speak freely."

"Demelza, I–I do not understand how, I mean, why..." He trailed off, trying to find the right way to express himself. Simpler was better, he decided. "Why do my emotions still exist?"

"Emotions are normal, Bawb."

"But I am a Ghalian. Twice in recent times I have reacted to something emotionally. I have allowed feelings to cloud my judgment and drive me to action. Not calmly decided action, but rather, fueled by emotion."

Demelza's hands slowed. She put the blade down and looked at her student, making sure he felt one hundred percent of her focus was on him. She nodded knowingly, a slight smile creasing her lips.

"Bawb, I appreciate your coming to me with this concern, and let me assure you that, while rare, there are plenty among us who, on occasion, have had similar issues. In fact, one of the most powerful Ghalian I have ever known is also by far the most feeling, with a depth of emotion I have rarely seen in our kind."

"Is this anyone I know?"

"Perhaps," she said with a knowing grin. "But anonymity is of the utmost value to a Ghalian, as you well know. And emotion can be used against you. You are wise to recognize this in yourself. It is a degree of introspection and self-awareness few possess at your age. But you would be wise to not allow this to be common knowledge. While I feel this makes you stronger, others may not feel the same."

"But this other Ghalian? The feeling one?"

"You know I will not speak their name."

"Of course. But can you tell me, how did they overcome it and drive it from their minds?"

Demelza laughed quietly. "Oh, Bawb. They are *still* the same person. In fact, I believe their well of emotion has actually grown larger in recent years. The difference between you is that their emotions are masked, and well-hidden. Essentially, achieved by doing what you are doing now. By being honest with yourself about your own inner workings, recognizing them, and laboring hard to correct what needs to be corrected while accepting all the parts of yourself for what they are. There is nothing wrong with feeling, Bawb. In fact, having emotions and recognizing them can make you so much more. You must simply not allow those feelings to become a liability. Do you understand?"

"I believe I do."

"Good. Then do not fret, my dear Adept. You will be fine, I am confident of it. Just be honest with yourself about any shortcomings you may find in yourself and labor to correct them."

"I will do my best. Thank you, Demelza."

"I am glad to have been of help, Bawb. Now, will you please hand me that short sword? I have a great many to repair today."

"Of course," he said, handing her the blade. "One thing."

"Yes?"

"May I stay with you for a bit and help? Surprisingly, I am actually finding the act of sharpening these quite relaxing."

Demelza's grin broadened. "Of course, Bawb. Stay as long as you like."

Level up: Introspection, the konus announced, but Bawb didn't need the device to know that.

CHAPTER TWENTY-NINE

Bawb and Usalla moved past the incident as if nothing had happened. In a way, nothing had, at least, not between them directly. They were still the same good friends as before, and they still enjoyed one another's company while pushing each other to excel in their endeavors. But their extracurricular training was a thing of the past.

It took a few days for Bawb to first get his emotions under control. What had happened to her had triggered a protective instinct he hadn't realized he possessed. At least, not to that degree. It was the sort of thing that could get a Ghalian killed, and that was not acceptable. It was for that reason he endeavored with all his might to overcome this shortcoming. And he actually succeeded, though not without a few hiccups.

Teacher Demelza had not betrayed his trust, but she did have a conversation with the other teachers, asking each of them to pay a little more attention to the Adept and intentionally pressure him with various triggers. She was confident he would overcome his issues, but if they could help speed the process, all the better.

It was something they were well-prepared to do, the Ghalian

having kept detailed records on each of their students over the years, noting everything of even the slightest significance, and especially those of greater impact. It was something they did not just with Bawb but with every student, and for good reason. To know what would get under each individual's skin was vital to their growth as Ghalian. If they could not overcome what made them uncomfortable, they could not progress in their training.

They learned quickly that Bawb was fast to adapt, pushing aside his visceral reactions and redoubling his efforts, focusing on his training and nothing else. In just a few short weeks, nearly all of their attempts to unsettle him began to simply bounce off him as if no more than minor annoyances.

A few more weeks passed without a single notable reaction elicited. Demelza spoke with the others, and it was agreed that the young man was ready. It was time to start sending him on more difficult contracts.

"It will be a challenging test of your skills," Master Orvus told him when he pulled him from his studies with a new task.

"I am ready."

"From what Imalla has told me, I believe you very well may be. But do not get cocky. This will require a great degree of stealth."

"I do not get cocky, Master. I merely know my abilities and am confident in them."

Orvus nodded, a slight grin creasing his lips. "Yes, I suppose it is another of your class who has an issue with cockiness."

Bawb knew full well he was talking about Elzina but kept his mouth shut. Criticism in private was one thing, but with a Master of the house it was quite another. Nothing good would come of speaking ill of her in this situation, so it was simply best not to speak at all.

"We have received and vetted a contract to eliminate an information broker."

"Powered?"

"No, they are not magical in nature."

"That sounds easy enough."

"It will not be. From what we have heard, several of the lesser assassin's guilds were hired to accomplish this task and failed miserably. Fortunately, they all perished long before reaching him, and therefore did not alert him to their true purpose. They seemed to be thieves, nothing more."

Bawb shrugged slightly. "If you wish for it to be done correctly, you must be willing to spend the coin to hire the best."

"Yes, it has cost them far more handling things in this manner. But that is their problem, not ours. The target is located, and our spy network has confirmed the basic details of his current residence."

"Then I will leave at once."

"Be warned, Adept Bawb, this must look like a death of natural causes. Anything else and it will draw unwanted attention on not only the Ghalian but also those who have contracted with us. There is a power struggle in play, and an obvious assassination could cause the matter to spill over into other areas, possibly even triggering a small-scale war."

"So, be very careful and make it appear as if I was never there. Understood."

"There are also traps and alarms, from what our spies have heard."

"Further details?"

"They were unable to acquire that information. Recon and intelligence gathering prior to your insertion will be up to you, Bawb. A ship has been requisitioned for you, and full details are waiting for you there. This is not simply an elimination contract. There is also a piece of sensitive information in this person's possession, written on a sealed scroll and hidden in their chambers. You must retrieve that and leave no trace. Set off no alarms. Only your target knows it is there, and as such, no one will question it going missing. But you must move quickly. There is to be a handoff within two days, so time is short."

"Ah, time is of the essence. Failures have put them in a bit of a bind. I now see the true reason they finally came to the Ghalian."

"It would appear that way."

"It will be done."

Bawb gave a slight bow and headed off to gather his things and prepare for the mission. This could be challenging, but in true Ghalian fashion, he was looking forward to testing his skills. That, and he had a new set of daggers he was planning on bringing for this one, as well as his standard kit.

Bawb found Usalla in the bunkhouse when he arrived, changing from her sweat-soaked attire into a fresh outfit.

"A difficult day?" he queried.

"In a good way," she said with a grin, sliding into her dry clothing. "As they always say, the more we sweat in training—"

"The less we bleed in combat. Yes, I know it well."

She watched as he began pulling out weapons, laying them on his bunk before beginning the process of concealing them on his body.

"You have a task, I take it?"

"Elimination of a troublesome individual and the retrieval of a hidden object."

"That sounds rather like most of what we've been doing of late."

"It does. But it also seems this particular target has proven difficult for others who were previously contracted for the task."

"We are not the first?"

"No. But we will be the last," he said, tucking away his weapons with quick efficiency and heading for the exit. "I will see you again soon."

"I look forward to it. Be safe, my friend. I would like to hear of your successful mission upon your return."

"And so you shall," he replied.

Bawb was walking the streets of the bustling metropolis his target called home less than a day later. He had flown in aboard a nondescript vessel piloted by a pilot-for-hire. No one knew who he was or what he was doing, just that he had paid for transit and would be returning within a day or two.

After thoroughly reviewing his mission brief in his small room, Bawb destroyed the contents and moved up to join the pilot, making small talk and letting slip that he was heading to an important meeting to set up a new trade partnership. He was hopeful it would be a fruitful venture as it was his family's business, and he wanted to make them proud.

He then delved into the insanely boring details of interplanetary commerce and the mind-numbingly dull products his make-believe family sold. Within ten minutes the pilot had glazed over, replying, "Uh-huh. I see," to him on autopilot just to be polite.

It was perfect. He was precisely the sort of passenger who would arouse no suspicion just in case anything did happen to go wrong.

Upon landing Bawb took his leave of the pilot and his craft with a cheerful wave as he headed off in the opposite direction of his real target. Several streets over he shifted his course and reversed toward his true destination. He planned to use a fair amount of magic on this trip out of necessity. Disguises would need to be switched quickly and regularly, and to do that with conventional means would be nearly impossible.

Instead, Bawb posed as a variety of personas and races, mostly sticking with the ones he was most comfortable with, but occasionally stepping outside his usual repertoire to break in a new character. This phase of the mission was the one time he could afford a little slip-up should it occur. Once inside the target's residence it would be quite a different story.

Bawb spent nearly a full day awake, gathering intelligence from every establishment his target's staff frequented. That meant he was visiting bars and taverns, massage halls and bath houses. Even a few houses of ill-repute where gaming, illicit substances, and pleasures of the flesh could be had for a price.

He had filled his pouch of holding with coin before heading out and was buying drinks, food, and the occasional romantic interlude for his new "friends" made over many drinks and much laughter. This was the easy part. Pretending to be a jovial fellow with ample coin he was happy to spend. Much as he had seen Hozark do, Bawb was rapidly becoming a dear friend of nearly everyone he met. And with the help of alcohol generously flowing in abundance, along with some very cleverly phrased inquiries, he soon gathered what he needed to know, the facts verified by multiple oblivious sources.

The residence was essentially like any other from the outside. But once inside, there were roving guards, traps and tripwires, and even beasts trained to sniff out intruders. All of these were things no one should have spoken of to an outsider, but none stood a chance against his expertly honed skills, the more unconventional of them learned courtesy of his favorite Master Ghalian.

Hozark had lived up to his word, spending much time with him as he grew, teaching him privately, setting him firmly on the course to becoming a Master one day. He also showed him things students his age were not normally taught, helping him gain control of his skills and refine them until he was functioning at a capacity well above his technical level.

Of course, Hozark did not tell the other Masters what he was doing, nor did Bawb. It was a silent agreement they had between them, and one the young man was ever so grateful for.

It was late afternoon the following day when Bawb finally paid off his last tab and stumbled out of the tavern he had been in for the last few hours. He staggered into an alleyway and changed disguise again, emerging in dirty farmer's clothing looking utterly unremarkable. He walked to his destination and "accidentally" dropped a small pouch of seeds.

"Ah, stupid me," he grumbled, squatting down to collect them.

There were a lot, and it would take him some time to pick them all up. More than enough time for anyone around to have passed and for those approaching to see and subsequently ignore the farmhand.

No one even considered that he was crouched next to the servants' door to the structure. And when he finally stood and slipped inside, none paid any attention at all.

Bawb immediately pulled his shimmer cloak over himself, standing utterly still, invisible to all who passed by. He breathed a silent sigh of relief when they did.

It worked.

He was fair at using the spell while stationary, but in motion he was still quite lacking. But he couldn't stand there hiding forever. Carefully, he crept ahead, stopping whenever he heard footsteps, until he reached what appeared to be a staff common room. He stood there, watching as they entered and exited, noting all the fine points of their garb.

Do it, already, his konus grumbled.

"I will. I just need to be certain."

You know what they look like. You're just stalling. Get on with it!

Bawb hated to admit it, but the konus was kind of right. He took a deep breath and cast the new spell, altering his appearance once more beneath his shimmer cloak.

"Here we go," he said as he emerged from hiding, appearing, he hoped, as one of the staff. He nodded to the woman who walked by in a hurry, clearly on some task, and was pleased to find she didn't even give him a second glance.

See? I told you.

"Yes, you did. Now, let us hope I can maintain this for the duration."

If you don't, you're gonna have more problems than questioning staff, the device noted.

He needn't have said anything. Bawb was all too aware what would happen. From here on, failure was simply not an option.

CHAPTER THIRTY

Getting in unnoticed was often the hardest part of a Ghalian's task. Beasts and guards, not to mention pesky spells, often protected the residences and compounds of their targets. But in this case, Bawb quickly learned that while the outside had not been so bad, it was inside he really had to worry about.

There were passcode spells and timed barriers, all of them laid out in such a way as to trip up any who didn't know exactly what they were doing or where they were going. Fortunately, he had managed to subtly extract much of that information from his new "friends" with the help of a fat coin pouch and a *lot* of alcohol. His minor persuasion spells and tactful questioning didn't hurt either.

It was because of that he was moving with confidence. Slowly and cautiously, perhaps, but he showed no hesitation. As a result, none of the other staff questioned his presence. Even if his disguise slipped and he accidentally presented an unfamiliar face, it shouldn't matter. Only those who were supposed to be here could walk the halls of the structure.

Bawb hurried his pace as he drew closer to the man's chambers, confident he would have at least a little time before he returned. This he had learned from one very drunken guard he had befriended at the third tavern on his all-night tour of the city's recreation spots. It had been exhausting, but ultimately worth it. Lay the groundwork and reap the rewards, Teacher Warfin would say. And what reward he would reap.

The scroll he had been tasked with retrieving would be in the man's personal suite of rooms, no doubt, an expansive area, he deduced by the doors leading to it and walls blocking it from other parts of the building. Whatever you might say about him, the treacherous fellow had good taste in living accommodations. What he seemed to lack, surprisingly, was a solid security system on his door.

Bawb made quick work of the two warding spells and slid inside, reapplying them with ease.

"I cannot believe he did not have something more robust for his—"

Bawb felt the hair on the back of his neck stand on end as every nerve in his body screamed at him to run. The fight-or-flight response was triggered and on fire by something very close by. He turned slowly and immediately saw the cause.

It was a Zomoki.

Not a full-grown one by any stretch—a space dragon of that size would require several more chambers having their walls removed to accommodate it. But the Zomoki the man had locked in his rooms was more than enough as-is, and good luck to any hoping to pass it to reach the inner chambers. No wonder the door was so easy to enter.

Despite his training, Bawb felt a knot of fear in his belly. Monsters and warriors, he'd faced them all successfully at one time or another. But a Zomoki? He's never been so close to one, and yet, this man was keeping one in his rooms as a pet. A pet, and one hell of an alarm system.

The Zomoki was lying flat, but its bright, golden eyes were

SCOTT BARON

sharp and aware, keenly watching the new arrival with a curious look but not immediately leaping to attack, affording Bawb a moment to better take it in.

The beast was massive, its scales deep green with a ruddy gold along their edges. A beautiful creature to observe under any other circumstances. Bawb knew he would never get the wards off the door before the Zomoki devoured him, so he did the only thing he could do. He raised his hands and moved closer, hoping the unexpected action might make the animal hesitate, buying him some time to think.

Amazingly, it worked.

"Hey, big guy," he said calmly, stepping closer. "I mean you no harm."

The Zomoki remained still, watching in that unsettling way of a predator deciding how and when it was going to kill its prey. But Bawb continued on, forcing his feet to move in spite of himself.

"If I have to die, at least this will be an impressive way to go," he rationalized, making the most of a terrible situation.

The Zomoki, however, did not strike.

As Bawb moved around it slowly, he noticed several lengths of scarred scales where the animal had taken a beating, a whip or some similar device gouging its flesh in younger years. Apparently, it had taken some doing getting it to comply. That meant it had been captured, not raised since birth. Then he saw something else. Something gleaming in the light. A golden control collar around the beast's neck. So, that was how it was kept in check, restrained from breaking its way out or worse. Of course, those without the spell specifically allowing access and protection would be subject to devouring, but otherwise, the Zomoki was as safe to be near as one could hope for from so mighty a beast.

There was just one problem.

Bawb, despite his expertly crafted disguise, did not have such permission. And from the look in the animal's eyes, it was quite well aware of that. It shifted, lifting its massive head to better watch the intruder.

"I do not wish for any conflict with you," Bawb blurted, reaching out with his innate empathic skills as best he could. "I am just here to collect something, then I will be gone."

The Zomoki glared at him, as if the words made sense. Then it rested its head back on the ground, its gaze softening to one of boredom rather than increasing interest.

"Are we good?" the comically small man said to the enormous beast.

The Zomoki snorted a hot-aired sigh, its body relaxing once more.

How in the world you did that, I don't know. But you most certainly just leveled up, the konus said, a shocked tone in its silent voice.

Bawb wasn't going to look a gift Zomoki in the mouth. He set to work at once, sliding past the beast into the next area and quickly deactivating the alarm tripwire spells directly in his path. The entire chamber was full of them. Any major movement, and certainly any large use of magic, would set off alarms that would rouse the entire building. Odds were, only when their owner returned home would they be disarmed.

As that was not the case, Bawb would have to work carefully. Carefully, unfortunately, also meant slowly.

"Where would I have hidden it if I were him?" he wondered, searching for secret hiding places for the scroll in question.

He was considering his options as he carefully navigated the hidden traps, only his years of Ghalian training and heightened sensitivity allowing him to make any progress, when a realization hit him. This man had a Zomoki in his home. Anyone with that sort of protection was bound to be confident. Overconfident, in fact.

Bawb shifted his search to more obvious locations. If he was so well protected, why not just put the scroll—

"Here," he said quietly, pulling open a drawer in the small table with parchments and knick-knacks atop it.

The scroll was exactly as it had been described, just sitting there. No elaborate hiding place, just tucked in a drawer. Even so, he cast a detection spell to make sure there were no additional protective spells on it. To his delight, there were none.

Bawb grabbed it and tucked it into his tunic, closing the drawer tight.

"This is easier than I—" he started to muse when the door opened, and his target stepped inside.

The man had turned to close the door out of habit, not bothering to look for intruders, but when he turned back around to release his alarm spells, he saw the unthinkable. There was someone standing in his chambers. Deep in his chambers, no less, his Zomoki guard failing at its one job.

He didn't care. This was his turf, and he was not about to let this go unpunished.

"You! I'm going to—" he began to shout, ready to raise the alarm, when suddenly, his voice fell silent.

Silent, but he couldn't tell. To his own ears he was shouting for the guards, but not a sound escaped the tiny muting spell Bawb had cast around his head with pinpoint accuracy. Shout as he might, no one would hear his voice.

It was an unheard-of use of that spell, and under almost any other circumstances it shouldn't have worked. But focused as he was on moving within the narrow confines of un-alarmed space, Bawb had been casting in a tight beam on instinct, and that allowed the spell to fly true.

The enraged man realized something was wrong a few moments later when no one rushed to his aid. This was not how things were supposed to work. Not at all. Bawb watched helplessly as he turned and raced to the door, unable to chase after him lest he trigger the alarms. He would be in the hall any second, and then it would be all over.

Without even thinking about what he was doing a flurry of daggers flashed from the confines of Bawb's clothing, the hidden weapons flying true, avoiding the tripwire spells as they thudded hard into the man's back. He might have let out a shriek, but if he did, no one would have been able to tell with the muting spell in place.

He took just one step then fell to the ground. Dead.

A new sinking feeling hit Bawb's stomach.

"Oh, no," he muttered. "No, no, no." This was not how it was supposed to go. This had to look like natural causes or an accidental death. No way were multiple dagger wounds in the back going to be mistaken for that.

Bawb's mind raced, taking in the situation, desperately looking for a way out. The Zomoki turned its head slightly, seemingly a bit more interested by this new event. Interested, and approving of its cruel master's demise.

Bawb realized something at that moment. The control collar would have almost certainly become deactivated when the man fell. That is, unless he had backup spells placed by key staff for just such an eventuality. Whatever the case, it gave him an idea.

"Okay, you'll behave now, yes?" he asked as he made his way to the fallen man and retrieved his blades from the corpse.

The Zomoki just watched him curiously with those big golden eyes.

Bawb used the man's clothing to wipe up any blood where he fell, then dragged the body to the beast, dropping him in a heap in front of it. Then he took a deep breath and stepped forward, reaching out and resting his hand on the Zomoki's thick neck.

"This may hurt a little, but I am trying to help you. Please, do not eat me."

The Zomoki blinked slowly but did not move.

"Well then. Here we go."

Bawb wrapped his hands around the control collar and began feeding as much magic as he could into it, trying to force the locking spell to release. It was as he had feared, while the main spell was negated by the man's death, there were at least two minor ones still active. His fingers smoked from the effort, the metal growing hot and burning his flesh as he pulled, his own spells flowing hard and fast.

The Zomoki watched him with great interest, holding still despite what was surely a painful sensation for it as well. Suddenly, the metal gave way, the collar unlocking and falling to the ground with a clang. Bawb stepped back and looked at his blistering fingers. The Zomoki, he realized, was watching him as well, saliva dripping from its mouth.

Bawb just hoped it would be painless.

The Zomoki lurched forward, its mighty jaws opening and snapping shut hard, bone and blood spurting onto the floor. Bawb took a breath, then another, slowly relaxing as the beast crunched on its former captor. It paused a moment, locking eyes with him, then set back to its meal. Bawb turned and maneuvered around the tripwire spells and out the door, making sure he left no bloody tracks in his wake. Then he opened the door and stepped into the hall, the Zomoki covering his assassination quite well. The body, whatever would be left of it, would show no signs of mere dagger wounds. He had gotten away with it. There was just one more thing to do.

"Come quickly! The master has fallen!" he shouted in a

panic, pushing the door open from the outside just as shocked faces of guards and staff came running.

They looked inside to witness the Zomoki devouring their master with relish. Whatever had gone wrong, the beast had gotten loose, and it had made quick work of the man.

"It's free! The Zomoki is free! Run!" one of the senior staff shouted in fear.

The others heard the words "Zomoki" and "free" and took off running without hesitation. It had been small when their master had first acquired it, but the beast had grown, and it would easily smash its way free when it had finished its gruesome meal. And if its control collar was truly gone, no one was safe. Everyone reacted immediately on raw instinct, fleeing in a thundering of panicked feet.

Bawb ran with the rest of the staff, shrieking in fear and scattering into the streets in a frantic rush to get as far from the creature as possible. He ducked into an alleyway and almost immediately emerged in a new disguise, this time a well-off tradesman.

"What happened?" he asked a wild-eyed servant, grabbing them by the arm with the confidence of an elite used to being respected.

"The master! The Zomoki! It ate him!" the servant blubbered.

Bawb released his grip, letting them flee with the rest, then turned and hurried back to his waiting ship, changing back to his original disguise and boarding in a calm and relaxed manner.

"How did it go?" the pilot asked.

"Better than expected. Not quite what I'd anticipated, but a very satisfactory result."

"So, more business for your family, then? Good for you. I assume you are ready to depart?"

"Yes, I am, thank you. I look forward to getting home and relaying my success," he said, feeling the hidden shape of the scroll tucked in his tunic. "I'm sure my family will be most pleased."

CHAPTER THIRTY-ONE

Bawb had gone on his mission prepared for the worst. It had been presented to him in a manner that had him expecting to be tested to his limits, and he had readied himself for precisely that. But fate, it seemed, had other ideas for him. Yes, it had been a challenging ingress, requiring him to wield his disguise magic with all of his skill, and he had also finally deployed his shimmer cloak in a real-world situation and come out on top, but the actual elimination of his target had been almost anticlimactic.

Except for the whole Zomoki part, that is.

That had been exceptional. He had only ever seen the creatures from a distance, and those had all been raging beasts wanting only to kill, eat, and fly free. This one, on the other hand, while not one of the long-extinct Wise Ones, did seem to nevertheless possess a spark of intellect. Perhaps it had just been tamed by years upon years of particularly strict restraining spells, forcing it to observe rather than react on pure instinct, but whatever the cause, his encounter had left him in awe of the creatures.

Thoughts of Visla Balamar were in his mind. The man had

formed a union with the ancient Zomoki and, together, they had lived together in peaceful synergy. While this Zomoki was nowhere near that sort of creature, the feeling of mutual understanding he had experienced with it was a heady sensation indeed. He could only imagine what it must have been like for Balamar, living in harmony with the legendary Zomoki who could actually speak.

He had always been fascinated with Zomoki, studying them far beyond the basic texts covered in class, and the stories of what had happened to Visla Balamar were well-known. The Council of Twenty had eliminated him with malice, along with the remaining Wise Ones, destroying a massive swath of fertile land he called home as well as the source of the Balamar waters in the process. While the waters were fatal to Wampeh Ghalian, Bawb nevertheless regretted that he could not visit the mystical place. That he would never meet one of the amazing animals in person.

Bawb's emotions had been triggered unexpectedly by the encounter, and as a result, he felt a bit introspective and kept to himself the majority of the flight home, quietly mulling over the events of the day. But when he stepped out into the familiar air of his home city, a sense of warm contentedness washed over him, leading him to stop and chat with a few food vendors as he strolled back to the compound, his mission complete and his spirits high.

He found Master Orvus talking with one of the teachers not far from the dining hall. The Master saw him approach, cutting his conversation short to welcome the new arrival.

"Adept Bawb, you are back," he said. "And in fine condition, I am pleased to see. Rested, whole, and I see you still possess all of your weapons. Surprising, given the nature of that task. Were there no difficulties?"

"Oh, there most certainly were, but I handled it. Life

sometimes presents us unexpected opportunities," he replied, pulling the scroll from his tunic and handing it to the man.

"That it does," Orvus said, opening the scroll, scanning the contents in a glance, then tucking it away in his pocket. "Well done, Adept. Very well done indeed."

"Thank you, Master. If there is nothing else, I was thinking I would perhaps get in a little training session before the evening meal."

"You will not be resting just yet," Orvus said, a curious look in his eye.

"I do not understand."

"I would not expect you to. This is rather unusual, Adept Bawb, but something of some importance has come up, and on a bit of a time crunch. You are fresh and prepped for action, and none of the Masters are available for the next several days."

"But I am only an Adept. The Mavens?"

"Yes, there are some I could call upon. But you have proven yourself, Bawb. And this is an opportunity for you to do so even further. If you accept the task, that is."

"Of course I will."

"I assumed as much. Gather food for the trip. We secured transit on a freighter, and the food aboard will be less than impressive, I am afraid."

"I will load up more than usual, then."

"A wise choice. I would have you well-fed for this task."

"I assume another difficult one, if Masters were considered for it."

"It might be, yes. There is a weapons dealer named Durggin selling dangerous and overpowered konuses and slaaps to Tslavar mercenaries on Phiralias. There has been unrest of late, and the Council has started to become involved. These weapons could turn the tide against those opposing them. He is a suspicious sort and keeps his contracts in his head rather than on parchment. As such, if he dies, so does the exchange."

"And the enemy of my enemy..."

"I would not call the one who ordered the contract a friend, exactly, but our goals do align from time to time. This is one such occasion." He pulled a folded piece of parchment from his pocket and handed it to the Adept. "All the details you need. Get in, kill him, and get out. This does not need to look like an accident. He is an arms dealer, after all. But he is also a very paranoid one, even for that line of work, so be careful."

Bawb hurried to the dining hall to gather up sustenance for the trip. He truly did feel quite good, all things considered. Yes, he had been a bit sleep-deprived during his recent quest, but aside from that he had suffered no ill effects. And with a bit of a flight ahead of him, he could catch up on that much-needed shut-eye on the way.

"I heard you were on a stealth run," a voice said from across the dining hall.

"Yes, Elzina, I was," he replied, stuffing food into a sack.

"Successful, I take it?"

"Indeed. And interesting."

"Oh?"

"There was a Zomoki."

For once, she actually seemed legitimately surprised. "An actual Zomoki? And you are unharmed?"

"Yes. Amazing, is it not? It was exhilarating being so close to it. And when I freed it from its control collar, it even seemed grateful."

"You freed it? That takes enormous power."

"My hands suffered, but I have repaired the damage."

"And you are clearly hungry as a result." she said, nodding to the sizable amount of food he was collecting.

"No, this is for the trip."

"Trip?"

"I am off on another assignment."

She looked at him with clear surprise and perhaps a little jealousy. "Another? So soon?"

"Yes."

She noted his weapons, still kitted out from his prior task. "Dangerous, I take it?"

"Yes and no. It is more of a time-sensitive thing. Some weapons dealer named Durggin. He is not a powered man, so as long as I am careful, this should go smoothly."

"Is it far?"

"Not terribly. A world called Phiralias. Have you heard of it?"

"No, but there are a great many we have not heard of."

"This is very true. In any case, I must go. Time is of the essence."

He hurried out of the dining hall, leaving Elzina to wonder why she hadn't been asked to do any exciting tasks of late.

Bawb made it to his ship quickly and settled into his seat. It was as Master Orvus had said. Not a particularly pleasant vessel. But it would get him from point A to point B, and that was all that mattered. He relaxed and dug into his food, filling his belly, then had a nice bit of sleep for the duration of the flight. He arrived at Phiralias in good time, exiting the craft with renewed energy and redoubled enthusiasm.

It was quick work finding Durggin, he discovered. Everyone knew the man, and it didn't even take any subterfuge to get directions to his compound. Apparently, he was very easy to reach, at least in the most superficial of senses. Getting closer, however, was another story entirely.

Bawb found out some new details the mission briefing had failed to mention. Namely, that Durggin, while lacking magic of his own, surrounded himself with moderately powerful lackeys. He had to admire the tactic. It was a clever means of defense for a man with an abundance of coin but no magic of his own. And while he had access to plenty of mercenaries as an arms dealer, it was never a good idea to sample from one's own supply. This way, instead, he had underlings who could use their own power to do his dirty work, keeping his business and private affairs cleanly separated.

It also meant Bawb would have to improvise a bit. He walked the area, taking in the doors and windows he could access, forming a plan. Soon enough he would be inside. Soon this contract would be executed and complete. And then he would return home, victorious, having proven himself worthy of Master Orvus's confidence.

CHAPTER THIRTY-TWO

Bawb was glad he still had his shimmer cloak on him when he was sent on the assignment. Without it, he realized that getting inside Durggin's compound undetected would have been nearly impossible—at least in any semblance of a hurry. As it was, it was not going to be easy. Not one bit.

Guards were patrolling in regular intervals. That was normal. What wasn't was the periodic appearance of the naturally power-wielding mercenaries. They were a variable that would have to be very carefully dealt with. And if any of them had cast any sort of robust shimmer detection spells, he could be facing a very difficult time indeed.

Bawb counted the unpowered guards. Six of them. No problem for an Adept of the Ghalian. He moved to a less-visible area of the structure and donned his shimmer cloak. It wasn't going to do much for him when he climbed to the window above, but it would allow him to wait patiently below it unnoticed. Only when the coast was clear would he make the rapid ascent and ingress through the opening.

He stood there for several minutes, motionless. No one was walking by, but one of the guards had chosen the nearest corner to stop and chat with a local. Just his luck. He felt the time drag on but concentrated and slowed his breathing further, leaning into the tranquility of the comforting security of the shimmer cloak.

It wasn't perfect, and he still had trouble maintaining it in motion, but he felt he was finally starting to truly get the hang of this one piece of particularly difficult magic. Some could train their whole lives and never perfect it. He had no intention of joining those ranks.

Movement caught his eye. The guard had finished her conversation and was walking right toward him. He pressed flat against the wall, holding his breath as she passed, oblivious to the assassin mere inches away. He watched her round the next corner and leapt into action, climbing to the second-floor window and hurrying inside.

So far, so good. It seemed fortune was in his favor today.

A strange feeling washed over him.

A shimmer detection spell, the konus announced.

Bawb didn't need the clarification. He knew it the moment he felt it. His camouflage was still intact, but someone had been alerted to its presence. He quickly shed the cloak before it could cause further problems, hoping his disguise spell would hold up.

"You there, did you see anything unusual?" a lean man with an icy gaze and charcoal-gray skin asked.

"What do you mean, unusual?" he replied.

A blade embedded itself in his leg, the guard lunging into an attack without warning. Bawb felt the magic flowing off him in waves as he mixed weapons and spell attacks in a dizzying display. Bawb felt multiple spells hit, his body taking the brunt of the magic despite his defensive spells. He cast a retaliatory spell, flinging a half-dozen of his small daggers behind it.

The caster blocked the spell and most of the blades, but two struck him, making him falter in his spellcasting. The next blade flew into his forehead, ending the fight in an instant.

Bawb retrieved his weapons and quickly dragged the body into the nearest room. He had no idea if anyone would find it there, but he had few options. He called up a moderate healing spell to stop the bleeding from his leg, holding back from fully repairing it. He needed all the magic he had. Complete healing would have to wait.

Resetting his disguise spell, Bawb pressed on, but only a moment later a pair of guards came rushing his way, and they weren't bothering with the formalities of asking who he was.

Their weapons flew, but at least they weren't casters. Bawb engaged, slaying one quickly as the other danced aside, barely dodging his blow as his injured leg hindered the strike. A brutal force spell hit him from behind, knocking him down hard.

Bawb sprang back to his feet, the unexpected attack actually working to his advantage, allowing him to drive a dagger into the guard's heart as he turned to look at whoever was casting the magical attack.

It was a woman. A Tslavar, no less, with deep green skin and lean, sinewy muscles. She was a natural caster. Highly unusual for her kind. Worse for Bawb, Tslavars were a very aggressive people, made evident as she charged him, spells a-flying. And with her natural intent being inclined toward violence, her spells carried an extra bit of force to them as she cast.

Bawb blocked and evaded as they closed the gap, each trying to land a stunning blow that would allow for a killing stroke as they clashed in passing. Neither did, but Bawb felt his ribs wet with blood as her blade sliced into him. The Tslavar staggered as well. Her hand went to her side, revealing blood. A lot of it. She fell to her knees, mortally wounded.

Bawb wasn't doing too great himself. Her blade had cut deep, and he was losing a fair amount of blood as well. Worse, he was nowhere near his target. He had to think fast.

Do what Ghalian do, fool, the konus urged.

Bawb felt his fangs sliding into place almost on instinct. Of course, the konus was right. He could take what power the caster had left and use it to mend himself, at least somewhat. With that, he could keep moving ahead.

He pulled her head aside sharply, sinking his teeth and stealing her power as her life faded away. He hadn't gotten much before she died, but it was enough to stop the bleeding from his side. The wound, however, would undoubtedly slow him in combat. Something he would have to take into consideration if he ran into any more—

A dozen guards appeared in the corridor, coming at him from both sides. Without hesitation he leapt into action, disarming and dismembering them as fast as he could. They fell quickly, unaccustomed to fighting in the confines of a hallway, but Bawb had suffered more injuries. His clothing was wet and sticky with blood, a fair amount of it his own.

He had no time to reevaluate the situation as two casters came at him from opposite directions. This wasn't any normal guard patrol. This was something worse, as if they knew he was coming. And if they knew a Ghalian would be in their midst, they would be prepared for his deadly tricks.

So Bawb shifted tack and remembered the spells of his youth, casting a shield spell in front and behind him, then firing off a series of annoyance spells. The itching rash spell was mostly dissipated by the casters' defenses, but as it was not a true attack spell, some of the magic got through their defenses, the spells tuned to negate deadly magic, not annoying. And that distracted them enough to allow more of the stinging insects spell to fly true.

Instinct kicked in and the two began swatting at nonexistent bugs before realizing what they were doing. It was only the briefest of lapses in judgment, but it was already too late.

Bawb had moved fast despite his injuries, closing the distance to the nearest of the two in a flash. It had cost him, a trail of blood now slicked the floor behind him, but the power he stole the moment his fangs clamped on the caster's neck made up for it, sealing the worst of the damage in a painful instant.

Bawb stopped short of killing them, instead pivoting their body to act as a living shield, allowing them to absorb all of their comrade's renewed attacks. Bawb stumbled back, the other caster advancing confidently. The Ghalian may have taken down his partner, but he remained standing.

Or so he thought.

He had stumbled right into the Ghalian's trap.

Bawb cast the freezing spell, turning his own pool of blood to ice, the caster's feet slipping out from under him in a flash. He hit the ground hard, knocking the wind out of him. And with no wind, there was no casting. He was only able to ponder that for a moment before he felt the sting of the assassin's fangs breaking his skin. A moment later he was stone dead.

Bawb stumbled to his feet. He'd been injured, and badly. Repeatedly at that. This was not a normal defensive situation. This was something more. Logically, he should have turned and fled, but not only did he believe whoever was orchestrating this fiasco would assume he would do that, they would also be ready for him with even worse surprises.

So, rather than do what was expected of him, Bawb did the unthinkable. Injured and operating at far below full capacity, he pressed onward, disguising himself as one of the fallen as best he could. Fortunately, the injuries being very real made it easier to get past the other guards. And there were a *lot* of them he soon discovered. The six outside were just a drop in the proverbial bucket. This place was a freaking garrison.

"Move toward the streets!" one of the officers ordered. "Look for a wounded Ghalian using magic to heal himself. Do not get within his reach!"

The guards hurried ahead while Bawb, as their injured comrade, was left behind. He turned and hurried for Durggin's most likely location. It was a secured chamber with no windows and thick doors. An easy place to hole up until the threat was eliminated.

He took down a few minor power-using guards as he went, stealing their magic but not killing them, merely leaving them to slumber for a few hours. The true casters would not be so lucky, but these unfortunate souls were just in the wrong place at the wrong time. That, and they happened to have something he very much needed.

Magic.

Bawb didn't use it to heal his wounds. He used it to refine his disguise, his injured mercenary appearance now locked firmly in place when he reached Durggin's safe room.

"The Ghalian has fled for the streets," he announced as he approached.

The muscular brutes standing on either side of the door saw their wounded comrade approaching and instinctively let their guard down to help him. Rather than attack, Bawb allowed them. His blood was not a spell, and it was soon coating their hands, making his disguise all the more solid. One took his skree and sent word that Zaphixx had reported in and the assassin was making a run for it. Who he was talking to, Bawb wasn't sure. Likely an open channel to the others in the compound.

Durggin opened the door a crack and peered out.

"What's going on?"

"Zaphixx reporting in, sir. The intruder has run for the exit."

"As we figured he would," Durggin said with a satisfied chuckle as he opened the door wider. "And this one? Will he survive?"

"Looks like it, though he's losing a lot of blood."

"I'll be all right," Bawb mumbled, nearly falling over.

The weapons dealer looked at his injuries, giving them a twice-over. "You took quite a beating, yet you managed to survive. And against a Ghalian, no less. Consider yourself lucky."

"Yeah, about that," Bawb said as his dagger lodged in the man's chest.

Durggin dropped to his knees then fell forward, driving the knife even deeper. The guards tried to react but Bawb pulled deep and cast a stun spell, affording himself just enough time to dispatch them both while he still had the energy for it.

Okay, you've leveled up. Now, can we please get out of here?

"Konus, for once we are in complete agreement," Bawb replied, hurrying to catch up with the other guards fanning out toward the exit in search of the Ghalian actually hidden in their midst. He would use this disguise just a tiny bit longer, then he would switch to something less obvious. That, and less bloody.

If all worked out, the dead man he'd been impersonating would take at least some of the blame. All that remained was getting off this world as fast as he could. And that would be no easy feat.

CHAPTER THIRTY-THREE

Bawb had managed to pull off an impossible escape from Durggin's compound, following the mercenary force as they swept the building in their assumed pursuit of the fleeing assassin. As he moved, blending in with the group, it became apparent a lot were very recent additions to the security detail. So recent, in fact, that he could use their unfamiliarity with all the new arrivals to his advantage.

He kept the dead man's face as a disguise a bit longer, but then shifted for a new identity, hiding the blood on his clothing with a simple masking spell. He was low on power and hurt, but he was making progress. More importantly, he had managed to get all the way to the landing site unmolested, the others treating him as just another merc in their ranks.

That was all well and good, but he quickly realized there was a new problem. Of course there was.

The ship he had booked passage on for his return trip was under scrutiny. For whatever reason, the mercenaries had taken a particular interest in that vessel, and at least two casters that he could sense were aboard it, casting unmasking spells in search of a hidden Ghalian. Bawb would have to shift course, and fast.

There were a fair amount of craft parked in the landing area, but most had their crews or security details milling about. One, however, appeared unguarded. It was just a small transport ship, but one of good quality. It was scheduled to leave soon but had not begun boarding yet. Small as it was, it would hopefully work for his needs.

Bawb peeled off from the others and headed to it, using his disguise to pass through the area without drawing any more attention than the rest of the dead man's guards. In this case, appearing as part of a large group was working to his advantage.

One man blustering his way past checkpoints was one thing, but when dozens of others were doing the same, it suddenly seemed far more reasonable. Safety in numbers was the key. Numbers that the average person did not question.

He strode aboard as though he had every right to be there and headed straight for the command compartment. This was where it could get tricky, but if his guess was right, this ship was likely run by a Drookonus rather than a team of Drooks. The size and design did not lend itself to large housing facilities, and the galley would not be set up for extended food service. All things that pointed to it being powered by precisely what he needed.

If it was a Drookonus, he could steal the ship, taking command and flying off without an issue. There would be a few alarm spells preventing that, but he had enough magic left to disable them. At least, he hoped he did. If not, it would be a very hasty and very ugly chase that ensued.

Bawb found the command compartment empty, as he had hoped. There were some refreshments off to one side, so it was clear the crew was somewhere about, but for the moment he was alone. More importantly, the Drookonus was exactly where it was supposed to be. Excellent. He slid into the command seat and felt for the device's power.

"What are you doing in there?" a voice demanded from the doorway.

Bawb fought the urge to simply kill the person, instead turning to them with a questioning look.

"What do you mean?" he asked, his mind racing for a clean way out of this.

"We're about to open up for pre-boarding. The captain's on her way back to the ship as we speak. She just skreed me to get things prepared. And then you lot are running around the landing area mucking about in people's business."

Bawb saw the opportunity and took it.

"I'm just following orders. Search the ships, they said. So that's what we're doing."

"No, you're sitting in the captain's chair."

"Oh, that," Bawb said, forcing himself to blush. "Yeah, sorry. I've just never been in one before. Didn't think anyone would mind."

"Well, we do mind. This is our livelihood, and we can't have non-pilots in sensitive areas."

"Right, right," Bawb replied, sliding out of the seat at an angle, knocking over a beverage container that had not been there a moment earlier. The contents splashed across the deck in a gush.

"Oh, I'm so sorry!" he exclaimed, rising and kicking the container as he did. "Let me help!"

"Just get out! This is why you people aren't allowed in here."

"I'm really sorry."

"Great. Thanks. Now get the hell out. I've got to clean this up before the captain gets here."

Bawb sidestepped them and made for the door. "Right. Again, I'm sorry."

"Go!"

He nodded meekly and headed toward the exit hatch with haste. His diversion had worked. While he couldn't take the ship, he had managed to surreptitiously disengage and steal the Drookonus, placing a small masking spell over the console so it would appear it was still there. It wouldn't stand up to close scrutiny, of course, but he didn't have the time or magic to lay that sort of complicated spell anyway.

Bawb moved fast, surprised there hadn't been an alarm spell on the device. He'd cast a negation spell in the command center just in case, but the Drookonus hadn't triggered anything. At least that was going his way. Now he just had to find another ship, and fast.

The exit lay just ahead, and from what he could see the search teams were still spread out far from this craft. He made sure his disguise was firmly in place just in case and stepped out into the fresh air.

A shrill alarm erupted from the ship.

You didn't think to check for a secondary alarm system? the konus asked. *Level down: Alarm detection.*

"Not now," he growled, silently kicking himself for his carelessness. He should have sensed it, but injured and low on power, he simply made a mistake. Hopefully one that would not cost him his life.

Mercenaries hurried his way from several directions. There was only one thing Bawb could do.

"In there!" he called to them, waving them over. "He attacked me and boarded the ship."

Bawb allowed his wounds to become visible once more, the blood seeping through his clothing adding to the effect.

"You're lucky to be alive," the nearest merc said.

"I don't feel so lucky," he replied, pressing his hand over the wound with a pained grimace.

"Well, you are. Get that tended to." He turned to the others. "Secure the exterior. No one in or out. My team, with me!" the man barked, the others quickly falling into their places.

Bawb stepped away as he had been instructed, supposedly to seek medical help, his eyes scanning the other ships in the area for anything at all he might be able to use. The misdirection would not last long. The ship was too small to keep the mercenaries busy for long.

Bawb walked fast, weaving through the crowd, taking in every craft nearby. Nearly all were big and run by Drooks, or smaller but with bustling crews mingling with searching guards. He needed something smaller, more personal. Something like—

"Oh, *hello*," he said quietly as his eyes fell on a very small, but very expensive ship. It was some sort of racer, the type of thing the ultra-wealthy flew around for fun, flaunting their wealth but not using it for any lengthy travel. They would have luxury vessels for that sort of thing. This was for showing off.

"That will do just fine."

Bawb's spirits fell a moment later as he sensed the powerful locking spell on the entry system protecting the ship. While he had been hopeful, it didn't really surprise him. For what the craft had cost, it was expected the protection system would be robust. And he had drained his magic almost entirely. This was not good.

Additional magic unlocked, the konus announced.

"What?"

You heard me. You know I contain far more power than you are allowed to access under normal circumstances.

"But now?"

Don't question it. Just use it and get us out of here.

Hozark had told him the konus was incredibly powerful, but he'd never felt any more than he was supposed to at his level. But for whatever reason the device had decided that just this once it was going to give him a taste of what it could truly do, and as Bawb pulled from its magic, powering his disarming spells with shocking ease and efficiency, he realized just how strong the nondescript konus truly was.

This was a Master-level device. Higher, even. And, if he managed to survive long enough, one day he would have access to *all* of its power. *If* he survived.

The alarm and locking spells fell to his efforts quickly, their protests overwhelmed by the Ghalian's specialized magic. Bawb raced aboard and sealed the hatch, dropping his stolen Drookonus into the ship's receptacle, hoping it had enough power to activate such a customized craft.

The ship came to life. A bit sluggish, as the Drookonus's power was far less than what it was used to, but it activated, nonetheless. Bawb lifted off at once and departed as casually as he could fly. He couldn't draw attention to himself. Not now. Bawb headed out of the atmosphere far slower than he wanted, fighting the urge to punch it and make his escape. But he knew he only had one, maybe two jumps before he would be in a whole new kind of trouble.

The problem was the relatively weak Drookonus he had stolen was draining fast, the luxury racer's power needs threatening to suck it dry like a hungry beast just getting a taste of a fresh meal and wanting more. He would have to be *very* careful. If not, he could find himself in a very difficult situation.

Out of power and drifting in space.

Once he was clear of the planet's atmosphere, Bawb slowly adjusted course, then finally activated the jump spell, hurtling himself to the safety of a new system. He arrived in a flash, but just as quickly, the Drookonus had been drained almost empty. Its power consumption was even worse than he'd expected.

His options were few. Try to find somewhere to land and

hope it would take his pursuers longer to find him, or see if the Drookonus maybe had enough juice for one more jump.

It was folly, the latter thought. He knew full well if he jumped again the Drookonus would fail, and he would be lost in space.

His eyes fell on the long-range skree mounted to the command console, an idea flashing through his mind. A way out.

There was one other option he hadn't considered. An emergency call he could place to the one lifeline he knew could get him out of this mess.

He just hoped they were listening.

CHAPTER THIRTY-FOUR

He wasn't exactly what one could call scared. Ghalian really didn't feel that emotion by the time they reached his level. But Bawb did have a sense of concern as he floated in the inky black of space. The Drookonus powering his stolen craft had been reduced to a barely functioning shell of itself, the sleek ship having pulled such a huge amount of power from it, and far faster than it was designed for. One thing about Drookonuses was true; they came in a variety of capacities and with differing degrees of robustness, and this craft required a specialized version for peak performance.

This one, however, was barely pumping out enough magic to just keep the ship habitable. Even with all of the fancy bells and whistles the expensive craft came equipped with turned off and running at the absolute minimum, the overtaxed device was hanging on by a thread.

Bawb didn't allow himself to worry. He had done what he could, and there was nothing left for him but to wait. So he sat quietly and meditated, feeding himself the slowest trickle of magic from his konus on a continuous stream to keep his wounds from reopening before he could be properly healed.

There were some very nice clothes tucked away in a storage compartment, and while they were not a perfect fit, he was at least pleased to find they were tailored for someone with two arms and two legs. In any case, it was better than his bloody attire by a long shot.

He soon lost track of time, easing into a relaxed Zen state as here, in the middle of nowhere, he was as alone as he could possibly be. There was no one else aboard the small racer with him, and he was far enough from any planet that the odds of the ship being stumbled upon were slim to none.

The slight shake that rumbled the craft as a much larger vessel pulled it close to its hull and locked it down with a clamping spell roused him from his rest, but Bawb was unconcerned. Relieved, even. He rose to his feet and made his way to the airlock and waited.

A minute later the hatch opened, sealed in a tight umbilical spell leading into the smuggler's ship.

"Heya, Bawb," Henni said with her trademark smirk firmly in place.

She and Bud walked into the stolen ship, taking in the ridiculously opulent interior.

Bud followed behind her and let out a whistle as he took it all in. "Wow. I've heard of this model, but I've never seen one in person."

Henni ran her hands across the nearest console, actually impressed for once. "Not exactly a subtle and stealthy ride for a Ghalian. You wanna tell us what this is all about?"

"Yeah, we got here as fast as we could," Bud added. "You made it sound kinda urgent in your skree."

Bawb gestured to the drained Drookonus, calling up the readout showing just how close it was to failure.

"Oh, shit," the pilot said with a little chuckle. "You really *were* in a bit of trouble."

"Losing power would not have been an ideal situation," Bawb replied with that trademark Ghalian calm.

Bud and Henni shared a look and laughed.

"In any case, I find myself in a bit of a bind here. I was hoping you could give me a ride back to the training house."

Bud nodded. "And this beauty doesn't have the power to get you there."

"Yes. That, and even if it did, I need to travel in a discreet manner. I am rather short on coin at the moment, but I will gladly trade you this craft for your troubles."

"This thing is worth *way* more than a ride, Bawb. Where'd you get it, anyway?"

"Ah, yes. About that. We should probably pull some power from your ship and cloak it."

"I see," Henni said with an amused tone, her brow arching upward as she immediately cast multiple spells, disguising the ship now stuck to their own vessel's hull while also encapsulating it in a muting spell of sorts, designed to block out any tracking or alert spells it might be emitting.

They were pirates and smugglers, after all, and they knew all the tools of the trade. And once they got their friend home, they could properly go over the ship and deactivate any alarms or trackers at their leisure. Then they could sell it off to one of their contacts who was always in the market for high-end vessels.

The duo nodded to one another, the decision made pretty much immediately. One, this was a great salvage, though technically more of an outright theft. And two, Bawb was Hozark's kid, even if he didn't know it, and that made him like family.

"Deal," Bud finally said. "But listen, Kid, are you supposed to be doing this?"

"Not exactly. But necessity births creative decisions, does it not?"

"That it does."

"And you *do* want this ship, I assume."

"You assume correctly. I mean hey, free ship," Bud said with a grin.

"Ya can't beat the price," Henni finished his thought. "You hungry? You look like you're hungry."

"I could eat."

"Well, you're in luck. We have one stop we have to make before we can take you home. Don't worry, it's close by, on the way, and it won't take long. And while we're there, I think a nice hearty traveler's meal would do all of us some good."

"What about the ship? Landing with it—"

"Don't worry about that. There's a moon close by we sometimes use to stash things. It'll be safe there until we come back for it."

Normally, Bawb would have questioned such a plan, but he trusted these two completely. More than anyone else he had ever known outside the order, Bud and Henni had proven themselves to be absolutely worthy of his full faith and confidence. And on top of that, one of the Five vouched for them, and that was as good a recommendation as anyone could ask for.

"If you say so," he said, his belly rumbling audibly. "A good meal sounds divine."

"Excellent. And, Bud, get him some regular clothes, will ya? We can't have him looking like that. Poor kid looks like he's wearing his wealthy brother's hand-me-downs."

"Of course. I've got plenty of things for you on our ship. You know where the lockers are."

"I do," Bawb replied, heading for the airlock. "And thank you, I was in quite a bind."

"That's what friends are for," Bud said as he added an additional clamping spell to hold the stolen craft in place if the Drookonus failed and caused it to vent some air.

Bawb stepped aboard the familiar corridors of their ship. It wasn't their largest one, but rather, the one they used most often. A smuggling vessel rather than a pirating one. And it was a comforting place that immediately set the wounded Ghalian at ease. He was safe. As safe as he could hope for, at least, and soon he would return home, his near-disastrous mission complete.

The planet they set down on was a relatively unremarkable one, calm skies and green landscape dotted by towns and cities without a sign of unrest. Given how Bawb was feeling, that was just the right kind of place. He didn't want to fight, didn't want to run. He just wanted to get through the day without any further conflict and enjoy a nice meal with his friends.

Bud and Henni had skreed ahead and set their meeting in their favorite tavern in the second largest city. It seemed their business was the sort that could be transacted in public for a change, and that meant they could kill two birds with one stone.

"It's just a simple exchange of goods," Henni explained as she slipped the heavy shoulder bag across her body. "Gorrik pays us, we hand him the bag, and all is well and good in the world."

"And we get a good meal out of it," Bud added. "With the trouble we went to getting this for him, damn straight Gorrik's picking up the tab."

The trio stepped out of the ship into the pleasantly warm sun's rays. The air was lightly spiced with the fragrances of cooking, but Bawb was still a bit sluggish in his first steps.

"Are you okay to eat?" Henni asked. "You're looking kind of rundown."

"I am just tired from my contract. It was draining, and I suffered some injuries in the process."

"We can bring you something back if you'd rather rest."

"No. A good meal with good friends would be most pleasant, and I could use the pick-me-up. Also, this will be good practice."

"Practice?"

"Yes."

Henni shrugged. "Well, okay then. This is the place up ahead."

"Marvelous! What a fine establishment! I cannot wait to sample their fare!" the Ghalian said with unexpected gusto, his skin tone changing in a flash.

Henni and Bud looked at each other, wondering what he was up to but carrying on with their business all the same.

"A table for three. No, four, my good fellow," Bawb said to the host the moment they answered, slapping him on the back and beaming a jovial grin. "I have heard amazing things about this place. Amazing, I tell you. And I am very much looking forward to sampling your wares."

The host looked at Bud and Henni. They just shrugged.

"Okay, then. Right this way."

He led them to a table in the middle of the establishment. Bawb joked and greeted everyone they passed on the way, treating each as if they were longtime friends he was thrilled to see. He was a jovial whirlwind of good cheer and wit, and he shamelessly flirted with any unattached person they passed, regardless of gender or race.

It was crazy, but rather than annoying people, his antics were earning him goodwill throughout the tavern. And when he ordered a round of drinks for one of the tables to which he paid an impromptu visit, his popularity only grew.

Of course, he had identified those particular patrons as a popular bunch, and by endearing himself to them and earning their fondness, he further elevated his social cache. It was quite the impressive act, and no one who engaged with him would have thought for a moment that he was a badly injured and exhausted assassin on the run. He was hiding in plain sight, and he was doing it with style.

By the time Gorrik came to make the exchange, Bawb had befriended nearly everyone in the establishment.

"Ignore him," Bud said as their contact took a seat. "He's just a really, *really* outgoing guy."

"I can see that," Gorrik replied, sliding a modest pouch across the table.

Bud checked the contents in a glance. Satisfied, he gave his partner a subtle nod. Henni slipped him the shoulder bag under the table. "Thanks for the business, Gorrik."

"Always a pleasure, Henni. Now, that out of the way, shall we dine?"

Food arrived shortly thereafter, and the four of them ate very well, Bawb's trader persona entertaining them all with tales of dealings across the stars. Bud and Henni knew he was just making it all up, but even so, they got a bit caught up in his impressive storytelling. For people who knew who and what he really was to almost believe his tales was the truest sign of his growing skill he could ask for.

Finally, much food and drink later, they headed back to the ship, full of belly and cheerful of spirits. The moment the door closed behind them Bawb let his disguise slip away, an exhausted sag washing over his body. He was wiped out.

"Okay, that was kinda nuts. What was that all about?" Bud marveled.

Bawb let out a tired chuckle. "No one looks for the loudest, most friendly person in the room."

"But no one was looking for us," Henni noted.

"Likely not. But in case we *were* somehow pursued, this would throw anyone off our trail."

Bud and Henni shared an amused look, leaving their friend a bit confused.

SCOTT BARON

"What is so funny?"

"Oh, nothing," Bud replied. "It's just that it's funny, is all. Your little show back there? It's really similar to a character Hozark likes to use. A fella named Alasnib the trader."

"I have seen him employ that role. And, point in fact, my character is also a trader, fashioned in part after that very persona."

"What do you call him?"

"The name varies."

"Well, one day you'll settle on a name for your favorite persona, and seeing what you just managed to do despite being beat up and exhausted, I'm pretty sure you'll slip into it as easily as your most comfortable pair of boots."

"That is the intent," he agreed.

"As it should be. But enough of this. You've had a pretty rough go of it and could probably use a good healing session. Let's get you home."

CHAPTER THIRTY-FIVE

Bud and Henni landed at the site closest to the Ghalian compound. It cost a little more in docking fees, but Bawb was wiped out, and they wanted to help him get back sooner rather than later now that their business was done. Also, it was business that had paid quite well, so a little extra expense wasn't an issue. And with the valuable racer ship stashed on their lunar hiding spot, they would have a fair amount of additional coin coming their way quite soon indeed.

The pair walked their Ghalian passenger to the mercantile shop that served as one of the hidden entrances to the training house. Through the back they walked, tucking into a service room and shutting the door. Bawb intoned the spell to unseal the hidden door in the opposite wall.

"Are you coming in?" he asked.

"Yeah, we're gonna visit some people," Henni replied. "You go on and get patched up. We know the way."

Bawb gave them a little bow. "Thank you both. Your help has been more appreciated than you can imagine."

"Aww, shucks. I bet you say that to all the pirates who bail you out of sticky situations," Henni chuckled. "Now get going. Those wounds aren't gonna heal themselves."

"Of course. And again, thank you."

Bawb headed off in one direction while Bud and Henni moved in another, the only two non-Ghalian allowed the freedom to walk these hallways unescorted. As for the injured Adept, he made straight for the healer's chambers, flopping down on one of the low beds as soon as he entered. This was as safe a place as he would ever be, and his latent stress washed off him like sweat from his brow in a post-workout shower.

"What have you managed to do to yourself this time?" the healer asked, sensing his many injuries as soon as she touched him.

"A difficult mission. Nothing more."

"Difficult would appear to be an understatement, Adept. I see that you attempted to mend your own wounds. Several times, in fact. But this is not good work. It is below your skill level. I know you can do far better than this. What happened?"

"I had only a limited amount of power at my disposal. I had to make the decision between mending my flesh or using it to complete my mission. I chose the latter."

"At great personal risk. You stopped the bleeding in most cases, but the underlying injuries are still significant."

"I am aware. Can you repair them?"

"You know full well I can. Now, lie back and relax as best you are able. As you know, this is going to be uncomfortable."

The healer spent an extra-long time working on him on this occasion. Normally, she would leave a little residual bruising and let the student deal with the discomfort, but this Adept had performed admirably in the face of adversity on an actual contract, choosing possibly crippling injury in order to complete his task. That level of dedication warranted only the best treatment.

Bawb was lying in the bed as his strength began to recover when visitors arrived to see him.

"Master Hozark? Teacher Demelza?"

"Bud and Henni are with us as well," Hozark noted, all four of them stepping close and surrounding his bed. "Master Orvus told me about your contract, and Bud and Henni filled me in on the more interesting aspects of it. What you did was very risky, Bawb. You could have failed."

"But I did not."

"No, you did not. But relying on sourcing a series of power users to steal magic from to continue on? It borders on reckless."

"If I may interject," Henni said. "I have to note that I may know another Ghalian who has done just that very same thing in the past. Just saying."

"Yes, Henni, we know," Hozark replied, almost showing a hint of sheepishness.

Almost.

"So, you completed your contract but were forced to make alternate arrangements for your return here," he continued. "Hitching a ride with these two? Hardly lying low, would you not agree?"

"Hey now, we were in the area, and the kid just needed a lift," Bud objected. "C'mon, Hozark. There's no harm in that. We've given plenty of Ghalian a ride over the years."

"Yes, you have. But he is an Adept, and he is supposed to rely on no one. Are you certain you only gave him a ride?"

"Of course."

"Nothing more?"

"I don't know whatever you could be implying," Bud said, turning to Bawb and flashing a knowing wink. "Just a ride, nothing more."

Hozark saw, of course, but he let it go, shifting his focus to the healing young man lying before him. "Just be careful in the future, Bawb. You are facing real risks now, and the price of failure, as you have learned firsthand, is steep."

"I understand."

"Good," Hozark softly replied. He held Bawb's gaze a long moment, resting his hand on the Adept's shoulder. "Now, recover and rejoin your classmates. Have a good meal tonight, and sleep early. Tomorrow you resume training."

"I look forward to it," he replied as his visitors turned and took their leave.

"Seriously, Hozark? No rest for the kid?" Bud marveled as they stepped out into the hallway.

"He is a Wampeh Ghalian. This *is* rest. Now, if you will excuse me for a bit, I have matters to attend to."

"We're still on for dinner, though, right?" Henni asked, led by her black hole of a stomach once again.

"In the Masters' dining hall, yes."

"Great. We'll see ya there."

She and Bud meandered off, leaving Hozark and Demelza to whatever it was they had to do. As soon as they were out of earshot, Demelza spoke.

"This was not a blown mission."

"No, it does not appear to be the case."

"There were stacked casters waiting for him. And hidden guards. Honestly, I am amazed he managed to escape."

"And complete his contract in spite of the odds," Hozark noted. "He was impetuous and took an enormous risk, but in this case, it happened to work out. Had it been any other, they likely would not have pushed on, and that would have led them right into the heart of the trap."

"And there is that word. *Trap*," Demelza mused. "Sometimes intelligence is not up to date. That happens."

"Indeed it does," he agreed.

"But this? There is the very real appearance that this was a trap. That someone clued in the target in advance. And more than that, someone spent a fair amount of coin in the process."

"So it seems," Hozark said, a metaphorical cloud hovering over his head as he pondered just what this all could mean. "We cannot afford to lose more of our number. Someone is leaking valuable information, and sooner or later, another of our brothers or sisters will fall. Bawb got lucky today. His skill held out, and he performed admirably, but there is no denying luck was on his side."

"Agreed."

"We must find who is doing this. Who the mole is."

"Do you have any ideas?" Demelza asked.

"I have spies checking on several leads. But for the time being, we will all take contracts as usual, but with extra due diligence on the part of our spy network to vet both the employer as well as the target. The other Masters and I will personally work to root out the traitor in our ranks. This has to come to an end, and sooner than later."

"And the boy?"

"He will continue his training, but I fear we may need to hold him back from higher-level missions, at least for now."

"He will not like that."

"No, he will not. But I will not have him perish when there is something I can do to protect him. Come with me. I wish to show you some communications I have received surrounding this incident with Durggin. Perhaps your fresh eyes will see something I have overlooked."

The two headed off down the corridor, their footfall silent out of habit.

Bawb stepped back from the door he had been pressing his ear to. A listening spell would have been detected. He had to eavesdrop the old-fashioned way. And what he'd heard was disconcerting indeed. There *was* a traitor in their midst. It was no longer a question. And this time, he was the one who had nearly perished. But with Hozark on their trail, heaven help whoever had been so foolish as to betray the order.

CHAPTER THIRTY-SIX

Bawb had healed up nicely, and with a few days of relatively light training, he felt as good as new by the time an unexpected announcement was made at breakfast.

Of course, as Ghalian, the unexpected was expected. The Adepts just didn't know exactly what sort of surprise they might find themselves facing. In this instance, much to their delight, it was a rather pleasant one.

"Adepts, you are going on an outing," Teacher Demelza informed the assembled group. "You have worked hard of late, and the Masters of the house have decided you have earned a bit of relaxation."

Albinius raised his hand.

"You know you do not need to raise your hand, Albinius."

"He knows. He just does it out of habit," Finnia said with a chuckle. "Always playing the role of the fool. I do not think he knows where the act ends and the real Albi begins."

"Hey!"

"That was not an insult, my friend. Just an observation."

Demelza slowly shook her head. These two had been at it

for years, but beneath all the ribbing lay a deep and trusting friendship. Perhaps a hint of something more, but the teachers had kept detailed records on every student's activities, and these two had not raised any eyebrows thus far.

"Regardless, you had a question?" she said.

"Yeah. You say we're going somewhere to relax, but we never really relax, do we? What's the catch? No disrespect."

Finnia smacked him, but Demelza raised her hand to silence her. "It is a reasonable question, Finnia. And to answer your question, Albinius, Ghalian *do* relax. We simply do so in a manner that is fitting our nature."

"So, we will be training?"

"Yes and no. Your class is to be flown to Vorkus, where you will be left to your own devices on one of its tropical islands for five days. You will need to craft shelter for yourselves, and you will hunt and gather your own food beyond the basics you may bring with. But other than that, you will be on your own. Should you wish to train, that is your prerogative. Likewise, should you choose to simply do nothing for a few days, that, too, is your choice."

"We can do nothing?" Zota marveled, the very concept of true free time something akin to a fairy tale at this point in their lives.

Mavens had it, as did Masters, of course, but Adepts were still expected to work hard, and pretty much all the time at that. They would train, naturally. But having the ability to do so at their own pace and in a truly relaxed manner without any teacher supervision would be a wonderful and novel experience.

"You may do as you wish, though I would expect, given your wishes to advance to Mavens, that you would continue your efforts at self-improvement even while enjoying your recreation."

"Teacher?" Elzina chimed in. "Will we be travelling armed?"

"You are Ghalian. You know the answer to that."

"I meant beyond our usual kit."

"There are no fight scenarios planned, so you may bring what you wish. Do be aware, there are bandit gangs that occasionally frequent the area, but you will be located in an area relatively far from their usual raiding grounds."

All of them had their own preferred implements they carried as second nature at this point, but the option to travel light was an enticing one. They also knew from their own experiences that the teachers loved to drop surprise challenges on them when they least expected it. Logic dictated it would only make sense to bring at least a few more substantial weapons.

"Gather what you wish and meet back here in the dining hall," she continued. "Eat up, and take what you wish to carry. But know there is ample game on the island, and as a mostly water-covered world, the ocean is rich with an abundance of seafood and natural springs are readily found. I will see you all shortly. Then your excursion will begin."

It was late afternoon when the Adepts finally reached the small open field on the island the teachers had chosen for their outing. The ship set down in a low hover, deposited the group, then lifted off, leaving them to their own devices with a simple set of instructions. Relax, enjoy their time in this beautiful place, but do not make themselves obvious. Their location was far enough from frequented areas that they should not see another soul during their stay.

The group worked together as a team, enjoying the relaxed nature of this experience and joining forces to build a communal shelter for them all. The air was warm and moist, the nature of tropical life, and as such, they were more concerned with rain and dew from above than keeping in any warmth. As a result, their shelter was open-walled on two of its four sides.

The design allowed for protection from the sun as it traversed the sky but otherwise was open to the elements, letting the comfortable breeze waft through the space. As for bedding, they formed an elevated structure of branches and large leaves then piled cushioning foliage thick before adding another layer of the large, waxy leaves on top. It wasn't quite the same as a bed back home, but they had all slept in far less comfortable environs, and often at that.

"I will seek game," Elzina said as the others finished putting the final touches on the structure. She had sharpened a long pole into a makeshift spear to take down larger prey, but knowing her proclivities, it seemed likely she'd just as soon get up close and dirty about it. "Finnia, why don't you collect edible plants?" she suggested.

Finnia, though firmly on the spy path and not possessing nearly the same killer instinct as her cohort, took the suggestion without offense, though Elzina had likely intended it. She had a fondness for pointing out the spy training in their midst was a lesser warrior. Finnia, utilizing precisely those spy skills of observation and tact, simply let her. There was no point getting into an argument with her. Elzina would always be Elzina, and there was no way around it. If conflict could just be avoided, that was the way to go.

That seemed to be the general consensus among her classmates as well. They'd hoped she might temper her attitude as she grew older, but that had been no more than an exercise in wishful thinking.

"I will see what I can find," Finnia said, heading off to gather what she could.

"And get firewood while you are out," Elzina called after her.

Bawb shook his head but let it slide. He wasn't about to step into that mess. He had been whittling a trident out of a branch, binding barbed prongs to its end with plant fibers. He hefted the lightweight weapon with a satisfied grin.

"I will head to the water and see what manner of game the ocean might provide us."

He headed out toward the coast at a quick jog. It would take some time to get to the water, but they had all the time in the world for a change. He reached it in less than an hour, his feet padding into the soft, warm sand. He shed his boots and headed into the clear waters, casting a bubble spell around his head and submerging to hunt.

Bawb had grown quite proficient in the water, and he managed to take quite a few large fish without drawing any reaction before he struck. His carefully used stealth spells seemed to function rather well underwater, and the poor fish didn't stand a chance. It was a wonderful sensation, using his talents in a new way. While his abilities on land were demonstrably quite solid, only the actual application of them in practice in this environment let him see how far he had progressed in the water.

Judging by the numerous fish he soon had strung together as he began his trek back to their campsite, he had come far indeed.

As he walked, he considered the use of a shimmer cloak and how it might function in water. It was something he had never even thought of doing prior to today, but now he found the idea of the novel application of the magical device a fascinating possibility. Of course, he was still only moderately talented with it on dry land, having to remain still for it to work properly, as he had not yet mastered the art of maintaining it in motion. But underwater one drifted and swam, both requiring less effort and more fluid motion. Perhaps that would make the spell work better.

Or it might simply suck underwater regardless of one's skill. Some spells just worked that way. Or didn't work, as the case might be. For now, however, that didn't matter. He had a sizable haul to share with his cohort, and that was the important thing.

Elzina had been successful as well, he found when he returned to camp. She had brought down a medium-sized animal that had more than enough meat to feed them all for a few days. It was a fortunate thing, as it saved her from spending too much time chasing down smaller prey.

Finnia had also had a productive go of it, and a modest but varied spread of berries and edible plants now lay before them on wide leaves. She had piled up a stack of wood and had nursed it into a blaze, feeding it until it would be ready to cook their meal. She tossed in another length of wood, but this variety snapped and sparked violently.

"What did you do?" Elzina demanded.

"I did nothing. It is just wood!"

Thick smoke began pouring out of the fire, wafting up into the sky in a dense plume.

"Put it out!" Usalla shouted, unsuccessfully casting an extinguishing spell. With the body of the fire around it, the lone piece remained stubbornly aflame.

Bawb and Zota leapt into action, each grabbing a length of wood and using them to leverage the troublesome piece out of the fire.

"Try again," Bawb commanded.

Usalla hit it with the spell once more as hard as she could. The smoke stopped but the wood still crackled. Martza and Albinius joined in, the three of them casting in unison. Finally, under the onslaught of their overlapping power, the wood finally fell silent.

"What the hell was that?" Zota marveled.

"Some strange kind of fungus or something grew inside the wood," Finnia replied, studying the hot remains. "It reacted with the fire. I've never seen anything like it. At least it does not appear to be toxic."

"It made a mess, though," Albinius said with a laugh. "And, Elzina, you should have seen the look on your face!"

"Shut up, fool. That could have become a real problem."

"But it didn't. So let's cook this stuff. I'm starving."

Elzina opened her mouth to fire off a rebuttal but let it go. She was hungry as well, and much as she was annoyed with him, as usual, there was no sense in delaying their meal over it.

She made quick work cleaning the beast and preparing it for the fire. Bawb did the same, gutting and skewering the fish then setting them over the embers where the flames had died down. In short order they were all eating, and quite well.

"I could get used to this," Zota mused, reclining comfortably and stuffing his face. "To actually relax for a change? This has to be the best outing we've had yet."

The others nodded their agreement, settling in and enjoying an incredibly rare respite from their typically difficult training regimen. As the sun set and they relaxed with their bellies full, the Adepts surprisingly felt something unusual away from home. They felt at ease.

"Bandits!" Usalla shouted late that night, rousing the few still sleeping in an instant.

The others were already fighting hard, greatly outnumbered by the camouflaged brutes who had descended upon them in the wee hours.

Elzina's worst fear had apparently played out. The smoke from the fire, no matter how brief, had drawn unwanted attention from the hostiles normally far away, and now they were engaged in a very lopsided battle against an unknown number of attackers. They were all cloaked in outfits that helped them blend into the environment with ease. Even with night-vision spells, the Adepts found themselves struggling against so many adversaries.

Bawb slayed two of them, their bodies spurting blood as they fell at his feet, his daggers wet and gleaming in the moonlight. The others were getting their footing now as well, dishing out a significant amount of hurt on the interlopers. They may have been relatively young and caught off-guard, but these youths were no pushovers by any means. In fact, their attackers quickly found they were far more trouble than they were worth.

A shrill whistle pierced the air, and as quickly as they appeared, the bandits turned and fled, blending into the night. A minute later silence rang out, deafeningly still where the cacophony of battle had just been.

"Is everyone okay?" Bawb asked, throwing fresh wood on the embers of the fire, giving them ambient light to take in the carnage.

Multiple bandits lay dead. The wounded had managed to escape, likely helped by their comrades so as not to compromise their ranks. The deceased, however, could spill no secrets.

"Everyone is fine," Usalla said as she looked over the group. "A few minor injuries, but nothing—wait. Where is Finnia?"

The group spun and searched for her, eyes scanning every inch of the area. But there was no sign of their friend. Finnia was gone.

"They took her," Bawb growled, his emotions threatening to bubble to the surface despite his best efforts.

He wiped his blades on a corpse's clothes and sheathed them, picking up the dead man's meager short sword and testing its balance. It was poorly weighted but would have to do. He turned in the direction the bandits had fled and started walking.

"What are you doing?" Martza asked.

He turned back to her, his eyes blazing. "I am going to get her back."

CHAPTER THIRTY-SEVEN

Bawb didn't wait for the others. He knew they would follow, gathering up the fallen raiders' weapons as well as their own before they came chasing after him. Unfortunately, it had looked like the enemy had taken their deceased comrades' blades when they fled. Bawb had only scored the short sword because he was standing right over the corpse at the time.

And now he raced ahead with singular focus. He was on the kidnappers' trail, and despite their relatively clever and efficient use of camouflaging magic to hide their tracks, he had a few tricks of his own up his sleeve.

While the imprints of their feet had been softened to barely visible, and the plants were carefully moved aside as they passed rather than bent and broken like a hurried animal might, Bawb didn't really care. His gaze was focused squarely on the ground and the one thing they hadn't thought to disguise. Something that left a clear path to anyone clever enough to use the right spell.

It was a variation of night vision Bawb had been working on in his spare time for several years at this point. A technique of his own making, though not quite refined enough to share with the Masters. But now, under pressure to make it work or else, the spell he had tweaked was working. It was not only picking up and amplifying any light no matter how small, as a night-sight spell would, but it was also reading heat.

Bawb's logic was that this was akin to light in a way. Power or radiation or whatever you wanted to call it, heat could be tracked just like light. Amplified into the visible scale and, in this case, leaving a very obvious trail despite the seeming absence of one at all.

He heard the others coming from behind, their muting spells silencing most but not all of their movements. In the hurry they were in, and with the enemy rushing before them, the emphasis on stealth was somewhat diminished, replaced with the need to catch them before anything bad befell their friend.

Bawb surged ahead for some time until he abruptly burst from the thick tree line onto an unexpected sandy beach bordered by steep black stone cliffs. It was a bit breezy on the ocean, and though the trail had been clear up until this point, the shifting sands blown by the cool wind off the water quickly had erased any sign of his targets.

He stood still, straining his ears for a sound of them. All he heard was the rumble of the waves. He breathed deep, hoping to catch even the faintest whiff of sweat, but there was nothing but the scent of salt in the air. He scanned every which way with his eyes and magical sensitivity, looking for anything at all that might give him direction.

He found none.

"Where is she?" Usalla asked as she and the others emerged from the jungle.

"Gone."

"Gone?"

"I tracked them to the shore, but I have lost their trail."

"They could not have fled into the ocean. We would see a vessel," Elzina noted, scanning the waters. "They have to be here somewhere."

Bawb's frustration was growing by the second. There was no Drook signature in the air, so no craft had been waiting for them. Something else was at play. But what? He stood still, forcing himself to slow his breathing and calm his mind. To unfocus his eyes and allow his instincts to guide him.

"What are you doing?" Elzina barked.

Bawb held up his hand for silence. Amazingly, she obliged.

He stood there a long while and was about to give up on this tactic when a flicker of movement appeared in the corner of his peripheral vision. Small. So small he'd have missed it if his eyes had been focused. But it was there, clear as mud.

A small, rodent-like animal had just emerged from what looked like a sheer volcanic rock face. The animal, unlike the Adepts, knew the trail and did not let its eyes fool it. A little grin pulled his lips upward. "Clever," he muttered, walking closer.

"What did you say?" Elzina demanded.

"Come. Look." He reached out his hand, passing it through what looked like solid stone.

Elzina stuck her head through to take a proper look. "A hidden tunnel entrance? Here?"

"It would seem that way."

"Then what are we waiting for?" she asked with a frustrated glare.

"Wait," Bawb urged. "We are woefully under-armed for a fight. We need more weapons."

Usalla saw where he was going with this. "What did you have in mind?"

"Back to the basics," he replied, picking up a piece of the volcanic stone and whacking it against a plain rock. It cracked as planned, exposing a razor-sharp edge of smoky glass. "A bit of crafting is in order."

The group fell to work in a heartbeat, their task clear, the objective plain to see. Compared to some of the more complex crafting they had learned over the years, this was easy, and in no time at all they had a healthy collection of spears and slicing instruments, all hewn from the volcanic glass. They might break in use, but so long as they performed their purpose that was fine. They were use-and-abandon implements of death, and the young Ghalian planned on meting out a lot of it.

The sky was growing lighter in the distance, the sun preparing to rise, but that would be of no help to them. Not where they were going.

"We do not know what waits for us inside," Bawb said as they stacked by the hidden entrance. "This tunnel could lead anywhere, so stay alert. Night-vision spells only. No illumination. We stay close, cover each other's blind sides." He glanced at his friends, noting the intense looks on their faces with great satisfaction. All of them were of the same bloody mindset. There was only one thing for them to do.

"Let's get our friend."

He led the way through the false stone wall into the darkness. Only, it wasn't as dark as he had first thought it would be. In fact, the faintly glowing moss lining the walls and ceiling cast enough light that they could even save their night-vision magic, at least for the time being. That was a pleasant surprise.

The *un*pleasant one was the direction the tunnel turned. In just a short distance it abruptly shifted downward and toward the water. This wasn't a normal tunnel. It was an old lava tube leading somewhere beneath the waves. They all knew how to cast bubble spells, but if they went far enough ahead and this tunnel flooded, there was no telling if they could maintain them long enough to swim the length of the tunnel to fresh air.

It was a risk they would have to take.

The Adepts moved fast and silent, any hint of their usual training banter long gone, replaced by grim resolve. Finnia needed them, and even Elzina seemed to have taken the abduction personally. Whatever happened to them in the course of a contract or training session was one thing, but to have a band of outsiders attack them as a group was crossing a line even she would not tolerate.

They descended into the damp, briny tunnel, feeling the invisible weight of incredible amounts of water above them, pressing down on the rock surrounding their comparatively fragile bodies. The footing was sound, the ground seemingly worked to provide grit for traction unlike the smooth walls. It was a good thing given the pitch. If it was at all slippery, they would have likely had a very fast and very direct ride to the bottom, however far that might be.

Down and down they traveled, weapons ready, moving in silence. Bawb slowed his pace as a brighter light illuminated the tunnel just up ahead. Their descent was coming to an end, it seemed, and as he cautiously stepped out into the underwater chamber, he couldn't help but feel a sense of wonder and awe wash over him despite the seriousness of their task.

They were standing in an enormous cavern, its domed ceiling high above and glowing with illumination. From what he could see, it was more of that moss, and a lot of it, as well as some spells blended in, amplifying the effect. But that wasn't the most amazing thing. In fact, it barely held a candle to the rest of the place.

This was not just a cavern, but a vast and magical city hidden entirely from the surface deep beneath the sea. Amphibious ships sat gently bobbing beside floating docks, each of them stretching out a long walkway to the shoreline and the town proper.

Out along the far wall, illumination of a different sort brightened the water, the morning sun's rays hitting the sandy bottom and reflecting upward. It seemed there was a wide opening below the surface, the ambient air pressure and likely a bit of specialized magic keeping the water level even and the tidal flow gentle.

Along a section of floating walkways, Bawb saw what looked like enormous underwater pens. The flashing shapes were familiar, he realized. These were fish hatcheries, or perhaps just holding areas for the day's catch. Whatever the case, it was an elegant system and one completely in tune with nature.

The smell of cooking food wafted toward them from the city proper. It wasn't that far, all told, and they could reach it quite quickly if they needed. Only a few fields of strange vegetables growing under magical illumination stood in their way, and the paths through and around them were clear enough.

"It is a whole hidden society down here," Usalla marveled quietly. "I have never seen anything like it."

"None of us has," Bawb replied, likewise in a respectable amount of awe. "And that means we must be cautious. We need to approach slowly so as to best determine how to disguise ourselves among the locals. To fit in. And then, once we can walk the streets freely, we find Finnia."

Elzina rolled her head, cracking her neck in a threatening way. "And then we make whoever took her pay."

CHAPTER THIRTY-EIGHT

The Adepts checked each other's impromptu disguises. They had been in luck. This place seemed to be frequented by a few races, not just the squishy, often tentacled ones they saw coming and going from the waters. Several bipedal ones lived here as well, and of them one in particular had a similar enough size and shape that they had all been able to shift their coloring to the blotchy greens and grays with ease. The stringy black-green hair was a simple addition.

The clothing was also rather standard in cut and fit, so all they needed were a few well-placed altering spells to make their own attire appear like the locals. All in all, it was as easy an infiltration as they could hope for. At least visually. Beyond that, however, they knew absolutely nothing about these people. Customs, habits, even language, all were a blank. They hoped the translation spells everyone in the galaxy used were just as effective here, but they also knew full well that the unexpected was called that for a reason.

"We have only one path in from this location," Martza noted. "We will be forced to travel in a group until we enter the city."

"A defensive strategy in the city's construction, no doubt,"

Dillar mused.

She shrugged. "Logical, given I do not see any additional entry points at this end of the cavern. But who knows what may lie along the other walls."

Bawb started walking. There was no time to waste, and if a bottleneck entry was how this place defended itself, so be it. They would just have to bluff their way in. That, or get very, very violent. Fortunately, he was quite confident in his cohort's abilities. Yes, they were armed mostly with primitive weapons, but that and the selection of quality blades they sported out of habit would be more than adequate against whatever civilians they might run up against.

As for the raiding party's success in the dark hours, they had managed to catch the group off guard. It was embarrassing, really. That they had taken their rest period for granted and that no one had thought to set a basic perimeter tripwire spell was a failure all of them had squarely on their shoulders. Someone should have done it, and to assume it was taken care of without verifying was inexcusable.

But they would address that mistake later. For now, their priorities were squarely on one thing. Getting their friend back.

The group devised a plan as they drew near the point where the trail opened into the city streets. They would split up into small teams, covering as much ground as possible as fast as they could without drawing suspicion. Then, when Finnia's location had been ascertained, they would regroup and make a single combined effort to free her and make their escape.

A lone guard sat up ahead, seemingly bored with his job but holding his post all the same. It was commonplace across the galaxy. Someone always got the shit detail, but that didn't mean they could slack off. To do so was to court disaster. Or, in this case, a group of trained killers. Regardless, the raiding party had to have passed by here, so there was no way he was unaware of their arrival. That meant the city guards themselves were in on the raids, if not carrying them out themselves.

"No luck?" the guard asked as the disguised Adepts walked past.

"Not today," Bawb replied with a casual nod.

The man looked up at him and his companions, a hint of curiosity in his eyes, but only just. "The land and the sea both give and take."

"That they do."

The fellow gave a little nod and settled back into his boredom, allowing them all to pass.

Apparently, their disguises had worked.

Once in the streets they encountered more people. It appeared to be a rather tight-knit community, which made sense given their very specialized locale. Blending in as a group would be a problem. New faces might appear once in a while as a trading vessel pulled in to sell their wares, but not a large group wearing local attire. It seemed they would need to separate into small teams sooner than later.

As the thought passed through Bawb's mind, a group of uniformed guards raced out of the adjacent street, taking up a position in front of them. Apparently, the sentry's comment had been a passcode. One he'd failed. As soon as they'd entered the city the alarm had been sent ahead and guards roused. There were only four of them, however. An annoyance, but not a problem.

The leader of the group strode forward, drawing a rather impressive sword from its scabbard. Only Bawb, Elzina, and Martza were carrying swords, and they were short ones at that. The rest had daggers and improvised weapons, but nothing that would fare terribly well against that sort of blade.

Fortunately, they knew they had both the skills and numbers to render that a moot point.

"Stop. You trespass upon Goolan soil," the man said, standing imposingly in front of them.

Bawb had to give it to him, the fellow showed no sign of unease whatsoever. That sort of confidence was both admirable as well as foolish.

"We are just looking for our friend," he replied. "Perhaps you saw her. A young woman, pale—"

"This is your one chance to leave," was the growled reply. "You will not be told twice."

"Oh, you do not know who you are messing with," Elzina hissed, a gleam in her eye as she drew her short sword.

The others in their group drew their weapons as well, but the man just grinned. "Neither do you."

And just like that he was in motion, his blade flashing at impossible angles with the speed and power they had only seen a few wield during their years of training. The three Adepts with short swords leapt into action immediately.

Bawb parried and swung a flurry of counterattacks as Elzina and Martza did the same, but each suffered slices from his blade. They redoubled their efforts, pouring their energy into each blow. The man blocked with ease, landing a solid kick square in the middle of Elzina's chest, driving her tumbling backwards.

Bawb cast a force spell, followed by a series of tripping ones, but their adversary deftly avoided them, all the while his blade swinging with aggressive power and blistering speed. Bawb was overwhelmed, as was Martza. They very quickly realized this was a master swordsman. Maybe better. No wonder the other guards hadn't even drawn their weapons. They were just standing back and watching the show. It seemed the intruders didn't have a numerical advantage after all.

Martza grunted in pain as the blade slid past her guard and drove through her body, withdrawing in a bloody flash and swinging at her neck. Bawb barely got his weapon up to protect her in time, slowing the strike enough to save her a killing blow. Even so, she suffered a long cut along her shoulder.

Elzina jumped back into the fray, her and Bawb's attacks giving the others a chance to pick up their fallen friend and run. This was bad. Very bad, and they knew it. Bawb and Elzina used every trick they knew, but the man handled them with ease, almost toying with them as he slowly wore them down.

But what mattered was Martza had been carried away from the action. Whether she would survive her injury was something they would worry about once they saved their own skins.

"Form Twelve," Bawb called to Elzina.

She knew what he meant and reacted at once, the two of them fanning out wide to opposite sides, risking getting the other guards involved but creating enough space for the odd spell they were about to cast.

"*Callonus nictu,*" they intoned in unison.

The ground at their feet rumbled and shook, cracking open in places as it split apart. *That* got the man's attention. They were underwater, after all, and any breach to the stability of their environment could possibly be fatal. He had just never expected anyone to use this sort of magic in this place. It was madness. Suicide.

Or a very clever Ghalian trick.

Bawb and Elzina turned and ran, casting every blocking and diversionary spell they could behind them as they raced away. They managed to veer down a small street leading deeper into the city just before their spell wore off. The broken ground abruptly appeared whole again, the whole thing no more than an illusion.

The guard wiped the blood from his blade with an appreciative chuckle. "Clever," he said. "Now, go find them."

CHAPTER THIRTY-NINE

Martza's clothing was wet with blood, her disguise spells falling away as her vital energy drained from her body. The konus she wore had power, but gravely injured as she was, she lacked the requisite focus and intent to keep it in place. She had been carried to a quiet spot in a small garden. It was far from ideal, but the plants were tall enough that it would keep her away from prying eyes. At least for the moment.

Bawb and Elzina raced through the streets, their keen senses and specialized spells allowing them to zero in on the only spilled Ghalian blood in this place besides their own. After seeing what the master swordsman could do, they hoped the rest of theirs would not soon join it.

They found the others crouched low around their fallen comrade, looks of concern on their faces.

"How bad?" Bawb asked, his weapons sheathed, his hands ready to heal rather than harm.

The look in Usalla's eyes said as much as her words, if not more. "It is bad."

He didn't hesitate. Pulling deep from his limited stores of

power as well as his konus, Bawb began casting healing spells, hoping to at least stop the worst of the bleeding.

"Everyone, I need your power. Help me mend her enough to move."

The others did as he asked without hesitation, each of them pouring all the magic they could spare into their overlapping healing spells. Some were better at it than others, and the pain from the different spells and magic mixing would be sheer agony for Martza, but the results were what mattered, pain be damned, and soon her profuse bleeding slowed to a trickle.

They wanted to help more, but each was well aware they would likely need to keep some in reserve beyond what was being used for their disguises. Their confidence had just been gravely shaken. While they'd all been on missions and performed contracts of varying degrees of difficulty as Adepts, their success rate had been excellent. They believed, and rightly so for the most part, that they were simply more skilled than those they would face.

In most cases, that was true. But that overconfidence had just taught them a brutal lesson in humility. Never underestimate an enemy, and never overestimate your own abilities. It was something they all felt viscerally now. While they were extremely skilled, they also still had a lot to learn. Their humiliation at the hands of a lone swordsman, and facing several of them at once, no less, made that abundantly clear.

But first things first. They had just landed themselves square in the sights of the city's guards, who it seemed could very well be tied in with the roving bandits, if not members themselves. Whatever the case may be, their disguises needed to change, and fast.

"Pirates," Albinius said as if reading Bawb's mind.

"What's that?"

"Pirates. There were a couple of ships moored out there that looked like pirate craft. They're notorious for not having uniforms, as well as pretty diverse crews. And they come and go a lot."

Zota nodded his agreement. "He's right. We can shift disguises pretty easily that way."

"And pirates get hurt pretty often," Usalla noted. "It will reduce attention as we evacuate Martza."

"No," Martza's weak voice said. "Find Finnia first."

Bawb shook his head. "You have been gravely injured. We must get you out of this place."

"I said no. I realize the situation, but Finnia is our friend, and we did not come down here, and I did not sustain these injuries, for nothing."

The group nodded as one, silently admiring her guts, especially as her literal ones had been run-through by a sword.

"Okay, we move fast," Bawb said, a plan already forming in his head. "It is going to be tough."

"Of course it is," Albinius said, managing a little grin.

"Finnia will likely be held in a relatively accessible place. As the bandits are in cahoots with the guards, there would be no need for them to hide her. And we can take a lesson from our own overconfidence. They will likely feel invincible, and that leads to carelessness."

Elzina didn't like his words, given how the two of them had just had their asses thoroughly handed to them, but she knew he was right. "We will need to be brazen. Confident. We must move as pirates move. Hesitation will lead to our discovery."

"So we do not hesitate," Bawb replied. "We are Ghalian. This is what we do. Everyone, change your disguise and walk the city. Interact with locals and learn what you can. Pretend to be gathering supplies for your vessel. Or perhaps taking a shore leave. Rather than run, we walk. Rather than hide, we operate in plain sight. Whatever you choose, move fast. I worry we do not have much time. Dillar, will you stay with Martza?"

"I will. Just be quick about it. We are in a hidden but rather precarious position."

"Understood. I think we can do something about that. Albinius, stir up a commotion at the opposite end of the city. Something that will draw a lot of attention but not seem like an obvious diversion. That should buy us at least a little time. Once we have Finnia, we make for the exit, no delays, clear?"

"I'm on it," he replied, heading off in a hurry.

Bawb looked at the faces of his remaining classmates. All were ready to do whatever it took to get their friend back. "The rest of us need to fan out and learn where Finnia is being held. Use your konus and cast a minor smoke spell if you find her. Thin and barely noticeable. The rest of us will converge immediately."

There were no rah-rah words of encouragement or lengthy speeches. The Ghalian simply moved out at once without a word, hyper-focused on their task. And they had to be. Finnia and Martza's lives depended on it.

Bawb headed toward the docks nearest the center area of town. There was a rather extensive network of the floating walkways, but odds were there would be more visitors, as well as more ambient chatter, in the middle area. He walked with blustery bravado, having spent plenty of time among pirates in the past. This was a disguise he could pull off in his sleep, and that allowed him to pay extra attention to the snippets of conversations around him.

As he had hoped, there were several groups of pirates and unsavory traders closer to the docks. He blended in without an issue, delving deeper into the seedy den of scum and villainy near what seemed to be a black market of sorts. Only a few minutes later he cast the faint smoke spell. Finnia was there, tied up in plain sight.

It was a slave auction, he realized with rising disgust, and their friend, bloody and beaten, had been bound in heavy ropes and sat upon a low platform for display. Bawb had coin in his pocket, a habit regardless of where he might be going, even a camping expedition. And now he hoped it would serve him well.

"How much?" he asked the burly mountain of a man with a toad-like body and long, greasy hair, who was overseeing the slaves.

"She's a fresh one. Strong and young. She'll fetch a good price at auction."

"No shit," Bawb snarled, leaning into his pirate act. "That's why I asked how much. I'd buy her now and have my fun, if you know what I mean."

"I do, but you're not the only one showing interest. Come back at the auction tonight and try your luck."

Bawb withdrew the coin pouch from his tunic and handed it to the man. "I would think this should be adequate."

The man gave the contents a quick look then tossed it back.

"I'll get more at auction. If you really want this one, go see if you can find more coin. If not, you're out of luck."

"Listen, I—"

"I said come back later. Don't make me call the town guard."

Bawb held his tongue and stepped back, quickly taking in Finnia's injuries. She looked worse than she was, clearly. To anyone else, they might see a beaten and broken young woman. To him he saw a pissed off Ghalian spy biding her time.

Bawb walked away, as if browsing the other slaves up for auction, but his attention remaining on Finnia. Eventually, the overseer walked away to talk to a rugged-looking fellow looking at another slave. This was his chance.

He moved in close, covering the distance fast but not so fast as to draw unwanted attention. Rather than pull a blade, he palmed a piece of sharpened volcanic glass from his pocket and slipped it into Finnia's hand.

"I have come to get you out of here," he said quietly as she set to work slicing the bonds behind her back.

"Caught you!" an enraged voice bellowed, a meaty hand slamming down on Bawb's shoulder. "Thought you could pull a fast one on me, did you? Stealing a slave is a grave offense."

"I'm doing nothing of the sort," Bawb protested, but the man wasn't having it.

"Lies. All lies. Guards! Over here!"

"I wish you hadn't done that."

"I bet you do. But the law's the law, and your freedom is forfeit. I'm gonna make good money adding you to the auction."

Bawb's eyes scanned the growing crowd watching the mess unfolding before them, a chilling grin spreading across his face. "There's just one problem."

"Oh? And what kind of problem could you possibly pose?"

"Not me. *Them*."

The disguised Ghalian Adepts stepped forward from the throngs, weapons in hand, moving in and encircling them both. Finnia's ropes dropped free a moment later as they helped her finish unbinding herself. To the overseer's distress, he saw that someone had also handed her a dagger.

Before she could extract her revenge, however, a dozen guards charged at them from multiple directions, drawn by the man's shouts, and some of this lot were still wearing their camouflage attire. These were the bandits after all, it seemed, and the Adepts leapt into action, eager to repay a debt of blood and violence.

The fight was over quickly, the guards falling in rapid succession, but something caught Bawb's eye that made his stomach knot and his blood run cold. The swordsman they'd encountered earlier was charging right at them from the far end of the waterfront slave market, and twenty or more guards were right behind him.

"Run," he said loud enough for his friends to hear but not so loud as to give the bystanders the courage to step in, knowing they were fleeing. It was a funny thing how that worked. The most timid could become a threat if they knew they were not alone. They had to get clear fast for that very reason.

The Adepts raced through the streets, casting diversionary spells with the limited magic they had left. It wasn't enough to slow the pursuing swordsman by much, as they had used too much power on Martza. But it had to be done. There was no other option. They all hoped that it would not lead to their demise.

Dillar and Martza were just entering the tunnel's mouth when their classmates came into view, running toward the city exit. They had seen the smoke and moved slowly toward their egress, killing the sentry on the way and hiding his body before heading to the lava tube exit. Their friends' approach was the final thing they saw before hurrying into the dimly lit tunnel.

The others raced ahead, charging into the tunnel at speed. Bawb, Usalla, and Elzina stopped and cast the most powerful blocking spell they could. It was the same sort of magic one would use in space to keep a hole sealed in case of a breach. If it worked as intended, the specialized bit of magic, layered in triplicate, no less, would buy them enough time to get at least close to the surface. They raced ahead into the tunnel, knowing they would find out soon enough.

What they were unaware of was the lone figure appearing out of nowhere at the city exit, standing tall and blocking the path.

"Out of the way or perish!" the swordsman bellowed as he ran right for him.

The blue glow of the Vespus blade lit up the area as Hozark slid his shimmer cloak back fully, twirling the powerful sword with a casual ease. He was not supposed to intervene in the Adepts' training. For that matter, he wasn't even supposed to be anywhere near them at the moment. But since the ambush against Bawb he had been keeping a closer eye on him, and now, with his son in danger facing an adversary he could not yet hope to defeat, he made the conscious decision to cross that line without hesitation or regret.

The guard faltered at the sight of the weapon. The others might not have known what it was, but he did, and the blue glow meant just one thing. This was a Ghalian, and a Master at that. He slowed to a walk, preparing himself for what he knew would be the greatest sword fight he would ever face. With the slightest of nods to his opponent, he attacked, ready for whatever would come. Victory or defeat, this was going to be a glorious battle.

CHAPTER FORTY

Martza was in bad shape when the Adepts exited the lava tube tunnel, but the worst of her bleeding had slowed. How much they'd managed to heal in their improvised healing efforts they could not be sure, but she was still alive as they carried her off the beach and began the long trek to their campsite.

They quickly gathered up their things and moved out, leaving markings only other Ghalian would recognize, informing them where the Adepts had gone. They'd managed to get away from the raiding party, but it was pretty much guaranteed now that they would be pursued. With a gravely injured comrade and facing unknown numbers, flight into the woods was their best, and pretty much only, option. To stay and attempt to fight would be courting disaster.

Bawb took point, leading them deep into the wilderness away from the obvious landing site areas anyone looking for offworld intruders might search. When their teachers finally did return for them, they would make the trek to whichever landing site they had chosen, but not before.

A full day of paranoia passed into night, the Adepts taking shifts watching and listening for signs of any pursuers.

Normally, they would have laid an intricate web of tripwire and alarm spells, but their magic was otherwise spoken for, those now actively watching for danger also slowly drip-feeding additional healing spells into their wounded classmate.

Martza's internal injuries were severe, and they simply lacked the raw power to even attempt to cast a proper healing spell that would fully mend her. Instead, they cast a little here, a little there, tracking problems and addressing them as they arose, trying to stay one step ahead of the reaper. So far, it had worked. Whether or not they could maintain for several more days was another matter entirely.

Bawb climbed down from the tree he had been using for an elevated lookout post and went to check on her, dreading what he might find.

"How is she?" he asked, resting his hand on Usalla's shoulder as she crouched beside her.

"The same. Weak, though she is a fighter. But the injury is severe. Despite our efforts, I fear she may not survive."

"If we had a proper healer she would be fine," he lamented. "But here, now, we are stuck without the resources we desperately need. We do not even possess enough power between us all to effect a substantial cure."

"It is what it is," she said with an exhausted sigh. "We have trained for all eventualities. Even this."

"Yes, but we could do so much more for her. We just need power."

"Which we do not have. Our konuses are nearly tapped out and will require a full recharge when we return to the training house. Unfortunately, we simply do not have any options."

Bawb's gaze drifted off into the woods, the spark of an idea growing into a blaze in the blink of an eye.

"Keep an eye on her. I will be back as quickly as I am able."

"What are you going to do?"

"Anything I can to help her."

Bawb turned without another word and took off at a jog, not rushing, not leaving any traces as he went, gliding through the trees, but moving like a ghost in the wind. He circled their former campsite from a distance but saw no pursuers. At least not yet. It was entirely possible they had assumed the intruders would know better than to return there and therefore took alternate routes in their search.

He was pretty much unconcerned with that, continuing on at a faster clip now that he was far from his hiding classmates. He pressed on until he smelled the sea air fresh in his nose. Bawb slowed his pace and carefully peered out of the treeline. There were dozens of footprints in the churned sand, but the hidden entrance to the underwater city was unguarded.

Then again, it made sense. The people they wanted were on the run. Only a fool would come back. A fool, or a very clever Ghalian.

Bawb applied a new disguise spell, using the last of his available magic to alter his appearance just enough to blend in with the guards should he encounter any in the tunnel. He made himself look bloody, as if he'd been in quite a serious fight, then stepped through the camouflaged entrance and began his rapid descent.

There were signs of a large group passing recently, but it seemed they had all exited en masse, fanning out to find the brazen intruders who had killed their sentry and made off with a slave. The city guards were out for blood, and everyone knew it, so when he stepped into the city proper, looking worse for wear, no one even batted an eye.

Bawb made his way through the streets quickly, following his instincts as a Ghalian, sniffing out the magic user he knew had to be there somewhere.

"Found you," he said to himself quietly as he caught their scent.

With his disguise firmly in place, he trudged the remaining distance until he could see his destination, verifying what he had sensed.

"Is the healer in?" he asked, stepping into the healing establishment.

"I am here," an old woman said, stepping out from a side room. "Oh, you've had a rough go of it, I see. The escaped intruders do this?"

"They're a handful, let me tell ya."

"I can see that. Come to the back, and I'll fix you right up."

"Thanks," he replied, the very last drops of his magic about to expire. As soon as that happened, his disguise would fall away. Worse, the healer would sense that his injuries were not real, that last bit of misdirection a very specialized bit of Ghalian magic few outside the order even knew existed.

To look hurt was one thing. To look hurt to one sensitive to such things was another entirely.

He drew close as he followed her. Sure they were alone, he let his fangs slide into place, their tips piercing the flesh of the woman's neck with the utmost ease. She passed out from the magic loss almost immediately. Bawb caught her in his arms and kept draining her, pulling hard until she was almost tapped out but still maintaining enough blood and power to mend and survive. She was an innocent who simply possessed what he so desperately needed right now, nothing more.

Bawb gently lay the old woman on one of her exam tables.

"Thank you for your gift of power," he said quietly. "I apologize for taking it, but you will mend in time, and my friend needs it far more than you right now."

Bawb stepped out and closed the door then applied a fastening spell, his body now flush with an abundance of power.

He turned and made quick time back to the tunnel and up to the surface, not encountering another guard the entire time. Once safely in the fresh air above ground, he dropped the disguise and took off at a run.

He could see the tracks of the raiding group and guards clearly now. They had gone in a parallel direction to the one the Adepts had taken. A fluke of luck, it seemed, and one that would take them far enough away that his friends would be safely out of sight for a little while, at least.

He ran fast, pushing himself hard, scanning for traps, tripwires, and any signs of their enemy, but fortunately finding none. In relatively short order he approached their concealed hideout. Movement from above caught the corner of his eye.

"Where did you go?" Finnia asked as he approached, dropping silently from a tree, weapons strapped to her body, hoping for a chance at some payback.

"I had to get something," he replied, hurrying to Martza's side.

Bawb crouched down and rested his hands on her body.

"What are you doing?" Zota asked from his seat beside her where he'd been trickling what little magic he had into his friend.

"This."

Bawb shifted his focus to the unusual magic flowing inside of him. He had taken power from all sorts of casters in the past —typically mercenaries and henchmen—but this was healer's magic, something he'd never thought he would steal. It was sort of an unwritten rule; leave the healers out of it.

But Martza was in dire need, and that outweighed all else.

His body shuddered as the different type of magic latched onto the intent behind his healing spells. With a jolt he felt it flow through him and out into his unconscious classmate. His hands itched and tingled as he actually sensed her flesh mending beneath his touch. Martza writhed in pain, rousing from her daze.

"Is it working?" Finnia asked. "She is in great discomfort."

"It is, I can feel it. Allow me to concentrate."

Bawb carried on, wielding the new magic clumsily by any standards, but doing far more good than harm. The leaking blood vessels in her body were sealing and reattaching where the blade had sliced them, her muscles and organs holding together where his amateur attempts had forced them to heal, albeit rather sloppily.

But the important thing was, it seemed she was out of the woods.

Bawb sat back, a bit dizzy from the effort. Healing, it turned out, was a very different beast when using healer magic. Not exactly something he wanted to make a regular practice out of, but yet another useful skill in his Ghalian toolbox.

"What happened?" Teacher Demelza's unexpected voice demanded as she appeared seemingly out of nowhere, her eyes scanning the injured students, Martza in particular.

"Where did you come from? I did not see you approach," Finnia marveled.

Demelza nodded upward. A silent shimmer ship was hovering directly above the trees, only the open hatch visible from below.

"I was checking in on you, as we teachers do from time to time. A good thing, it seems." She crouched beside Martza and assessed her status. "Who did this to her?"

Bawb shook the fuzz from his mind. "Bandits. Bandits who are aligned with the guards of a nearby underwater city."

Demelza shook her head, clearly annoyed. "They should not have been a problem. They should have remained far away and unaware of your group. We leave them to their business and they to ours."

"Not this time."

"Clearly. But I see you suffered no losses. How did they fare?"

An angry grin creased Elzina's lips. "Not so lucky," she said with open malice.

Demelza nodded but said no more about the matter. They had clearly been through a lot. There would be plenty of time for a debriefing back home. Right now, their extrication was the priority.

"I will take Martza back with me, but the shimmer ship is too small for all of you."

"We will be fine," Bawb said, rising back to his feet. "We can take care of ourselves."

"Just avoid them until you are retrieved. We do not need any further conflict."

"Understood."

"I will skree for a transport to come at once. You will be off this island by morning."

Demelza bundled up their fallen classmate in her arms and activated a pulling spell, lifting her up through the trees and into her ship. The hatch sealed a moment later, the craft once more invisible. Then, they assumed, she was gone.

"What now?" Albinius wondered. "What if they find us?"

"Then we kill them all," Finnia replied with a cold look in her eyes.

"They have headed in a different direction, at least for now," Bawb informed them. "So we should get some rest and await our ride. I will keep first watch."

The others didn't bother protesting. They'd all used up their energy to a dangerous degree. A bit of rest would do them all good, though none would sleep soundly. Soon enough they would be home, however, and there they would be able to sleep deep and sound, safe in the heart of the Ghalian compound.

CHAPTER FORTY-ONE

Bathed and rested, safe in their training house, the Adepts were given the rare free day to do with as they pleased. Whether inside the compound or out in the world, they had faced and survived a daunting challenge and had not only come out on top, but also shown exceptional teamwork and quick thinking in the face of adversity.

In this sort of situation, the informal Ghalian code of working alone was very much set aside, and on occasion, even Masters would sometimes join forces if the situation warranted it. Solo operations were the standard most definitely, but also certainly not the hard rule.

Finnia had been summoned for a long debrief with Master Imalla upon her return, and the anger dredged up in the process shocked her. She had thought herself past all that, but being kidnapped, beaten, and nearly sold into slavery had caused her to reassess. As a result, she spent her free day training hard, letting the thump of her fists and knees on the padded targets and clangs of her blades on their mobile practice dummies drain at least some of the feelings from her body.

She would be fine, the Masters had decided. In fact, this

incident could actually prove beneficial for her, as she was on the spy path. More than any other Ghalian, they were the ones most likely to be put in those sorts of situations. And while they typically didn't wish for Adepts to be captured and tormented like that, the girl had persevered and come through it with flying colors. In fact, it seemed likely she would be an even better spy because of it.

In an odd way, it had helped her overcome the one thing they could not teach. The spy students had trained and prepared for this sort of thing, naturally, but having experienced it first-hand, it seemed that what was previously a worrisome possibility had just had its threatening mystique evaporate in an instant. She knew what to expect now, and she was stronger for it.

As for Elzina, she had reacted to their defeat the way one might expect of her. Namely, she sulked off in a huff to go take out her aggressions on some of the more dangerous beasts lurking in the deepest dungeon levels of the training course. A violent sort of mediation, one could say.

For Bawb and Usalla it was a very different sort of vibe. They had spent the morning talking. Nothing more than that, just two very good friends spending time together. Without the pressures of training or missions, it was a refreshing change of pace for both of them. One that left them mentally recharged when they parted ways. She was heading to relax in the thermal baths on the second level. He, on the other hand, just wandered the halls, replaying what had happened over and over with an almost compulsive repetition.

Different as they were in almost every way, one thing was the same for Bawb as it had been for Elzina, though he handled it differently. Even after talking it through with Usalla, running over all the variables this way and that, he was still taken aback at their abject failure, albeit against a far superior swordsman.

He had allowed himself to become overconfident in his abilities. Not cocky, but not as cautious as he should have been. They all had. And they had all very nearly paid the ultimate price as a result.

You did as well as you could, given your level, the konus said, uncharacteristically polite in its tone.

"We nearly died."

But you didn't, and that's what counts, am I right? I mean, sure, you got your butts kicked, and good at that, but as the one keeping track of your progress, trust me when I say you were still punching well above your weight on that one. He was just better than you. A lot better.

"He fought all three of us like it was nothing. And Elzina and I are the top of our class."

Yeah, I didn't want to mention it, but there was that.

Bawb shifted his course, a new objective firmly in mind.

He found the objects of his interest in one of the smaller sparring courtyards, enjoying some fresh air as they moved through their forms. Even for Masters such as Hozark and Demelza, training was a constant part of their existence. It was the only way a Ghalian could ever hope to see old age.

"Hello, Adept Bawb," Demelza greeted him, halting her form. Hozark did the same, giving him a little nod in way of greeting.

"Train me."

The two looked at each other a moment. "You *are* being trained, Bawb," Hozark said, picking up on a troubling energy about the young man.

"No. I mean *really* train me."

There it was. He was acting in anger, his emotions riding high. They both knew what had happened, of course, and being upset was understandable. But Ghalian must not become emotional. In this instance, however, both Hozark and Demelza came to a silent agreement. They would help the boy excel beyond his Adept training if they could.

Hozark gave Demelza a little nod.

"Very well. But only if we deem you ready. Let's see what you can do," she said, tossing him a sword, twirling hers with a relaxed ease that looked almost effortless.

Bawb did not need nudging. Not after what had happened. Not today. He lunged into an attack, using more force than necessary in his emotionally charged haste. Demelza parried and countered in a flash, slapping his flank with the flat of her blade.

"Focus, Bawb. Calm your emotions. Try again," Hozark chided from the sidelines.

Again he pressed an attack, and again Demelza countered him, but at least he seemed to be doing his best to get his emotions under control. A slight grin curved her lips. "Better. Again."

They went on like this for several more rounds, Bawb forcing himself to focus while Demelza subtly ramped up the speed until they were moving far faster than the Adept realized he could.

"Enough," Hozark called out. "Not bad, Bawb. Not bad at all."

"Thank you, Master. And thank you, Teacher."

"It is my pleasure to help you improve," she replied, but also giving him a slightly pensive look. "I am curious about something. Take my sword." She offered him the Vespus blade grip-first.

He reached out and gently took the razor-sharp weapon from her hands, feeling the power thrum in his palms as he wrapped his fingers around the grip. The blade reacted to him, not in a brief flash as had happened before, but generating a steadily growing blue glow. He watched it, fascinated, feeling the power of the weapon mingle with his own. Whether it was the healer's magic still in his system causing the reaction or something else he didn't know. What he did know was an Adept was not supposed to be able to do that.

Demelza and Hozark were actually smiling when he handed her back the sword.

"We will train you, Bawb," Hozark declared. "But how far you progress depends entirely on your own efforts. Your own drive and will to succeed. We can only provide you the tools."

"That is all I can ask."

"Then it shall be so. But realize, this will further eat into what little free time you may have."

"Worth it. When do we begin?"

Hozark drew his blade and walked toward him. "Now seems as good a time as any, would you not agree?"

Months passed in a flash for Bawb, the training indeed taking up a great deal of his limited free time, his every waking moment not actively studying in class, training with the others, or out on a mission, now spent practicing and perfecting his swordplay.

He met with both Hozark and Demelza frequently now, working until his arms felt like rubber from his efforts, then doing it all over again. And in short order the hard determination began to pay off. So much so that Master Hozark would have him spar not only with normal weapons, but also with his Vespus blade, a weapon whose heft, balance, and stored power he soon came to know as if the sword was his own.

Hozark warmed to him in those sessions, acting less like a stoic Ghalian and more like a caring friend as his training progressed. A bond was forming between them, forged over sweat, blood, and sore muscles, and Bawb even stopped considering him "one of the Five," but rather, "Hozark, my mentor." More than any adult he had known, Bawb came to cherish his relationship with the Master Ghalian more than he ever thought he could.

And Hozark's feelings for the boy were clear as well, something Bawb found unbelievable yet true. The most skilled of the Ghalian, Master Hozark himself, *liked* him. This was not just a duty to him. He genuinely wanted to help.

To that end, Hozark did more than just train the young man. He went so far as to vouch for his new skills even though he was still an Adept, getting him sent on increasingly difficult tasks that a Ghalian of his rank would simply not normally be given. And all this while Hozark still carried out his own contracts, performing the same duties he had always done as a Ghalian regardless of rank, but also never failing to make time to spend with Bawb.

It was a relationship blossoming into something special, and the Adept realized just how lucky he was. Hozark was more than a teacher or Master or even mentor. He was a friend. And Bawb's life would never be the same.

CHAPTER FORTY-TWO

With accelerated training came increasingly challenging contracts, and Bawb found himself reveling in the intensity of the new experiences. He had hit his stride in the past several months, his sessions with Master Hozark in particular truly ramping up some of his skills to well beyond his current level. In addition, the legendary Ghalian had been teaching him many of the hidden arts of the Ghalian in increasingly frequent drips of information.

These weren't just any skills. These were techniques and spells only known to a handful, even among the Ghalian. Students at the highest levels might eventually learn some of them, but only those groomed for consideration for the Five ever learned them all. Those who were more than just students. Those whom a Master found worthy of the rarest of honors in the order.

To become an apprentice.

Master Hozark had not officially declared Bawb's apprenticeship. To do so would have drawn more attention to the young man, possibly distracting him just as he was finding his groove. But more than that, he had never taken an apprentice before, and to do so with this young man could very possibly lead to someone discovering his true provenance. With enough digging and putting together of the fine threads of the story, Bawb's origins could be unearthed.

If they learned that Hozark was his father, that could be worked around, though a bit uncomfortably, given he had kept that secret hidden from even the other members of the Five. But if they learned that his mother was none other than the alleged traitor and former Ghalian Master Samara, *that* could pose serious problems for him moving forward.

Having lineage tied to one of the only Ghalian Masters to ever leave the order, a woman who had worked for the enemy, albeit under duress, could mark him as unworthy of the honor. And at this age, knowing what he did of their techniques and secrets, expulsion would not suffice. He knew too much, and death would be the only option.

That his mother was also one of the most talented swordsmen the Ghalian had ever seen was inconsequential. And only Hozark knew her true reasons for fleeing the order. It was a secret he had sworn he would take to his grave. Ghalian did not bond with one another, and they certainly did not have children. And yet, here in these halls, excelling beyond his years, was the result of that forbidden union. Bawb. Son of Master Hozark of the Five and the traitor Master Samara. A regular student so far as the others knew, and Hozark was going to keep it that way.

Demelza knew, as did Bud and Henni, but they had been with Hozark during the tumultuous events leading to his discovery that he had fathered a child. It had never been explicitly declared to them outright, but they were privy to just enough information by direct proximity to piece it together themselves. But incredible as it was, this was a tale they simply could never share. With all of the blood and sweat spilled together in their many battles and brushes with death, the three swore among themselves to keep his secret safe. And now, as they had watched the boy grow into a fine young man any would be proud of, their dedication to that secrecy only grew stronger.

Bawb was carrying himself a little differently of late, and the Masters noticed it, no matter how subtle it may have been. He moved with the confidence of one who was both aware of their skills but also their shortcomings, ready and eager to learn more and face whatever challenges might be thrown his way. It was something they saw eventually in each student who would progress to Maven and beyond. Bawb just happened to be evolving a bit earlier than normal.

It was enough to give them reason to heed Hozark's backing the boy for more challenging missions, and they had an interesting contract that had just been vetted by their spy network. Not the most difficult in terms of brute strength and fighting skills, but rather one that would require a flexibility of mind as well as combative abilities.

"Adept Bawb, there is a new contract for you," Master Imalla told him.

She had been directly interacting with him more and more these past months, debriefing him after missions herself, noting the progress he was making with great pleasure. This student, she was certain, would grow to be quite an asset to the order.

"Whatever it is, I am happy to oblige, Master."

"As I knew you would be. A shimmer ship has been dedicated to you for this task. You will find the details aboard."

Bawb felt his heart beat just a little faster, though he restrained his blush reflex with well-practiced skill. "A shimmer ship? But I am an Adept."

"You are, yes. And you will almost certainly be unable to attain full cloaking of the craft. But the best form of practice is to simply do it. Masking your presence will not be crucial in the landing phase of your contract, but this will afford you the opportunity to test your shimmer spellcasting in a real-world situation."

"I gladly accept the offer, Master Imalla. Thank you for the confidence."

"You have earned it, Bawb. Your progress of late has been most impressive. I hope you continue along this track. I am confident you will grasp the fine points of shimmer casting soon. It is just a matter of time."

Spirits high, Bawb was in the air in less than an hour, sitting at the helm of a shimmer ship solo for the very first time. Hozark had been giving him lessons for some time now, but to be on his own without the training wheels was something of a rush.

He arrived at his destination world after several long jumps. The ship had a very robust Drookonus, and there was no need to conserve power where transit was concerned, but taking his time allowed him to fully brief himself on the contract at hand. Rushing would achieve nothing, and he would just have to sit and plan on-site rather than en route. The difference was minimal, so he decided to save the ship's power even though it had plenty to spare. A good habit well worth having, for it would not always be like this.

He pored over the details of the mission several times, absorbing them like a sponge, eager and quite looking forward to discussing it with Hozark when he got home. A shimmer ship? And this sort of unusual infiltration? It was an exciting outing he could not wait to talk about.

But first, he had to actually achieve his goal. No sense getting ahead of himself, after all.

As it turned out, once he landed and got to see the linked structures and the surrounding network of guard facilities and subterranean escape tunnels linking it all together, Bawb realized this was going to take longer than he had anticipated. A *lot* longer. With quiet resolve, he set to work, modifying his plan and putting it into action.

It took five full days for him to track and replace one of the facility staff he learned was not so vital as to be noticed missing, but not so low on the rankings as to lack or be denied access. The person had been taken out quietly, hit with a powerful stun spell then administered a hefty dose of a sleeping toxin. When they awoke, it would be days later, and Bawb would be long gone.

Bawb approached the main entry gate, a large double-doored affair with steely-gazed Zarfin beasts on either side. The animals were chest-tall and possessed a thick, slate-gray coat of fur that possessed a degree of metal in its matrix. That made them particularly difficult to fight, which led to their widespread use as guard animals. That and their well-documented ferocity.

But the guards did not know one crucial thing. Of the various animals Bawb had learned his empathic connection abilities worked on, Zarfin were particularly open to his communication. And after his first few encounters, Bawb had learned they were quite happy to let him pass if he simply provided them a few treats. They were treated like monsters, rough-handled and to be feared. Being handled like something else, and with kindness, no less, went a long way.

Teacher Griggitz had told him that it was a rare gift he possessed and that empaths were typically not found among Ghalian. Bawb downplayed his abilities, but the teacher's words inspired him, driving him to seek out more encounters with animals to hone his skills. One day all that work would surely pay off. As it turned out, today was that day.

"Hello, my friends," he said, approaching calmly, a sizeable Banziki legbone in each hand. "I have brought you something you might enjoy."

The guards were inside the guardhouse at the gate,

confident the Zarfin would handle any intruders and alert them whenever someone arrived. It made handing them each their treat that much easier.

"Enjoy. You are deserving of the best, you know. I am sorry the people you work for do not appreciate your full worth," he added as he passed the contented creatures. They didn't speak back— that was an ability they lacked—but the looks in their eyes conveyed more than enough. "Maybe one day you will be free to live your lives as you wish, not chained to the walls of this place. I wish you the best. Be well, my friends."

He knew they'd likely never achieve those ends, but planting that seed in their minds would only help him if they decided to make an attempt at escaping their servitude. That bit of added chaos would help cover his tracks, as would their simply eating one of the guards before they managed to trigger a control spell.

In any case, his passing the guardians told the gatekeepers that he was staff cleared for entrance better than any pass phrase ever could. And wearing the familiar face of someone they recognized at a glance, he was admitted without them even pausing their conversation.

He was in. It had taken nearly a week, but he'd gotten within the walls. Now the hard part began.

Once inside he discovered the true nature of the place. For one, there were a lot more guards walking the grounds than he anticipated. There were also more Zarfin, though he knew he could handle those with relative ease and no bloodshed. He noted a few other creatures as well and made sure to steer clear of them. While he could communicate with the Zarfin, these others did not seem to react to his attempts. Just one more surprise to deal with. But that was Ghalian life. Adapt, overcome, prevail.

The thing about the spy network was it had gotten a truly great deal of information, but there were always tidbits they simply could not attain without a lengthy and costly infiltration. Taking the identity of established staff was one thing if it was only for a few days. Becoming an actual part of the employee group was another entirely, and one that took weeks, if not months or even years. That sort of access and the information that came with it could almost never be gotten any other way.

Bawb did not have weeks. He had a few more days, at most, before his stunned victim would rouse and return to work, albeit a bit confused at the missing days of their life. That meant he had to find the item he had been tasked with stealing sooner rather than later.

It was a skree, but no ordinary communications device. This was tied in to the Council of Twenty's secure network, and as such, possessing it would allow the Ghalian to learn their plans in advance as well as possibly help them discover whether the mole in the organization was in fact communicating with them directly, as they thought.

He had a replacement with him. Identical to their long-range skree but modified to fail and self-destruct when used. Sometimes, magic failed, and when it did, especially in secure locations like this, no one thought much of it. They would simply replace the device and toss the defunct item in the scrap heap, none the wiser they had been compromised.

But first, Bawb had to find it. And that would take a bit of work.

Resigned to his task, he set to it, delving into the underground tunnel network with the external confidence of a long-time staffer, following his instincts as much as his limited intel as he began his search for the secure skree. It would be in a specialized holding area, no doubt. Perhaps even a secret room. Whatever the case, he would find it, swap it out, and make his escape. There was simply no other option. Whether he would be discovered in the process or not remained to be seen.

CHAPTER FORTY-THREE

Blending in was easier than Bawb had expected it to be. It seemed that once you were inside, getting around was actually almost completely unrestricted. As a result, the massive amount of guards on-site didn't really have much to do, but they patrolled continually regardless. Bawb quickly learned their routes and schedules and did his best to be conveniently where they were not.

That part was relatively simple.

The difficult part was something none of their intel had prepared him for. Different tunnels, corridors, and buildings had unique passcodes and mechanisms to gain entry. Anyone could walk up to them, but to get in was another thing entirely. And to make an incorrect attempt would mean a very quick up-close-and-personal introduction to the guards and their Zarfin.

This was going to take a while.

Bawb made the rounds for a few days, doing his best to observe and capture the various entry protocols. It was akin to codebreaking, which he had been quite good at in class, but this required piecing together the snippets he managed to catch over the course of many observed entrances.

He got them, eventually—there was little doubt that he would—and he made his entrance with stealth and efficiency, searching each location for the tell-tale power signature of the device he sought. Progress was being made, but it took far longer than he had originally anticipated.

Worse, he had managed to gain entry into nearly two-thirds of the restricted areas before he finally came upon what he was looking for. Any longer would have been a serious problem. The stunned person he was impersonating would be waking soon, so that was fortunate timing on his side. Unfortunate were the multiple tripwires and warding spells locking down the otherwise normal-looking set of drawers he felt sure the skree was housed in.

Another full day went into accessing the drawers, proving himself correct, then freeing the skree from the intricate web of protections, replacing it with the dummy device, and finally resetting all the wards and tripwires just as he had found them. By the time he stepped out of the compound he had been awake for nearly four days and was utterly exhausted. Exhausted, but victorious as he climbed aboard the shimmer ship and lifted off into space.

He jumped once to get clear of the planet just in case anyone noticed him, as unlikely as that seemed. Then he crawled into the lone bunk space and fell sound asleep, drifting in the frozen black of deep space. Bawb had pushed himself hard, and his body needed the rest badly, and as a result, he slept for nearly sixteen hours straight. He finally roused himself, ate a filling but not overly heavy meal, then napped for another three hours.

That finally seemed to have done the trick, the Adept waking with greatly renewed energy and clarity of thought. It was one thing to be sleep-deprived, but being so while engaged in heavy brain work was far worse. The sheer amount of energy it required to stay alert, maintain the disguise spells, and avoid discovery, all while simultaneously scanning for the faintest magic signature of a well-hidden device was significant. The drain was made even more pronounced because it was unrelenting. Days of that, non-stop, would test anyone's resolve, and most would fail.

But Bawb, of course, was not like most others.

He sat a long while in the command seat with a warm cup of soothing modinza tea, staring out at the billions of specks of light in the inky black, each of them a sun with its own solar system, and a few of those planets scattered among them actually habitable.

Small was how he felt drifting in the endless black. Not in a depressing way but rather an introspective one. In all of the immense galaxy of empty space and complex matter, he was no more than a speck in the vastness of it all. And yet he had life and consciousness. The ability for rational thought and emotion. Even at this age, the wonders of life still amazed him sometimes, and he was glad for it.

A few hours of meditative pondering left him absolutely energized and ready to return to the training house, victorious in his endeavor, even if he was arriving more than a week later than expected. But that didn't matter to him. Not with his spirits so high. It had been a fantastic mission, and difficult in novel ways. And despite the challenges he faced, Bawb had been successful.

His mood bright and satisfied, Bawb finally fired up the Drookonus and began the series of jumps that would take him back home. There was one thing he wanted to do first, though.

He detoured a few times along the way, taking the time to delve into the atmosphere of uninhabited planets to practice the ship's shimmer spell. Boosting his spirits even more, the magic actually felt like it was finally starting to take hold. As if shimmer cloaking an entire ship was no longer out of his reach.

The ship's shimmer cloak never fully engaged, of course, but for whatever reason, the use of it now actually seemed to be clicking to a degree. Like learning to whistle, now that he had gotten the slightest bit of success it was making sense. His ultimate goal didn't seem so far away anymore, and it was a satisfying feeling.

He couldn't have asked for a better mission outcome, and as a result, Bawb was positively glowing with contentedness when he walked into the training house. Master Imalla would be expecting him, naturally, but he swung by the dining hall on his way to see her and grabbed a small snack first. He had done a good job, and the extra few minutes of delay would not upset her, he was certain.

Stepping back into the hallway, he bumped into Usalla's familiar shape. He beamed wide, happy to see his dear friend and eager to tell her about his mission's great success. There was an odd look on her face, however. One he hadn't seen her wear before.

"Hello, Usalla," he said with uncharacteristic cheer.

"Bawb," she replied almost timidly, which was something he'd never known her to be.

"You sound odd."

"I am as fine as I can be, I suppose. But you... are you okay?"

"I am. Better than okay, in fact. I completed my contract without a scratch. No injuries whatsoever."

"No. That is not what I mean. I mean, are you *okay*?"

"What are you talking about, Usalla? You are acting rather strangely."

Her eyes widened slightly as she realized he didn't know. "You need to go speak with Teacher Demelza."

"What is going on?"

"See Teacher Demelza, Bawb."

"Very well, if you insist. But first I need to—"

"No. You must see her *now*. Promise me."

He thought about it for only a split-second. Whatever was up, Usalla thought it was urgent. He trusted her implicitly and would do as she asked. Master Imalla could wait a tiny bit longer.

"Very well, I will go find her."

"She is in her chambers."

"Her chambers? Then I should wait until she is—"

"Go there, Bawb," she said, her voice low with uncharacteristic emotion. "Go now."

He heard something worrisome in her tone, and the remnants of his jovial cheer evaporated in an instant. "I will at once," he replied, then hurried down the corridor, wondering what in the world was upsetting her so.

CHAPTER FORTY-FOUR

"Enter," Demelza's voice called out when he knocked on her door.

Bawb stepped across the threshold into her private chambers, more than a little uncomfortable doing so. This was off-limits to students. A teacher's place to separate themself from the workplace. He looked around at the spacious suite of rooms, taking it all in for what he assumed would be the only time.

Demelza had traveled far and accomplished many things in her years, and a tasteful collection of art and decorative items adorned her walls and shelves. She had kept her rooms relatively empty, opting for a less-is-more approach to her living space, and it gave the whole area a very clean and open, yet cozy and intimate feeling.

Her personal collection of specialized weapons hung on a wall dedicated for the purpose, her mighty Vespus blade not prominently displayed in the center, but rather just hung up in a utilitarian manner along with the other items. This was a tool, not something she cared to brag of. A tool she undoubtedly valued above all others, but one she still did not make a big deal about. Typical Ghalian behavior, in other words.

He stepped further into her rooms and saw her kneeling on a cushion in front of a small, low table. A lone candle burned in front of her, the deep red wax letting off a strange scent the likes of which he had never encountered before. Beside it was a simple wooden box. She took it in her hands and rose to her feet. If Bawb didn't know better, he would have sworn there were traces of tears in her eyes.

"This is yours now," she said softly, handing him the container.

"I do not understand," he said as he pulled back the lid. His confusion grew even greater when he saw what was inside. "This is Master Hozark's shimmer cloak. Why are you—" But he knew the answer before the words left her lips.

"Master Hozark was killed several days ago on the planet Radzor. Betrayed by someone with intimate knowledge of our network."

Bawb felt as though a tidal wave of ice had just crashed over him, slamming him hard and pinning him to the bottom of the sea. He fought to regain his breath, adrenaline, emotion, pain, and rage all swirling within like a tsunami of despair.

"What happened?" he managed to say, his throat tight with barely contained emotion.

"It was an elaborate setup. Someone went to great lengths to ensure he was outnumbered and overpowered. Few details have made it our way at this point, but our spies are prying for more information."

"It cannot be. He is too powerful. Too skilled."

"He was. But even the best of us will fall someday. We only hope to do so in a glorious manner. From what we have managed to learn, we can at least take comfort in the knowledge that he made whomever was involved pay dearly, leaving dozens of corpses in his wake, casters and mercenaries alike. The exact details are still unknown, but the bodies seen being removed from the scene tell the tale. It was a fate worthy of one of the Five."

"Master Hozark's remains?"

"Gone. But they were just a container for his essence. We do not need his body to pay our respects."

Bawb's face remained blank, his expression calm and utterly normal to anyone who would have seen it. This was the culmination of his Ghalian training, but in a way he never anticipated. The anger, the grief, were all condensing into a ball of white-hot rage, but rather than exploding outward, he took that hard lump and buried it deep within himself, his body using it and refining it, sharpening his intent to a razor's-edge hone.

"Are you okay, Bawb?" Demelza asked, locking eyes with him.

"Yes. If you will excuse me, I have something I must deliver to Master Imalla. Thank you for being the one to inform me of our loss. I know you and he had a long friendship, and I am deeply sorry for your loss."

"Thank you, Bawb. And I am sorry for yours."

He nodded once and quickly stepped out before his emotions could flare up and show themselves. Master Hozark was dead, his body taken and discarded by his killers, his Vespus blade lost forever. The only reason his shimmer cloak remained was he had not required it for his contract. At least, so he had thought.

Bawb walked to his bunk and deposited the cloak with his possessions then sank down and sat quietly a long while, processing as his world spun around him. Finally, he rose to his feet, took a deep breath, and headed to see Master Imalla, the specialized skree in-hand. When he entered her chamber, however, he was surprised to see several other Masters there with her. More surprising, Bud and Henni were there too, as was a woman he had never seen before.

"Bawb, you have something for me?" Imalla asked.

He placed the skree on her desk and stepped back, standing attentive but at ease. She looked the device over, nodding solemnly. "Well done, Adept. You have yet again proven your worth beyond your years."

"Thank you, Master," he replied, his expression neutral.

She studied him a long moment, as did the older woman sitting beside her.

"Are you okay, Bawb?"

"Why would I not be?" he replied, well aware of Henni's presence so close by. She was a reader, and he had no idea if she was picking up what he was keeping bottled up inside. Whatever the case, she remained silent.

Imalla nodded then glanced to her side.

"Adept Bawb, we have not met before," the newcomer said. "I am Master Corann."

He knew the name, of course. Hozark had mentioned it, as had others. And now the leader of the Five was here, talking to *him*.

"An honor," he said with a little bow.

"I have heard a lot about you over the years, Adept Bawb. And I now see with my own eyes you are every bit the Ghalian I expected to find. You have completed a contract well above the level of one your age," she noted, picking up the skree and turning it over in her hands. "I see Hozark taught you well."

"Thank you, Master Corann." He hesitated, then spoke. If ever there was a time to overstep, this was it. "Master? Do we have any idea who did this to Master Hozark?"

Corann hesitated a split second, assessing him in a flash. Should she share details with a mere Adept? In this one instance, she felt an exception was warranted.

"We do not know for certain yet. Whoever it was who is responsible for this act, they have access to vast resources and yet have managed to keep themselves hidden from our prying eyes."

"So we do not have any leads?"

"It will take time, Bawb. But rest assured, the Ghalian will avenge Hozark's death."

From what details he had heard, the young man did not feel so confident. His friends, clearly distraught, apparently felt the same.

"And what if you guys don't find the piece of shit responsible for this?" Henni growled, her eyes sparkling with rage.

"Control your emotions, Henni," Corann chided. "Rein in your power."

Amazingly, Henni seemed to listen to the woman, forcing herself to calm down. Bawb was a bit shocked. He had never seen anyone have that sort of effect on her. Apparently, Corann was the exception to the rule.

"Sorry, Corann. But listen, I want to get these bastards as bad as anyone, but from what I have heard so far, they left nothing to track them by. Aside from a heap of dead bodies, that is, and even those were taken away and disposed of."

"And it seemed all of them were muscle for hire," Bud added. "Whoever coordinated this did it in a way that couldn't lead back to them. All of our contacts are hitting dead ends. They left no trace."

Bawb turned to his pirate friends, calm resolve forming within him. "There is always a trace," he said with certainty. "Master Hozark taught me that."

"And he's dead, Bawb," Henni shot back, tears in her eyes. "They fucking killed him."

Bawb's emotions threatened to burst forth like the pressure

of a surging wave cracking the foundations of his internal dam. Somehow, he managed to force them back. To keep them in check. And as he did, all of that energy, all of those feelings, condensed and coalesced in his belly, added themselves to the growing knot in his gut.

I know this is a shitty time, but I thought you should know, Level up: Resolve, Self-control, Intent. More power has been unlocked for your use.

Bawb took the information in stride, his mind already racing, planning ahead. Master Hozark was dead. The man who had supported him since his youth. The one who took him under his wing and helped him grow beyond his ranking. Who showed him he could be so much more.

A cool resolve washed over him, his destiny now a certainty in his mind and heart. Bawb would become one of the Five no matter what it took. Not now, clearly. Hozark's death meant someone else would step up to fill that role at this time. But some day, when he was ready, he would ascend.

For now, his first order of business was to do all he could to help avenge his mentor. But a concern weighed on him. What if the Ghalian could not find who did this?

You know the answer to that, his konus said quietly.

And he did.

A calm confidence like he had never felt before flowed through his body, aligning his mind and spirit with utter certainty in his success. The feeling faded quickly, but it had been there, and he knew it for what it was. This must be what it felt like to be a true Ghalian. A Master. To be completely at one with your mind and body and power.

His konus flashed something new on his invisible display. Not unblurring one of the skills he had long wondered about, but rather, a new branch to the tree of abilities he had never even seen before. And while the konus remained silent, the words were clear. *Path to the Five*.

With that, he knew he was on the right course, his actions clear. *If the Ghalian cannot find Hozark's killer*, he thought with certainty, *then someday, no matter how long it takes,* I *will.*

CHAPTER FORTY-FIVE

Bawb, Demelza, Bud, and Henni sat alone in the dining hall, sipping on the drinks they were sharing in remembrance of their friend. As for food, no one had much of an appetite.

"A truly good one," Henni said, draining her cup.

Bud nodded solemnly. "One of the best."

Bawb only sipped on his drink. He wanted a clear mind as he processed all of the new information he had just had dumped on him. He had always been good at spotting patterns. Hidden messages and things others might overlook. If there was something to find, he would damn well find it.

"I do not understand how, with all the resources at our disposal, the network of spies and informants, we do not yet have so much as an idea who was responsible for this," he grumbled. "He had enemies, of course. Anyone in our line of work would. But we are anonymous. Untraceable. Who could possibly know to target him in such a manner?"

Demelza was good friends with Bud and Henni, having shared a lot of spilled blood with them in her younger years. Speaking plainly with them was a given. But Bawb was an Adept. Yes, an exceptional one, as well as the son of the

317

deceased, but nevertheless, a student. Today, however, she would speak openly.

She drained her cup and refilled it, Bawb noticed. That was unlike her.

"There are *some* signs," she said.

Now Bawb thought *that* was an interesting twist that would have been good to know earlier. "Why did no one mention this?"

"Because if they are correct, there is nothing to do. No one to exact revenge from." She glanced at Bud and Henni with a knowing look. Bud's face paled as an impossible realization gut - punched him.

"No. You can't be serious. *Maktan*?"

"No way," Henni blurted. "No fucking way!"

The name was familiar to Bawb, as well it should be. "There is a Visla Yoral Maktan. A young, low-ranking member on the Council of Twenty."

Demelza shook her head. "Not him. He was but a boy when this would have begun. I speak of his father Tozorro Maktan."

"That son of a bitch?" Henni growled. "He's dead. Like, *very* dead. Hozark killed his ass."

"Indeed he did, and a long time ago at that."

"Wait," Bawb said, confused. "You knew a visla personally?"

Bud's fingers paled as he clutched his cup, his anger clear. "Yeah, you could say that."

Bawb shook his head, confused. "If he's dead, his involvement would be impossible."

Demelza took another drink. "One would think, yes. But there are whispers, just the faintest of hints, that before his demise Visla Maktan put a contingency plan in place in the event of his death. One with the full resources of his estate backing it."

"What sort of plan?"

"A small team of specialized agents loyal to him would seek

out his killer, no matter how long it took, and one day, they would exact their revenge. Of course, if this rumor is true, that would mean they have been working quietly all this time, hunting in secret, gathering information at a slow pace until the absolute best opportunity presented itself. It would be a work of years, you see, Bawb. One that was put in place before you even joined the order." She let out a pained chuckle. "The funny thing is, they were very Ghalian-like in their execution of their plan. Patient. Cunning. Stealthy. For that, even Hozark would grudgingly give them credit. It was a masterful use of subterfuge, violence, and trickery."

Bawb's head was spinning, and not from drink. A long-dead visla, and formerly one of the Council of Twenty, no less, had quite possibly had his friend and mentor killed from beyond the grave? It was ridiculous to even consider, but Demelza thought it could be true, so he had no choice but to give credence to the possibility. But if that was the case, what justice could be had?

"I do not know what to say," he croaked, his voice breaking for the first time since hearing the news. "How can this be allowed to pass?"

"It will not," Demelza replied. "No matter what, we will seek out the ones who carried this out. Those who oversaw the attack itself. And we will exact our price, as well as the name of the ringleader who directed them and devised the plan. It is only a matter of time. And while the killers may have been cautious in their planning and covered their tracks with considerable skill, the Ghalian are very patient in our endeavors as well. One day, we will find what we seek, however long it takes."

"I've got word out, but there's nothing," Bud griped. "No one's heard anything. And as for the surviving mercs who participated, it's like they've vanished. They've gone to ground."

"Or were just given a cushy gig somewhere far away to keep their mouths shut," Henni added.

Demelza didn't seem so sure. "Perhaps. Our spies are searching out leads, and a dedicated team has been surveilling the Maktan estates as best they can. Despite being a full-fledged member of the Council of Twenty, Tozorro Maktan's heir was only a boy when his father set this plan into motion. But now that he has reached adulthood, there is a possibility his father's servants will report what happened to him."

Bawb did not like the up-in-the-air sound of that. Not one bit. He wanted revenge and he wanted it *now*. "And if they do not report to him? If those responsible simply go about their lives as if nothing happened? What then? Do we allow them to draw breath until they die of old age?"

"We *will* find them, Bawb," Demelza assured him. "While Ghalian sometimes die in the performance of their duties, this was different. This was the culmination of a targeted attempt. One that has claimed several others along the way. Only because the Master taking a particular contract is often undecided until the job begins, did the others find themselves on the receiving end of this treachery. There is a mole somewhere in our order, and they are sure to go silent now that this goal has been achieved. We will let them think their life is normal, but rest assured, we will be looking for them. Watching. Waiting. Confirming any suspicions and acting upon them when the time is right. I know you are upset, Bawb. We all are. But we must do this the Ghalian way. And that may take time."

The young man hid his agitation as best he could, but a tumultuous storm was raging inside. "I understand, Teacher. And I thank you for your honesty. Now, if you will all excuse me, I feel the need to go outside for a bit. Get some air."

"Of course. We are all processing this loss in our own ways."

"Cheers to that," Henni said, draining her cup again and refilling it to the top. "Revenge, kiddo. That's all that matters now. We'll find the bastards. I don't know how, but we will."

Bawb simply nodded once and stepped out, making his way to the city streets to walk, think, and plan. The Ghalian would do things their way, but he would not sit idly by and wait. An extra set of eyes would never hurt, and he was going to do a little digging on his own whenever he had free time. Other endeavors seemed unimportant now. Trivial, almost. This and this alone would be his life's goal for now, and he would leave no stone unturned.

CHAPTER FORTY-SIX

In the days following Bawb's unfortunate discovery of his mentor's demise, the young man appeared to be in a calm frame of mind. Surprisingly so, in fact. To any who didn't know him, that is. Those who had spent years in close contact could tell he was hurting inside despite his best efforts. He was hiding his grief well, and for that they gave him high marks, but he and Master Hozark had grown close, and a student's bond with his mentor could be a very powerful thing indeed.

He was still only an Adept, just a young man, really, and he needed to mourn in his own way and in his own time. It was to be expected. Even the most senior of Ghalian had felt the blow in one way or another. No one, not even a Ghalian, was devoid of emotion. They simply learned to control and hide theirs much better than everyone else. It was something all of them had mastered over their years as friends and associates inevitably fell.

But Bawb had always been far more emotional than his classmates, even if he did eventually learn to keep it under wraps. It was partly what made him so much better than the others. The sheer willpower and control required to keep pace with his cohort while also molding himself into what he wanted to be. And from his efforts it was clear; Bawb was on the path to the Five, and it was clearer to see in him than any other prodigy in recent history.

Even so, he was young and still had his limitations, and his progress could derail if he lost focus and allowed it to do so. And the death of Hozark was just the sort of thing that could do just that. He was strong, no doubt, but he would be tested in ways he had not yet faced in his relatively short life.

The teachers, Master Imalla, and even Master Corann, discussed the issue and decided it would be best to keep the troubled Adept busy, but not on any missions of critical importance or exceptional risk. Yes, he had more than proven himself capable of handling far more difficult tasks than his years should allow, but for now, at least, he would be kept from harm's way as much as they could.

So it was that Bawb found himself sent on lesser missions. He would deliver messages and retrieve items for the order, focusing on disguise and diversion rather than infiltration and battle. And though it might have been perceived as a boring shift for most, Bawb excelled at it far better than they would have expected. So much so that after just a few short weeks he seemed to be back to his old self.

Calm. Collected. Focused. He had faced the trauma head-on and beaten it, coming out the other side stronger for it, ready to get back to his life and training. Master Imalla waited another two weeks before allowing him on more challenging tasks. And to her great delight, he outperformed her expectations. Hozark's prodigal pupil was back.

Bawb set his sights on self-improvement beyond the mere training performed under the guidance of the teachers. He now pushed himself hard during his every free hour, training with his friends, his teachers—those willing to do so on their off-time, that is—and even visiting outside facilities when he had a large enough block of time.

Demelza spent the most time with him, the hours upon hours of one-on-one swordplay accelerating his natural abilities even further. It was all starting to click into place. To feel second-nature. To be as easy as breathing, just as she had told him it would eventually become one day.

It seemed that day was today.

Despite his newfound expertise with bladed weapons, Bawb still operated with the greatest of stealth on his contracts, avoiding detection and conflict whenever he could. And when there was no alternative but to fight, he ended the altercations with the utmost speed and precision. This was not the time to play. It was the time to win.

His tasks took him to many worlds, and on each of them he reached out to the network of Ghalian spies, picking their brains for what details they might have unearthed and asking them for the oddest of favors. Information on the faintest of interconnected threads of intrigue he had mapped out in his mind. Threads the Masters did not think were worth following, but that he saw value in nonetheless.

Most of them agreed to do as he asked. It wasn't as if it would require them to alter their routines in any way. All they had to do was note any variable within the parameters he had described. But a few of them pushed back.

"Why do you keep at this?" a man named Aogal asked. He was a dark-blue-skinned Bambatza, with their characteristic barrel chests and wide waists, along with the second set of arms growing from just above their hips. Not a Ghalian, but a member of their spy network able to go where magical disguises would be detected.

"I keep at this because someday someone will slip up. And when they do, I will have them."

"This is not according to the wishes of the order, is it?"

"Not exactly."

"So, this is an independent side quest, is it?"

"In a way. But the results sought align with what the Masters wish for."

The man shook his head. "I can't help you. Not against the order's wishes. And besides, what's done is done, and the Masters know best. You shouldn't go around acting against their wishes."

"I simply seek information. The truth. Nothing more."

"Well, good luck with that. I'm afraid I can't help you any more than I already have, for reasons I'm hoping I've made pretty clear."

"You have, and I will respect your code."

Aogal seemed pleased his words had an effect on the Ghalian. "I'm glad to hear it. So, you'll be heading home now, then?"

"Home? Oh, you misunderstand. I respect your code, but I must follow my own," he replied, then turned and walked away, determined to follow any lead, any hint of a clue, as long as he had to until one day, somehow, some way, he would uncover the mastermind behind Hozark's death.

He would live his life as before, training and carrying out missions, but never without an eye and an ear also scanning for clues, hints, and answers. And then, hopefully, one day he would avenge his mentor. One day.

CHAPTER FORTY-SEVEN

Bawb began upping the intensity of his contracts in the coming weeks and months, and to everyone's great delight, he was still performing admirably. Even so, he would, on occasion, take an assignment a bit below his blossoming skill set. No one questioned these minor variations as he had taken Hozark's death harder than most. An occasional need for a so-called easy gig was understandable, and he was still young enough to be allowed the leeway to get his feet, and his blade, wet on the occasional easier mission.

When a client brought a desert assassination to the order, Bawb requested he be assigned to it immediately. It seemed like a fairly straightforward but somewhat lengthy task. As an unusual type of magic protected the skies, the desert's sandy winds making it impossible for any craft to fly in undetected, he would need to infiltrate a caravan to pass undetected across the burning sands and eventually reach his target, the infamous Zaftal, a modestly wealthy tribal chieftain-warlord who controlled much of the region.

Apparently, he had managed to overstep the precarious peace agreement terms with several of his neighboring warlords, minorly in some cases, and with outright disregard in others. He needed to be taught a lesson. And that lesson was going to be one that saw his territory carved up and divided amongst his enemies upon his imminent demise.

It seemed like a good opportunity for Bawb to get some time away. Pretending to be someone else and immersing himself in a new identity for a while would do the young man wonders.

"Approved," Master Imalla said, handing him the details. "This may take a while."

"I understand, Master."

"I know you do. Be safe, and good hunting."

Bawb gave a slight bow and departed immediately. It seemed he was going on a desert adventure. Little did anyone know, for him and him alone, this was a dual-purpose mission.

It just so happened that this world was part of the informal network of spies and informants Bawb had loosely arranged, many of them not affiliated with the Ghalian whatsoever but all of them keeping an ear out for details that might earn them coin.

Importantly, some of what he'd learned from them was potentially useful. It seemed his people had located someone within Zaftal's city who might be of interest to him. A woman who had let slip nothing more than a lone statement whilst in a drunken revelry one night. Just a single sentence, ignored by most but one overheard by ears on his payroll. A few words hinting about a friend helping out in some super-secret mission with dozens of mercs and casters. Just like the trap Hozark had faced.

Naturally, he wanted to talk to them up close and personal-like. And now he was being afforded the opportunity to pay them a visit in person.

Of course, he would be anonymous in his approach. For that matter, even his own network did not know who he was. Their patron was just some faceless person paying anonymously for their services. But he knew who they were and where their information pointed. And he had learned a few *very* interesting tidbits over the months in this fashion.

As is often the case when one person spends all of their mental energy focused on something others gloss over, the amassed data looked like a bunch of gibberish to anyone not in the know. But to him, the finest threads of a pattern were beginning to make themselves known, like an image slowly revealing itself in the tea leaves. Every new piece of data added only served to add to the picture that only he could see. And now he had the opportunity to further jumpstart things.

Naturally, he would still have to kill the man—that was the official reason for his visit to the area, after all—but that would prove quite simple once he was in his presence, though the trek across the sands to encounter him would not be the most pleasant of journeys. But that was life on a desert world. Hardship, sand, and heat.

"So be it," he said to himself, resigned to his task as he boarded his ship.

Yakkotz was the name of the world, and the vast Sabbia desert was where he would begin his trek. Bawb set his course and lifted off, eager to begin, hopeful this lead might go somewhere. Might lead him a vital step closer to Master Hozark's killers.

He landed in a bustling trade site near a small, winding river at the edge of the barren sands. It was the only easy source of water as far as the eye could see in any direction and had as a result, become a gathering spot on this world. All manner of craft dotted the landscape, their owners doing trade in the sprawling marketplaces that sprang up along the river.

Bawb stepped out into the hot, dry air, the sting of sand on his face and the heavy rays of the sun beating down from above.

It was uncomfortable, but he smiled to himself, more than ready to begin his trek. But first he had to infiltrate a caravan heading the right direction.

He made quick work of that particular task, blending in and befriending a caravan group that fit the bill perfectly. He was carrying a minimal amount with him, only the choicest of items that would be of interest on this particular world. The disguise was a familiar one that he had no difficulty maintaining in even the most difficult situations. He might have been mourning on the inside, but to all he encountered he was wearing the jovial face of his favorite trader. One he had given a definitive name after Master Hozark's demise.

Binsala the trader, he was to be called from now on. Quick to smile and quicker to drink and make merry, he befriended everyone he met no matter the world or situation. He was acting, and he was damn good at it. In fact, it was a skill the konus had recently informed him he had maxed-out, his display showing he had achieved the highest level possible.

It was unsurprising. The truest test of an actor was putting on a smiling face when they are actually broken up inside. And he had been doing just that for months.

And so it came to be that Binsala the trader found himself trekking across the vast Sabbia desert in the company of pilgrims, traders, and travelers, all of them either moving on foot, their feet protected by broad sand shoes that gave them more purchase as they stepped, or riding atop the beasts of burden carrying their supplies and personal effects if they had the coin for it.

Bawb, aka Binsala the trader, was one such person. While he was in peak fitness and did not mind the trek one bit and would have actually enjoyed the exertion, his disguise was that of a man a bit loose with coin who took pleasure in the nicer things in life. It would only make sense he would ride rather than walk if afforded the chance. So it was that Bawb rode atop one of the lumbering beasts, the upside of which was he would be saving all his energy for later when he might actually need it.

Each day was spent in relative silence, the caravan focusing on conserving energy and ensuring they remained on the correct heading, using the sun for navigation. While travel by night would have been far cooler, the dangerous creatures living beneath the sand only emerged in the dark, hunting for the scarce game that could survive this environment. People and their beasts were safe in a close group, but the risks of stragglers being taken at night were simply too great to chance it.

As a result, Binsala the trader had ample opportunity to regale his fellow travelers with stories of mischief and adventure as they ate, drank, and sat around the night's fire—a simple thing more powered by magic than any combustible given the lack of wood in the desert. After a pleasant evening, they would then turn in early, restoring their strength for the next day's leg of the journey.

The caravan traveled for five days out into the shifting sands, following the route that would eventually get them to the oasis town that fell under Zaftal's rule, when the unexpected came upon them. A marauding band of raiders from one of the competing warlords swooped in under cover of night, attacking out of nowhere.

The alarm was raised, and the members of the caravan grabbed what arms they had and set to defending themselves against the onslaught. Bawb roused in a flash and immediately cast his night-vision spell, a dagger ready in each hand. He watched a moment and counted the attackers. There were fourteen of them. Not a huge force, but enough to cause problems, especially against an untrained and vulnerable group like this.

He saw the man he'd been merrily talking with just that very evening fall in a spray of blood but forced himself to stay his hands. He had to let this play out. He could not reveal who, and more importantly, *what*, he truly was. Maintaining his cover was paramount.

Another fell, then another. Despite doing their best, the travelers were taking a beating. Bawb stared at the downed bodies and saw a flash of Hozark in his mind, outnumbered and fighting for his life. Before he realized what he was doing, he had slain four of the attackers in a brutal flurry of blows.

Careful, Adept, the konus warned.

He knew it was right. He looked around and saw that, fortunately, no one was in a position to have observed what he did. No one still alive, anyway. But now there were corpses to deal with and explain away. Bawb quickly sheathed his blades and moved the bodies of two of the fallen travelers close to those he killed, placing them and their weapons in such a way that it would appear they had managed to kill the men, albeit at the cost of their own lives.

They would be remembered for dying as heroes, and in so doing, would maintain his cover story.

Bawb cast a spell at his feet, immediately giving himself better agility on the soft sand. He moved through the chaos, fighting off bandits with subtle violence, hiding his actions to his comrades by appearing to flee or be in a panic as he doled out violence upon the attackers. He was helping the travelers he could while avoiding any overt, open engagement with their attackers. As he worked through their numbers, injuring most enough to make them have second thoughts about this attack, he realized that in so doing, he now was the only one of his group unharmed in any way.

"It must be done," he told himself, resigned to the fact as he drew a blade and gave himself several impressive-looking but not dangerous cuts and slices. They would be easy enough to bind, and he could heal them properly at any time with the magic in his konus. For now, however, he needed to fit in with the others. And that meant he'd have to be as bloody as they were.

The raiders took what they could carry and hurried off into the night as quickly as they'd appeared, leaving the bodies of the dead behind for the desert to claim, their spirits gone leaving lifeless meat for the food chain. Just one more meal in the circle of life.

"Everyone, together," the caravan leader directed when it was clear the attack was over.

The group gathered themselves and formed a circle with three taking positions as sentries, watching for any sign of further attack. The others set to work binding one another's injuries as best they could. Come morning they would assess the damage fully, but for now the priority was to stop bleeding and triage the survivors.

Somehow, they had come through the attack alive. They thanked their gods, but it hadn't been a deity that had saved them. Bawb, however, was perfectly content to let that fact go unnoted.

CHAPTER FORTY-EIGHT

With the rise of the sun came a clearer picture of the carnage of the night before, the bodies of travelers and bandits alike lying in their own drying blood, soaking into the desert sands. The bandits would be left there to be claimed by the wasteland. Within days they would be stripped bare.

The slain travelers would be bundled up and taken to what was now to be their final destination, their family members able to either give them a proper send-off or arrange for their return home.

It took some time to properly sort through and salvage the debris of their caravan's belongings—the bandits had been more destructive than efficient and thorough—but by late morning everything had been gathered that was worth keeping, the deceased loaded onto makeshift litters to drag behind the beasts of burden to continue the journey.

Bawb lamented his injuries as loudly as the rest of them, along with concern over their stolen water supplies, playing it up as a distraught trader would. Restricted rations were nothing new to him, but civilians tended not to fare well with those sorts of discomforts.

The raiding group had certainly done a number on them, worse than they'd initially realized. In addition to lives, they had lost much of their necessary survival equipment and supplies. Fortunately, some things were still of use, and they gathered up anything they could. Bawb had the luxury of riding atop an animal, and that meant he could carry a few additional items as well. One was an oddity, but potentially life-saving. A bottle that he now urinated in rather than upon the sands.

The idea was to collect precious fluid in case he needed to fabricate a solar still. He had already designed one in his mind from the bits of debris they had, and if absolutely necessary he would be able to ride with it camouflaged among the things on the animal's back, evaporating and condensing water as they jostled along.

It would be far less efficient that way, and he was bound to lose some of the clean, condensed water in the process, but by nightfall he would have at least a mouthful, if not two. In a desert, that could make all the difference. It was on the second day of reduced water for the travelers that he put the device to use. They were close to the oasis, but he was not about to let his energy drop this close to his target.

Bawb did, however, alter his magical disguise, adding a darker tan to himself, both making him look a bit more weathered from the ordeal while also protecting his naturally pale Ghalian skin from the sun's rays. The konus found this a clever use of disguise magic and leveled him up for creativity, but dealing with the heat and fighting off dehydration as best he could, Bawb paid it no heed.

The next day they stumbled upon a group of desert people living in a tiny oasis hidden among the dunes. This was a place of survival and not on the maps. Only locals knew of its location, and it was something they guarded fiercely. Had this been any other caravan they would have driven them off without hesitation. But seeing the injuries and overall state of the travelers, the laws of the desert overruled their natural inclination to turn them away. Reluctantly, and with a fair bit of rude attitude, they took in the weary gaggle and provided them with water and food, which those with coin gratefully compensated them for.

It would have been free if they had none, however. The law stated those in distress would be given water and a place to shelter from the heat. It was an odd dichotomy, but while raiding and killing were perfectly allowable, the very same people who may have been trying to kill you just the other day would obey this one rule.

Fortunately, these were not those people, and the caravan was quite glad for it. Sheltering with those who had killed your companions just days before would be awkward, to say the least.

The next day they set out early, resupplied and rested enough to make the push in just two days if they moved fast. And that they did. All of them were quite motivated to get to their destination as soon as possible and get on with their lives.

It was an effort, but as predicted, in two days the vast oasis finally came into view. Not a mirage on the horizon, but the actual city thriving under Zaftal's thumb. And it was a sight for sore eyes. Even if they hadn't just endured the trials of the desert, the beautiful oasis would have been impressive. It was mostly one and two-level huts for those who had coin for construction, a panoply of colorful tents, yurts, and awning-covered marketplaces, restaurant stalls, and open-air cots for rent, no need for insulation in the year-round warm temperatures.

The group was met by local security, all members of Zaftal's police force, the group responsible for maintaining order as well as his complete control over the area. As soon as they heard what had happened to the travelers, healers and a free cot to sleep on were arranged for all of them that night and the following one. Two days to get themselves right. Beyond that, they would then be responsible for making their own way.

Bawb told the others to get tended to first. He would see the healer after the more seriously injured had been helped. It sounded like a generous offer from their friend Binsala. In actuality, he just did not want to have a healer poking around and possibly discovering he was actually a Wampeh Ghalian in disguise. Not all were sensitive to that sort of thing, but it was always a possibility to be wary of.

Bawb finally healed his wounds while changing his appearance in one of the public bathing stalls he rented to clean himself. He washed the sweat and grime off his body as he applied the healing spells, mending the sliced flesh with ease now that he didn't have to worry about not fitting in with the others. The man who stepped into the clean clothes on the shelf beside him looked nothing like Binsala the trader. *That* man would not be returning to the others until later. *This* one had a pressing task at hand.

Walking the paths and weaving between the tents and huts, Bawb allowed himself a moment to clear his thoughts and relax his body as he headed to the last reported location of the person of interest. A set of tents near a public bath house.

"Perhaps I will have a bath in the process," he mused, the thought of a warm soak while extracting the information he required a rather pleasant one.

But as luck would have it, after a quick survey of the area he confirmed that his target was not in the baths but rather a small tent not far from them. He stopped just outside, casting a robust muting spell on the fabric of the enclosure, then stepped inside.

A startled woman with broad shoulders and meaty fists jumped up in alarm, charging him rather than attempting to flee. He was glad for it. No need to chase her down to disable her.

The spell he used was an unusual one, even by Ghalian standards. One that caused paralysis for a few minutes while leaving the victim fully awake and able to speak, albeit softly. Normally, it was for working on livestock, freezing them in place and making them numb so any injuries could be tended without requiring an extensive tranquilization spell.

In this case, it just so happened to also function on the woman's particular race, stopping her in her tracks. Bawb ensured she wouldn't topple over then stepped in front of her where he was quite sure she could see him clearly.

"Speak."

"Fuck you," she said, her eyes wanting to shout but her voice no more than a whisper.

"Good. Thank you."

"What the hell do you want with me?"

"Funny you should ask," he replied, shifting to his natural form and letting his fangs slide into view.

The dampness between her legs spread quickly as her bladder emptied at the realization she was face-to-face with a Wampeh Ghalian. It was precisely the reaction he had hoped for. Fear sped things along so much easier, he'd found.

"Ah, I see you are ready to cooperate."

"What does a Ghalian want with me? I'm a nobody."

"A nobody with information. Tell me what I wish to know and you walk out of here intact. Fail and you will not be so fortunate."

The menace in his eyes made it clear he spoke true.

"I don't have information. I'm just a transport pilot."

"Oh, you can do better than that."

"It's the truth."

"Is it, though? Or is it a bit of a massaging of the facts?"

"What do you mean?"

"You know exactly what I mean. But let's discuss what interests me the most, shall we? You have a friend."

"I have lots of friends."

"One who was vital in a recent action involving dozens of mercenaries and casters."

She said nothing, but he saw her face go pale.

"You will give me their name."

"I can't."

"You can."

"Not going to happen. Do what you will, I won't sell out my friends."

Bawb didn't have the time for this. He still had his real contract to complete as well as dealing with this fool. He would have to improvise.

"You misunderstand. Yes, the Ghalian are interested in your friend, but only because they are privy to information we desire. No harm will come to them, or you. This is just an information collection assignment. I mean, do you really think they would send just one of us if it was of vital importance? Of course not. Look, just help me out here, and I will get out of your hair and let you get back to your day."

It was a lie, of course, and they both knew it. But the hope for survival was enough to make the most desperate convince themself of something they knew was not true. Nevertheless, it took Bawb several more minutes of careful manipulation before he had the name. It made sense. This person was a smuggler, and a certain degree of resistance to questioning was to be expected. But, eventually, she gave in. They always did. And her friend? It turned out he was a fellow named Kitzoff, an arms dealer. One he hadn't heard of but who was now most certainly in the center of his sphere of attention.

Pointed in the right direction, he could now complete his

contract and get back to his real mission. And he would even let this one live. A cautionary tale about why one should be careful who they do business with. Arms dealers were most certainly a good source of revenue, but the risks, as his slowly recovering victim realized, far outweighed the rewards.

"Thank you for cooperating," he said, turning for the tent's exit flap.

"You're just going to leave me?"

"You did as I asked. As I said, I was only seeking information."

The woman sighed heavily, relief clear in her face. "Oh, thank the gods. I knew delivering those weapons to Radzor was a bit risky, even for me."

Bawb froze, his stomach clenching tight. "Did you say *Radzor*?"

"Yeah. Some big job there needed extra gear. I was happy for the work, honestly, but that was a bit sketchy."

"And who did you interact with on Radzor?"

"A fella by the name Tinx met me to collect them."

Bawb knew the name. One of the mercenaries he had tracked down when he abruptly went missing after some super-secret job. He vanished, but Bawb found him. Or, what was left of him. Someone was tying up loose ends, and now there was one less.

Bawb quietly cast the spell he had in mind, then turned and left. His captive breathed a sigh of relief but started to feel a bit woozy. Was that normal when the spell wore off? She looked down and realized the cause. Her blood was pouring out of her, the warmth of it destroying the ice dagger embedded in her chest. A moment later she toppled to the ground, the rest of the weapon melting away in the desert heat, leaving her just another victim of desert intrigue.

Bawb really had been planning to let her live. But she had

inadvertently admitted that she'd played a direct role in Hozark's demise. Maybe she didn't know who she was delivering those weapons to, but at this moment in time that wasn't something the angry Ghalian even considered important.

Level up: Ice weapons.

"I do not care," he growled, ready to take out his anger on whoever got in his way. Lucky him, he had a perfect target already in mind, and Zaftal didn't stand a snowball's chance in, well, the middle of the desert. Precisely why he had prepared to use ice weapons, the moisture of the oasis's water source providing all the material he needed to craft them.

Murder on his mind, Bawb set to work on his official job, eager to finish it and then set off to find this Kitzoff person, and through him, the ones truly behind the plot.

CHAPTER FORTY-NINE

Zaftal was an unpowered, perfectly normal sort of man, albeit a thick-skinned one who towered over most of the other races living in his area of control. His kind were naturally hardy, with durable bones and dense muscle underneath that protective layer that was closer to leather armor than a normal epidermis.

The whole package made him very difficult to hurt and near impossible to kill, which was part of the reason he had managed to wrestle control of so large a swath of the region, including the coveted oasis city, from his competitors.

His imposing physical attributes could have made him free and easy with his own personal protection, but he recognized the precarious nature of his position and knew full well that others, if given the chance, would do whatever they could to seize his domain from under him. It was almost refreshing, seeing a ruler actually pay attention to that sort of thing and not get overconfident. Only in his inner sanctum was Zaftal truly alone, and that was the one place he had paid handsomely to have layered with protective wards, the magic specifically geared to shield him and him alone. Heaven help anyone else who happened to be in there when those spells triggered.

Bawb didn't care one way or another.

It was early in the morning when Bawb set out to complete his task. He moved through Zaftal's city with the speed of a man set on a path, absolutely certain he would achieve his goal and that nothing would stand in his way. He had a solid lead to move him closer to Hozark's killers now, and Zaftal was just an annoying task standing in his way and slowing him down. He would be done away with quickly and efficiently, and that was all there was to it.

Bawb changed disguises on the fly, his magic flowing with absolute ease, his intent crystal clear. He would step behind one of the colorful tents or a pile of crates and another would emerge mere seconds later, a partial confusion spell added to the mix of rapidly changing magic, making sure that any who might have caught a glimpse of him before and after the change would chalk it up to a trick of the light or something in their eyes.

As he drew closer to Zaftal's compound of outer tents and inner huts surrounding his central structure, made up of interlinked buildings that formed a ring around the inner sanctum, a few guards did stop him to carry out an informal identity check as he was now in the protective zone around their master's home.

Bawb disarmed and stunned them with a single spell, pouring alcohol on their slumbering bodies and dropping a half-empty bottle next to them as he passed. The whole thing took mere seconds, leaving him free to go while barely breaking his stride, the guards seemingly drunk and nothing more. It would draw attention sooner or later, but he would be long gone by then. And equally important, even in his singular drive, he would not kill innocents, even if they were guards. This was just a job for them, nothing more. But heaven help those who would try to stop him by force.

Arriving closer to the structures surrounding Zaftal's central sanctuary, he snatched up a small sack of root vegetables from a vendor stall, dropping coin in its place while no one was looking, not stopping to haggle over the items. He was moving fast and not about to slow his progress. He then shifted disguises again and took on the look of a lowly servant, down to the identifying brand each wore on their exposed shoulders, the need for sleeves in this heat nonexistent.

Into the ebb and flow of minions he went, registering and cataloging everyone's look, rank, and movements as he moved deeper into the structures and closer to Zaftal's personal area. He sensed the warding spells from a distance. These were substantial, and he could not simply blow through them. Not without a massive expenditure of magic. And as Zaftal was not a natural magic user, he would not be able to replenish himself from his blood.

Bawb shifted tack immediately, a new plan forming as his feet carried him around the structures, looking for a gap in the protective spells. He found none. That meant long-range weapons would not work. Not against Zaftal's thick skin. Too much velocity would be lost by the time they passed through the warding spells. And if he attacked him up close the wards would trigger and injure him greatly. Possibly fatally. Only two options remained. Wait for the man to come to a more vulnerable location, which could take days, or try something unusual. Unusual and disgusting.

Bawb didn't hesitate, redirecting to the stink of the grating he had passed in his circuit of the grounds. It would be a fair trick of magic, but his plan should work. Fortunately, this part of the compound was not one protected by any magical wards or detection spells. He lifted the grate and cast hard, a full-body bubble spell encasing him from head to toe, then slipped inside, lowering it over himself.

The drop wasn't far, and the sound of his splash into the flow of raw sewage was small and lost in the noise above ground. Bawb held his breath, conserving the air in his bubble as he'd trained over the years. But covering his entire body with it was way beyond the spell's normal parameters. But for whatever reason, his unusual use of it cast as he'd hoped, his intent absolutely clear in its function, as was the steady power flowing to feed it. He and his konus were working in tandem perfectly as never before. He was moving with singular purpose and speed, and nothing would deter him from his goal.

He swam and crawled his way to the toilet within Zaftal's personal space. The man would be waking soon, and, if Bawb was lucky, he would come to relieve himself before starting his day. He sensed the magic sealing the toilet from the stench below. It was strong against smell but otherwise items could pass through with no resistance.

Perfect.

The Ghalian then did what he didn't want to. He stopped, sat, and waited. He wanted to move, to make progress, but also knew patience was part of the job, and sometimes, no matter how much you wanted to be in action, you just had to stop and wait.

He allowed himself a single deep breath, filling his lungs with clean air from within his expanded bubble, then slid into a semi-trance-like state, slowing his heart and bodily functions to a crawl. He *could* just breathe the air in the sewage network, but he knew the fumes and stench would get to him eventually. It would also make his egress a bit more difficult, as he would have to mask the odor upon his exit, calling attention to himself if he didn't. Given what he had in mind, that was the last thing he wanted.

He sat in his meditative state and waited, only taking a breath every ten minutes or so, his bodily functions slowed as if immersed in ice water. Finally, sound from above roused him, and judging by the weight of the footsteps, it could only be one person.

Zaftal had awakened and was coming to relieve himself.

Bawb focused hard, forming the very unusual intent firmly in his mind, fixing it as he drew upon his konus's magic stores to power his spell. The light from above vanished as an enormous ass took its place upon the throne above. A blast of flatulence vibrated the air, but Bawb grinned. This was what he had been waiting for.

Zaftal was dead before he could process the utterly wrong sensation coming from his rear, the pointed ice shaft formed of frozen feces and urine avoiding his tough hide, driving through his anus up into his body, piercing vital organs on its way to his heart.

Bawb was already on the move, heading to the grating as fast as he could. The frozen waste would act as a cork for the time being, but when it melted, a hot rush of blood and guts would come pouring out of the dead man in a violent expulsion of his innards. Odds were he would topple over at that point, and that, in turn, would most likely trigger one of his many alarm spells.

The assassin, however, was not concerned. By then he would be well out of the city and on his way back across the sands, leaving this world with his task complete and a vital new lead to follow up on in the bargain.

CHAPTER FIFTY

Bawb returned home, his mission complete, if perhaps a few days overdue. Such was the nature of their work, and they all knew that things did not always go according to plan, so no one was at all surprised by his delayed arrival. What had been something of a shock was when the details of his ingress and execution of the contract were revealed.

Bawb was pushing hard, driving himself to excel as a Ghalian, which they were glad for. But unlike a healthy work ethic, this was becoming something of a fixation. An all-consuming focus that was a bit unsettling. So much so that the Masters, along with Bud, Henni, and Demelza, each spoke with him, assessing his mental well-being as best they could. Even Usalla pried a bit, seeing what she could make of her friend's state.

But the young man's responses to all of their inquiries seemed to indicate he was acutely aware of his issues and, unlike most people following a trauma, was actively working to address them. It would take time, naturally, but his response was all anyone could ask. Worries allayed, so long as he wasn't actively harming himself in his immersion in training and work, they would support him in every way.

What they didn't know was that Bawb was planning in secret, directing the network of informants he had amassed under the somewhat murky auspices of being on Ghalian work to find this Kitzoff person. The arms dealer had provided the additional weapons used in the trap for Master Hozark, and that meant he was quite possibly the one holding the key to this whole affair he so desperately needed. Finding him was of paramount importance.

Unfortunately, Kitzoff had gone dark. All Bawb could do was wait for his people to find word of them. Until then, he would simply train and take contracts, appearing to the others to be back to his usual routine.

One thing, however, still bothered him. A little something nagging the back of his mind. *That*, at least, he could address. With extreme prejudice, if required, though that would undoubtedly be frowned upon by the Masters, the reason being it was a fellow Ghalian he intended to question. One he felt could very well be the mole in their ranks.

Bawb surprised Elzina in the hallway leading to the third lower-level obstacle course. She was on her way to her usual morning warmup. A routine. Something they were trained not to develop. But here, within the safe walls of the compound, she had gotten sloppy.

"Elzina," he said, stepping in front of her, blocking her way.

"Move, Bawb. I am busy."

He stood his ground.

"I said *move!*"

She pushed him, only to find herself flung backward with far more force than she expected.

"Oh, it is like that, is it?" she growled, her trademark simmering anger bubbling to the surface in a flash. She lunged at him, intending to show him just how wrong he was to push her. Bawb, however, met her attack with force, ready and even eager for this particular fight.

His fist cracked into her jaw as a hard knee rose up into her gut, sending her into a wall. Elzina's expression was one of surprise. She expected a bit of a brawl, but Bawb was not holding back. If that was the case, neither would she.

Her kick snapped out hard and fast, a move that almost always connected. *Almost.*

Bawb caught her foot and drove the ball of his own into her upper thigh, forcing her base leg out from under her and slamming her to the ground.

"I have questions," he said icily, circling as she scrambled back to her feet.

"Yeah? You could have just asked," she replied, diving into a flying knee.

He slapped it aside as he spun into a rear elbow, the strike hitting hard enough to make her see stars and taste blood. He didn't stop there, an immediate low kick slamming her thigh just above the knee, driving her to the ground once more. Bawb stopped the attack, letting her get up.

Elzina did, and fast, but there was a new look in her eyes. An unfamiliar one. Elzina was actually concerned.

"You were meeting with Council agents," he said. Not a question but an accusation.

Her pupils involuntarily twitched, reacting in the tiniest way, the only outward sign she made. It was enough.

"I did no such thing," she spat, attacking hard and fast, using magic as well as fists and feet.

Bawb had already cast his counter spells before she finished her first attempt, while his body moved with the newfound speed and violence of action he had drilled into himself since Hozark's demise. His elbow slammed into her face, his knee to her gut, driving her into the wall. Bawb did not relent, landing knee after knee until he had knocked the wind out of her.

Again, he stepped back. He would mete out this beating as long as it took.

"Why, Elzina? Why betray the order?"

"I would never do that!"

She attacked again, but she knew in her heart she was no match for him. Somehow, incredibly, Bawb had grown exponentially more powerful than before. She had no hope for victory. But that didn't mean she wouldn't give it her all.

Bawb countered her moves, beating on her with precise force, making her acutely aware that he could have done more damage if he wanted to but was holding back. She couldn't help marvel at what he had become. At the level of skill at which he was fighting. This wasn't the Bawb she had bullied all their lives. This was something else. And he was *angry*.

"You lie to me, Elzina," he said as she hit the wall hard from his stomping front kick. "I *know* you were with Council goons. I saw it with my own eyes."

"You do not know what you saw," she shot back, spitting blood and wiping her mouth.

"You are a traitor," he replied, laying another beating on her then stepping back yet again to await her reply. The look in his eyes said he would be perfectly happy chipping away at her like this all day. Elzina realized this and made a choice. She would have to come clean, like it or not.

"I am not a traitor. Never."

"I saw you."

"Yes, okay? Yes, you saw me meeting with Council agents. But it was not what you think. I would never betray the order."

Bawb held back his attack. "Oh? Then why? What possible reason could you have?"

Elzina was clearly torn, not wanting to speak but having no

real options. "I was taking contracts outside the order," she reluctantly admitted.

Bawb stared hard but she met his gaze.

"What? You find it hard to believe I would do such a thing?" she challenged. "I want to work, Bawb. I want to excel. To be the best of the best. But you. You and your stupid extra lessons. Don't think no one noticed. We all did. And you usurped my top spot in our class because of it."

Bawb's rage was simmering just beneath the surface, his fury clear in his eyes. A blade appeared in his hand faster than she could register him moving.

"And Master Hozark perished because of your acts," he growled, the weapon poised not to injure but to kill.

Elzina, normally bitchy and a pain in his ass, displayed a look of genuine horror. The first time he had ever seen that expression on her face, her control over her emotions slipping in spite of herself.

"You think I was responsible for that?" she said, her tone far more placid than before. If he thought she had been part of the killing of his mentor, she was in far more danger than she had previously thought. It also explained his enraged reaction. "Bawb, I swear on my life, I would never do such a thing. I only sought to improve my skills. To take contracts outside the order while I was still an Adept. To do so as a Maven would be utterly unthinkable, as would ever betraying anyone of our order. Even you, Bawb. We have had our differences, but I would never, ever do that."

Bawb lowered his hands, his blade sheathed and his rage calming in an instant, the flames quenched and only a low smolder remaining. For now, anyway. He was a good judge of people's emotions, and in this rare instance of her defenses dropping, it was clear she was telling the truth. He realized he had just attacked her on a hunch, not hard facts. Elzina may have deserved it, or at least some, but Bawb felt ashamed of himself regardless. He was better than this. And from this point on, he would endeavor to be just that.

Better.

"I apologize, Elzina," he said, his body still tingling from adrenaline. "I misjudged you."

She wiped the blood from her trickling nose with a casual nod, her life no longer in jeopardy, and her respect for his skills now most definitely bolstered. He had made easy work of her. It was a hard pill to swallow, but even she had to admit, Bawb had moved to an entirely different level.

"You've improved, you know," she said. "I have never seen you fight like that. Not even in our most pitched sessions."

"I have been practicing. And I have been *very* motivated."

"Clearly." She stepped closer and extended her hand. "No hard feelings."

He grasped it and shook firmly.

"Thank you, Elzina."

"Of course. And, Bawb, if ever I can be of assistance in bringing whoever truly did this to Master Hozark to justice, you have my blades and hands at your service."

With that she released her grip, turned, and walked away, sore from her beating but not letting it show, her pride simply not allowing it. Bawb watched her go, marveling at the shift their years-long rivalry had just undergone.

Life's funny like that, Adept, his konus said.

"That it is, my friend. That it is, indeed."

CHAPTER FIFTY-ONE

Bawb's severe overreaction where Elzina was involved had given him quite a slap in the face. One that pulled him back from the precipice he hadn't even realized he was inching toward. Now as the honest realization of just how far he had gone had sunk in, he vowed never to lose control of himself like that again.

He would keep working toward his goal, of course, that much was never going to change. But he would look before he leapt, so to speak. For now he would wait for word on his next target. Until Kitzoff the weapons dealer was located, his only choices were to train, analyze whatever clues he had, and complete contracts with brutal efficiency.

Bawb did all three to excess.

Where the data analysis came into play, he spent most, but not all, of his free time studying the web of tiny clues. Some were just hints of a whisper, rumors on the wind. Others were abruptly truncated, as those involved were now deceased. It seemed someone had been cleaning up their trail one link at a time.

As for training, he pushed himself even harder now. Teacher Demelza gave freely of her time, happy to help the young man further his skills with the sword. He was beginning to show his father and mother's natural propensity for the bladed arts, though he didn't know it, coming into his own much as they had at around his age. It wasn't until a good two months into their frequent sessions that, to both of their surprise, he actually defeated her in single combat.

Bawb had apologized, saying it was a fluke. A mistake. But Demelza put an end to that nonsense in a hurry.

"You won, Bawb. In an even and fair contest, today you prevailed. Do not downplay your achievement, and do not doubt your win. Even the greatest among us did not *always* come out on top, especially in training."

"It is just unexpected, is all."

"It should not be. Your skills are compounding at quite an impressive speed, and your dedication is, in large part, responsible. I am glad to have lost to you, Bawb. It was a long time coming and I am proud of your accomplishments. You should be too."

"Thank you, Teacher. I cannot overstate how grateful I am for your tutelage and the gift of your time."

"It is my pleasure and honor. Master Hozark did as much for me, and I am pleased to be able to do the same for you. It is as it should be. Full circle, in a way."

"What do you mean?"

"Just that it is something we do. The Masters teach the teachers, the teachers teach the students, this is the way of things," she replied, cleverly avoiding the topic of his lineage she had sworn never to reveal. "Now, would you care to prove to me this victory was not a fluke?" she asked, twirling her sword in a dizzying blur.

Bawb grinned. "It would be my pleasure."

They trained daily thereafter, with Bawb actually winning matches more frequently. Demelza didn't say anything to him about it at the time, but she had initially thought once or twice it might be a fluke, just the beginnings of his skills manifestation. But when she found herself losing with regularity, it became clear Bawb was truly advancing beyond his age and rank. Something within him was aligning, the pieces falling into place. It was time for the next step. And she knew exactly what that should be.

Ser Baruud welcomed his young gladiator pupil back to his training grounds with as close to pleased emotion as he ever showed. In this case, a hint of a grin when he saw the boy return to him.

"Good to see you once more, Drenn. And on your own. A free man I see."

"Ser Baruud," Bawb replied with a respectful bow.

"And where is your Master, eh?"

Bawb's jaw twitched involuntarily, but he otherwise maintained his composure. "He is no more."

Baruud nodded solemnly, studying the young man's demeanor. "He was a good man."

"He was."

"And he took good care of you as well."

"He did."

"Well, then. What can I do for you, *Drenn*?" he asked. Bawb didn't know how, but he was certain the man knew he was not what he claimed to be. He also knew in his gut that it did not matter one bit to Ser Baruud. Drenn or any other name, this was a pupil he respected.

"I seek to test my skills. Swordplay in particular, but all other forms as well."

"Any particular reason?"

"Merely to improve myself."

"For?"

"Improvement."

"Or possibly revenge?"

Bawb's face remained neutral, but his pupils twitched. It was enough. Ser Baruud nodded sagely, considering the request.

"Very well. You shall be run through the gauntlet, as you request. A *true* test of your mettle and skills. You will surely come out injured, and you could even die as a result. I must make that perfectly clear. You are a free man, not a slave."

"I am aware, and I accept your terms."

"Very well, then. We begin at once."

Bawb followed Baruud to the advanced student training area and selected a weapon from the racks. His teacher summoned over four of the toughest fighters, one of whom he knew from his previous visit.

"Drenn, my friend! It's great seeing you again!" Borx hollered across the training field, rushing to give his friend an enormous hug. "What're you doing back?"

"My master died, and I am a free man."

Borx cocked his head like a puzzled pup. "I don't get it. If you're free, why in the gods' names are you here?"

"Because, my friend, I have been training."

"I can see that. You've muscled up, all right."

"Yes. And I need to push myself harder. To see what I can really do."

Borx realized what he had been summoned for, and his smile faltered. "You want a no-holds-barred contest? Against all four of us?"

"I do."

The gladiator glanced over at Ser Baruud. "I have already summoned the healer to be on hand," he informed them. "Now, Drenn wants to fight, and fight he shall. I shall leave it to you four to decide the order you will face him."

Baruud took a seat on a simple stool off to the side, ready to watch whatever might unfold.

After some chatter among themselves, the gladiators decided that Borx would be the last to fight, his hope being his friend would be exhausted or hurt enough to not want to face him. He liked Drenn, and he didn't want to hurt him. But he would do just that if it came down to it.

As it turned out, he would do no such thing.

Bawb's skills had leveled up far beyond anyone's expectations, and the healer did not have to do much work at all, the young man's killing blows pulled back, only barely breaking the skin. One after another he moved through the best gladiators in the camp with ease. After Borx's rapid defeat, something different happened. Something rarely seen within these walls.

Ser Baruud rose and crossed to the weapons rack. He selected a sword, gave it a few cursory twirls, then stood calmly in front of their visitor.

"I could not," Bawb protested out of respect.

"You have no choice," the master gladiator replied with a rare joyous smile spreading across his lips before launching into action.

Their blades rang out loud, the metal hitting hard, attacks and counterattacks cast and parried in blurring speed. Word got out the moment Baruud stepped forward, and now the far doorways were filling with curious faces. The master was fighting, something they couldn't believe and had to see with their own eyes.

Bawb and Baruud noted them but did not slow. In fact, they only increased the intensity, their combat now incorporating other martial styles as well as swords. Punches and elbows, knees and feet, every body part was a weapon, and all of them were being used in a dazzling display of all-out combat.

Baruud had the advantage of decades of experience, but Bawb was younger and stronger. On top of that, he was fast, his body moving at great speed, driven by the newfound fire constantly burning in his belly. He wanted to learn. To grow. To hone his body and mind into the absolute best version of himself he could possibly be. And this had nothing to do with becoming one of the Five. This quest was an entirely different endeavor, and that freedom of thought allowed him to achieve even greater heights.

He pushed the attack, feeling that Ser Baruud, despite all his impressive skills, was starting to tire. It was then that Bawb knew in his gut that he would win this battle. His opponent knew as well but would never submit. The two locked eyes, combatants in vicious battle yet also bound by endless respect.

Bawb abruptly shifted stance, his sword's guard slipping down as a result, Baruud's blade slicing into his flank. Bawb dropped the blade and gripped his side.

"Healer!" Baruud called out, summoning them to the ring.

"The master is victorious!" one of the younger gladiatorial students cried out, and a cheer rose in the air.

Ser Baruud spun and glared at the faces crammed in the doorways. The students immediately turned and ran back to their training. He then shifted his attentions to his opponent. He watched silently as the healer mended his wound, the young man not even flinching as the painful mending of flesh was done.

"Thank you," Baruud said, sending the healer on his way. He put his arm around Bawb's shoulder and walked with him to the front gates. "You were winning. You could have defeated me."

"Never on your soil," Bawb replied respectfully.

Baruud gave a slight nod. "Your skills have dramatically. Even for your kind, you show exceptional promise."

"My kind? I am merely a free man, no longer bound in servitude."

SCOTT BARON

"Call it what you wish, Ghalian."

Bawb's stride nearly faltered. He glanced at the man and saw his face showed no fear. Baruud cracked a little grin.

"Yes, I know what you are, as was your alleged owner, or should I say, Master, before you. Rest assured, your secret is safe with me."

Bawb already knew he spoke the truth. "I have no doubt, Master."

"Do not call me that. I am a Wampeh, yes, but not one of your ilk, though I have spent my life fighting. But now I am just an old warrior past his days of service."

"Service in battle, perhaps. But the knowledge you impart to your students has saved many lives, mine included. You do valuable work here."

"Perhaps. But so, too, is yours," he replied, opening the gate. "I hope this has answered your question and put to rest any self-doubt."

"It has."

"Then you are ready for whatever may come next. And now I bid you farewell. For now, at least. You are welcome in my walls any time you wish to train with us, Drenn."

"My name is not actually Drenn."

"Of course it isn't," the old gladiator said, patting him on the shoulder in an almost familial way. "May the gods watch over you and protect you on your journey. I am sure it is to be an impressive one."

CHAPTER FIFTY-TWO

Bawb returned to the Ghalian compound he called home with a renewed sense of purpose, accompanied by a robust feeling of drive and vigor coursing through him. He had challenged himself. Tested his limits against the best. And unlike any Adept before him, he had been victorious where one so young should have failed.

Neither Demelza nor Baruud would speak of their defeat, but not because of any sense of shame for having lost to a student. They realized they were witnessing the birth of something special. This one was different. This one could become legendary.

Of course, Bawb knew none of this. He was simply focusing on his goal, taking contracts as they came available, selecting those that happened to be nearest to where he needed to go to follow up on a lead, no matter how slim. In this way he was able to hop around the galaxy, performing his duties as expected while serving his own purposes.

He needed spare time to do that, however, and it was the pursuit of that cushion that led him to accelerate his speed on even the most difficult of tasks. Akin to when he would sandbag a lesson as a young Novice to afford himself a little time to study a particular skill on his own while the others moved ahead to the next lesson, Bawb was now creating a new version of that practice, albeit in a completely opposite manner.

Rather than move slowly to create a gap, he now raced through his actions with laser-like focus, always following the correct guidelines for his jobs but accomplishing them with increasing efficiency. In addition to that, Bawb was improvising new techniques no one had used before in the rushed furtherance of his goals, their creation birthed by necessity. He was blending the most unlikely of styles, using unconventional spells in the most unexpected of circumstances. Anything he had to do in order to wrap up a contract as quickly and efficiently as possible to free him up to spend as much time as he could following up on his own leads before he had to report back in.

As a result his number of successfully completed jobs was skyrocketing. In addition, he was gaining quite a reputation for his speed and stealth. Even his shimmer cloak abilities were nearly there. Perhaps not yet perfect, but starting to click into place well ahead of schedule.

The lone Ghalian assassin leaving a trail of the dead had begun to be considered something akin to an avenging spirit by those who had been in the vicinity of his completed contracts, somehow entering locations, completing his task, and exiting without so much as a trace. No one knew who he or she was, but word began to spread across the systems of some mysterious Ghalian who came and went like a geist, leaving a trail of the dead in their wake.

Bawb didn't care about the reputation. He was just working toward a very important goal. But soon after he had completed several particularly high-profile contracts with impossible stealth, the nickname stuck for good, and the legendary Geist was born.

Bawb did find it amusing that he actually had nothing to do with many of the deaths now being attributed to him, but he was not about to correct people's assumptions. The Geist was becoming a name to be feared, like the boogeyman, but one whose bloody work was more than a myth. And that could work to his benefit in the right situation. Like when he finally tracked down the elusive Kitzoff.

Despite his best efforts and many new leads confirming the man's involvement, however, the arms dealer was nowhere to be found. Vanished without a trace. He hoped he was merely operating under a low profile. If Kitzoff had been eliminated to cover his role in all this, he would be back searching at square one. But Bawb would keep looking.

The search, unfortunately, would take far longer than he had hoped for.

In the meantime, however, Bawb continued to work and train as usual, pushing himself physically as well as mentally, honing his skills and seeking out the most talented non-Ghalian masters of the martial or magical arts across the systems to further expand his knowledge. His own fighting style had come together a while ago, but as a result of his new endeavors, it was now shifting into something new, the change fueled by his newfound purpose in life.

He put those talents to good use in his work, finishing contracts with stealth and speed, always hoping to catch a break and receive word of the man he was searching for. The one person he had managed to learn of who was peripheral enough to the actual killing of Hozark to have been overlooked for liquidation. After all, the delivery of weapons would have been done well before the actual ambush, and as a result he would have been long gone by the time Hozark actually fell. That may well have saved his life. If only Bawb's people could find him.

As for the Ghalian, their investigation had still come up empty for the same reasons as Bawb's. The spy network had uncovered plenty of leads of their own, but all of them were dead ends in the most literal of senses. Someone had done a very thorough job cleaning up after themselves, and the Ghalian were no closer to an answer than before.

So it went for nearly a year, the order's spies coming up short and Bawb's own people quietly searching but finding nothing.

Until they finally did.

Bawb had been waiting so long, but when the word reached him that Kitzoff had been located in a quiet township on a quiet moon in a backwater system, he leapt at the chance, flying out fast and jumping continuously and with such haste that he nearly burned out his ship's Drookonus in the process. But he had a spare, and he could not afford to let this man slip away. Not after so long.

Bawb landed in the site closest to the township, unconcerned about a stealthy approach. His ship was nondescript, and he was in disguise. Just another traveler stopping on this moon for a bit of rest before continuing on his way. It was a disguise that required almost no effort whatsoever.

He was ready to do some digging to unearth the man but found him in the most anticlimactic of ways, sitting in the local tavern, drowning his sorrows. Bawb put on a cheerful grin and ordered a drink, then flopped down at the bar beside him.

"Whew, it's a hot one today," he said, downing the drink in a single quaff, the liquid magically appearing some distance away in an alleyway.

"Eh, it's been hotter," Kitzoff replied, a bit lost in thought.

"You okay, friend? You seem down. Let me buy you a drink. Another round, and whatever he's having."

The barkeep quickly served them, his tentacles moving in a well-practiced blur of activity. Bawb took a smaller drink this time, only draining the mug halfway. Kitzoff barely touched his.

"What's troubling you? You seem out of sorts. Is there anything I can do to help?"

"You don't even know me," the man replied.

"True. But I always make a point of helping those in need if I can. What goes around comes around, I say. Everything is reciprocal."

"Well, I appreciate the generosity, but I don't think you can help me. But I do thank you for the offer."

"How do you know I can't until you tell me what you need?"

"Trust me, you can't."

"Humor me," Bawb persisted.

Kitzoff sighed. "Fine. I need a ship. Loaned mine to a friend to run a little side hustle while I took some downtime, and it was destroyed. Now I've lost a ship, a friend, and I've been stuck here for longer than I can remember. A trader with no way to move his goods. How ridiculous is that?"

Bawb realized why no one had word of him for so long. He seemingly *had* been targeted for elimination, but whomever had done the actual deed had not verified he was aboard his ship when it was destroyed. It made sense he would have been, but to not confirm was simply sloppy assassination. But that worked in his favor, and an opportunity to get him alone had just presented itself.

"You say you have goods waiting to be transported?"

"Aye. A lot of 'em too."

"You know, with collateral like that, a ship should not be hard to come by."

"There's more to the problem, but I'm not gonna bore you with the details. Suffice it to say, not a single ship that's come through has been interested. This is a stopover point, not a trading outpost. Anyone who lands here is already full-up."

Bawb made a face as though he was weighing options in his head. A moment later, a bright smile emerged on his lips. "Listen, friend, crazy as it may sound, you may actually be in luck."

"I wouldn't call it luck."

"No, you misunderstand. What I'm telling you is, I've got a transport that I am about to sell. In fact, I was flying it to Orgaza for that very purpose when I decided to stop here for a break. But if you're a trader, maybe we could come to a mutually beneficial arrangement."

He had set the bait, now he just needed to give Kitzoff enough time to take it. He could see the gears turning in his head. Kitzoff clearly suspected he had gotten off lucky not being on his ship when it was destroyed. It was one of the risks of his line of work, and he'd managed to avoid it. But despite that close shave with death, the possibility of pulling himself from the ashes of his formerly profitable career was too much to just let slip by. Even if his subconscious was screaming at him to let it go as he had for the better part of the last year, having this opportunity drop in his lap was simply irresistable.

"A ship, you say? Is it fast?"

"Quite. And plenty of storage room for cargo. Since it's headed for sale, it's empty too. You want to take a look at it? I have it parked close by."

Kitzoff's energy seemed to perk up. He drained his drink and slid off his stool, his spirits renewed. "You know what? Yeah, I do."

"Excellent. Follow me."

Bawb led him out of the tavern, making small talk and charming the man with tales of finance and trade. It seemed the out-of-luck arms dealer had just stumbled upon the perfect silent partner to rebuild his business empire.

Or so he thought.

Once aboard the ship he found himself in a *very* different situation.

"What the hell are you doing?" he demanded when he awoke, bound to a chair and most definitely in space. "Where are you taking me?"

"Not far, do not worry. In fact, we are just outside the moon's atmosphere," Bawb replied. "Holding a low orbit for now. I wanted privacy for our discussion."

"What do you want with me? Why are you doing this?"

"Because, you have information I desire. Be forthcoming and I will spare you the pain of its extraction. There is no sense making this unpleasant," Bawb said with a friendly but cool grin. He wanted to persuade the man, not scare him. Not yet, at least.

"You're with the Council, aren't you? I knew I never should have gotten involved with their mess. Is this about that job last year?"

"Do you mean the one where you dropped off a large quantity of weapons on short notice?"

That was all he needed to confirm his fears. If only he knew the truth.

"Look, I did what I was hired to do. I found a lot of weaponry, and quick too. Flew out there and delivered it to your person just as requested."

This was news to Bawb. It sounded as if the exchange had occurred on the planet itself. Sloppy, to say the least, if true. Someone had been in a bit of a hurry, it seemed. Of course, if they were uncertain this was the mission Hozark would be on personally, they would have to be once they received confirmation.

"Ah, the handoff. The transfer took place on Radzor's surface."

"What? No, we did it in low orbit, as contracted."

"Right, of course. But there was a problem with your goods," Bawb improvised. "All appeared to be as requested, but after you departed some irregularities were noted. Damaged goods."

"They were pristine!"

"That is not what we heard, but I wonder..." Bawb said, slipping a look of doubt onto his face for good measure. "Could they have been damaged during the handoff?"

"Ask Skrillat. He's the one who took possession personally."

"In orbit, you said."

"Yeah, aboard that pirate bitch's ship. A pain in all our asses, that one is. Always stealing from our convoys."

Bawb maintained his facial expression, but the shock of those words sank in deep. He knew only one person who fit that description.

"Nixxa."

"Yeah, her."

"She can be a difficult one to deal with at times, indeed. But she serves a purpose."

"Like ferrying weapons and spies around for the Council from time to time, right? I know what you all are doing, and I tell ya, after that job, I don't want anything more to do with it."

Bawb nodded, the pieces all clicking into place.

"Do not worry," he said, pulling him from his seat and tossing him in the airlock. "You won't." Bawb almost pitied the man, but he had played a vital role in Hozark's death, and mercy was not an option. It wasn't even a consideration. But he had spoken freely. Tricked into doing it, but he'd been honest and saved Bawb a lot of time. Sparing him a miserable death seemed the right thing to do.

"Hey, can't we—"

Kitzoff fell silent, his neck snapped, killing him in an instant. Bawb jettisoned the body to burn up in the atmosphere. So far as the Council knew, he had died on his ship, and no one would ever be the wiser.

"Skrillat," he mused as he slid back into his command seat. "We need to have a little talk, you and I."

Of course he knew him. Skrillat was a name used by one of the Ghalian's top spies, embedded deep within the Council's ranks. A well-paid non-Wampeh who had sworn loyalty to the order and been one of their most useful agents over the years. But now it seemed things were different than they appeared.

Skrillat was a double agent, and he had used his high position within the spy ranks to help arrange Hozark's death. It was something he would pay for, no doubt, but first, he would be brought before the Five to reveal who had been pulling the strings behind the ambush. Only after would he pay the price.

It would be the last thing he ever did.

CHAPTER FIFTY-THREE

Bawb was eager to seek out Skrillat and bring him to justice before the Five, but there was just one problem. The master spy had infiltrated so deep within the Council of Twenty that he had effectively gone dark with no way to reach him. When there was intel of value, he would find a way to get it out of the secret facility he now called home. But getting a message in? Impossible.

Bawb had to plan, finding some way to reach him, and that would take time.

The base was hidden inside a massive asteroid and had no formal name, making matters a bit more difficult. Council vessels were irregular in their visits, and while he could determine which carried the most likely cargo to be transferred there, it seemed there were no regularly established Council craft for delivery duty. Also a significant difficulty.

Only one realistic opportunity presented itself, and it would take quite some effort to achieve. Bawb would have to infiltrate Nixxa's very own command ship. Unfortunately, she was always on the move these days. More than that, her defensive protocols made penetrating her craft unlikely, even for a cloaked ship. She was *very* paranoid, and it had served her well. It also meant a lot of work lay ahead of him if this was truly to be his path. He looked for other options but soon determined that the pirate craft was the only non-Council vessel reported to make the run, and even then only sporadically.

And he already had quite a history with the woman.

She was still pirating, of course, stealing from pretty much anyone she could, her happy and growing band of followers both in space and on safeworld planets keeping the bulk of the wealth taken for themselves but distributing a large amount to those in need as well. It was part of her psychological makeup to do so, not merely generosity or convenience to garner goodwill. And as she was on their payroll of late, the Council of Twenty was now turning a blind eye to her actions.

It seemed she had gone from being quite the thorn in their side, raiding their vessels without regard to who they belonged to, to a novel new position. That of paid contractor of the Council of Twenty. Say what you might about Nixxa, she was a shrewd businesswoman, and whatever deal she had struck, it was a certainty she was being paid *very* well for her services. As a result, hers was the only vessel he could count on making a trip there eventually. Sneaking aboard a Council ship in hopes it might be making that voyage would just be a guessing game and roll of the dice.

Bawb knew what had to be done. He just wasn't happy about it.

He prepared as usual, then took a difficult contract. One that would take a long time, if things didn't go just right. He thanked the Masters for their confidence and headed out, ready to take on the challenge. As it turned out, he accomplished the goal in no time, taking down a troublesome emmik protected by layers of guards and casters. Nevertheless, he managed it, but somewhere after his contract's completion, the young Ghalian vanished.

It pained Bawb that the others would think he had perished in the line of duty, but he had to do what he had to do, going silent and beginning a long infiltration. When he finally returned with Skrillat in hand, revealing his role in Hozark's death, all would be forgiven.

He spent the first month of his absence disguising himself as various crewmembers aboard several lower-level Council ships, killing a crewmember and taking their identity, and stowing their body in a stasis spell until he was ready to move on. Then later, when he was provided the opportunity to move to another ship higher up in the food chain, he would release the body, leaving it to appear the victim of a depressurization incident or other accident, making his sudden absence as that person go unquestioned.

Again and again he would repeat this over the first month. By the second, however, he was moving up to more powerful vessels. This meant spending more time aboard one ship, and on some occasions, he would be forced to take the identity of another Wampeh. With the robust detection spells and powerful casters aboard some of the Council craft, he had to resort to practical makeup to alter his naturally Wampeh features to match those of his victims. In those instances, his was the one race he could copy with just a bit of makeup without much difficulty.

Unfortunately, that meant he was unable to select freely from any of the crew he wished to impersonate. While Wampeh were a common race among the many represented aboard most ships, they would typically make up a handful of the crew. The Geist made it work, and he did so flawlessly, his stealth unrivaled as he leapfrogged from ship to ship until, one day, the opportunity he had been waiting for finally presented itself.

Nixxa was being summoned to take some sort of highly secret cargo off their hands and deliver it to the mysterious Council base. His post aboard this ship was not one that afforded him very much in the way of higher-level access, but he did manage to hear that the transfer would occur in two weeks, after they had first secured the cargo themselves from a clandestine transport ship. When queried why they couldn't just deliver it themselves, the ranking officer made it quite clear that very few knew the location it was being delivered to, and even fewer had clearance to actually land. Most craft were held at a distance, locked in the defensive system's kill box. And if they approached without permission? *Boom.*

Bawb worked his figurative magic, infiltrating areas of the ship and eavesdropping on conversations, learning which of the crew would be handling the transfer. Mostly it would be Nixxa's people retrieving the cargo from the Council ship, but a few Council crewmembers would be present for the handoff. It was one of those whom Bawb would have to become.

It would be difficult and risky, requiring the killing and stowing of his chosen target's body in the cargo bay itself, ready and waiting to appear to be the victim of some unfortunate accident. But not too soon. It had to be timed just right. And he would have to ensure his current disguise's corpse would also suffer a tragic but unsuspicious demise in the same limited window.

He planned carefully, setting several interlocked spells together over the days, each of them so small and cast far enough apart that the ship's casters would likely not sense a thing. Individually they were minute. Together, however, they would trigger a pair of incidents. Ones that would look like accidents and do exactly what he needed them to.

Bawb carried on with his cover identity's daily duties, cracking jokes, making small talk, and basically fitting in as just

SCOTT BARON

another cog in the machine, doing his job and getting by. Inside, however, he was running calculations constantly, ready to adjust his plan on the fly if need be. There would be but one shot at this, and he was damn sure going to make it count.

At the appointed time and place, Nixxa's pirate craft jumped out of nowhere, appearing dangerously close to the Council vessel. Of course, she was a very seasoned pirate, and her piloting skills were second to none. Not to mention pirates used tactics like this all the time to take their prey by surprise. A risky move, but one that worked. And those who perfected it often had very profitable careers. Those who didn't, well, on occasion they would meet a most unfortunate end when their jump deposited them a little *too* close to their target. In those cases, the destructive results went without saying.

"Where is it?" Nixxa bellowed out, striding into the cargo hold in front of her team of lackeys.

Bawb surveyed them quickly, noting size, gender, rank, position in the group, and if they possessed power of their own. It was a quick calculus, and he made his selection in mere moments. Now the hard part. To sneak aboard their pirate ship and dispose of the man, taking his place without notice.

"Nixxa, how lovely to see you," the loadmaster called out in reply, crossing the deck to meet her.

"Yeah, lovely, my ass. I've been summoned to play ferry ship for some Council crap yet again."

"It is an honor to be afforded such a degree of trust."

"Screw trust. I'm in it for the coin," she spat back. "So? Where is it?"

"There. Five crates, each quite heavy."

"Whatever. My people'll make short work of it. Pollix, get the gang moving. We're on a schedule."

"You got it, Cap'n! You heard her, get to work, you lot!"

Bawb remembered the man. He had shown him kindness

when he was but a boy. Lucky for Pollix, he was too close to Nixxa to be a good target. At least not now. For now, Bawb simply needed to hitch a ride and be as unnoticed as possible. Once he had acquired the traitorous spy, then he could see about having words with the woman responsible for ferrying him around and seeing what additional information she might possess.

But first things first. He had to get aboard her ship, and the window was small and closing fast as her team began moving the enormous crates, lifting them with hover spells and maneuvering them to the airlock joining the ships via a sealed umbilical spell. Just as he had anticipated.

Bawb's plan had grown a little more complex when he took the identity of the worker helping guide the visiting pirates back to their craft—he now had one more body to dispose of, but that one was in their bunk, apparently dead of a heart attack. Unusual, but it happened.

His current one would be more difficult. And it would require an expert application of camouflage magic like he had never before attempted. The crates bumped slightly as they hopped from the ship's deck into the short umbilical spell locking the craft together. It was a powerful spell, and one used often. But that wasn't to say it never had problems. Problems like the one Bawb had concocted.

The tripwire spell started the reaction, disconnecting the umbilical from the Council ship, setting them floating, precious air blasting out all around them. Now was the moment he had been preparing for. He yanked his shimmer cloak from the top of the crate, and with it the body of the man he was impersonating, sending him tumbling out into the void.

The pirates and Council crew alike were hanging on for dear life, struggling to reconnect the spell as their training had taught them. In that moment, while they were all focused with singular intensity on the danger in front of them, an assassin moved in their midst, removing one of the pirates from the equation and quickly hiding his body atop a crate, covered by the shimmer cloak, blending in to all but the most scrutinizing observation. It was all done so fast, no one even noticed. The Geist at his finest.

"Get the gap sealed!" Nixxa bellowed.

"Trying, Cap!" Pollix shouted back as he and the others calmly moved through the motions, casting their spells in unison while simultaneously sending tether spells behind them, making sure their booty, or in this case, cargo, would not be lost to space.

Bawb cast right alongside them, now disguised as their comrade. No one had noticed the switch. He had pulled it off.

He fought hard alongside them, casting and casting, knitting the breach bit by bit. That he had secondary and tertiary spells stymying their efforts just added to the diversion, giving him that little extra time to lock in his victim's look, voice, and mannerisms. He had only been afforded a few minutes to learn as much about them as he could. Now, as they sealed the rift and resumed the transfer of the cargo, he would have to improvise.

Bawb was now a part of Nixxa's crew, with all that entailed. Most importantly, though, he would be taken right to their destination. And he wouldn't have to sneak in. He would be invited as they docked as familiars.

Bawb maneuvered the crates along with his supposed comrades, safely ensconced in Nixxa's ship. Next stop, the secret Council base.

CHAPTER FIFTY-FOUR

The delivery run to the secret Council base turned out to be more complicated than even Bawb had initially believed. Once aboard Nixxa's ship, he quickly learned the reason so few knew where the base actually was and why it was so hard to find.

The facility was not stationary in an asteroid field, but rather, moving through space. Their landing site was a moving target.

He had to give the Council some credit for this one. Normally they were a bit rigid in their thinking, following the ages-old traditions of constructing robust fortresses and compounds across the various systems as not only the residences of the Council of Twenty's leaders, but also safe havens as they moved around their realms.

This, however, was something new. Someone was thinking outside the box. No one aboard the ship seemed to know who had come up with the idea, but Bawb made a mental note to do some digging when this was all done. Whomever that person was, their spies would need to keep a closer eye on them.

But that was for later. The pressing matter now was to remain blended in with the crew and make it to the Council base without discovery. There were always some particular ways about different pirate crews, and each had their own shorthand and lexicon, partly out of habit, but also as a means of sussing out interlopers. It was a pretty good system and one that didn't require much thought once put in place, all of it becoming second nature to the entire crew.

That meant they rarely, if ever, changed any of it. And that worked to Bawb's advantage.

When he was a boy, he had infiltrated Nixxa's ship, and it was the same one she flew now, though a great many upgrades and modifications had been made to it over the years. Robust shielding spells had been woven into the hull, as well as blocking wards against breach and intrusion. Pretty much anything to make her craft as secure as possible against enemies and would-be intruders. Only those specifically permitted were allowed inside.

Without realizing they had done so, Bawb had been included in the entry spell during the cargo transfer and now had free access. At least until they changed the spell again in a week or so.

But more than just that, his prior visit had given him time to observe her crew. Nixxa had unwittingly taken in the Ghalian as a boy, and in that brief time among them the attentive youth had learned a great many of their pass phrases and crew-specific speech patterns. And as this was the same crew, albeit with some additions and losses over the years, no one had ever thought to change them.

He didn't know all of the minutia, of course, but he knew enough to blend in upon his arrival, and he immediately began listening to and memorizing every new irregularity of speech he heard, echoing them back to the others he interacted with until they all just accepted him for who he was. No outsider would know to speak like that, after all.

Unless that interloper was a disguised Ghalian with a particular bit of specialized expertise, that is.

Bawb fully embraced his role, acting as a pirate, eating and drinking as a pirate, carousing and merry-making as a pirate. But he had to do so with caution. While he had been able to observe the person whose identity he was now wearing for a few moments during the cargo swap, he had no idea how they acted in a less formal group setting. It was easier to downplay it a little and ramp up his persona rather than the other way around, using a stomach bug or some such excuse if anyone commented that his energy seemed low.

As it turned out, he more or less nailed it on the first try, and from that point on he just had to memorize the names and faces of the crew, which was easy enough for a Ghalian of his level. Beyond that, it was business as usual aboard Nixxa's ship.

He discovered the person he was playing was fairly highly ranked and, as a result, had a great deal of free time when they weren't engaged in some sort of action. It made sense. They had been part of the small group tasked with retrieving the secret cargo, and only Nixxa's most-trusted crew would be allowed on so sensitive a task. And as he had hoped, the same people would be doing the offloading as well.

So Bawb settled in for the flight and took walks around the ship, noting every last detail in his mental catalog. Where chambers were, what sort of emergency egress routes existed, and most importantly, what sorts of magical wards were in place *within* the ship itself. As it turned out, Nixxa's paranoia extended mostly to the outer parts of the craft, warding off intruders with powerful spells pretty much everywhere.

Inside, however, she did not seem to have anything excessively difficult to deal with at all, save for the robust wards around her personal quarters. After Hozark's visit to her many years ago, she had been sure to reinforce those compartments immediately. But with a solid week to chip away at them, devising a disarming sequence, Bawb was unconcerned. Normally, he wouldn't be afforded that sort of leisure, and in that case they would be quite formidable. Time, however, was a great equalizer.

As for when Nixxa traveled *outside* the ship, her casters went with her, using their natural magic to bolster her own robust konus should she need them. But Bawb had met them, first getting a feel for their magic from a distance, and he had determined they were not readers. They could not sense his disguise. That was to his benefit. But then, he also had a different target in his sights, at least at first. Nixxa would go unbothered, for now.

Bawb moved the stasis-frozen corpse of the man he was impersonating on his second day aboard, having located a good place to stash it for later use, covering his tracks. This not only gave him one less thing to worry about when things got moving, but it also let him reclaim the shimmer cloak for his own use, though he was still a bit concerned about using it in motion. He'd gotten better, yes, but that last bit had not yet clicked all the way.

So he would practice when he had free time and could find a private spot in which to make his attempts unbothered. Beyond that, he was content to simply ride it out, saving his mental, magical, and physical bandwidth for the most difficult part of his quest. Once he reached the asteroid base, all bets were off. There would be powerful casters. There would be robust defenses. And he would be going in utterly blind.

The ship was jumping periodically, but much of their transit was done via regular flight, albeit at a very high rate of speed. The team of Drooks powering the ship were impressively powerful. He could sense them even through the hull, but when tracking a moving target like the asteroid across such vast distances, it was important to reassess and confirm one's trajectory regularly lest they travel in the wrong direction.

The call to their stations roused Bawb from his meditation. As they drew closer to the traitor, he had tucked himself away in a quiet storage area, the imminent encounter bringing up memories and making him even ponder the riddle Hozark had posed to him as a boy and a few more times over the years. *A fire blazes, dead without embers. Storms rage, yet a feather floats.*

Now he would never be able to ask him what that meant. He ran it through his mind over and over, feeling the meaning was so close, just on the tip of his consciousness, yet out of reach. No amount of focusing and mentally preparing for the challenge that was coming next could force it before they arrived, and by the sound of it, that time had finally come.

Bawb hopped to his feet, ensured his gear was secure and his disguise firmly in place, and made his way to the cargo area. The others on his delivery team were gathering as well, all of them wearing their most serious faces. This wasn't some free-wheeling pirate gig. This was the most vital of deliveries, and to a place few even knew existed. Nixxa was making a huge amount of coin from these runs, and she spread the wealth among her crew. No one wanted to mess that up, nearly as much as they wouldn't dare disappoint their captain.

Say what you might about other pirates, this bunch was loyal to the death. And from the talk among the group, that was exactly what would happen to them if they strayed out of the base receiving area. There and there alone they were allowed to set foot. Anywhere else was an instant death sentence.

Just the sort of odds Bawb expected.

The plan was to bring the cargo off the ship and settle it in the location designated by the receiving loadmaster, then immediately head back aboard their ship. Nixxa would stay off the ship and be accompanied into the base proper for the evening, dining with the commander and top aides. Then she would depart, returning to her ship much wealthier and with a belly full of the finest gourmet food.

That left a slim but manageable window for Bawb to infiltrate, locate and snatch the traitor, then bundle him back aboard the ship unconscious and locked in a small container for delivery to the Five. Impossible? It would be, even for most Ghalian. But Bawb was not most Ghalian.

Only one risk variable remained, the weak link in his plan. The one that no matter how he labored, he just couldn't quite get to work. Now it seemed he would just have to try his best and either succeed or perish. There was no middle ground. Bawb had concealed Hozark's shimmer cloak on his person and was as ready as he'd ever be, focusing on his intent, needing the spell to work to its full capacity just this once.

For some reason, Hozark's cryptic words kept creeping back into his thoughts, repeating in his head like some sort of mantra. *A fire blazes, dead without embers. Storms rage, yet a feather floats.*

"Oh," he gasped as his mentor's words suddenly made sense. "Oh, I see!"

It's about time, his konus chimed in, the shimmer cloak icon on his display registering a level up at long last. It also unlocked an entirely new series of obscured skills that hadn't even been visible before, blurred or not. He realized there was still a *long* way to go in his journey. But he was most definitely on his way.

Hozark had left him his powerful shimmer cloak. Not a training cloak, but the tool of a Master Ghalian, and one of the most vital ones at that. But he had drilled it into Bawb's head over and over and over; making a spell work was not about force. It was about calm and sure focus, no matter the strength of the magic involved. Even the most dangerous and powerful spells required the same thing.

A raging fire, full of strength and power, was nothing

without the embers calmly smoldering at its base. The very substance upon which it was born. And no matter how strong a storm's winds might be, a feather did not fight them, but rather floated at ease, becoming part of the storm, one with it rather than opposing its might.

Bawb felt the shimmer cloak react even before he activated it, as if it recognized him, having only been waiting for him to use it properly for the first time.

"Let's move," Nixxa called out to her people, setting the procession in motion.

The cargo was bulky but manageable, the enormous crates floating into the base with relative ease. The loadmaster directed them where to place the freight and left them to it. They did just that, making a few trips then returning to the ship as their captain was escorted into the base.

No one noticed one of their number was not with them, assuming he had simply gone on ahead.

Invisible, moving as quietly and smoothly as possible, Bawb followed Nixxa inside, staying close to her as the entry security spells pulled back for her, closing behind her as she was shown to her meeting with the base commander. It was only because eyes were everywhere and this base was seen as impenetrable that the gap existed, and he took full advantage of their error.

Bawb's shimmer-cloaked form quickly hugged the wall and waited. He still wasn't perfect at using the cloak in motion, but it had worked well enough for gaining entry. And once he was alone, he would begin the next step in his mission, confident he could carry his target out unseen, a calm happiness in his gut as he used his mentor's gift as he'd surely intended.

"Thank you, Master Hozark," he said quietly. "I will see you avenged."

CHAPTER FIFTY-FIVE

The funny thing about super-secure top-secret facilities is that they are often so difficult to access that once you are inside, the security is far more relaxed than a normal location that has sensitive areas scattered throughout it. Those types of places have guards and wards and all sorts of security systems to keep people from the unsecure areas from wandering into places they do not belong.

But when the entire base is one giant secure area, designed with chokepoint entry systems and robust defenses, once you are inside those kind of locations, further precautions and checkpoints tend to be largely disregarded. Essentially, the logic being, if you're inside, you're supposed to be there, and the thought of anyone making it that far who wasn't was almost laughable to those designing the security measures.

It was a quirk that benefitted Bawb enormously as he began his race to find the traitorous spy Skrillat. While the shimmer cloak was working well for him, he was still not fully proficient yet. Yes, it was clicking and making visceral sense now, but even so, it would still take a bit more work to become truly expert in its use. Bawb realized, as he finally connected with the right intent for this particularly tricky and powerful bit of magic, that as he embarked on this deadly endeavor, several other lessons Hozark had imparted to him now applied as well.

"Being still is being active," he had once said. "And moving slowly is also moving fast."

At the time it had seemed like some mystical guru mumbo-jumbo, but Bawb had been quite young and hadn't yet learned to glean the lessons from the Master Ghalian's words. Now, however, it all made sense. Children would naturally take those words literally, but as an adult, the layers revealed themselves.

For now Bawb was on the move in disguise, having adopted the appearance of one of the base guards he had seen escorting Nixxa to her meeting with the commander. It wasn't one he wanted to use if he could avoid it—that person was somewhere else right now in the same facility, and that could lead to questions—but in the interest of speed he made the compromise, hoping to avoid more than a passing greeting with others if possible. He was saving his shimmer magic for when he needed it most. When he smuggled the spy's unconscious form out of the base. If he timed it right, no one would know he was missing until they were long gone.

Skrillat was certainly using his own form rather than a disguise for this infiltration. To maintain a false appearance for the months upon months, or even years, it would take to burrow this deep into the Council's ranks was simply not feasible. So Bawb had that going for him. The man looked the way he should, making visual identification easy. But he didn't know for certain what name he was currently using, nor what his duties were aboard the asteroid base. Ideally, it would be a position where his absence wouldn't be noticed, but without those details he would just have to wing that part and hope for the best.

After a solid half-hour of searching, Bawb realized this was not going to work. He was blindly seeking out one person in a massive facility, and as it was a top-secret site, things were not labeled as they would be elsewhere, nor were there easily accessible records of the crew staffing the base. He was going to have to try something different. Different, and a bit out of his wheelhouse.

Try it, the konus urged. *What've you got to lose?*

"Besides my life, you mean?"

Nothing ventured, nothing gained, Adept. You know the spell. You know you do.

The konus was right, of course. He did know the spell. He just hadn't ever used it before. But as he was running out of time and options in a hurry, it seemed there was a first time for everything, and today was that day. Again.

"Excuse me," he said, approaching what appeared to be a middle-ranked officer. The type who oversaw a fair amount while not actually getting their own hands dirty if they could avoid it.

"What is it?" the man asked just as the dazzle spell hit.

Bawb pulled him into a restroom chamber he had noted prior and shut the door. The spell had worked, but he didn't know how long it would last. Normally, the victim would not remember anything of the last several minutes or longer, depending on the power and skill of the caster. In his case, this was his first real-world attempt. The spell could last a while or mere seconds. He would have to extract the information as fast as possible.

"You will answer me as concisely and quickly as possible. Do you understand?"

"Yes."

Amazingly, the spell was still working. Bawb was casting so much above his rank it actually made him nervous as well as thrilled, but he also knew he had to work quickly. He described

Skrillat and demanded that person's name, duties, and location. For once, fortune was on his side. He was called Tonzio, and his quarters were very close by. Better yet, today and tomorrow were his off-duty days. No one would even notice him missing.

The man started blinking faster. The spell was wearing off.

"*Boto pa,*" Bawb intoned, the spell knocking his rousing victim into a deep sleep. Locked in the restroom, he would remain undisturbed for at least a little bit.

Bawb raced down the halls as fast as he could without drawing attention to himself, now wearing the slumbering man's identity, confident that at least now no one would see him in two places at once. He reached the spy calling himself Tonzio's quarters in no time.

"Yes?" a voice called when he activated the door chime spell.

"Tonzio, I need to speak with you."

The spy opened the door and was hit immediately with a powerful stun spell. It drove him back, but amazingly, he stayed on his feet. Apparently, he was wearing a defensive spell at all times, powered by his konus. Clever, Bawb had to admit.

Bawb slammed the door, casting a powerful muting spell in a flash, silencing the chamber to the outside world. And it was a good thing. Tonzio began shouting for help, attempting to trigger an alarm spell. The muting spell held, blocking it, but only barely. The man had some serious skills at his disposal. It made sense, given his rank as a spy, and Bawb realized he would have to be very careful handling this one.

"Who the hell are you? You're clearly not Zorfin," the spy asked, a blade appearing in his hand. He wasn't a Ghalian, but he knew the craft well.

Bawb let the disguise slide away, revealing his true form.

"Of course," Skrillat said with a little chuckle. "A Ghalian, naturally. I wondered if you would eventually come for me." He wasn't even trying to hide his guilt. For a Ghalian to be here it was a certainty he'd been found out.

"I have, and you will come with me," Bawb replied coolly. "Unconscious, of course."

"My, my. So brazen. Bawb, isn't it?"

"How do you know who I am?" Bawb asked, hiding his confusion expertly.

It didn't matter.

Skrillat had been at this game a long, long time and was a master at reading people, and he most certainly knew how to push their buttons. It was only natural, after all. Being a spy, he had perfected his many manipulation skills long ago. A little grin creased his lips.

"You cast a muting spell, I see."

"Of course."

"Clever boy."

"I am a *man*, and a Wampeh Ghalian, *Spy*."

"And yet you let so little a thing make you emotional. It makes sense, of course, given who you are."

Bawb grinned but felt no mirth. He slid his fangs into place slowly, a cold look in his eye. "And how do you know who I am?"

"Oh, put your fangs away, boy. I know as well as you that my blood is useless to you."

Bawb actually did. This man knew the Ghalian intimately. It was why he was able to set up his mentor's demise.

"Good. Now that's showing some sense. And to answer your question, young Bawb, Hozark spoke of you often over the years. It was all casual chatter, of course, but his interest seemed a bit more keen than with other young Ghalian. So much so that I did a little digging. I must say, it was *fascinating* what I found, though it wasn't easy, I assure you. But, for one such as me, that was just a fun little added challenge. Getting my answer to that question was a given, in time."

"I do not care about your treachery. You are coming with me."

"You plan on taking me to the Five, don't you?"

"You know what awaits you."

"Perhaps. But what is before me now is just a young Ghalian. Poor Bawb. So sad. So alone."

"You are not getting a rise out of me, if that is your intent. And I am not sad, nor am I alone. My brothers and sisters alike await justice. Justice that will be served when you are before the—"

Skrillat launched a flurry of magic and hidden blades without warning, the sheer ferocity of the attack making it quite clear how he had survived so long in this deadly business. Bawb reacted fast but was forced to use far more power than he wanted in doing so. He cast a counterattack but Skrillat was already in motion, batting it aside and moving in with yet more blades in his hands.

Bawb drew his as well and parried the strikes, marveling at how fast and nimble the older man was. But it made sense. He may not have been a Ghalian, but he had been trained by them, taken into the fold as one of their most trusted agents.

"You betrayed the order," Bawb grunted, landing a punch to the man's chest.

"What can I say? I got a better offer," he replied flippantly, though it was clear from his body language that he was beginning to struggle, his calm demeanor a mere façade.

"Coin? You betrayed one of the Five for *coin*?"

Skrillat and Bawb locked blades, their faces inches apart as they struggled against one another.

"What can I say? Coin and friends in high places aren't a bad thing to have."

"What friends? Who ordered this?"

"You know I'll never tell you," he shot back, kicking out Bawb's leg and hitting him with a force spell.

Bawb spun, the spell deflecting harmlessly away as he let loose a flurry of his *real* martial skills. He had been trying to take the man in unharmed, but he'd had enough of that. Skrillat was a good fighter and dangerous. But more than that, he was pissing him off. Bawb's punch spell snuck in through his enemy's defenses after a distracting peppering of projectile spells set him up to miss.

The spell hit hard, slamming the spy into the wall. With the muting spell in place, no one outside heard a sound. Bawb realized, however, his konus was running low on power. He'd drawn from it for so long on this quest that when it came time to battle, it was sadly lacking.

Skrillat moved fast and redoubled his efforts, locking magic with the Adept. And he was *strong* in that regard. So strong that Bawb faced the uneasy realization that had he actually found this man when he first started his quest for revenge, he would surely have fallen to his skills.

But this was a different time, and he was a different Ghalian.

Both were bleeding from their edged weapons now, but Bawb held a distinct advantage where blades were concerned. He was going to win. But Skrillat, always a tactician at heart, realized this as they crossed blades again, and he still had a few extra special tricks up his sleeve.

"All this to avenge your Master," he said with a forced laugh.

"He was a good man. My mentor," Bawb growled back.

Skrillat's eyes sparkled with unexpected amusement. Enough so that Bawb was taken aback by the reaction.

"Your mentor? Is that all? Priceless. You didn't even know he was your father, did you?"

No matter how much training he'd had, the words struck harder than any weapon or spell. Bawb's resolve faltered as shock ran through his body. A sharp pain ripped through his side, Skrillat's blade driven deep.

"And now you'll perish just like the man who sired you," he said with open malice.

Bawb felt his strength waver. He was hurt, and his magic was nearly out. There had to be a way. Hozark was his father? It seemed impossible, but he knew in his heart that was not a lie. And he absolutely could not let him down. Not now. Not so close to finding who ordered him dead.

Level Unlocked: Family

Bawb had never heard of that level, nor any powers that were associated with it, but the konus didn't care. A massive amount of power flooded into him, released as the blocks placed on the device fell away, triggered by his now-accepted familial bond.

The knife twisted in his side, and Bawb nearly fell from the pain. Instinct kicked in, and he cast hard, an ugly, violent spell let loose out of pure self-preservation.

Skrillat didn't have so much as a moment to make one final snarky comment before his body exploded, vaporizing into a mist, chunks spraying the walls and ceiling.

Bawb staggered back and pulled the dagger free, the magic now available to him easily knitting the injury. He looked around, staring at the carnage in shock. This was supposed to be a prisoner taken to the Five. This was his lead to Hozark—his father's killer. And now?

A bit of overkill, I'd agree, the konus said. *But the bastard deserved it.*

"What happened, Konus?"

You released the largest block to my stored power, the same as when Hozark wore me when he was a boy. Each Ghalian has a different trigger, of course. In your case, it was the truth of your origins. He knew you'd find out one day, quite possibly after his demise. And when that day came, he wanted you to be ready to protect yourself completely.

The words hit Bawb like a slap across the soul. He had been training with his father all this time. Spending countless hours with him. Learning secret techniques known only to a handful. The sort of thing you'd expect to be handed down to the closest of relations, not just an apprentice.

The sticky-wetness of bloody reality crept back in, pulling him from his thoughts. He could ponder this later. Right now, he had to get the hell out of this place, and fast. But first he had to clean himself thoroughly. He hurried into the showering stall and washed the blood and gore away, drying off then leaping across the crimson pool to the doorway, not dirtying his boots with the blood.

There was so much of it, and the scene was horrific. There was no way he could cover up this mess. No plausible story to explain it away.

Bawb made a decision then and there. He wouldn't even try. Rather, he'd do something quite the opposite.

He cast a small spell, burning a message into the slick floor itself, confident and empowered, ready for whatever came next. He was the man who made it in and out unnoticed, unseen, slaying without fear of repercussion. This was who he was now.

Bawb opened the door and stepped outside, sealing it tight with multiple spells, leaving behind the mark of the Geist.

CHAPTER FIFTY-SIX

Bawb's magic was firing on all cylinders, the power flowing freely from his unlocked konus bolstering his shimmer cloak with ease as he raced down the hallways of the Council base. He had been exceptionally careful getting in, and he was equally cautious on the way out. The only difference was he had just left one of the base staff reduced to a puddle of muck, and though he was confident he had secured the room thoroughly, and he knew that Skrillat was not due to be at work for some time, things could always go awry. All it would take was one person checking in on him and the jig would be up.

If that happened, he damn well needed to be aboard Nixxa's ship instead of trapped within the base.

Of course, they would lock everything down and search from top to bottom, but her ship was far easier to maneuver around to avoid detection if it came down to that. The base, on the other hand, would be an inescapable death trap.

Ideally, they'd be long gone before any of that became a problem, and with that in mind and with no prisoner to carry, Bawb moved as fast as he could, the shimmer cloak heeding his very clear and very powerful intent, making him invisible to all even in motion.

It was a speed run of sorts, taking the most direct route back to the pirate vessel. Bawb had to avoid the wards of the more restricted areas of the base, but that was easy enough. The hard part was a variable he hadn't counted on.

The beasts the two guards were leading through the facility were small compared to most guard animals. But what they lacked in size they made up for in razor-sharp teeth and long, retractable claws. With sharp eyes and keen hearing, the creatures were natural hunters, well-built for the task. He had encountered their kind before and dealt with them on a few occasions in his training. They were quite difficult to fight due to their extreme flexibility, allowing their bodies to twist and turn in ways that made landing a killing blow tricky.

But they had a weakness.

Despite all of their natural gifts and attributes, one of their senses was not as sharp as the others. Relying on sight and sound to pinpoint their prey, the beasts had evolved a rather rudimentary sense of smell. It was an unusual shift for an animal, as most tended to have exceptional olfactory talents. But these were visual hunters first and foremost. And with his shimmer cloak functioning robustly, Bawb would be able to avoid detection. He just had to stay utterly still and not make a sound.

The Geist held his breath as the guards and their animals padded past him without notice, his scent masked by a simple spell as an added precaution, his form perfectly hidden beneath his shimmer cloak. He waited until they had been out of sight for a few minutes before finally moving once more. The labyrinth of corridors soon took him to the trickiest part of his escape. The sealed door leading to the cargo dock.

This was a particularly robust spell, and it had to be released by one of the guards in charge of the area. The loadmaster was also able to do so, however, and it was that persona he quickly adopted, shifting his appearance and walking into the guards' office with an angry look on his face.

"What's this I hear about one of those newly delivered crates being damaged?" he growled menacingly, copying the man's voice and tone as best he could, hoping the fear his sudden, angry appearance caused the guards would make them overlook any irregularities.

"Sir? I hadn't heard—"

"Did I ask for your input? Get out there and verify the condition of every last one of them! If there's damage, I damn well expect a full report on who caused it and why."

"Yes, sir," the guard said, lurching to his feet.

"But don't go wasting my time if there's nothing there. I've got better things to do. No damage, no report, is that clear?"

"Clear as day, sir."

"Then get to it. And let me tell you, if this turns out to be nothing, *I* will handle the fool wasting my time with it personally."

The guard jumped to it, releasing the door spell and hurrying out to survey the containers. Bawb seized the opportunity and cloaked himself once more, slipping out unseen behind him and making his way across the cargo area, being sure to steer wide of the man working to ensure he would not face his superior's wrath.

Of course, there was no damage, and the whole thing would be no more than an exercise in futility for the guard. But it had served its purpose. Bawb had accessed the final restricted area, and no report would ever reach the loadmaster's desk. Best of all, like all Council goons, unless their higher-up mentioned it, the guards wouldn't speak of the issue again.

Bawb cleared the crate storage area in a flash and rushed

back aboard Nixxa's waiting ship with ease. At least that one part of this ordeal wasn't a challenge. They were at the most secure base in this part of the galaxy, and the pirate crew were the ones not allowed *out* of their ship. There was no need to secure the door Nixxa would be using to come back in.

Bawb shifted into his pirate disguise and made his way to the mess hall just in time to join the others for dinner. He was greeted with the usual shit talking one found among their ilk, dishing out a bit of his own and taking a seat at one of the long communal tables. He ate heartily, his large portions and matching appetite not something he had to fake. He'd burned a lot of energy in a short period of time, and the recharge was very much appreciated.

On top of that, as he had remembered from his visit all those years ago as a fresh-faced boy, the food was amazing. Nixxa spared no expense when it came to seeing her crew was well-fed and happy. These people would sometimes be in space for months with no shore leave that whole time. Excellent food was one of the things that kept their spirits high. Say what you might about the pirate captain, she knew how to take care of her people. They would lay down their lives for her if it came to it, and it was because of the myriad ways she showed her appreciation to her people. They weren't just crew. They were family.

Bawb marveled at their little ecosystem. It was almost Ghalian-like, in a way.

He was finishing up his meal when Nixxa strode into the mess hall to the uproarious cheers of her crew. It seemed her dinner meeting had gone smoothly and quickly. And most importantly, no one had noticed the dead man's remains.

"We're done here," Nixxa called out to the assembled crew. "A good run and even better pay. You'll all be getting bonuses."

Another cheer and a few toasts to their beloved captain ensued, and despite being quite full from her meal, Nixxa indulged in a tall drink, downing it in a single quaff.

"Okay. Pollix, Dinbar, with me. Let's get the hell out of here. The sooner we put this place behind us the better."

Pollix was on his feet in a flash. "Aye, Captain."

Nixxa looked at the assembled crew, a happy little smile on her lips. This was her home, and she couldn't think of anything better. It was clear the faces looking back at her felt the same.

"All right, you all can take the day off, but don't overdo it. We're stopping on Grovvix tomorrow. I think a bit of shore leave is in order."

She exited the mess hall to the cheers of her team, heading to the command center with a smile on her face.

Bawb waited a few minutes then took his leave, walking casually down the ship's corridors with a grin firmly in place, as if he hadn't a care in the world. They would make landfall soon, and he would make his return to the training house. And then he'd explain his lengthy absence, along with why he'd kept his quest secret, to the Masters. And given what he'd learned, they would welcome the information and shift some of the spy network's focus in a new direction. One that would hopefully get them closer to finding the one pulling the strings behind his father's demise.

The ship shuddered slightly as it pulled free of the Council base's tethering spells and into open space. A slight feeling of relief hit him. They were clear.

The Geist, eh? the konus said. *I like it. Sure to strike fear in the hearts of whoever hears the name.*

"That is the plan, though the moniker was not of my doing."

True, but it serves the purpose all the same. And after this, the legend will only spread farther. Faster. It may be a secure facility, but there is no way news of something as brazen and impressive as this does not leak out.

"We shall see."

Level up.

The konus stopped at that.

"You did not say in what, konus. Are you actually at a loss for words? That would be a first."

No, I'm actually just marveling at what you've accomplished.

"Thank you."

You don't catch my meaning. You have leveled up, Master Bawb.

"You mean Adept."

No, I do not.

A whole new group of Master level spells appeared on his hidden display, along with all the Maven ones.

You have achieved what no one ever has. Not ever. Incredible, really.

"What are you talking about?"

You have skipped the level of Maven and achieved the level of Master, is what I'm saying. Only barely, mind you—and you still need a ton of work on all the Maven-level skills—but what you have accomplished on this outing and the expertise with which you wielded your abilities has overridden my normal constraints.

"I was only doing what needed to be done."

And in so doing you've become a Master Ghalian. Not officially, of course, but you can trust me on this. I am an impartial device, and as such, my assessment entirely objective.

"But the Masters are unaware you exist."

True. And so it's going to stay. And as for you, you'll remain an Adept to them. But know this, Bawb, son of Hozark, Master Ghalian and one of the Five. You have lived up to your potential. You are a Master. It is incontrovertible, and I should know. Your actions have proven your worth, and having spent so many years on his wrist before yours, let me say, your father would be proud.

Bawb felt a warmth in his chest, but his eyes remained dry. He quickened his pace slightly, heading toward the final piece in this particular puzzle.

"Thank you. But I am not done yet."

CHAPTER FIFTY-SEVEN

Nixxa was sitting quietly in her quarters, relaxing with a pleasant glass of a fine Orlatian wine in her hand. She'd bathed and put on something far more comfortable and less restricting than the formal outfit she'd worn to her dinner meeting. She had to look the part for the Council big-wigs, of course, but now, safely locked in the warded and sealed confines of her personal chambers, she could let her hair down, literally as well as figuratively.

The ship was running like a dream, as always, and their course was plotted and set. Now she could just relax. The Drooks and her flight team would get them there without needing to bother her. All in all, a good end to a good day.

A shape emerged from nowhere, the wiry Wampeh appearing as if from thin air.

"Do not bother with your alarms. I have disabled them," he said calmly.

Nixxa didn't move, forcing herself to look calm and composed even as the realization set in that if he was in her chambers here and now, that meant he had been aboard her ship for the entire trip. More than long enough to learn her countermeasures at his leisure. She did, however, pale a little at the threat she now faced.

Nixxa had always been a fighter. Tough, scrappy, she'd taken on plenty of men and women many times her size and always come out on top. But she didn't need to see this Wampeh's fangs to know what he was. She'd known a few Ghalian in her day, and his utterly unflappable, calm demeanor said all she needed to hear. Against a normal man, she would have stood more than a fighting chance, but facing a full-fledged Ghalian? She'd been in the game long enough to know her odds were slim to none.

Bawb was pleased at her reaction. She wouldn't be a problem, and he could extract the information he wanted from her without an issue. He could smell her fear clinging to her, the faint scent pungent to his sensitive nose. There wasn't much of it —she was a seasoned pirate captain, after all—but this type of danger was a different sort than her usual fare. This wasn't the kind she could fight or run from. And that left her with a feeling of helplessness she hadn't felt in longer than she could remember.

So Nixxa resigned herself to do the one thing she could do. She sat quietly and waited.

Bawb watched the gears turning in her mind, giving her time to settle into the reality of her situation, staring at her in a most disconcerting way the entire time. When he felt she was at her peak discomfort and would be most receptive, he finally spoke.

"I have some questions for you."

"You can ask what you want. Can't say I'll be much help, though. I'm just a pilot."

"Please. You and I know you are much more than that. And you are in possession of knowledge. Do you remember a Ghalian spy named Skrillat?"

"Oh, that was a while ago. I hadn't dealt with him before, nor after. It was a one-off assignment."

"So you say."

"But Skrillat's a very connected man. If you go after him, you know they'll come after you."

"Not likely. I assure you, Skrillat is quite dead."

"Dead?" she asked casually, keeping her face neutral but knowing if he had reached the supposedly untouchable spy, this man was possessing of the highest skills among his kind.

"By my hand. Yes."

"How? Why?"

"The how is thanks to you. You delivered me to his latest location."

"The Council base?" she asked, unable to fully conceal her shock.

"The very same. I could not have reached it without you, so again, my thanks. Now, as for the why, do you remember a man, a Wampeh Ghalian named Hozark?"

"It rings a bell, but I'm not sure I—"

"Please do not lie. I know you remember him. He visited you in the past, and Master Hozark was one to make quite an impression."

Nixxa shrugged, letting out a nervous chuckle. "Well, it was worth trying."

"And I do not blame you for it," he said, moving a little closer but in a non-threatening way. "Nixxa, I do not intend to harm you. You were only the pilot ferrying the parties involved and their cargo from place to place. And I know full well that you are not a stupid woman. You may rub many the wrong way with your actions, but even you would not knowingly act against the Ghalian. Of that I am sure."

"Oh, thank the gods."

"But I *will* get what I came for."

If it was anyone else she would have subconsciously covered

herself, but this was a Ghalian on a quest, and he was most definitely not after her body. He wanted something else.

Information.

"You have quite a reputation, you know," he continued, slowly pacing in front of her. "But then, you always have. It took me a very long time to figure out it was you who was present when the most crucial parts of this plot to kill him came to fruition. It was a very, *very* secretive affair, but you were present at a key moment. And now you will tell me everything you recall of that day. Who was there. Who was in contact with those present. Who arranged Master Hozark's death. If you do this simple thing for me, you will go free and unharmed, and I will never reveal that you cooperated with me in this matter."

"Y-you'll really let me live?"

"You have my oath."

Those were words a Ghalian did not say lightly.

"I believe you, and I accept," she said, a feeling of safety washing over her with those words. "A Ghalian's word is his bond, this much we all know. But I'll admit, I didn't expect you to show mercy to a pirate, even one innocently drawn into this mess."

"About that," he said, flashing an amused little grin. "You were kind to me once. Showed your better nature. And that memory has remained with me to this day."

"I did *what*, now?"

"I was very young, but I am sure you will remember me. I stole a Drookonus from you when I was but a boy."

Nixxa's face flushed as she looked closer, taking in the man's features. Yes, his face had changed over the years as he grew, but now that she knew what she was looking for, it was clear as day. A look of dislike briefly flashed through her eyes, along with a renewed impetus to find a way to kill this man if she could.

"Fucking *Boddik*," she growled. "Ate my food, took my clothes, and even accepted my coin, then stole from me."

"Ah, I see you *do* remember me."

"Oh, I do. A lot of trouble you caused me. That Drookonus you took was a hard to come by and very powerful."

"Yes, Nixxa, I realize that what I took from you was not the item stolen from the Ghalian I had set out to recover but a much more valuable one. But I assure you, it was a young boy's foolish mistake."

"Sure. Whatever. So, I assume Boddik isn't your name."

"Of course not. But you may call me the Geist."

The moniker was relatively new, but even she had heard tales of the Geist's exploits. Her rage extinguished in an instant, her hopes of any chance at revenge gone in a flash. She was as good as dead if he wanted it, and she knew it. Bawb watched her process the news with amusement. It seemed having his newfound reputation precede him truly did have its benefits.

Nixxa resigned herself to her fate, even if that meant helping the not-so-little shit who stole from her all those years ago.

"Fine. I'll tell you what you want. But you can never say it came from me. I have a sweet deal with the Council that lets me feed a lot of my people."

"Always playing both sides. Stealing from the wealthy and redistributing it to the poor."

"We've gotta do what we feel is right."

"At least you have a code, odd as it is. And the less fortunate and downtrodden should be helped if possible. On that we agree."

"Great, we're on the same team," she replied sarcastically. "Can we get on with this? You said I'll go free if I tell you what you want to know."

"And you will. None will know of our conversation," he replied, but wondered just how much the discovery of the dead body on the Council base might throw some looks her way. Knowing Nixxa, she'd handle it with her trademark poise. She'd been with the base commander the whole time, after all, and none from her ship but her had been seen entering the base.

"Fine. So those names? That's all you want to know."

Bawb felt a tingle of excitement creep into his gut. Finally, after so long searching, he would have what he'd been looking for. If not a direct link to Hozark's killer, at least the next best thing.

"Yes. I seek the identities of those who directly or indirectly were involved in the planning and execution of the ambush for which you helped deliver weapons. Nothing more."

"All right. There were a few involved, but I actually heard them say who was running it all behind the scenes. The person you want is—"

Nixxa dropped dead at his feet, like a marionette with its strings abruptly cut, her eyes staring lifelessly up at him.

Bawb stood over her, looking at the corpse at his feet, the slightest twitch of frustrated emotion in his eye. But he was a Ghalian. A *Master* Ghalian at that. Losing himself to uncontrolled emotion was beneath him. He put his emotions on lockdown and set to work.

First, he took a breath then crouched down to examine her body. He knew it wasn't suicide. The question was what had happened? He lifted her and moved her to her bed, then stripped her nude. There wasn't a mark on her.

"This makes no sense," he muttered, racking his brain for a possible explanation.

Her quarters had no lingering kill spells, and there was no trace of poison residue he could detect on her anywhere. But somehow she'd dropped stone dead. And right when she was about to—

The realization hit him like a punch in the gut. Dreading

what he would find, he cast a modified illumination spell, the light emitted veering hard into the ultraviolet spectrum. He leaned close and moved her body again, searching every inch of the dead woman's corpse. Only at the last spot he checked did he find what he was looking for.

"There you are," he said as he separated her legs exposing her innermost thigh, not wanting to but needing to. Nixxa was a fierce woman, and no one would ever see this part of her body without her express permission. The perfect place for someone to have hidden a kill rune.

It was tiny and not terribly powerful, but it was powerful enough. The magical rune was formed with pigment invisible to the naked eye in normal light, undoubtedly placed there without her knowing by someone who wanted their identity kept secret no matter what. When she was about to speak their name in this context, the spell triggered, killing her in an instant.

It was an old trick, stunning someone, usually while they were drinking to excess, and marking them with a kill rune, but it was incredibly uncommon these days. First, most would be detected, as few had the power and skill to successfully place one to begin with. And second, to do so with this sort of pigment, all while hiding the magic's power signature from any sort of accidental scan and discovery? It was the work of a powerful individual. Powerful, talented, and willing to kill anyone they had to without a second thought.

Bawb tucked her into her bed and closed her eyes.

"I am sorry, Nixxa. You did not deserve this," he said quietly, then shimmer-cloaked himself and stepped out into the corridor, sealing her quarters behind him. By the time someone came looking for her, he would be off the ship along with the rest of the crew on shore leave and flying home.

. . .

The next day he did as he had planned. The crew was gregarious as they fanned out across the city, eager to enjoy their time off the ship. Bawb pretended to be overjoyed along with the rest of them, then, when the opportunity presented itself, he slipped away, shifted to his normal form, and boarded the first ship home.

He sat quietly in his seat, pondering the amazing events that had unfolded. The traitor was dead, and in the process, he had leveled up faster and higher than any Ghalian before him. Even Hozark. His father.

That was the revelation of a lifetime and one he wanted to scream from the rooftops. But no one could know. It was to be his not-so-little secret. One that he already felt inspiring him to excel even more. To do his father proud.

Unfortunately, the purpose of the entire mission was ultimately a bust. Skrillat was dead, and Nixxa had joined him on the other side, and with their demise the trail was now cold. Once he got home, he would have to start all over again, back to square one. The killer was still out there, and one day, he would find them, no matter how long it took.

The Geist was a patient man, and when it came to revenge, he had all the time in the world.

PREVIEW - ASSASSIN: DRAGONMAGE
THE BOOK OF BAWB 4

It wasn't rain showering down upon the clashing warriors. At least, not of the water variety. The droplets were accompanied by chunks of meat. Meat formerly belonging to the bodies of the defenders atop the walls of the fortress on the embattled planet of Xenthix. Defenders who had been lax in their defenses for just a moment too long, allowing the most brutal of killing spells to breach their ranks, exploding their bodies into a pink mist, sending their remains flying every which way.

The fighters didn't slow their attacks. In fact, by this point in the conflict, they were numb to such things, having seen equal and worse over the course of this drawn-out affair.

The battle was epic in scale, spanning much of the region at one point, the warring factions on both sides possessing both significant numbers of fodder as well as a sizable quantity of magic at their disposal. Aerial battles raged with casters plucking craft from the sky as best they could, their overlapping spellcasting affording them at least a modicum of defense against the relentless barrage.

Even so, bodies littered both the battlefield as well as the parapet walls of the fortified keep belonging to Visla Kormin.

While the conflict had started with open battle between Kormin's forces and those of Visla Hurvey, Kormin had retreated to the safety of his thick walls, protected by years upon years of defensive magic layered into an impenetrable barrier that allowed him to send out wave after wave of fighters to engage his enemy while directing them from the comfort and security of his fortress. Once within those walls he was untouchable.

It had been weeks since the tide shifted and Visla Hurvey had begun pushing his adversary back on his heels. Had he been able to strike him dead before he reached his fortress the conflict would have ended with far less bloodshed and damage to the innocent civilians of the region. But fortune had not been on Hurvey's side, and now Kormin was regrouping, resting his strongest troops and sending out reinforced attack parties to chip away at Visla Hurvey's forces.

It was folly, this conflict, and a great many were suffering needlessly for it. The power struggle between the two powerful vislas could have been handled the old way with a simple duel between them, but they had both grown lazy in their power. Lazy, and reluctant to risk actual harm to themselves despite their own inherent abilities.

The two were both relatively high-ranking members in the Council of Twenty's regional governing body, but as was so often the case, rather than working together toward more efficient and profitable rule, each of the men wanted all the power for themselves. And eventually the kindling of that desire burst into an open flame of conflict. Now the populace was needlessly suffering as the battle raged on into yet another month of brutal fighting. It had become a pointless war of attrition. One the Wampeh Ghalian had been contracted to end.

Infiltrate an impenetrable fortress protected by decades of layers of deadly spells, dozens of powerful casters, tens of thousands of troops, guards, and mercenaries, and, of course, one of the most powerful vislas in the region? It was suicide to even consider the job. Naturally, when the contract was agreed to, only one Ghalian came to mind.

The Geist had earned his reputation over the twenty-plus years since he had first been given that moniker, rising to the rank of Master Ghalian with a frightening speed and efficiency. He may have had his troubles as a youth, but once he accepted his calling and embraced it fully, he began regularly accomplishing the unfathomable, reaching targets no matter where they were entrenched, seemingly coming and going through walls without a trace. But even for Bawb, this one would be a challenge.

"You say the fortress is utterly impenetrable?" he asked Master Corann, the leader of the Five and overseer of the handful of top Masters controlling all Ghalian affairs across the galaxy.

"Quite," was her reply. "Even before this conflict we had attempted to place a spy within its walls to keep tabs on Visla Kormin."

"With no success, I take it."

"Indeed. Many have tried to breach his defenses, and many have failed. The visla is a very cautious man, and the sheer number of disguise-detection spells as well as wards and traps on his fortress made it a fool's errand at the time."

"I take it the Five have determined it would have required considerable effort to have one of our non-Ghalian allies infiltrate, then?"

"Considering the issues surrounding this particular location, yes. But none expected this little conflict to escalate into the problem it has become. If we had, we may have possibly managed to place someone within the lowest-ranking staff— given enough time and a sizable amount of coin. But war is upon the factions, and there is simply no way to do so anymore. That option, tenuous as it was, is gone."

Bawb stroked his chin, pondering the situation, studying the parchment detailing the layout of the fortress, its various forces, and the geography of the battlefields and terrain surrounding it, taking it all in with his usual calm and keen eye.

"So? What do you think, Bawb? Can you manage it?" Corann asked. "Can you penetrate the impenetrable and end this war?"

He paused a moment, considering the facts. Walls he could not breach, spells he could not counter, and literally thousands of skilled adversaries between him and his objective. He looked closer at the maps, soaking in every detail, the seed of a nascent plan already forming in his mind.

"I will embed myself within Visla Hurvey's forces to get close enough to properly survey the situation and my options. If it is simply difficult, I will handle it right away," he said. "If it is *impossible*, well, that will take a little longer."

Bawb geared up and flew his shimmer ship to Xenthix, powering up his shimmer cloak while still in space with the skill few Ghalian would ever attain. Master Hozark had taught him well, and with practice he had exceeded even his mentor's abilities. The shimmer cloak held up through his entry into the planet's atmosphere, a few carefully placed cooling spells added to the mix keeping the craft from forming much of a heat signature at all. In no time at all he was flying safely in the cold air high above his target continent, invisible, but like a beast of prey, very much on the hunt.

He guided his ship with calm confidence, skirting the aerial battles, not for fear of discovery and attack, but rather, because he knew full well that a misfired spell or projectile could still take down even the most skilled of pilots. In head-to-head combat he was unrivaled. That didn't mean fluke misfortune could not befall him.

It was this awareness and understanding of the quirks of luck that had kept him alive this long. And with his current contract, he would need every last bit of fortune to complete his mission and remain so.

He had been tasked with ending this battle. This sprawling war between two of the most powerful vislas within several solar systems and their massive armies. Bawb. One man. Obviously, he could not single-handedly stop the surging waves of tens of thousands of combatants as they clashed, bled, and died. And even if he could, that would not end this conflict. But he *could* cut off the serpent's head, so to speak, and the resulting power vacuum would bring about an abrupt resolution to this whole ordeal.

Without one of their power-hungry leaders pushing them to fight, one side would have no reason to spill any further blood, and the war would finally come to an end. Unfortunately, the man the contract was placed on happened to be safely ensconced within his utterly impenetrable fortress. A stronghold that many had tried to enter, and all had failed horribly in their attempts.

They were not, however, the Geist.

Bawb landed behind a rocky formation in the landscape, securing his shimmer ship in one of the few locations that would not accidentally be demolished by errant spells as the tide of combat churned this way and that. The spell hiding the craft was robust, and the shielding left in place on top of that would guarantee that all but the most powerful and directly focused attacks would simply bounce off it should the shifting battle somehow reach the area.

He intended to be done with his job and long gone before that could even become a possibility.

It's a friggin' mess out there, his konus noted as he applied layers of disguise spells on top of his practical makeup and prosthetics, all of them making him seem no more than just another soldier on the battlefield in the chaos of war.

"It is at that," he agreed, mentally calling up the massive list of spells and skills he had gained mastery over in the course of his adventure-filled life. All were clearly visible and maxed out. All but two. Two that remained annoyingly blurred to his eyes, though he'd been afforded the briefest of glimpses of one of them years prior. The one that informed him he was on the path to becoming one of the Five. The other, he had no idea about, but with every completed mission he hoped to see it clearly.

For decades now, that had not been the case. Not even a glimpse.

Stop dwelling on that, the konus chided, reading his mind as it had always done. *Get in there and get to work.*

"I *am* working," he silently replied as he navigated his way through the troops, making his way closer to the leadership encampment where the top generals and Visla Hurvey resided, surrounded by hundreds of guards, all ready to die for their leaders.

It was the general, a fierce, stout woman named Trayxa, who had secretly reached out to the Wampeh Ghalian in hopes they would accept her contract. She was not one to shy away from battle by any means, and her reputation was that of a great warrior and keen tactical mind. But she had seen too many of her soldiers perish in a senseless war that could rage on for months, if not years, now that their enemy was holed up in his fortress. She was perfectly willing to sacrifice thousands to achieve her visla's goals, but this wasn't a clean battle. It was attrition, and she knew full well that even if they won, her visla would be vulnerable to other challengers, having greatly diminished his forces in this foolish conflict.

So it was with that in mind that she hired the Ghalian to put a quick end to this, if they could. Her discretionary funding had been emptied in the process, but that could be replaced relatively easily. The integrity of her position and those supporting it, however, could not if her visla perished.

"Where are you going?" a dozen guards challenged as Bawb drew near the outer line of defenses.

He put on an exhausted look, the blood smeared on his uniform adding to the appearance of a drained and confused soldier.

"I got separated from my unit," he replied, squeezing out the last drops of his water skin with an exasperated sigh.

The guards remained alert—anyone could be an enemy infiltrator—but one offered him her water skin. Bawb accepted with a grateful nod and drained half of it like a man who'd just spent a month in the desert, then handed it back.

"Thank you," he said, wiping his mouth with the back of his hand. "The fighting has been fierce."

"That would be war," one of the other guards said. "You aren't supposed to be here. The front is that way."

"I was hoping to cross over to rejoin them without heading through the middle of the hot spot."

"Not this way," was the reply. The man's set jaw made it clear he was not about to change his mind.

That was fine. Bawb had seen all he needed. He knew where his employer was. Now he just had to complete his contract.

"I understand," the disguised assassin replied, turning and heading off through the masses once more, moving in the direction of the main battle, though at a bit of an angle. One that would take him over a small section of uneven rocks.

Both sides avoided it, as the footing was too treacherous for anyone to gain an advantage. If they were going to kill each other, at least they could do it from the comfort of relatively flat ground. That meant the area was shockingly empty considering all that was going on around it. Perfect for Bawb's purposes.

He clamored through the rocky field, the topographical map of the area firmly at the front of his mind's eye. A large, angled rocky mound confirmed his location, the landmark helping guide him on his path. Bawb moved to the far side, counted out seventy-three paces, then began lifting heavy stones, tossing them aside. He was breaking quite a sweat after just a few minutes, but he didn't dare use magic to move them. Not with so many casters and guards so close. He needed to go unnoticed, and this was the only way.

He labored for nearly an hour, slowly making his way deeper into the ground, breaking up larger rocks with repeated impacts of smaller ones when needed then tossing the shattered bits out of the makeshift pit. He slammed a large rock down onto a flat slab at his feet as hard as he could. The stone cracked, but unlike previously, this time he felt a gust of cold air rise to his face.

Bawb smiled to himself and continued his labors until an opening large enough for him to fit through had been hammered out of the rock. He leaned down and listened. It was faint, but the sound was unmistakable.

Rushing water.

Carefully, he lowered himself into the hole then cast the smallest of spells, tumbling rocks he had piled to one side over the opening, sealing him in and disguising his prior efforts. He was inside now, and he was committed.

Slowly, he climbed deeper, minding his footing on the damp rocks. He allowed himself an illumination spell now. The thick rocks above would block anyone from noticing his small expenditure of magic even if they were specifically looking for it. And with the battle raging, that was certainly not a concern.

He squeezed through a narrow gap, following the sound of

water and the breeze it caused. It was getting louder now. Bawb was close. He did not rush, however. That was how mistakes were made. How one would die in the most foolish of ways. He'd seen it plenty of times over the course of his career, and he had taken those hard lessons others had learned to heart, certain not to repeat them himself.

Not bad, the konus said as he pressed into a small, domed chamber with a body of clear water flowing through it. *Good luck.*

"Thank you, Konus," he replied, then set to work preparing himself mentally for the challenge ahead of him.

The konus had given him endless grief as a youth, talking trash and being overall unhelpful. But as he grew in skill and power, proving his worth, the device not only unlocked more and more power for him to tap into, it also began treating him with respect. Almost friendship. At least, as much as a *technically* non-living but somewhat sentient device could develop.

Bawb took a series of thirty slow, deep breaths, filling his lungs and readying his body as best he could. His plan was an audacious one and risky as hell. The dangerous and seemingly impossible sort of thing no one would even consider. No one but Bawb, that is. It had taken a fair amount of research to find the ancient survey of the aquifers flowing through the region, feeding into one another, and, eventually, connecting with the subterranean water source for Visla Kormin's stronghold.

Even with the assistance of the flowing water, the distance he would have to cover was great. Far greater than anyone could hold their breath to travel. But Bawb had a few tricks up his sleeve. And if he had gauged his calculations right, he would soon penetrate the impenetrable.

If he failed, he would be lost forever, his body trapped deep below the planet's surface, leaving his friends and colleagues to wonder what ever became of the man they'd called the Geist.

THANK YOU!

Thank you so much for joining me on this wild ride. It's really meant so much and has made even the sometimes daunting slog of keeping storylines straight across 30 interconnected books almost a joy. So, from the warmed cockles of my heart, you have my deepest appreciation.
Now, that said, if you could do one little thing before heading on to book 4, please leave a rating/review if you have 20 seconds to spare. It makes a huge impact for us indie authors.
Y'all are the best :)

~ Scott ~

ALSO BY SCOTT BARON

Standalone Novels

Living the Good Death

Vigor Mortis

The Clockwork Chimera Series

Daisy's Run

Pushing Daisy

Daisy's Gambit

Chasing Daisy

Daisy's War

The Dragon Mage Series

Bad Luck Charlie

Space Pirate Charlie

Dragon King Charlie

Magic Man Charlie

Star Fighter Charlie

Portal Thief Charlie

Rebel Mage Charlie

Warp Speed Charlie

Checkmate Charlie

Castaway Charlie

Wild Card Charlie

End Game Charlie

The Space Assassins Series

The Interstellar Slayer

The Vespus Blade

The Ghalian Code

Death From the Shadows

Hozark's Revenge

The Book of Bawb Series

Assassins' Academy

Assassin's Apprentice

Assassin: Rise of the Geist

Assassin and the Dragon Mage

The Warp Riders Series

Deep Space Boogie

Belly of the Beast

Rise of the Forgotten

Pandora's Menagerie

Engines of Chaos

Seeds of Damocles

Odd and Unusual Short Stories:

The Best Laid Plans of Mice: An Anthology

Snow White's Walk of Shame

The Tin Foil Hat Club

Lawyers vs. Demons

The Queen of the Nutters

Lost & Found

ABOUT THE AUTHOR

A native Californian, Scott Baron was born in Hollywood, which he claims may be the reason for his rather off-kilter sense of humor.

Before taking up residence in Venice Beach, Scott first spent a few years abroad in Florence, Italy before returning home to Los Angeles and settling into the film and television industry, where he has worked as an on-set medic for many years.

Aside from mending boo-boos and owies, and penning books and screenplays, Scott is also involved in indie film and theater scene both in the U.S. and abroad.

Made in United States
North Haven, CT
31 January 2025

65168677R00255